MW01672804

THE SHADOW CABINET

THE SHADOW CABINET

BY

HAROL MARSHALL

STORYTELLER
A Publisher of Quality Fiction

ISBN-13: 978-1-938833-01-4

Author Website
http://www.harolmarshall.com

Give feedback to:
harolmarshall@gmail.com

Cover art by Kathey Amaral
http://kattnboys.deviantart.com

Back cover photography by Robert Scoble

Storyteller Publishing
www.storytellerpublishing.com
Email: info@storytellerpublishing.com

Printed in U.S.A

ACKNOWLEDGEMENTS

I take full responsibility for any errors or mistakes that might appear in *The Shadow Cabinet*. However, I want to credit those who've been especially helpful to me over the course of writing the novel. I appreciate the input I've received from my family including editing assistance from my daughter Sharol Gauthier, encouragement from my son Dale Hoffman, and feedback from my husband Jerry Meisner and my cousin June Grinter. Particular thanks goes to my friend Rob Furr for all his great "tech support."

I have many good writing friends who have kindly read and reacted to all or parts of the book and I thank them all, including: the Triad Writer's roundtable (Trudy Atkins, Karen Fritz, Emogene Joyner, Lynette Hall, Dixie Land, Dave Shaffer, and John Staples) and the Writer's Group of the Triad (WGOT) Mystery Writers I (Betty DiMeo, Nancy Gotter Gates, Helen Goodman, and Dorothy O'Neill).

Finally, I am grateful to Storyteller Publishing and Editor Goldie Browning, whose editorial suggestions have improved the book considerably. I'm proud to be one of their authors.

DEDICATION

To Jerry, as always

An intelligence service is the ideal vehicle for a conspiracy.

~ Allen Dulles

Chapter One

EX-VICE-PRESIDENT REITERATES STANCE ON USE OF CIA INSIDE THE UNITED STATES
By Arlan Skeels | ASSOCIATED PRESS

Washington, D.C. Former Vice-President Frederick McGuire, appearing on CAB News television, reiterated his position in support of a Congressional amendment to the Patriot Act allowing the Central Intelligence Agency to spy on American citizens. On questioning, McGuire went beyond his previous statements to say…

Bluemont, Virginia
Mount Weather

A canopy of shape-shifter clouds threatened the Blue Ridge Mountains as the barometer dropped with lightning speed, and a single thunderhead that blotted out the mid-morning sun hovered ominously over Mount Weather. Three stories underground, beneath a nondescript building near the edge of the FEMA weather facility, storm clouds of a different sort gathered in the mind of ex-Vice-President Fred McGuire.

He'd spent the past two hours studying the previous day's copies of the national intelligence brief. The more he read the more irritated he became. Even the silence of the soundproof sanctuary annoyed him, reminding him of his lonely childhood and the days he spent playing in his room with toy soldiers his only company.

The ex-Veep thumbed through the two communiqués spread over the mahogany table in the President's Conference Room and shook his head in a fit of frustration. Neither was good enough, not even the brief the CIA's Director of Intelligence had redacted for the President. McGuire flipped to another section of the report, glancing through it with unmitigated disgust. *Too soft on America's enemies*—Iran in particular, the country that kept him from sleeping at night. Where was the intel supporting a strike on Iranian nuclear sites? *What about the*

Israelis? Had they caved to U.S. demands?

The new President is too naïve, too trusting. Hasn't the guts to face down a disingenuous, two-bit dictatorship like Iran. What happens once they've stocked their underground bunkers with nukes? What does the President think he can do then? The ex Vice-President took a deep breath, trying to relax.

The subtle scent of lemons from the recently polished table turned his thoughts to his favorite cocktail, a prohibition-era Sidecar. He could use a drink right now, except that he no longer drank before noon, thanks to his meddling cardiologist. McGuire knew his heart might give out on him again. He didn't need someone constantly reminding him. Taking a deep breath, he resumed his signature posture. Tenting his hands, he reflected on the best eight years of his life. The paramount accomplishment of his tenure as Vice-President had been establishing the COG, the Continuity of Government plan—that strange doppelgänger of the Federal Government over which he now presided in his role as Shadow President. The importance of this, his most momentous decision, became more apparent every day.

The young President can't control his own party, let alone the country or the world, McGuire thought. With economic pressures from China and India, and nuclear threats from Iran and North Korea, the country needed a strong leader, not a "negotiator," a compromiser. America was facing its greatest set of pressures since the beginning of World War II, and McGuire had no confidence in the ability of the current administration to rise to the challenges. They lacked any sensible plan for restoring America to its rightful place in the world, never mind containing the myriad threats to the country's safety. *A catastrophic event could wipe out Washington tomorrow.*

McGuire shoved aside the papers with a disdainful sweep of his hand. *I'll prepare my own Intelligence Brief for the Cabinet meeting, and I know exactly the approach to use.* Having made his decision, he reached for his black leather briefcase, sliding it across the table's gleaming surface. As he formulated in his mind the revisions he would make, he stuffed the CIA reports into an opening in his briefcase. He would capitalize on the brewing unrest in the country, turn it to his advantage. Americans were too preoccupied with the prevailing economic and political turmoil to make decisions in the country's best interests. He would make the decisions for them. One day, they would understand and thank him.

He snapped shut the case and gave the keypad an extra twist. For the next few minutes, he sat in the comfortable upholstered wing chair at the head of the table and contemplated the upcoming Shadow Cabinet meeting, considering how to frame his arguments to prevent opposition in the unlikely event anyone dared raise an objection. Only one person concerned him. They'd tangled before, but McGuire felt confident in his ability to sway the man. If not, other methods could be deployed to deal with him.

Satisfied his meeting would proceed according to plan, McGuire rolled back his chair and glanced around, absorbing the ambience of the high-ceilinged room with its marble floor and expensive wood furnishings. Glass or maybe Plexiglas "windows" at one end of the room overlooked a Washington, D.C. street scene projected from webcams mounted on the side of the Congressional Office Building. If he hadn't known better, he'd believe he was sitting inside his favorite conference room on Capitol Hill rather than being entombed in the basement of a civilian command center designed to shelter up to two thousand critical government employees in the event of a cataclysmic attack on the country.

An insistent rapping from across the room interrupted his reveries. He stood up, stretched his limbs to relieve the kinks in his muscles from sitting, and prepared to meet his visitor. On the way to the door, he crossed to the room's lone mirror where he smoothed back the sides of his thick, black hair now flecked with gray. Steely blue eyes returned his dispassionate gaze. Lifting his chin with an admiring twist of his broad head, McGuire straightened his silk Armani tie, adjusted the knot and fluffed the matching silk square in his jacket pocket. After a final approving glance, he turned away from the mirror and pushed up the shirt cuff on his left wrist to adjust his Rolex, facing it inward before continuing in the direction of the conference room's steel-reinforced door. He lifted the engraved brass handle and swung open the door to admit his impatient guest.

"I presume you're the bearer of bad news," McGuire said, ignoring Zak Browning's outstretched hand.

Chapter Two

Shortly before noon, the black BMW carrying Zak Browning, the CIA's Director of Intelligence, rounded the sharp curve along the tree-lined country road in Virginia's Fauquier County and climbed the low hills into the Blue Ridge Mountains. The DI could have taken the subway to Mt. Weather, but he preferred to drive and avoid a record of his visits. The razor-wire fence came into view with its faded signs warning away visitors. Zak ignored the warnings and pulled up to the main gate.

In what he considered an egregious anomaly, given the site's wide-ranging secrecy, a branch of the Appalachian Trail ran by the main gate. Two hikers stood on the trail next to the sign that read: U.S. PROPERTY NO TRESPASSING. Zak waved his hand in front of the windshield, impatiently motioning the couple to move along, uncertain whether they could see him through the dark tinted windows of his vehicle. He hoped they weren't taking pictures, since he had no interest in a photo of his car decorating some amateur *I Spy* website. His license plate would show up on a U.S. spy satellite eventually, but since he controlled the flow of intelligence gathered from the government system, erasing the image would be no problem.

The chain link gates into the protected compound slid open. Zak's BMW crawled by the white aluminum sheds and followed the snaking macadam road past a nondescript series of FEMA weather observation buildings to a parking lot at the edge of the ridge. He hadn't bothered to lock his vehicle knowing he was in one of the safest locations in the world. Entering the gray metal storage shed, he crossed to the tunnel entrance where he pushed the button that activated the iris scanner. Leaning close, he peered into a set of binoculars mounted on the wall to the right of the door and pressed the *Start ID* button.

As he waited for the system to confirm his identity, he wondered how long before the credit card companies would employ iris technology. *Probably still too expensive, like wireless electricity.* What impressed him was the complex set of mathematical algorithms developed to compare one image with another and unequivocally identify the iris's owner. No "closest match" that relied on expert testimony, as with DNA or fingerprints, but rather, precise mathematical equations. Too bad the President's daily intelligence analysis couldn't be produced with such precision.

Iris matching would be ideal for a national ID card, Zak mused, tucking the idea in the back of his mind as the lock whirred. The five-foot-thick steel door guarding the Mount Weather tunnel entrance swung open, permitting him to enter. He walked over to the bank of elevators and pushed the Down button, the only direction to choose. Inside the elevator, he pressed number three for the third floor, the bottom floor of the complex and the most secure level. His thoughts turned to his upcoming meeting with the *Raptor*, Fred McGuire's Secret Service handle. Zak sighed at the prospect of a difficult meeting ahead.

The elevator deposited him into a corridor that emulated the halls of Congress. He passed by a series of conference rooms, including the Pentagon's war room and the White House situation room where he turned right, heading for number 336, the Raptor's favorite meeting room. He knocked on the door and waited, checking his watch every few minutes, pacing the floor in front of the residential apartments belonging to the President and Vice-President.

The ex-Veep liked to keep people waiting, which Zak attributed to his megalomaniacal need for power, the kind of power he'd enjoyed over the past twenty-five years as the *éminence grise* of the country's richest and most powerful political party. The gray ghost, as he was known, called all the shots—or so he believed. After several minutes, the conference room door opened with a sudden sweep, and McGuire greeted Zak with a snarky comment about being the bearer of bad news.

"Killing the messenger isn't wise," he replied in response to McGuire's rude greeting. Zak walked over to the conference table and placed what looked like a copy of *USA Today* at McGuire's place at the head of the table. The paper was an exact duplicate of the President's Daily Intelligence Brief. "This one should make you a little happier."

McGuire picked it up with a dismissive wave, motioning Zak to be seated. Waiting for the ex-Veep to thumb through the report, Zak amused himself watching the pedestrians and motorists passing by the Congressional Office building in D.C., blissfully unaware of the cleverly hidden surveillance cameras mounted in the crevices of the building's walls. Symbolic, he thought, of the public's ignorance of the inner workings of their government.

McGuire pushed the papers aside. "I assume you hand-delivered this for a reason, because at first glance it's not much better than yesterday's pap."

"A few small, but significant changes that should please you when you delve deeper," Zak said, "but that's not why I'm here. We've run into a glitch."

"What and where?"

"Honolulu. Our team has been compromised."

"Then take care of it."

"Already in the works. I wanted to give you a heads-up."

"Don't bother me with details. Just get the job done. Chun's scheduled to fly to Hawaii in a few days for some damn Asian-American goodwill conference. I want him returning to D.C. in a box."

"It's as good as done," Zak said, "and we have a backup plan in place, in case the Vice-President cancels his trip and decides to remain in D.C."

"We can't change the schedule without Nilsson's okay," McGuire barked.

Bile rose in Zak's throat at the idea of kowtowing to Bjorn Nilsson, CEO of Sigma Services. "I have a meeting scheduled with Nilsson tomorrow, but we don't take orders from him, we *give* the orders."

"Keep in mind, his damned army is the largest paramilitary organization in U.S. history. Hell, it out-ranks the U.S. Marines when it comes to money, men, and equipment. He's dangerous. Got to pamper him."

Zak needed no lecture on Sigma Services. He knew them inside out. The organization had thrived during the Iraq war, but with the new administration and its efforts to draw down land wars, Sigma had seen its income stream diminish substantially. Consequently, as Zak knew from personal conversations with the man, Bjorn Nilsson harbored an intense hatred for the President. Zak also knew the feeling was mutual. He'd sat through more than one meeting in which the young President expressed his distrust and dislike of contractors and their exorbitant salaries, insisting their compensation should not exceed that of the military's own men and women who willingly served their country for far less.

"I'll take care of it," Zak said, repeating his reassurances in an effort to appease the Raptor. Zak wasn't worried about dealing with Sigma.

He had enough evidence on Nilsson to put him away for twenty years.

McGuire glanced down at the lined yellow tablet in front of him and placed a checkmark next to one of the items on his list. "Where do we stand on our false flag operations?"

"Sigma's on it, starting with Europe—"

McGuire interrupted. "Meaningless, unless we follow up with appropriate actions here, and by here, I mean D.C. The President will sit up and take notice when the danger arrives on his doorstep. Since we haven't convinced him to bomb the hell out of Iran's nukes, we need to frighten him into heading for the hills where he'll be under our control."

Knowing the Raptor enjoyed humor if it enhanced his ego, Zak smirked. "And by "hills" you mean Mt. Weather."

"Precisely. Now bring me up to date with your D.C. plans, which you need to run by Sigma whether you want to or not."

"We have an Iranian assassin stashed in a safe house outside D.C.," Zak replied with calm efficiency, even though he was seething inside. "He crossed into the U.S. from Canada. Walked over the border in an obscure village in northern Maine. No record exists of his arrival."

"Can we trust him?"

"Absolutely. He's Mojahedin-e-Khalq, a fanatic and trained MEK killer. He hates *Iran's government.* An attack on them by the U.S. would be a dream come true. He'll do whatever he can to bring that about, including admitting to the assassination. We said we'd arrange an escape and transfer him out of the country, if he's arrested. He's agreed, but it won't come to that. Sigma will take care of him long before it's a worry."

"Spend a little more time checking up on the Iranian before we proceed. Another job you can hand over to Sigma. They've got contacts in all the right places."

Zak gave McGuire a disdainful look, trying to keep his patience in check. "We've already vetted him and no one has more contacts than the Agency, not even Sigma."

"Don't lecture me. When you talk to Nilsson, put him on it. We'll kill two birds with one stone—find out if Sigma can deliver on their promises *and* see if they turn up information the Agency's missed. You and Henry Larson aren't exactly bosom buddies these days and even if you were, the DCS doesn't like to share."

A feeling of intense hatred filled Zak's soul at the mention of the CIA's Director of National Clandestine Services. "Information flows through my Directorate," Zak snapped, "and when I know something you'll know it, though I admit Henry's a concern. He doesn't play by the rules."

McGuire chuckled. "And you do? Anyway, Henry's not a worry for long. We may have him out of the way before we get to Chun."

"How?"

"It's need to know, and you don't need to know. Just be glad I'm managing it for you."

"I'm all for getting Henry out of my hair," Zak replied, unable to hide his satisfaction despite McGuire's refusal to share information. He understood the ex-Veep's paranoia, and if McGuire could eliminate Larson, more power to him. Henry and Zak had been enemies for years, and there was no one he despised or feared more. He looked forward to a world without Henry Larson, a world where Clandestine Operations, as well as Intelligence, were under the complete control of Zachary Browning, future Director of the Central Intelligence Agency.

"Is that everything?" McGuire asked, checking his watch.

The Raptor must have a date with one of his lady friends, Zak thought, aware of the Raptor's wandering eye. He'd heard the rumors about McGuire having to settle for older mistresses since his quadruple bypass, most of whom served his political agenda more than his personal needs.

Zak was happy to have the meeting cut short. He had bigger problems on his mind today, which he did not intend to share with McGuire. He could play the secrecy game too. "Is the Executive Cabinet meeting still on for later this week?"

"Yes, but I'm handling it on my own. Don't want you showing your face yet. I'll let you know if we run into any difficulties. I'm anticipating one possible holdout. If I'm right, we'll turn the problem over to Sigma."

"They'll need to be careful," Zak cautioned, worried about raising red flags. "We can't afford an investigation at this stage."

"There won't be anything to investigate."

"Okay, but call if you need me."

"I'm not worried," McGuire said, ushering Zak to the door.

Chapter Three

Falls Church, Virginia

CIA analyst Malcolm Hall blew a kiss to his wife Cheryl as she hurried out the front door on her way to choir practice. He crossed the foyer to his first floor study and turned on the computer. Anxiety constricted his chest, a common experience since the death of his son in Iraq. Waiting for the machine to boot, Malcolm stretched his arms over his head, one of his relaxation exercises. *I need a Valium.*

The computer prompted him for a password. He bent down and typed it in. *Scanning for viruses*, the computer said.

"Thank you," he whispered. Talking to his computer calmed him.

Malcolm wished he could get by without the tranquilizer, especially after a year of counseling. More than fifty, one-hour sessions on how to heal a broken heart. Terrible thing when your worst fears are realized. First, your only son announces he's entering the military, then the military appears at your front door unannounced, telling you he was blown to hell and back by a roadside bomb. The counseling helped with his depression, but nothing dispelled the lurking sense of doom. His wife submerged her grief in the church and scrapbooking the memories of her beloved son while Malcolm exercised and wrapped himself in his work. *Easy to do at Langley. The place churned out workaholics.*

A linguist by training, Malcolm was proud of his reputation as one of the Agency's star analysts. He'd entered the CIA in his late twenties shortly after marrying Cheryl thirty years ago. Thinking about his marriage to his beautiful wife nearly brought tears to his eyes. Ironic that no one who knew him back then would have predicted his career choice. He'd avoided anything military. Hated football and most other team sports. A fitness addict, he practiced yoga and watched his diet and read incessantly, sometimes to the detriment of his relationships. Fortunately, he had a tolerant wife who supported his endeavors. What led him to join the Agency he never explained to her, and she never asked. It was one of his many secrets. He wished she were here right now. He'd take the time to tell her.

Too many secrets, Malcolm thought. As a CIA analyst, he delved into secrets every day, secrets of other countries and just as often, secrets within his own. His latest, a heart-stopping secret, fell into the latter category. He'd discovered it on his own without the aid of outside intel. No FBI files sent over from the Counterterrorism Center, no overseas documents pointing to home-based terror cells, but a secret deliberately hidden away inside the Agency he served. Discovered by accident some might think, but he knew differently. In his world, there were no accidents, no coincidences, only anomalies to be analyzed and explained, then written into reports with or without recommendations and sent to the appropriate people to handle as they saw fit. What happened after that was out of his hands. Malcolm wondered what his son would make of today's secret if he could tell him, but of course, he couldn't.

Take the Valium

Still leaning over his computer, Malcolm opened an application and typed in a second password. The app would take a few minutes to start. He left the study and walked into the kitchen where he kept his pills. Filling his water glass, Malcolm stared out the small-paned window over the sink. *Had something moved in the garden?* He leaned closer, squinting into the darkness. Were his eyes playing tricks? Glass in hand, he walked the few steps to the back door and flipped on the spots, surveying the lighted yard from a different angle. Only stillness. His imagination again. *Or maybe a neighbor's dog.* He should stop being so skittish.

The Valium.

Malcolm swallowed the pill and carefully placed the glass in the sink before heading back to his study. He needed to concentrate his thoughts on the upcoming meeting. He wished he'd tried harder to contact Dan Chavez, his closest friend and former colleague, but they'd played phone tag all day and never managed to connect. He thought about calling him again, inviting him over, but he'd see him in the morning, no need to bother him now. He'd share his suspicions with Dan over breakfast when he had more to tell him, including the results of tonight's meeting.

After failing to reach Dan, Malcolm turned to the only other colleague whom he felt he could trust implicitly—the person he and Dan dubbed *Shotgun* for his love of hunting. Like Malcolm's son,

Shotgun had served in the BRO, *The Big Red One*, the Army's First Infantry Division. A sick feeling overcame Malcolm as he thought about his son defending his country in northern Iraq in Washington's War on Terror. Shotgun had also served in Iraq, in Operations Desert Shield and Desert Storm in the early nineties, but he'd returned alive. Malcolm's son and Shotgun were BROs, brothers, even though they served at different times and never met. "BROs have each other's back," Malcolm's son once told him. And so, Malcolm relied on his son's judgment and turned to a BRO.

Headlights reflected off the wall in the study. *Not Shotgun this soon.* Malcolm rolled his chair over to the window in time to see a car inching by, not one he recognized. *Looking for a house number?* He took another deep breath. The Valium should kick in by the time his guest arrived, calming him enough to discuss his unusual finding in a business-like manner.

Malcolm reached up and closed the window shades. Returning to his desk, he opened the top drawer and retrieved the small revolver, tucking it into the right front pocket of his khakis. He wasn't a gun fan, but the sense of protection helped him breathe easier. His son had given him the gun, shown him how to use it. They went target practicing together. Malcolm sighed, wishing he could think about his son without feeling so much pain.

Back at his computer, Malcolm straightened the pencils strewn about the desktop, lining them parallel to his keyboard. One of the neat-freak habits his wife teased him about. He checked his watch, thinking back to late afternoon when he'd informed Shotgun about his discovery.

"Sounds crazy, I know," Malcolm had said.

"What do you think you've found?"

"I think it's a conspiracy." Malcolm had paused, assessing his boss's response. No reaction. Malcolm continued, "involving the Agency."

Shotgun reached for a pen and paper. Must have been a while since Security swept the office for bugs, Malcolm thought.

Shotgun handed Malcolm the paper. *Let's meet at your place to discuss it. Tonight?*

My wife has choir practice, Malcolm had written back. *She leaves at 8:00.*

Malcolm checked his watch again and rubbed his eyes. The Valium was making him sleepy. He turned back to his computer and logged into one of his secure email accounts. Sent off a message. When he finished, he fired up his disk-erase software and programmed it to wipe all traces of the day's activity. While the software churned, he leaned back and closed his eyes.

Chapter Four

The doorbell rang and Malcolm jumped. *Never heard the car.* Checking the window, he saw a dark Escalade parked in the driveway. Looks like an Agency car, he thought. *Shotgun must be returning to the office after leaving here.* Malcolm pushed himself out of his chair and walked to the front door.

"Thanks for coming over," Malcolm said, shaking hands and pointing the way to his study.

"No problem, Buddy. I'm concerned." Shotgun stepped into the tidy home office and glanced around, seeing it for the first time.

Malcolm patted the back of the room's only armchair, a comfortable, black leather that looked well used. "My favorite reading chair. Have a seat."

Malcolm's guest eased himself into the club chair. "You're right. Comfy."

"Can I get you something to drink?"

"Not now."

Malcolm tried to hide his anxiety. "Where do you want me to begin?"

"Wherever you want. This is your party."

My party? Malcolm sat back, trying to unwind. His desk chair slid and he pulled on the arms to keep it from rolling backward on the slick plastic rug protector Cheryl had installed for him.

"I was going through the Agency's archived mission files when I stumbled across something I couldn't access."

"Files you couldn't access?"

"Insufficient clearance. I knew that couldn't be right, so I contacted Security," Malcolm explained, referring to the Office of Security in the Mission Support Directorate.

"Who did you talk to in OS?"

"One of the top IT techs over there."

"He gave you access?"

"She. No. She said she'd look into it and get back to me."

"And?"

"She stopped by my office today. Said as far as she could tell, the classification level was correct and she couldn't help me."

"Why is that a problem? You don't have blanket clearance, do you?"

"I know, but I am cleared for the files in that database. So why would I be denied access to the information in there?"

"Is that what this is about? You want me to move you to a higher security level?"

Shotgun's tone irritated Malcolm. If Malcolm wanted to move to a higher security level, he would fill out the necessary paperwork and submit his request. Other people might use political means or friends to achieve their ends, but not Malcolm. If anyone was upfront in his interpersonal dealings, it was Malcolm.

"No, that's not it."

"Not it. Then why don't you tell me what you found and how you found it."

He's talking to me like he's a damned therapist and I'm his patient.

"I did a workaround," Malcolm took a deep breath, hoping Shotgun wouldn't report his hacking of Agency files, "which gave me access to some of the files, but not all. I think we've got an honest-to-god conspiracy emanating from inside the Agency," Malcolm paused, "aimed at political targets."

This seemed to catch Shotgun's attention because he sat forward leaning closer to Malcolm. "A conspiracy. What kind of conspiracy?"

The comforting therapist voice again. "Assassination plot."

"An assassination plot hatched inside the Agency. Is that what you're telling me?"

Malcolm found Shotgun's response unsettling. *Did he already know about the plot? Were his people investigating it? If so, he could keep it under wraps until he decided to release the information. If that's what he wants, he should say so.* Disconcerted, Malcolm hesitated. "Are you sure I can't get you a drink?"

"On second thought," Shotgun bent down and unzipped his briefcase, "how about I treat you? Always keep a couple of airplane bottles of my favorites stashed in here." He looked up at Malcolm and grinned. "For emergencies," he added, bringing out two small bottles of Single Malt Scotch, which he held to the light.

Shotgun liked his liquor. Malcolm wondered how many he'd had before he arrived. "Hang on, I'll get you a glass."

"I've got glasses right here." Shotgun reached into his bag and pulled out two expensive shot glasses.

The man always travels first class. "I think I'll take a pass," Malcolm said, admiring Shotgun's style.

"Not joining me?"

"Took a Valium earlier. Cheryl won't let me combine alcohol and tranquilizers. Problem with marrying a nurse."

"One shot won't hurt. I do it all the time." Shotgun poured two drinks, one from each bottle.

Malcolm gave in, not wanting to offend. "Okay, sure," he said, watching Shotgun manipulate the contents of his traveling bar and wondering if his boss was a closet alcoholic. Shotgun's proclivity for booze was well documented.

Malcolm reached out for the shot glass his boss offered.

"*Salud*," Shotgun said, downing his drink in one long gulp while Malcolm held onto his glass, thinking about how to phrase what he had to say next. "From what I could determine … " he hesitated, "the operation's aimed at taking out high-level government officials, starting with the Vice-President." Malcolm put the shot glass to his lips and swallowed the Scotch, enjoying the burn as the liquid slid down his throat.

Shotgun's face wore a look of disbelief that worried Malcolm. "Assassination conspiracy. You said that earlier, but these were archived files, right? Meaning they're old files from some past training exercise."

"Not according to the time stamps."

"Time stamps?"

"Time stamps tell you when the files were last opened, last modified. The dates are recent, starting about two months ago and running up to the present."

"And you found a list of names of government officials you say are targeted for assassination?"

"No names, just numbers." Malcolm's head started to pound. He knew he wasn't making sense. Maybe he should have listened to Cheryl's warnings, not taken that drink on top of the Valium.

"And you believe these files are solid evidence of a high level assassination plot." A statement, not a question. The skeptical look again.

"Not solid, solid. But I plan to follow up on the information. If there's an investigation in progress, I can help."

"Have you told Chavez about this?"

Why does it matter if I've told Dan? "No one. Haven't mentioned a thing to Dan."

"What about your wife?"

"No, I said. No one." Malcolm could feel his blood pressure rising. His head throbbed.

Shotgun nodded. "That's good. Means we can keep this matter between the two of us."

Not the response Malcolm expected. *What was happening?* He had trouble thinking straight. "The pain," he moaned, grabbing his head with both hands. "It's about to explode … and my chest … " He registered Shotgun's vacant stare before his arm bumped against the pencils beside his computer, scattering them across his desk. " Call an ambulance," Malcolm managed to say before the world went black.

Chapter Five

The annoying jangle of the telephone persisted, waking Dan Chavez from a deep sleep. He checked the digital readout on the nightstand clock and fumbled the handset from its cradle. 6:23. *Who the hell's calling me this early?* He glanced at the caller ID. *Malcolm. Must be important.*

"What's up, Malcolm?" he said, trying to suppress the sleepiness in his voice.

"It's Cheryl."

"Cheryl. Everything all right?"

"Dan." A long pause filled the dead air space. "Malcolm died last night," she finally said, her voice cracking. "Heart attack."

"Oh God, no." A jolt of adrenalin shot through Dan's body. He sat upright.

"I need some help. Can you come over?"

"Of course. Right away. God, I'm sorry. I can't believe it."

"Neither can I." Cheryl choked back a sob and apologized, "I'm sorry, I'm … I've only been home from the hospital a short time. They couldn't help him. I don't know what to do."

Dan climbed out of bed, digging for his jockey shorts in the clothes on the floor. "I know, I understand. I'll be right over. Damn it. I can't believe this. Just hang on, I can be there in fifteen minutes."

"It's, I don't know, I'm … I need to talk to somebody. Thank you." Cheryl hung up.

"Damn," Dan said, speaking to the dial tone. "Good goddam." He wanted to throw something, punch somebody. He picked up a shoe and slung it across the room, hitting the bottom drawer of his dresser. "Dammit all to hell."

Dead of a heart attack? Malcolm? Mr. Physically Fit? Cheryl sounds a mess. First, their boy and now… Dan tried to shake off the grief flooding his body. *Nobody deserves this, and especially not Cheryl.*

He threw on his clothes from the day before, ran a toothbrush across his teeth and gums and without bothering to shave rushed out to his car, driving the eight city blocks to Malcolm and Cheryl's house in less than five minutes. She opened the front door before Dan could reach for the bell.

"Thanks for coming."

Dan hugged her to him, stroking her head as he would a child. "I can't believe it. Let's sit down and talk," he said. Cheryl led him into the living room and sat beside him on the sofa. He put his arm around her in a half hug. "Tell me what happened."

"I came home from choir practice last night and found him unconscious on the floor of the study. He was barely breathing. At first, I thought he was dead, but I found a slight, irregular pulse. I called 9-1-1 right away and administered CPR until they arrived. The EMTs worked on him all the way to the hospital and then the emergency room doctors," she paused and sucked in her breath, "but they couldn't revive him. The doctor said he'd had a massive heart attack. I can't stop thinking that if I'd just stayed home last night maybe things would have been different."

"You can't blame yourself. If the doctors are right, you couldn't have saved him.

Cheryl nodded numbly and placed her finger to her lips signaling silence.

Does she want me to be quiet or careful? Is someone else in the house, Dan wondered, still asleep?

"Excuse me a minute," Cheryl sniffed up her tears, "while I get some tissues and blow my nose."

Dan watched her leave the living room and cross the hall to Malcolm's study. His chest tightened when she returned with a pen and a small note pad, jotting down a couple of sentences and passing the paper to Dan. In barely legible handwriting the note read: *I think Malcolm was murdered and my house might be bugged. Can we go out for coffee where we can talk?*

Cheryl blew her nose loudly, her eyes begging Dan to believe her.

"You could probably use some coffee," he said, "and so could I. How about we go out for breakfast?"

"I'm not sure I can eat, but maybe a cup of coffee. I can put a pot on here, if you'd like."

Dan continued the ruse. "No, no. Let me take you out to breakfast."

"Okay. Hang on while I grab a sweater." Cheryl retrieved the note pad and stuffed it inside her purse on the sofa beside her. Buttoning the black sweater she'd worn when Dan arrived, she motioned him to the door.

"Thanks so much for coming over, Dan," she told him again as she locked the front door on the way out. "I really appreciate it."

Dan followed her down the sidewalk. My Honda could use a bath, he thought absently, reaching in his pants pocket for the car keys. *God, what kind of a damned situation is this?* He closed the passenger door after Cheryl and moved around to the other side of the car, lost in thought.

Settling into the front seat, Cheryl removed the note pad from her purse and laid it on Dan's lap as he buckled his seat belt. He looked down at the words she'd written: *We might be followed.*

Handing back the note pad and starting the car in one motion, Dan backed out onto North Van Buren trying to decide if he should head straight for the highway or wind around the neighborhood. No winding around, he thought. If Cheryl's suspicions were correct, which remained a large question mark in Dan's mind, he wanted to ensure her safety and not increase the threat by letting anyone know he suspected a tail.

Clearly, Cheryl assumed Malcolm's death had something to do with Agency work if she thought the house might be bugged. Dan reviewed their recent projects. Before his transfer to NCTC, he and Malcolm had worked together on a number of projects, but nothing of significance recently, nothing dangerous enough to support Cheryl's assumptions. Besides, Malcolm suffered a heart attack, not a violent death. *What led her to conclude murder? Sure, he was a fitness freak, but Malcolm wouldn't be the first damned exercise nut whose heart gave out. Has to be more than that.*

Bizarre thoughts ran through Dan's mind as he tried to make sense of the events of last night. *Was Malcolm involved in some sort of subversive activity?* He rejected the idea immediately, wondering why the notion even occurred to him. Not Malcolm. The best foreign agent in the world couldn't turn Malcolm.

Dan checked the rear view mirror. Two cars behind them. He slowed down, noting the color and style of each vehicle. At the next crossroad, he signaled his upcoming right turn. Both cars turned left. Just past the intersection, a third car pulled onto Van Buren behind him. Classic handoff, he thought, beginning to worry. He knew the range of high-tech listening devices these days. *Better to be safe. Keep a normal conversation going.*

"Are you doing okay?"

"Trying to hold myself together," Cheryl said, rummaging in her purse. "I can't thank you enough for coming over. The grief comes in waves. I can hardly stand the pain. Every ten minutes I go on a crying jag."

Dan reached over and laid his hand on Cheryl's shoulder. "I'm here, whatever you need."

Third car turned off. Less than a minute later, car number one appeared in his rear view mirror. *What the hell's going on here?*

Chapter Six

Cheryl removed a set of car keys from her purse and dangled them in front of Dan. A quick nod of his head let Cheryl know he understood. *Malcolm's private security car, the one he used for travel. I remember.* Dan turned the car toward Arlington and the parking garage on Fairfax where Malcolm, for reasons known only to Malcolm, stored his "security car" despite the sky-high monthly rates. Dan had once asked if he kept a mistress nearby, but immediately regretted the question when he heard Malcolm's response. Malcolm loved his wife and son more than anything in the world.

Cheryl scribbled down the car's location. *Third floor next to the elevator.*

Dan glanced at the note. *She'd make a good operative.* The thought almost brought a smile to his lips. Dan could feel the beat of his heart slowing to a normal rate. *This will work.* He felt almost gleeful at the idea of outwitting the bastards following them. The chase brought back memories of his early days working as a case officer in Eastern Europe. Exciting times, but hard on married life. He used to wonder how much the stress of his job had impacted his first wife's disease. The guilt had been hard to erase, but at least it no longer ate at him.

Just past the two-mile mark, Dan turned left onto Fairfax, entering a canyon of office buildings. *Almost there.* He checked the rear view mirror. Tail stayed with them the whole way. *Damn you to hell. I'm gonna feel good losing you bastards.*

Cheryl removed a parking card from her purse and laid it on the dash.

Good girl. The card will speed us through.

Dan took Malcolm's car keys from Cheryl's hand and slipped the ring over his index finger curling the keys in the palm of his left hand. The car exchange needed to be fast. Cheryl held her purse in her lap with both hands. He could see her readying herself for a quick exit.

Approaching the garage, Dan pressed the button to lower his window, grabbed the parking card and swung into the garage, barely stopping long enough to swipe the card as the gate lifted to let them through. He raced up the ramp to the third floor, thankful for the early hour and lack of traffic. A vacant spot two cars from Malcolm's provided easy parking. Dan slid the Honda into the slot. He and Cheryl jumped out and raced to Malcolm's SUV, the one with the dark-tinted windows.

As soon as Cheryl climbed in Dan started the car, motioning her to duck down. Malcolm's old baseball cap lay on the seat. Dan slapped it on his head, pulling it down so it barely covered his eyes. He backed out, turned the corner under the exit sign and spotted one of the tag cars coming up the parking ramp. *He'll see my Honda and assume he just missed us entering the elevator.* Dan slowed the SUV to seem less suspicious. *Need to give the outside wait car time to receive a report about the elevator.* When they get the report, they'll head for the hotel restaurant, he thought. He now understood Malcolm's choice of parking garages. *Lots of getaway options here. What was Malcolm involved in, anyway?*

Rounding the corner onto the lower second floor level, Dan caught sight of an empty space sandwiched between a van and another SUV, black like Malcolm's. *Just what we need.* He pulled in, adjusted the side bar mirror to reflect the traffic lane and kept the engine running. Starting up the car might tip their pursuers to their presence.

"My back's starting to cramp," Cheryl whispered.

"Just a few more minutes," Dan said, "hang in there." She wasn't in shape for this kind of action. Not a fitness addict like her husband. "Any breakfast place ideas?" The question provoked a laugh, given their circumstances.

"Starbucks on Lee Highway not far from here," Cheryl whispered. "It's in a shopping mall, easy access."

"I know the one," Dan whispered back as he monitored the side mirror. *So far, no evidence of the tag car. The occupants are probably on the elevator by now.* "Time to get out of here," he told Cheryl. "Stay down until I tell you it's clear."

§

Inside Starbucks, Cheryl moved to a table in the corner where she could watch people coming and going. She sat off to the side, scanning the room while Dan stood in line for their order. Everyone seemed to belong, stopping for coffee before work. She tried to relax, knowing Dan expected an explanation she couldn't provide. She'd tell him what she knew, or suspected, and hope he could take it from there. At least she'd managed to reach her minister from the hospital to postpone the funeral arrangements. She glanced over at Dan holding his cell phone to his ear as he paid the bill. *I wonder who he's talking to?* She checked the parking lot again. *All clear.*

Dan walked back with one tray and set it on the table. He handed her the coffee first. "It's hot, careful. Bought some muffins in case you're hungry." He took the seat that faced the front door.

"Are we out of the woods yet?" Cheryl felt too exhausted, too nerved up to eat, but she'd try. If nothing else, a jolt of sugar might restore her energy reserves.

"I don't know," Dan said, "but let's talk. Tell me why you think someone murdered Malcolm."

She took a deep breath. "First, I think he must have been investigating some terrorist plot or something, but you'd know more about that than I would."

"Not unless he was working on something I'm not privy to. What did he tell you?"

"Nothing, of course. But you know how paranoid he was. I used to think the security car was such a waste of money, and it wasn't his only safeguard. He regularly gave me instructions about what to do if anything happened to him. How to know an accident wasn't an accident. Things like that."

Dan interrupted. "Interesting. He insisted on a system with me, too."

Cheryl noticed how Dan's eyes never left the front door.

"What messages did he leave you?"

"I found my first clue, a small one, in the kitchen." She prayed Dan would understand its importance. "Malcolm turned a water glass upside down in the sink. Maybe he saw something outside? I don't know, but Malcolm would *never* leave a glass in the sink, let alone face down. Something happened in the kitchen, or perhaps he noticed something in the backyard."

"If he was distracted as you say, he might have forgotten about the glass."

"You're right, and with nothing more I might have concluded the same thing, but there's more. Another signal of his was to rearrange things. You know how obsessive he was, like the pencils on his desk? He always lined them up alongside his keyboard. Sometimes, I'd rearrange them just to tease him, which I did before I left the house last night. I know he would have straightened them the minute he sat down at his computer, but when I got home, they were scattered all over the desk, almost like he sent them flying on purpose."

"Lined up his pencils at work, too," Dan grunted. "Anything else?"

"Yes. His gun was in his pocket, which meant he'd had it out for protection or moved it there to let me know he was in danger. I checked his computer. He, or someone, wiped yesterday's files. No record of file modifications or applications opened, yet he was on the computer from the time he came home until we ate dinner. And when I left for choir practice, he was on his way back to the study for more computer work."

"Malcolm probably wiped the files. He was obsessive about that."

"But leaving the security car keys on top of his dresser was deliberate, not accidental. It was a coded message telling me I needed to escape. My instructions were to contact you if I ever found those car keys lying on his dresser. *Get away from the house, and ask you for help.*"

"Malcolm, the methodical." Dan gave her a thoughtful look. "Sounds like you're on to something. Clearly, he was under some kind of duress. Let's hope we can learn what it was before we find ourselves in the same boat."

On hearing Dan's words and knowing he believed her, a sense of relief swept over Cheryl despite the ominous reminder of their plight.

Chapter Seven

Starbucks, Lee Highway
Arlington, Virginia

"If Malcolm left messages for you, then he may have sent a message to me," Dan told Cheryl, continuing their breakfast discussion. "He emailed me last night about 7:30. I never saw the message until I checked my account before hitting the sack."

"What did he say?"

"Wanted to meet me for breakfast, which meant he had something on his mind. And if you're right about his death, he may have queued additional messages. Hang on while I check my account again." Dan ran his fingers over his cell. "Nothing's come in since last night's message. I'm worried about making the case for murder based on the evidence you've outlined, so let's hope we can turn up something more."

Cheryl cocked her head to one side. "It was enough for you. You believed me."

"I do believe you, but I knew Malcolm almost as well as you did. I'm worried about convincing people to open an investigation because this is something I can't handle on my own."

Cheryl nodded. "There's more. Again, it's indirect evidence, but aside from the clues he left, the main thing bothering me is the *way* he died."

"The heart attack?"

"He died of a heart attack, but here's the thing. When I walked in the house last night, I found him unconscious on the floor of his study. I bent over him and smelled alcohol on his breath. But he was on Valium. He wouldn't have been drinking, at least not of his own accord. I felt his pulse. It was very faint and slow, but it was there. In someone as healthy as Malcolm, the medical procedures should have been able to bring him back by speeding up his heart with drugs, but nothing worked."

"Well, if he'd had a massive heart attack … "

"In that case, he would have died instantly. He was alive when they got him to the hospital. That means there was still time. Unless, and this idea only occurred to me this morning, unless a poisonous substance brought on his brachycardia. Then, the medications would have had no effect. In order to save him under those conditions, the doctors would have had to know which poison was involved." She paused and wiped tears from her eyes, "and even then he might not have survived, but he would have had a chance." Her voice trailed off. "Ironic, isn't it? As if all his life he'd had a premonition."

Dan reached across and squeezed her hand. "Now you've hit on something tangible. There are tests to answer that question and we can arrange for them … " Dan sucked in his breath as two military types walked in the front door, their gaze drifting past Cheryl and Dan's table. " Don't look, but we have company," he said. "Two ex-Marines, by the look of them. We need to stall. Take your time drinking your coffee. They'll have to be careful, can't be too aggressive. That's our advantage."

"How did they find us?"

"I don't know, and I'm not certain yet they're bad guys. Might be the genuine article stopping by for their morning joe."

Cheryl looked over her coffee cup at Dan. "If not, and if they're the ones after us, how are we getting out of here?"

"Sit tight," he said. "I've got it covered. Old Indian rescue plan."

"I feel sick to my stomach."

"Rest room's right here. While you're in there, see if there's a window." Dan gave her a grim smile. "I won't go away."

§

Dan snapped his cell phone shut as Cheryl returned to the table. He reached over to pull out her chair, keeping his eyes glued to the front door. He could sense her apprehension.

"Those two ex-Marines, or whoever they are, are scaring the hell out of me," she said, sliding the remains of her blueberry muffin across to Dan. "I can't eat the rest of this.

He reached for the muffin, ignoring her comment about the military men now paying for their coffee. "I'll work on it, but I'm not very hungry, either. We need to behave as though we never spotted those two. Let's see whether they leave with their order or hang around."

"What are they doing now?"

"Just carried their trays to a table near the door. They're staying, apparently. If they're following us, they're trying hard to be cool about it, but I don't like their demeanor."

"Meaning?"

"They're not relaxed and chatting." Dan let his gaze roll absently around the room as he spoke, monitoring the behavior of the two out of the corner of his eye. "They haven't spoken a word to each other, and they take turns glancing outside and then back here, pretending they don't see us. My guess is contractors, not regular military. And they're here for us. Don't know if it's only to keep an eye on us, or they have other plans."

"I hope *you* have a plan," Cheryl whispered.

"I do," he said. A police siren sounded on Lee Highway, drawing the attention of the Starbucks customers, including the two military contractors. Dan could see the blue light flashing over the tops of the parked cars as the prowl car entered the parking lot. The strobe grew brighter as the vehicle pulled up to the Starbucks entrance.

"Are they coming for us?" Cheryl asked. "On some trumped-up charges? Malcolm told me it happens."

"Stay calm," Dan said, drawing another long swig of coffee. "I think the cavalry's arrived."

A lanky Virginia State Trooper entered the coffee shop and looked around. The two military types slid back their chairs and stood up. The Trooper ignored them and walked to the back of the store, stopping in front of Cheryl and Dan's table. The two military grunts followed two steps behind.

"I hope I'm right," Dan whispered, his heart beginning to race.

"You Mr. and Mrs. Larson?" the Trooper asked.

Cheryl shook her head, but Dan cut her off. "Yes, we are."

"Please come with me."

Dan took Cheryl's arm. "It's okay."

She gave him a worried look. "I don't understand."

"Henry Larson to the rescue. I'll explain later. Figured if anyone could help us, Henry could. Besides, you need to talk to him."

They stood to leave, but the two contractors moved in front of the Trooper, blocking the way. The Trooper stepped forward and pushed the pair aside, but they held their ground. The closest one thrust an ID in the Trooper's face.

"Excuse me, but this couple belongs to us," he said. "Military takes precedence over civilian."

The Trooper, who had a good six inches on each man, leaned

forward and squinted at the ID card. "Whose military?"

"Sigma Services, government contract."

The Trooper shoved him out of the way and Dan reached out and grabbed the man's partner, snapping his right arm behind his back.

"Federal agent," Dan said.

The Trooper nodded to Cheryl to move forward. "Car's out front," he said.

By the time Cheryl reached the exit, Dan heard a third police car scream its way into the parking lot, sirens blazing.

"We have custody here," the first Sigma contractor argued.

The Trooper spun around, his face to within an inch of the contractor's nose. "So sue us." As the Trooper turned to leave, the Sigma contractor made the mistake of grabbing his arm. "Touch me again, and I'll take you in for resisting arrest," the Trooper snarled.

"Where are you taking them?"

"Same place we'll take you if you interfere again. Class D felony. Care to risk it, wise-ass?"

Dan tried to hide a smile as he and Cheryl climbed into the back seat of the Dodge Charger registered to the Virginia State Police. "You have to admire Henry's style," he told her, watching their savior stride to the driver's side door. The Trooper leaned over the front seatback and introduced himself, nodding to Cheryl and extending his arm to shake hands with Dan.

"Dan Chavez, Cheryl Hall," Dan said.

"Not Mr. and Mrs. Larson? Must have arrested the wrong couple." The Trooper grinned, obviously enjoying his joke. "My orders are to drive you to the main gate at Langley and wait for Henry Larson to show up. I assume one or both of you have Agency ID so we'll have no problem at the gate?"

"Correct. And thank you," Dan said.

"Yes, thank you," Cheryl added. "You may have saved our lives."

"Just doing my job, Ma'am."

Cheryl turned to Dan. "I guess this explains your phone call."

"Lucky to find Henry in the office when I phoned," Dan said. "Not sure what I would have done, otherwise. Couldn't have a better boss than Henry. He's one tough sonofabitch. Exactly the person you want on your side if you're caught in a tight spot."

"Malcolm told me Agency people call him *Mr. Wizard*."

"They do, but he hates the nickname."

As the patrol car pulled away from the front of the coffee shop, Dan noted a second Trooper engaged in a conversation with the two Sigma Services men. He wondered about the lies being exchanged. "I'm looking forward to reading the report on those two," he said, more to himself than to Cheryl.

"I hope you'll be able to tell me about it."

"We'll see," Dan told her with a shrug, knowing she'd never be privy to a word of it. "Though I expect it'll be *need to know*. I'm hoping I get to read it."

Chapter Eight

Falls Church News-Press
Obituary: Malcolm Leighton Hall
Author Vince Becker
Published: 6:00 AM
Last updated: 7:10 AM

Falls Church resident Malcolm L. Hall passed away at his home last night. Funeral arrangements have been postponed until family members can be notified. Donations in support of the American Heart Association can be made to the Malcolm Hall Memorial Fund, P.O. Box…

7TH FLOOR, LANGLEY
OFFICE OF THE DIRECTOR OF NATIONAL CLANDESTINE SERVICES

Hours earlier, inside the new headquarters building at Langley, Henry Larson pushed aside the newspaper announcement of Malcolm's death and reached across his desk for the stack of memos that had accumulated over the past week. He'd arrived at 6:00 a.m., earlier than usual, for the sole purpose of catching up on paperwork before the weekend. His early appearance surprised his workaholic assistant Connie Lang, who prided herself on starting her workday by 7:00 a.m..

With the exception of an early morning telephone call and a ten-minute break enjoying his morning coffee while shooting the breeze with Connie, Henry had glued himself to the executive chair in his office. By 8:00, he'd managed to wade through half the pile. Most of the remaining items dealt with internal politics, and he was happy to put them off to a later time. He pushed his chair back and stared at the papers littering his desk, trying to remember a time of more turmoil at the Agency.

Investigations into the torture debacle had everyone on edge, even though the controversy had died down among the general public and the mainstream media. Inside the Agency was another matter. Henry knew the issue would be around for a long time, though he wasn't personally worried. Covering his ass was second nature. Other heads might be on the chopping block, but Henry Larson would not be going down for following illegal orders, especially ones that came in writing—with witnesses.

At the time, he'd seriously considered joining the fifty or so officers from his Directorate who had turned in their resignations in protest. But rather than resign, Henry had decided to stay on and fight. In his opinion, the Operations Directorate was a lot cleaner than the public believed. They held themselves to the highest standards, hence the spate of resignations. In many ways, he hoped the current investigations would result in cleaning up the corruption and weeding out the bad apples. There were enough of them left, Henry thought.

When the subject of the name change had come up, he'd agreed to it, despite the wishes of nearly everyone in his Directorate. If the switch from *Operations* to *National Clandestine Services* made his Directorate more palatable to the outside world, he supported the window dressing. As long as no one used it to gloss over the Agency's more serious problems, a point he continued to press home in upper management meetings.

The phone call from Dan Chavez had interrupted his early morning routine.

"Henry. Sorry to bother you, but we've got an emergency here. Don't know if you heard about Malcolm Hall's death last night."

"Got the message just before midnight. Heart attack, I heard. Big surprise to me, given his fitness schedule."

"That's just it, Henry. We need to talk, but right now I need your help. His wife is suspicious. Called me this morning. Thought her place was bugged, so we left. We've been followed, and I'm afraid I haven't shaken the tail. Anyway, we're at the Starbucks on Lee Highway in Arlington. Near Kirkwood."

"Little shopping center?"

"That's it. Can you send a car and get us out of here?"

Henry recognized the urgency in Dan's voice. A taut Native American with a sardonic grin, Dan's whole body bespoke his Apache ancestry. No soft-spoken, measured persona, Dan Chavez was wound tighter than a powwow drum. Henry took a deep breath. *No time for questions.* "Okay, I'll get right on it. Don't know who will show up for you, but they'll ask for Mr. and Mrs. Larson. Call me if anything else happens."

"Thanks, Henry." Hanging up with Dan, Henry put his thumb on the disconnect button only long enough to sever the connection.

"Connie, get me the Arlington station of the State Police and hurry. Tell them it's an emergency, and be sure to let them know who's calling." *Troopers will reach Dan faster than a car from here. They're a lot closer, and they can mobilize more firepower.* A brief discussion followed between Henry and someone at the Arlington station, after which Henry buzzed Connie a second time. "Have Security bring a car around for me. Tell them we won't be going far."

§

The patrol car carrying Dan and Cheryl pulled up to the main gate at Langley. Henry stepped out of the Security Protective Service car parked opposite. "Looking for me?"

"Damn, Henry. Can't remember the last time you looked so good," Dan said, climbing out of the car and shaking Henry's hand.

"Mrs. Hall in there?" Without waiting for an answer, Henry walked over to the police car. He offered his condolences to Cheryl and thanked the Trooper. "I owe you one, Lieutenant."

"Just doing my job, sir. But I might collect on that IOU some day." The Trooper grinned as he held open Cheryl's door, tipping his Smokey Bear hat before sliding back into the front seat of the police cruiser.

Henry led Cheryl through the gate, joining Dan alongside the SPS vehicle. "This train is bound for my office," Henry said, paraphrasing an old Woody Guthrie tune as he pointed to the open door. "Hop in."

Chapter Nine

Inside Henry's office, Dan pulled out a chair for Cheryl as Henry set out three cups of coffee.

Connie stuck her head in the office, holding the door partway open. "Let me know if you need anything," she said, giving Henry a coy smile and ignoring his visitors.

"We're good," Henry told her, turning to Dan. "Okay. Let's hear your story, and don't forget, our conversation is being recorded."

Dan and Cheryl detailed their versions of the events surrounding Malcolm's death, starting from the time Cheryl left for choir practice the previous night until Dan's call from Starbucks. Henry listened intently, stopping them periodically with questions, reviewing their descriptions and burrowing in for added detail, all in his traditional, low-key style.

"One more thing," Dan added. "Around 7:30 last night, Malcolm sent an email to my regular account. I checked it before I hit the sack. Found the message from him asking me to meet him for breakfast this morning."

"Was that unusual?"

"Not really," Dan sat forward, his arms on his knees, "but we normally had breakfast together only when one or the other of us wanted to discuss a delicate matter away from the office. I never thought to look for anything else since I expected to meet him this morning and hear about everything then. This morning I found that he'd sent the same message fifteen minutes later, but to a different account."

"Non-Agency account?"

"Yeah. Malcolm thought we should have secure accounts where we could contact each other if one of us were in trouble."

"Did he ever tell you what he meant by trouble? What worried him?"

"Just said our work had an element of danger to it, and we should take precautions. He was a little paranoid, but that's part of the reason he was so good at what he did. Besides, we're all a little paranoid after working here, aren't we, Henry?"

"If you aren't when you arrive, you will be by the time you leave." Henry reached around to switch off the recording device. "Any idea what's behind all this?"

Dan took his time answering. Henry hoped he could recall previous conversations with Malcolm that might shed light on his message.

"I have no idea," Dan finally admitted. "I'd have expected him to leave more information, tell me why he was in danger, who was after him, or who he *thought* might be after him if it were personal. The clues he left for Cheryl meant he knew he was in danger, but all his actions at home were quickly reversible, except for erasing his computer files. Suggests to me he had doubts about whether or not the danger was imminent. My bet is he knew his killer, maybe intimately."

"I'll take your guesses over mine when it comes to Malcolm," Henry said, "and we don't know whether *he* wiped the files or someone else did, but we're having a look at his computer today. I told Security to deliver it back here to Bob Randolph. Maybe we'll learn more when Randolph examines it."

"I doubt you'll find anything. Malcolm was obsessive about wiping his files, but I'll be glad to have a look-see, too."

"If anybody, other than you, can restore the information on that hard drive," Henry said, "Randolph can do it."

"I'll be glad to give him a hand if he needs it."

"I know, and I'll give him a head's up. In any case, you have me convinced. Here's what I propose. First, check your email accounts again from here. See if Malcolm's left any additional clues for us."

"No problem."

"Connie can set you up in my conference room. After that, I'd like you to take a walk downstairs and look around Malcolm's workspace, including his desktop computer, if you can manage it. And don't leave the premises without coming back up here. Your life may be in danger, too. I have an interest in keeping you safe."

"I can take care of myself, Henry."

"I know, but whatever you find, keep it between us," Henry added as Dan disappeared through the door into Connie Lang's office.

§

"Cheryl," Henry's voice softened once Dan left the room, "I know you must be exhausted, and you have a lot on your plate at home with phone calls, funeral matters, etcetera. I'm ordering a security detail to accompany you home. They'll sweep your place for bugs and block all traffic on your street that isn't local. Feel free to ask them to help you out with anything you need, including packing."

"Thank you, Henry, though my neighbors might not appreciate it. Did you say packing?"

"When you get home, tend to whatever's essential, and then pack a suitcase. Enough to last at least a week if you were going on vacation. When you're done, let the security people know. I'll make arrangements for a place you can stay until I learn what this is all about. I'm sorry to put you through more aggravation because I know how tough this is on you. And I wish for all the world I could bring Malcolm back."

Cheryl wiped away the tears flowing down her cheeks. "I appreciate your help, Henry. Malcolm would have appreciated it, too."

"Your husband was a great guy and a brilliant analyst. Intelligence will miss him. He was their superstar. We'll all miss him." Henry punched in five digits on his desk phone. "She's ready to go."

Chapter Ten

After Cheryl left with Henry's Security detail, he asked Connie to put through another call to the Trooper station in Arlington.

"Just calling to say thanks for helping us out today."

"Anytime. Glad it all worked out."

"I understand your men ran into a couple of Sigma boys."

"The Lieutenant's writing up the report now. I'll send you a copy."

"What'd they have to say for themselves?"

"Said they'd been hired to provide security for Mrs. Hall."

"Security? Who hired them?"

"Told us we'd have to go over their heads for that information. Hinted they were employed by the Agency. Given where her husband worked, it sounded logical to us, but we were left wondering."

Henry wondered, too. "I'll ask around."

"Right hand doesn't know what the left hand's doing?"

"Possibly. Let me know if you hear anything more definitive."

"Will do."

"And thanks again." Henry stared at the phone, thinking about the trooper's last comment. Something's going on here and I don't like being kept out of the loop. He picked up the phone. Better start with Intelligence, Henry thought, putting a call through to the Director. See what the DI has to say about the death of one of his analysts. Zak likes to play his cards close to his vest. Not the person to ask for information, despite his title, but maybe he'll volunteer something.

Zak Browning picked up the phone. "Morning, Henry. Guess you heard about Malcolm."

"Damn shame. I know he was one of your best. He'll be a big loss."

"Damn right he will."

"I have a unit over at his house."

"What?" Zak's outrage reverberated across the phone line like an out of control tuning fork. Henry tried to keep from smiling. "He's *my* employee, not yours," Zak sputtered.

"*Was* your employee, and I have intel on a connection between

Malcolm and a foreign op we're working on."

"I'm taking this to Whit," Zak said, referring to CIA Director Edward Whitworth. "You've gone too far this time, Henry."

"Already took it up with Whit. I was hoping for your cooperation." Henry turned on his soothing voice. "No sense making a territorial case out of a terrible tragedy that affects us all."

Silence greeted Henry on the other end of the line.

"Hard to believe he'd go like that," Henry continued. "Wish half my people were that physically fit."

"Exercised too much, if you ask me. Probably had an enlarged heart and never knew it."

"In that case, I'd think his annual physical would have caught it."

"You have something on your mind here?"

Henry could feel Zak's annoyance, and he bit back another grin. "Just wondering what Malcolm was working on."

"Nothing critical, and nothing you don't already know about. Check your Intelligence briefs."

Henry backed off, letting Zak save face. He knew he'd won the battle, no sense waging war. "Just called to extend my sympathies and let you know I'm involved. Trying to wrap my head around what's happened. Let me know if there's anything I can do to help your operation. Always liked Malcolm."

Henry knew he was rambling, but it was a useful strategy for keeping people off balance, and if there was anyone he wanted off balance, it was Zak Browning. The two men had never gotten along, one of the reasons Zak left Operations years ago and moved over to Intelligence. Even now, their relations were testy, at best.

"Nothing going on here we can't handle," Zak said, still sounding annoyed, "but keep me in the loop with your investigation, Henry, or I'll see there's hell to pay. Got another call coming in." He hung up, dismissing Henry with less subtlety than usual.

Henry's hand lay on the receiver as he re-ran the conversation in his mind. He was an adept listener. His years in the spy business left him with a sixth sense, the ability to spot a lie, uncover a half-truth in the briefest of conversations. When it came to Zak, the question never was *is Browning lying*? But rather, *what's he lying about now?*

Lots of arrangements to make, Henry thought, his mind absorbed with the details of the task facing him, which was getting around the heads of other Directorates. This would be one of the trickiest operations of his career. After surmounting that problem, he'd pour his Directorate's resources into uncovering the reasons behind Malcolm's death. His instincts told him Cheryl and Dan might be right. Malcolm hadn't died of natural causes.

Henry's stomach grumbled and he checked his watch. A little early for lunch, but he hadn't eaten breakfast, and he always ate breakfast. Intent on beating the morning traffic, he'd dressed quickly. Navy blazer, gray slacks and a button-down shirt. His ex-wife called it his uniform. "You look more like an accountant than a spymaster," she'd once told him. Henry told her to watch her language, and they'd both laughed. *A long time ago, another life.*

Today would be an early lunch day. He'd spend his lunchtime figuring out how to tackle the first of several questions: *What was Malcolm involved in that got him killed? And who hired the Sigma goons to protect Cheryl and why?*

Chapter Eleven

Dan waited in Connie's office for Henry to return from lunch. He wished he had more substantive information to report to his boss.

"Turn up anything?" Henry asked as he entered.

"A couple of things," Dan replied.

Henry held the office door open and waved Dan inside. "What'd you find?"

"An email from Malcolm," Dan said, sitting down. The day was only half over and he felt exhausted from the emotional stress. "Arrived in my account shortly past noon."

"You think someone's using Malcolm's account?"

"No. It came from one of his secure accounts that runs off an external server. Malcolm must have queued the message yesterday and set it to go out at noon today. But that's not all." Henry raised an eyebrow. "When I got downstairs and walked into Malcolm's office? Damned place was cleaned out already. Computer gone, file cabinets gone, like no one ever existed in the space."

"That was fast. Means Zak knows something," Henry said, "and he's intent on locking us out. Did you run into him down there?"

"No. Zak's a damn snake in the grass, in my opinion. I avoid him as much as possible, which brings me to my next question. I'd like a transfer out of my liaison position at NCTC and back into Ops, Henry. I'm hoping you'll give the okay on it."

"I put you in that liaison position for a reason, and not because I knew you wanted a shot at a desk job and regular hours."

Typical of Henry, Dan thought. "And here I thought you were doing me a favor, but that's not the point. I want to get to the bottom of what happened to Malcolm … " Dan left his sentence unfinished, the pain striking deep in his heart every time he thought about his friend's untimely death.

"You can do a better job of investigating Malcolm's death by staying where you are. As long as you're at the Counterterrorism Center you can come and go in both places. Besides, you've got a direct line to the

Bureau over there. At some point, we may need their help."

Dan listened, bristling at the stonewalling he'd encountered in his new job. Cooperation wasn't part of the FBI's vocabulary. "I've gotten nowhere with the Fibbies, other than a superficial interaction with one or two of them. As for the rest—never see 'em, never talk to 'em. They're invisible where we're concerned."

"They'll get over it, eventually. Tell me about Malcolm's email.

"Cryptic message: *Code 21, 731db. Assassinations?*

Henry let out a low whistle. "What's 731db?"

"Refers to an old training exercise database. Mostly archived material. Don't know why he'd be working with it."

"Something's in there, and Malcolm found it. Use my computer. See what you can find," Henry said, vacating his chair and picking up the *In Box* from his desk. "I've got plenty to do while you work." He walked over to the conference table with the box of papers and settled into the straight-backed desk chair designed to support his bad back.

"I'll see what I can turn up. Shouldn't take long."

"I'll be here."

Within minutes, Dan looked up scratching his head in frustration. "Damnedest thing. Found a folder labeled *Code 21*, but I can't access the files. Tells me I don't have clearance. I can try a hack—"

Henry stopped him. "Let me see what I can do," he said, crossing back to the desk. He logged into the system and followed Dan's instructions.

"Lets me access one file, then tells me I don't have clearance," Henry said. "I don't understand. My clearance is higher than the damned President of the United States."

Dan pointed to a line of numbers in the one file Henry managed to open. "Can you make sense of this?"

"Looks like a list of government job classifications. Third one down is mine. Vice-President Chun's is at the top. The rest I don't know."

Dan paced the room, struggling with the only conclusion that made sense, in light of Malcolm's "assassination" question. "For reasons we don't know, Malcolm accessed those files and concluded he'd found a hit list targeting government officials."

"Pretty flimsy evidence, if this is all of it."

"Is the President's number on the list?"

"No."

"This can't be all Malcolm saw. Don't know if I'd have given an archived database a second glance. One look and I'd have thought: *another outdated document misfiled, so what if I can't access it?* Why a training mission file? Doesn't compute," Dan said. "On the other hand, something led Malcolm to his conclusion. Maybe it *is* a plot that's designed to mimic a training exercise in order to draw in the military. They believe they're engaged in a mock mission when in fact, it's the real thing."

Henry nodded. "I like that idea."

Dan wandered over to the window, lost in thought. He could see the Potomac from this height. In fact, he could see most of Langley, land stolen from his people 300 years ago. And here he was defending that land. He shook off his negative thinking. "Let's hope we learn more when we get our hands on Malcolm's home computer."

"We could be barking up a dead tree here with archived files," Henry said. "Maybe we're wrong about Malcolm's death."

"Not a chance. Here's what we do know." Dan ticked off the points with his fingers. "One, Malcolm thought he uncovered some kind of assassination plot in the Agency's files. Two, he felt the discovery threatened his life. And three, he's dead. That makes it murder, in my book. I know we can't prove cause and effect here, but to tell you the truth, it scares the hell out of me, because whoever killed Malcolm is an insider. They may assume he told me what he knew. May think he told Cheryl, too. I can take care of myself, but I'm worried about her. We need a safe house for her that's not connected with the Agency."

"I'm already on it. I'll be staying with her tonight and set up a rotating guard I can trust until we get this sorted out."

"Thanks, Henry." Dan felt an immediate sense of relief. Cheryl was a good friend. She'd been indispensable in helping Dan's new wife adjust to D.C., and Dan owed her. "When I get back to my office, I'll contact the Secret Service about additional security for Chun. You need to pay attention to security, too, Henry. Remember, you're number three on that list."

"*If* it *is* a hit list. But don't worry," Henry moved his papers from the conference table back to his desk, "I've got a long history of watching my back. After you leave, I'll ask Connie to check on the government number in the second slot so we know who else to warn. Looks like we have some planning to do."

§

Once Dan left, Henry sat at his desk toying with the idea of going straight to the new DCI with Dan's theory, but the issue of trust stopped him. He and Whitworth were strangers, even though their offices occupied the same floor, and they'd participated in weekly meetings together over the past few months. Henry had too many unknowns when it came to Whitworth. If a conspiracy arose within the Agency, a newly appointed Director of Central Intelligence would be Henry's prime suspect. Was Whit in on the scheme or being kept in the dark? That was the $64,000 question. The latter wasn't inconceivable, and it wouldn't be the first time, particularly in the case of a new DCI.

Henry's nature was averse to trusting someone he barely knew. Not when his life and the lives of his friends might be on the line. He trusted Dan, whose life was on the line too, but Dan would have to play this out carefully. Couldn't trust his colleagues any more than Henry could. They needed a third player, someone with the right contacts, someone who no one knew was in the game, which is why Henry set about making arrangements to bring home Evan Phillips. He'd have to do it in a way that raised no suspicions about Evan's mission or the reasons for his return.

Evan was one of the CIA's top field officers in counterterrorism. He'd worked for Henry in the Middle East and in Eastern Europe. Memories swept over Henry of his time as Eastern Europe Station Chief working with Evan, his best operative, and the circumstances surrounding Evan's assignment to Prague where he'd fled following a painful divorce. Henry had called in chits on Evan's behalf because in some peculiar way, he'd felt responsible.

To Henry's great relief, Evan quickly settled into his Eastern European lifestyle and loved his work, despite the dangers. He ran an exhaustive counter-intelligence, counterterrorism network. Every important agent in Eastern Europe and in the Russian satellite countries belonged to Evan, adding one more obstacle to Henry's efforts to return him to the States surreptitiously. Henry knew he'd pay a price, but he hoped by then they'd know who killed Malcolm and why.

Henry picked up the phone. "Get me Prague 6," he told Connie, leaning back in his chair and contemplating the consequences of recent events in the U.S. The country seemed to be moving into another McCarthy-type era, the new demons being abortion, taxes, and gay marriage. Even the old communism bugaboo was being resurrected and reframed in terms of socialism.

Waiting for Prague to pick up, Henry ran a nervous hand over his bald spot. Maybe he was getting too old for this job or too cynical. After the phone call, he'd travel to the safe house where he planned to stash Cheryl Hall, a place no one in the Agency knew about. He looked forward to spending the night there. Cheryl was a nice lady, and Henry hoped to get to know her better. He could kill two birds with one stone here, he thought, trying to quiet his fears as he realized for the first time in his thirty odd years in the Agency that he was scared shitless.

Chapter Twelve

NEW PROTESTS OVER OLD DOUBTS
by Staff Writer | Associated Press

Honolulu, HI. Passions among Birthrighters are running high. Constituents booed long-time Hawaiian Congressman Kono Pukui at last night's town hall meeting for affirming the citizenship of Hawaiian-born U.S. Vice-President Allen Chun. "He's Chinese, not American," one woman shouted, "I want my country back!"

Honolulu, Hawaii

Hawaiian Airlines Flight 151 from Kahului landed on the hot tarmac at Honolulu International Airport ten minutes ahead of schedule. Alicia Michel pressed her cheek against the window of her first class seat and relived her past while she waited for the plane to taxi to the jetway.

A diorama of people and places played across her mind's eye. The happiest times of her life were spent on this island. Carefree years when the future looked brighter and happier than it turned out to be. Why had she traded life in this paradise for college and a career in Washington, D.C.? Two reasons, she grudgingly acknowledged, both of which had made sense at the time: a full ride to George Washington University to study International Affairs, an opportunity no one in their right mind would decline, followed by an exciting job offer from the CIA.

"Is this home for you?" The question came from the moon-faced businessman sitting in the seat beside her, a coach flyer lucky enough to move to first class after the flight attendant spilled coffee on his tie.

"No, just visiting." Alicia paused before adding, "but not for the first time." She flashed him a tight-lipped smile and turned away. Half-truths rather than outright lies prevented slip-ups, a lesson she learned early. She continued staring out the window, discouraging her seatmate from more conversation.

The full scholarship to GWU had been welcome news at her high school graduation. She'd worked hard for it, but an element of luck infused every university bureaucrat's decision, and she knew she'd been fortunate. Her father insisted she'd made her own luck and to some extent, he was right. Like him, she possessed the gift of recognizing opportunities and turning them to her advantage, a principle that guided her in the college application process. The near absence of Hawaiian born students in eastern elite schools, including George Washington, had made the scholarship almost a given. Her SAT scores hadn't hurt, either.

The plane's overhead speaker crackled with the voice of the flight attendant, stirring Alicia from her reveries. She reached down to gather her bag, only half-listening to the familiar patter.

"The current temperature at Honolulu International is a balmy 85 degrees," the attendant crooned. "Please watch your step as you exit the plane, and thank you for flying Hawaiian Airlines. Enjoy your stay in Honolulu. Aloha!"

Alicia stepped off the plane onto the gray-carpeted jetway and accepted the flower lei she'd ordered for herself when she booked the flight, ensuring the appearance of a genuine tourist. No one would be waiting for her at the baggage claim, but it never hurt to prepare for unexpected eventualities. She thought about her mother, who would be furious to know her only daughter had arrived in Honolulu without contacting her family.

Her parents would complain loudly if they ever found out. *What business is so important you couldn't find time for your family?* Alicia wasn't worried. They would never know about her visit, even if they happened to pass her on the street—an unlikely event. Honolulu was a big place, but her disguise was so perfect Alicia barely recognized herself in the bathroom mirror earlier that morning. She glanced at her wrist, checking the time on her new Veneto watch, a tasteful accessory that had set the Agency back about $10,000 if authentic, which she doubted. Her boss told her to keep it when she finished the job, reinforcing her suspicion of a Chinese knock-off.

Striding past the gates inside the airport, Alicia checked her reflection in the three-story windows overlooking the runway. She liked what she saw. With her index finger, she pushed her oversized sunglasses higher on the bridge of her nose in a gesture of approval for her new look. The short, bobbed hairstyle freed her blonde bombshell personality, which she normally kept hidden inside her fictive bookworm persona—her studied look with the rimless, square glasses and long, dark hair. She wondered if she would enjoy anything about her Honolulu assignment other than the new hairdo. *Given the circumstances? Probably not.*

§

Alicia located the nondescript Toyota in a nearly empty section of the airport parking garage and clicked the key's *Open* button. The car's taillights blinked. She tossed her bag in the back, settled into the driver's side and reached into the console to fish out the employee-parking card. Glancing over, she noticed a University of Hawaii baseball cap and neatly folded jacket lying on the passenger seat beside her.

She reached into her purse and removed a long, brown wig. After tucking her hair under the tight-fitting hairpiece, she donned the hat. She slipped on the jacket, zipped it and turned up the collar. After exchanging a pair of large, black-rimmed sunglasses for her Prada wraparounds, she felt ready to face the security cameras at the garage gate.

"Honolulu, here I come," she whispered as she exited the garage through the automated turnstile and followed the arrows pointing to Honolulu. Turning south onto the Lunalito Freeway she checked her rearview mirror for a tail. No vehicle left the airport garage with her, and no one followed her onto the freeway. She decided to double-check, anyway. Coming up on Kalihi Street she left the freeway, drove three blocks and made a quick U-turn, noting the color and make of cars passing in the opposite lane.

With one eye on the rearview mirror, she headed back to the freeway taking King to Liliha. A block from the Freeway entrance she noticed a black SUV two cars behind. *Was it a tail?* She made a quick turn into the Liliha Square Shopping Center and drove slowly, pretending to hunt for a parking place. The SUV followed her into the lot. Alicia swung into the nearest empty spot and waited. The SUV parked nearby. A young woman got out and looked around, then slid open the rear door and pulled out a stroller. Alicia watched her struggle with the stroller, trying to open it.

Who is she? Is she following me? Alicia's handlers had counseled her not to worry. Their mission hadn't been compromised so far, they told her, no need to expect trouble now. It was a meaningless assertion to Alicia, who took nothing for granted.

The SUV's shaded windows provided no clues to the presence of a child belonging to the stroller. Alicia removed her baseball cap and jacket without taking her eyes off the woman. *So far, no kid. That's trouble.* She opened the car door and stepped out, feeling in her shoulder bag for the semi-automatic. As she moved toward the SUV, she took note of nearby parked cars she could use as shields. If a bullet sailed her way, she'd keep enough metal between herself and the SUV to save her life, or at least give her a fighting chance.

Three cars from her quarry she heard, "Mommy, hurry up."

Alicia fumbled with her purse as the woman from the SUV lifted a towheaded three-year-old to the ground. *That was a close one.* A sense of relief swept over her. *Take good care of that kid*, she murmured to herself on her way back to the car. Inside the Toyota, she removed the wig, fluffed out her newly styled blonde hair and checked her phone. *Dinnertime.* No wonder she felt hungry. She headed back to the Freeway and her hotel, still wary.

Chapter Thirteen

Honolulu, Hawaii

The hot pink *Aloha Hoy* name stood out against the sign's bright blue background. It screamed bad taste, but Alicia approved of her target's breakfast place when he came to Honolulu. The fisherman's reef ambience was a bit over the top, but she loved the restaurant's fried poke omelet. And so did he. She knew exactly where he sat. He always ate breakfast alone, accompanied by two or three newspapers and a similar number of cups of coffee. She knew all about his tastes.

She entered the restaurant and spotted him immediately. An empty table sat next to him, a bit of good luck that might save her a second trip. She indicated her seating choice to the hostess who led her to her chosen table.

The target looked up from his newspaper when Alicia sat down. *Who wouldn't stare at a stunning blonde?* Amazing what makeup, expensive clothes and hair styling can do. She'd never considered herself beautiful, but she had a pretty face and a good figure. The Agency makeover had produced surprising results. He never would have noticed her if she'd appeared sans make-up and flashy clothes, her hair its natural medium brown and her eyes their normal hazel-green. She knew that for a fact, because in one of her previous visits she'd sat near him *au naturel,* so to speak. He never gave her a second glance. Lucky for her, some men were fools. Apparently, her target was one of them.

Alicia scanned the menu, casting a discrete glance every now and then at the dishes on her target's table. He caught her looking once and smiled. She returned the smile and quickly averted her eyes, focusing on the menu choices. After an appropriate delay, she leaned in his direction.

"Excuse me. I'm sorry to interrupt your breakfast, but this is my first time visiting Oahu. A friend recommended this restaurant, but never suggested what I should order. Can you tell me what poke is?"

The target grinned. "First, it's pronounced *pokay.*" He answered as if she were a child. She blamed it on her blonde hair, an attention getter with a downside, especially in Hawaii. "And second," he added, "it's every Hawaiian's favorite food." He acted like a native-born Hawaiian rather than an interloper who only visited a few times a year, despite owning a beach house on the island.

"Then, for sure, I'll give it a try. Which *pokay* dish would you recommend? And I still don't know what it is."

"I like the omelet."

She knew that, too.

"Poke is a fish dish," he added. "It's usually served raw, but in the omelet they sear the fish ever so lightly. It's delicious. You won't be sorry you tried it."

"Thanks, I'll let you know." Shameless in her professional pursuits, she winked at him when she said it, just barely, so it might have passed as a slight eye twitch.

The waiter arrived to take her order, and she decided to flirt with him, too. From the corner of her eye, she noticed another grin cross her target's face and wondered how quickly the grin would disappear when he realized she was there to terminate his life. Only fitting that a blonde would be hired to kill him, she thought.

"I'll have the poke omelet, coffee and some fresh papaya," Alicia told the waiter.

"Yes, ma'am. Can I interest you in a side of fried rice?"

"Sure. I hadn't thought of it." Alicia glanced up from the menu and smiled at the waiter, who grinned back. She could see her target watching her. Exactly the reaction she wanted.

He's a handsome man. Chiseled face that reminded her of the late JFK, Jr., only older and more wizened. Crystal blue eyes that danced when he grinned. They seemed to look straight through her. She knew his background because she had a copy of his dossier. Educated at Brown, with an MBA from Harvard.

She knew about his stint in the military and his foray into the family business, but from there, his connections to his family seemed to end. Afterward, he supposedly signed up with Sigma Services. However, new information turned up a different story, including evidence of ties to gunrunners supplying arms to terrorist groups in Eastern Europe. He was a hired assassin, and he had to be stopped. Her job was to stop him. If not, the consequences would be disastrous. According to the latest intel, he was coming close to achieving his goals. Too close.

"Cream and sugar?"

"Thanks, I take it black," Alicia told the waiter, rewarding him with another gleaming smile as he poured her coffee.

"No problem," he said. "Your order will be out in ten minutes."

The target leaned over and placed his left hand on her table. No wedding ring. Not a surprise. "If you're not expecting anyone, why don't you join me?"

Alicia couldn't believe her luck and credited the blonde hair again. "I'm not expecting company, and I'll be happy to join you," she gave him an apologetic look. "If I'm not interrupting your reading."

"I can read newspapers anytime, but breakfast with a beautiful woman? Who can pass up an opportunity like that?"

He was smooth, but Alicia knew that about him, too. He liked beautiful women, which is why they deployed her, the Agency said. She'd worried whether she could carry out the assignment, but the job was beginning to look easy. At least they hadn't asked her to carry out the killing, only to get him to the right place at the right time. She'd suffered a few pangs of self-doubt when she stepped on the plane at Kahului this morning, but the hardest part was over. She'd made contact.

Alicia picked up her Agency-supplied Marc Jacobs purse from the chair beside her and stood up, extending her hand. The target was on his feet giving her an appreciative once-over. They shook hands. "I'm Alicia Michel," she said. "I go by Ally."

"I'm pleased to meet you Ally. I'm Tom Kerrigan, and I go by Tom." They both laughed. He held out her chair and waited until she sat down. As he sat, he leaned forward and added, "I'm *very* pleased to meet you, Ally."

Alicia looked down, slightly embarrassed at her instant attraction to him. *I wish we could have met in another life*, she thought, with a touch of guilt. *I might have liked you.*

"So tell me, where are you from and what do you plan to do on your visit to the glorious state of Hawaii?"

Alicia pulled an itinerary from her purse and handed it him. "These are my proposed activities."

Tom reacted with a grin as he read over the neatly typed itinerary. "Even my assistant doesn't hand me a schedule this tightly organized."

"Well, I'm easily distracted, so I set out the perfect schedule for myself. What I plan to do is to purposely fail to meet each of the goals on my list so I can know I'm truly on holiday." She gave him a mischievous grin.

He tipped his head at an angle that matched hers. "And how do you go about failing to meet your goals?"

"Each day of my vacation I review my schedule and ask myself, 'do I really want to do this or that?' More often than not, the answer is no. It's such a good feeling to blow off one activity after another and only do what I really feel like doing at the moment."

Tom Kerrigan laughed out loud. "I'll have to say, this is a new one on me, but I like your ingenuity. I may do the same thing on my next vacation. And I'll ask my assistant to schedule it for me. That way, I can doubly appreciate doing exactly as I please."

Alicia's food arrived, and Tom asked for more coffee, adding papaya when he saw the plate the waiter set before Alicia. "Bring me the same fruit plate you brought the pretty lady."

"Do you do this on a regular basis?" Alicia asked, knowing from his dossier that he did.

"Order papaya or invite strange women to join me for breakfast?"

"Both." She smiled at him.

"Now and then." He startled her with the honesty of his answer. "I like beautiful women," he added, surprising her again. "Now, enough about me. Let's talk about you."

Alicia recited her cover identity, and he commented on everything. By the time she'd finished her breakfast and her third cup of coffee they'd decided to spend the day together. He said he could use some time off because he'd been working too hard and besides, he added, she wouldn't find a better guide in Honolulu, so she shouldn't let this opportunity slip away.

It was all too easy. Alicia began to worry.

Chapter Fourteen

Prague, Czech Republic

Evan Phillips eased himself off the bed and slowly crossed the safe house room to the only window. He gazed at the sea of orange roofs cascading down the hillside below. Shadowy voices in his head urged him to climb out and ride the tiles to downtown Prague and the Vlatava River, the drug's effects still playing tricks with his brain. He strained his eyes, searching the panoramic view for familiar landmarks, trying to clear his mind and focus his thoughts.

The watcher looked up from his newspaper. "The window's nailed shut, mate," he said, reading Evan's mind. "Breaking the glass will set off an alarm. You wouldn't want to do that."

"I know. What day is it?

"The tenth."

The slant of the sun and shadows suggested late afternoon. "Time?"

The watcher moved the paper aside and checked his watch. "4:23. I believe you slept in."

The watcher's dry humor escaped him. Evan rested his arms on the windowsill, examining the bruises on his elbow and wrist that stretched over to his aching fingers. One was covered with a bandage that needed to be changed. "I think I'm coming out of it," he told the watcher. "At least now I recognize the symptoms."

"Tomorrow will be better." The watcher turned back to his copy of the Prague Daily Monitor.

Better than what? Evan wondered, his memory of recent events foggy, at best. *Who did this to me and how many memories have they erased?* At the moment, he had no way of knowing, but he sure as hell intended to find out.

"Prague here," the watcher said, lifting his vibrating phone to his ear after checking caller ID.

"Get your friend on the line and then excuse yourself," Henry said.

"Hang on a minute, he's in the can. We'll switch places when he comes out."

Evan emerged from the bathroom, and the watcher handed over his phone.

"Phillips."

"Evan, it's Henry. I hear you're not in very good shape."

"Could have been worse."

"I'm bringing you home."

"Not now, Henry. Please. I've got work to do here. Besides, I want to get the bastards."

"We'll get them, I promise. And I'll help you, but your cover's been blown."

"Jesus, Henry. I know I owe you a lot, but please don't bring me back now. I'm not leaving here without a head in my hands."

"How bad off are you?"

"Mostly bruises. Nothing that won't go away in a week or two, but they fucked with my mind, Henry. I can't remember much about the whole incident. I can barely recall their faces. Don't know if I'd recognize the fuckers if I ran into them on the street, but at some point I'll meet up with them again, and they'll wish they'd never been born."

"Jeez, I'm sorry. Nobody told me about the mind thing, only that you got beat up. That's a pisser, but we'll get them. I hope our friends are treating you well?"

"Sure. It's the fucking Ritz Carlton here, Henry, but I want out."

"I know, and I appreciate how you feel, but you know what happens under these circumstances. I can't take responsibility for your life right now, and neither of us can risk losing somebody else because there's a bead on you. You've got to trust me on this partner, and you *can* trust me. You know that. Have I ever let you down?"

Evan sucked in his breath. Henry was calling in the IOU, and Evan knew it. He had no choice but to go along.

"I've got you booked on a military transport out of Stuttgart at midnight," Henry continued. "A car's picking you up at six."

"Fuck you, Henry."

"Dan Chavez is meeting you at the airport. I'm looking forward to seeing you. Have a good trip."

"As I said. F you."

§**

A passive Evan Phillips sat in the rear seat of the black Mercedes SUV, the watcher beside him while the young driver with the military haircut headed west down the hill. Away from the Vlatava River and out of Prague. Evan calculated their ETA. Normally five-and-a-half hours, but at the rate this cocky driver was going, he would probably shave off at least forty-five minutes, maybe an hour.

The Agency car had arrived at 6:00 on the dot, which gave them plenty of time to make the midnight flight, barring an accident or a problem at the German border. The likelihood of a delay was slim, given the EU open border treaty and the Agency's talent for forging foreign ID's. Someone had stripped Evan of all of his papers. He wondered what the watcher planned to provide in their place. The lost papers would have normally held up the trip. The Czech Republic was a signatory to the Schengen Agreement, but they hadn't joined the open borders policy yet. Thus, Czech papers required a customs check. Evan asked the watcher about the nationality of his new documents and received a noncommittal shrug. Better than the response to earlier questions, which were greeted with glaring silence.

He tried to strike up a conversation with the driver, but got nowhere fast there, too. The driver said he couldn't talk and operate a vehicle at the same time. *Wonder if the grunt could unzip his fly in time to piss?* Typical monophasic military type these days. Can't hold two competing ideas in their heads at the same time. Damn military. They let the good ones go, only to have them join up with independent contractors and make ten times the money without the discipline or the rules. Made his job a helluva lot harder.

The watcher's head bobbed against the back seat. Evan glanced over at his sleepy companion. Looked like a local. Baggy shirt, tan pants, not quite stylish but not quite out of date, either. Local haircut, too—a little too long and curling around the ears. Clean-shaven. Evan guessed his age at early forties. Accent wasn't local, though. A hint of Aussie in it. The guy had *agent* written all over him. Evan wondered who recruited him and where. The Agency didn't operate in Australia. Maybe MI6 out of England? Evan knew the signs, knew how he would behave under similar circumstances. He tried to draw the man out, test him, but the guy was good. Like talking to a robot. Evan wondered if that's how he appeared to other people. An automaton, a mechanoid—no emotion, no feelings, only intellect.

Feelings are for civilians, Henry once told him. Evan understood the message. Neither he nor the watcher was a civilian, both warriors fighting a deadly game against an often-anonymous enemy. He wondered where the watcher came from in Aussieland. He'd never seen him before, and he ran all the agents in Prague and the surrounding areas. He also knew all of the Brits' people. So where did Henry find this guy, and why didn't he use one of Evan's men? He wondered again how the watcher had rescued him, or if it was the watcher who set him free. He couldn't remember.

For their first few hours together, Evan had no idea whether he was still in captivity awaiting a second beating or had been placed in protective custody, as the watcher claimed. Maybe it was a trick to win his confidence. He wasn't sure. But then the call came in from Henry. It was the first time he knew with certainty he was in a safe house and in trustworthy, if uncommunicative, hands. How he got to this point was the question uppermost in his mind, and the first question he'd ask Henry: *how did you find me, and how did you get me out?*

Henry's answer would provide the starting point for his investigation, the first step in learning who blew his cover and how, learn who captured and beat him and messed with his head. He hoped that person was ready to meet his maker. If the perpetrators belonged to one of the Iranian terror cells he'd been investigating, they never would have let him get away. They'd have tortured and killed him in less than twelve hours.

The Iranians were a threat to Europe, but even more so to Israel and the United States, their premier targets. The number of Iranian cells turning up in Eastern Europe was a worry. He hated turning over surveillance to underlings, even for a temporary trip back home. And that's all it would be, as far as he was concerned. A short trip, a new cover, and he'd be back in business. He hated being pulled away from this operation.

He ran through the scenario of his capture hour by hour, straining the memory synapses in his brain to retrieve the missing events. He remembered dressing for dinner, tying his striped tie, then untying it and tossing it on the bed as he decided to go more casual. He selected his best dinner jacket, a dark silk. Women sent appreciative glances his way whenever he wore it. Funny how so muted a color could draw so much attention. *Where was the jacket now?*

The message left at the hotel desk said his Agency contact would be female. Tall, slender, and wearing a red blouse and white slacks with a paisley shawl over her shoulders. He remembered leaving the hotel and waving off the taxis, opting instead to walk to the Mlynec Restaurant.

An enjoyable fifteen-minute stroll from his hotel, downhill all the way.

He'd arrived on schedule. She was late. He waited over an hour for her; spent the time enjoying the scenery, sipping wine and dawdling over his appetizer. She was easy enough to spot when she finally entered the restaurant and looked around for him. He could still picture her walking in, the Old Town Bridge Tower in the background like a movie scene or a photo shoot from an ad campaign for Skale, his favorite wine and the best of the Czech reds. He remembered drinking it that night.

He also remembered the feel of the soft breeze flowing over the terrace, bringing with it indescribable scents of the river. His memory of the evening was sharp enough to recall the shape of the stones on the supports of the Charles Bridge, but he couldn't recall what he ate for dinner. Probably lamb chops or maybe the giant shrimp, his two favorites. The woman moved toward him in his mind. He stood, helped her remove her paisley wrap. She wore her long, dark hair swept up and away from her face. Her fair skin contrasted with the almond shape of her eyes, suggesting Asian ancestry. Roma, maybe. He struggled to recall her name, even though he knew she would have used an alias. Elaine, maybe. Or Ellen. It started with an *E*. That much he remembered.

When the waiter arrived, Evan had ordered the same wine for her. She said it was her favorite, too. He remembered how she accidentally dropped her purse when she adjusted her shawl over the back of her chair. He bent down to retrieve it, noticing the fine feel of the leather. His training had taught him better, but he mistakenly believed they were on the same side. He handed her the purse. She smiled at him when she thanked him, and that's where his memories ended. He realized later that she must have dropped something in his drink. He also knew that she was good at her job.

When he returned to Prague, the Mlynec would be his first stop. He wanted to know everything about the incident on the night he passed out. What did the beautiful woman do? Who arrived to collect him? What did she tell the restaurant employees? After that, he would find out who left the message at his hotel desk and then figure out how they learned his code, the one that changed daily.

"Border's coming up," the driver said, "need your ID cards."

The watcher stirred, and the driver repeated his request. Digging through his pockets, the watcher produced three nationality cards identifying the car's occupants as French citizens. "Let's have your best French," he cautioned as he leaned over the seat and held out the cards for the driver.

"*Oui*," the driver responded, cracking a smile for the first time.

Not a military grunt after all, Evan thought. Henry was good. He couldn't help but smile at his boss's attention to detail. The best, he thought, but that wouldn't stop him from questioning Henry about the person or persons who'd blown his cover and how Henry had tracked Evan's whereabouts and brought him to safety.

Chapter Fifteen

7th Floor, Langley
Office of the Director of Information

Pretty Bird has landed, the note read. The CIA's Director of Intelligence took the piece of paper and smiled at the message, amusing himself at the old-fashioned way he handled business these days. Hand-to-hand communication. As effective as disappearing paper, if you managed it right.

"And just in time for lunch," Zak said, waving the note in the air. "Gotta go. Can't keep our esteemed politician waiting any longer." His messenger left through the door to the back hall. Zak sat for a few minutes staring at the expensive artwork lining his office walls and thinking about how to handle the obnoxious visitor waiting for him in the outer reception room.

Congressman Jake Harper had invited himself to lunch with Zak and former Vice-President Fred McGuire. *I wonder what the Raptor has in mind,* Zak thought, as he tucked the "pretty bird" note in his pocket. Before leaving, he walked over to the liquor cabinet on the wall opposite his private bathroom and removed a key from his pants pocket. He bent down and clicked open the antique door with its inlaid Browning family crest.

The cabinet was a birthday gift from his wife, who'd pulled every string in Washington to have the piece delivered to CIA headquarters. It wasn't a gift her husband appreciated. He preferred calling in favors for matters of far more consequence. Besides, the whole transaction was a waste of the Agency's time, having to check out the furniture and institute a raft of special delivery procedures. *A major embarrassment.* One of several times in Zak's marriage when he would happily have ordered a hit on his wife and never felt a pang of guilt. For a few minutes he stood looking at the cabinet, savoring the thought of life without the burden of his overbearing spouse.

Barely glancing at the bottles in the cabinet, he reached for the

Macallan Single Malt Scotch from the stash he kept on hand for visits with important people. McGuire loved his Scotch whisky. Bottle in hand, Zak opened the front door of his inner sanctum and walked out to the reception area beyond, quietly closing the door behind him. He extended a hand to the visitor impatiently waiting on the settee in the outer office.

"Time for lunch, Congressman. I hope you're hungry." Zak shook hands with Congressman Harper and raised his left hand to display the Macallan's. "I'll be back by two," he told his assistant with a wink as he escorted his companion into the empty hallway. The two men strolled away from the DI's office on the seventh floor of Langley—one talking, the other listening with feigned deference.

Outside the building, they entered a waiting SUV, courtesy of the Agency's *Security Protective Service*, for the five-minute drive to the home of the ex-Vice-President. Barely enough time to chat about the usual topics: baseball, weather, the stock market. Two modest, well-dressed citizens, upholders of family values, the cause of freedom and American hegemony in the world, Zak thought with a smile as he glanced at his lunch companion.

The SUV passed through the main security gate and waited for traffic to ease and allow them to make the right turn onto Dolley Madison Boulevard. The tinted windows barely allowed enough light for the vehicle's occupants to see each other, which suited Zak. The driver eased the vehicle onto Dolley Madison, remaining in the right hand lane for the upcoming turn onto the Georgetown Pike. Rounding a corner into a nearby residential area only a stone's throw from Agency property, the SUV pulled up to a typical red brick McMansion. *No imagination*, Zak thought.

The driver and his front seat companion got out and opened the back doors for their passengers, neither of whom moved to open the doors for themselves. The agents escorted them up the front steps and onto the large porch. Zak was aware of the surveillance equipment invisibly monitoring their every move. The front door opened automatically before anyone rang the decorative doorbell mounted next to one of two Ionic columns framing the ostentatious entry. Zak wondered if the doorbell even worked.

He and Congressman Harper entered the two-story foyer where Zak's hunting companion, former Vice-President Fred McGuire greeted them.

"Pretty Bird's in place," Zak told McGuire, handing him the bottle of Scotch. "We should hear something soon."

"Good news," the former Vice-President replied, shaking hands with the Congressman. "Let's sample the Macallan's and have lunch." He turned and led the way to the dining room, glancing back at Zak. "Stuffed quail from our last hunt," he said with a sardonic grin. "*Sans* lead."

Chapter Sixteen

McLean, Virginia

"Best quail I ever ate," Zak said, licking the last bit of flavor from his fork. "What was in the stuffing besides rice? Spectacular. Some liver, maybe?"

His companion nodded, obviously savoring his last bite of the tender bird. "Damn good," the Congressman said, turning to Zak. "You shoot 'em and he cooks 'em, is that how it works?"

Zak nodded. "There's a reason they call me Shotgun."

McGuire looked pleased. Zak knew stuffed quail was the Veep's signature dish, reserved for close friends and special guests. "Perceptive taste buds. I'll let you in on the secret if you promise to keep it between us."

"I bet you say that to all the girls," Zak said, appealing to McGuire's exaggerated view of his sex appeal and his lingering vanity.

"No, no. I spill my secrets only for the two of you," he replied, with a dark grin. "For four quail, I sauté about a quarter pound of *foie gras,* add a couple of shallots, some mushrooms and my secret seasonings. Then I brown the SOB's on top of the stove and pop 'em in the oven on low for ten minutes." A smile lightened McGuire's normally morose features. His watery blue eyes glinted, matching the sheen on his thick mop of carefully coiffed hair. Clearly, he enjoyed discussing his culinary achievements.

Congressman Harper chimed in. "Best damn meal I've had in a month. Even the skin tastes good, and I usually pull off the skin. I'm not big on mushrooms either, but these are damn fine."

A momentary look of distaste crossed Zak's face, but he tempered his reaction. *What can you expect from a Texas Congressman?*

"Do we have you on board?" McGuire asked.

"Well, I'm still in the thinking stage." Harper popped another dinner roll in his mouth and continued talking while he chewed. "With the election coming up next year, I gotta be careful what I sign onto and how many secrets I keep. And, o' course, I gotta spend a lot of time raising money for the old campaign coffers and all. You know how that goes."

Zak knew what he meant, and he expected McGuire knew, too.

"Let's not discuss your campaign coffers right now," McGuire said. "We want to know if you'll sponsor the western states' farm bill with our little package tucked inside."

McGuire's *little package* characterization amused Zak. He hoped the amendment tacked onto the farm subsidy bill would attract little attention. Few, if any, Congressional staff would even read the bill, their aides assuming it was the same old same old. But a rider attached to it expanded the power of the executive branch under conditions of severe threat levels to the country. Most important was the clause allowing the CIA to spy on Americans inside the country and detain them indefinitely without counsel for charges of terrorism.

"Easy for you not to worry about my campaign bank account," Harper huffed, "but I need to know in advance what my support amounts to in terms of do-re-mi. I know we're safe from listenin' ears here, so I'm gonna be frank. I'm in some hot water, and it'll take a pile of cash to get me re-elected."

Zak noticed McGuire's embarrassment. "If you'll excuse me, I'll see how the kitchen is coming along with our dessert," the Veep said.

Zak leaned back in his chair. Once the kitchen door closed he addressed Harper. "What'll it take to get your support?"

The Congressman removed a cigar from his inside pocket and lit up, relaxing his shoulders and sitting back in his chair. With his free hand, he flicked a cotton thread from his expensive slacks and bent down to wipe some imagined specks of dust from his twenty-four-hundred-dollar alligator cowboy boots. The he said, "Ten million."

The DI watched him in a state of shock, his mind reeling at the Congressman's demand. McGuire wouldn't be happy about the size of the request or the cigar. Congressman Harper was an accident waiting to happen. He might say the right things in his political speeches, but he couldn't be trusted. No one played both ends against the middle better. From Zak's point of view, the Congressman's current situation made him ripe for a double cross. Zak wasn't about to let that happen. Harper's ridiculous request was the opening Zak needed to put the final nail in Jake Harper's coffin and end any further arguments over the Congressman's loyalty, or his fate. They could buy a handful of

Congress people from either party for half of Harper's asking price. Zak knew exactly who could handle the problem for him.

"We've been counting on you to shepherd the farm bill through Congress. I thought you were on board," Zak said, struggling to keep the anger from his voice. "Am I mistaken?"

"No, you aren't mistaken, but I'm in trouble here and I need help. Tit for tat, as they say."

The DI sucked in his breath. Listening to Harper's demands infuriated him. *Who does he think he is? And who does he think keeps him in power? He's out of control. Success and money can make people feel independent and untouchable. When that happen, they need to be brought in line. Congressman Harper would serve as an object lesson to the others.*

Zak watched Harper suck on his cigar. The man acted like some third-rate dictator instead of what he was—a two-bit horse trader who got lucky. Zak was not in a charitable mood. To characterize his opinion of Congressman Harper as dislike understated the intensity of his feelings toward the man, recent disclosures only accenting his animosity. After a long minute of toying with his silverware for the purpose of keeping the Congressman in suspense, Zak gave his answer. "Okay," he shrugged, letting Harper know the extent of his displeasure. "You've got a deal."

Apparently satisfied he'd bagged most of what he came for, Harper leaned back in his chair and took another drag on his cigar, rolling the smoke in his mouth before exhaling miniature smoke rings into the air, much to the annoyance of his companion.

"Now, I got one more issue," he said, like a character out of Tombstone pushing his luck with the new sheriff in town. Zak raised an eyebrow, waiting for the next shoe to drop. "Does Whitworth know what you and McGuire got in mind? Because if he doesn't, you sure as hell better fill him in before I have to go back over to Langley and request a sit-down with the boss, myself. I don't mind kicking ass, but I ain't no goddam traitor."

"Nothing to worry about, Congressman," Zak said, hoping to stop Harper from running at the mouth. He was sick of the sound of the man's voice. *What was Harper thinking trying to extort money from McGuire? The Congressman's ability to make a truly significant contribution to the cause had terminated with this latest scandal. He should be here begging forgiveness and pleading for any opportunity to redeem himself.*

If nothing else, this ridiculous request should convince McGuire to end his dealings with Congressman Harper. They didn't need Harper to move the farm bill through Congress. Maybe the opposite, given the latest revelations about his propensities. Harper's involvement might make the opposition sit up and take notice. Exactly the opposite of what he and McGuire wanted to happen. Harper posed a threat and Zak planned to make exactly that point to McGuire.

"I'm not here asking for a handout for myself, you know," Harper went on. "I'm not a crook. Hell, I'm in Washington for the sole purpose of protecting the interests of the good people of the God-fearing State of Texas, and on their behalf I expect to get some guarantees about my own ass. Texas needs me and they won't like me supporting a bunch of spooks runnin' around the world assassinatin' every Tom, Dick and Harry we don't like whether or not we're at war with their goddam country. Furthermore, I don't like this business about what the Agency can and can't do on American soil. Opens the door to home-grown political assassinations by the federal government, if you ask me, and I'm *agin* it, plain and simple."

"You've got my word that won't happen, and you have my word on the money." Zak stuck out his hand in another effort to placate the Congressman and end the discussion, but Harper ignored the gesture.

"I want more than promises from you. I want to hear it from Whitworth."

"Can't be done." Zak was seething inside. "The Director of Central Intelligence can't talk to you about this legislation, even if he wants to. Comes too close to lobbying and as you well know, it's against the law for a federal employee to lobby."

Harper gave him a withering look that said *since when are you worried about the law?* "Then I want the Raptor's assurances," Harper said. Zak could see the Congressman's anxiety levels rising, "and not just a goddam handshake, either. I want something in writing shipped to my office that gives me some satisfaction my ass is covered if something goes wrong."

Zak tried to keep his voice calm and his annoyance in check. "I'll let him know when he returns to the table."

Congressman Harper was one large pain in the ass. He would take up the matter with the Raptor after the Congressman left.

The door to the kitchen swung open and Fred McGuire emerged, his left hand balancing a tray containing three small round dishes. In his right hand he held a crème brûlée torch. Zak watched the ex-

Vice-President set the tray on a square wooden cutting board atop the antique buffet.

"Everything settled?" McGuire asked.

"Depends," Harper replied, ignoring Zak's warning look.

"The road's a little bumpy," Zak said to McGuire's back, "but I think we can put together a trip that will make everyone happy."

"I'm glad to hear that." McGuire lit the small torch and passed it over the tops of the custard in the white porcelain cups.

Harper nodded his head as if to say, *now, we're getting somewhere.*

"Mileage is steep. Around the world and back ten times." Zak's voice altered slightly as he spelled out the amount of Harper's request.

McGuire stopped moving and held the torch in the air as though he were lighting an altar candle. "That's quite a trip," he said, still facing away from his guests.

Harper was watching the Raptor's' reaction with the eye of an eagle assessing its prey as Zak continued to spell out the conditions. "We'll need to invite Whit," Zak said, adding, "and provide receipts."

"Take care of it, then." McGuire flicked the torch to the off position and lifted the tray of desserts, turning around to face his guests with his usual cocky grin. "My special Grand Marnier crème brûlée. I hope you like it." He placed a small white cup in front of each guest. "Enjoy," he said.

"Will do," the Congressman replied, digging his spoon into the soft custard and slurping it into his mouth.

Zak and the ex-Vice-President exchanged glances as Congressman Harper attacked his dessert.

Chapter Seventeen

Washington, DC

Congressman Jake Harper stepped out of the black SUV onto the sidewalk along Independence Avenue and hurried away from the curb without thanking his Secret Service chauffeurs or even acknowledging them with a wave good-bye. He hurried along the sidewalk, ignoring the reporters staked out in front of the building.

"Congressman, are the rumors true?" one shouted.

"Congressman, Congressman, CAB News, would you talk with us?" The reporter shoved a microphone in his face. Jake hit it away with the side of his arm, ducking under the camera. "Congressman, is it true that you're gay?" The reporter persisted, nearly tripping the Congressman in his efforts to keep up with Harper's long strides.

"You have my statement," Harper said, stalking up the broad, marble steps and into the confines of the House of Representatives Office Building. He was fuming. *Little piss ants.* He used to think of the CAB News channel as a friend, but no longer. Like other victims targeted by yellow journalists, he felt they deserved the appellation of *Cock-And-Bull News.* Once inside the building, he hurried across the marble floor without stopping for his usual chats with colleagues, reaching his office in record time.

A chorus greeted him as he entered the reception area of his oversized office, which he'd decorated in early *War of Northern Aggression* memorabilia. A Confederate stars and bars flag signed by Jefferson Davis hung prominently above his administrative assistant's desk. On either side of the room's two long windows hung framed photos of the Congressman with Lyndon Johnson and Jimmy Carter, two southern Presidents whom Harper considered traitors to the cause and their country. But they were southerners, and the photos lent prestige to the office. But the one with him standing between his true idols, President W. and Governor Perry—now *that* was a photo with bragging rights.

He glanced over at the large wooden frame hanging on the back wall between two columns of Texas cavalry unit photos. He'd placed it there for the benefit of his home-state visitors. If ever he'd wished Texas had successfully fled the Union, today was the day. On display inside the rustic, mesquite wood frame was a handwritten quote from the 1861 Texas Ordinance of Secession:

> *"That in this free government all white men are and of right ought to be entitled to equal civil and political rights; that the servitude of the African race, as existing in these States, is mutually beneficial to both bond and free, and is abundantly authorized and justified by the experience of mankind, and the revealed will of the Almighty Creator, as recognized by all Christian nations."*

"Afternoon, Congressman." More than a dozen people, including his administrative assistant, waited to see him. "I've a number of messages for you," she said.

"Can't do anything right now. Have to hit the can, then make a few phone calls." With that, he disappeared into his corner office. He wondered how many people waiting to see him knew about the most recent revelations. The people back home would never believe the accusations. Nothing but a passel of rumors on the part of a left-wing conspiracy intent on destroying him, he thought. *Hell, it was like tossing gay accusations at the ex-President. Unthinkable.* He felt confident his constituents and the majority of the rest of the country believed his side of the story. Unfortunately, a number of highly placed people did not, several of whom had somehow obtained evidence contradicting the Congressman's position, or so his lawyer recently informed him.

Harper picked up the phone and dialed Bjorn Nilsson, CEO of Sigma Services. He needed to let Nilsson know he could pull his weight, convince him not to drop his support. Once Nilsson heard how the meeting went he'd be on board again. Harper needed to let the Sigma head know that while Nilsson might have greased the skids, ole Jake Harper clinched the deal.

Nilsson's administrative assistant answered.

"Congressman Harper here," he said. "Let me talk to the boss."

Nilsson came on the line immediately. "Jake. How'd it go?"

"Just finished my meeting, and McGuire agreed to the terms. Ten mill, cold cash."

"I knew you'd get the job done for us. Did he put up much of a fight?"

"None. He turned down my request for assurances from Whitworth."

Nilsson interrupted. "What assurances?"

"I told him I wasn't no goddam traitor, and I wanted it in writing from Whitworth that this whole matter had his blessing. If I push through this amendment, I don't want it to be abused. I told him I wouldn't be responsible for establishing a hit squad inside the U.S. government. I'm not stupid, and neither are a lot of other people. There's a way you can read this bill that'll let the federal government do anything they damn well please, anywhere they want inside the country. All they need is a smart lawyer to back 'em up and there's plenty of those kickin' around D.C."

"Now, why did you go and do that?"

"CYA. To cover my ass, that's why. I'm not interested in spending my retirement behind bars."

"That'd never happen, you know that."

"Tell that to Duke Cunningham. You should be thanking me. They're coming up with a pile of money for those contracts you want."

"What about your little incident?"

"I'll want some of that money, o' course. Enough to beef up my re-election campaign account and grease the skids from here to Texas and back. There'll still be plenty left over for you."

Nilsson whistled. "I've got to hand it to you. Never thought you'd get them to agree to that much. Good work. Should take care of everything, so the rest is up to you. Keep your nose clean. At least you weren't flying off to Peru banging some dark-eyed Latin mistress. Your constituents might have bought a story like that. Harder for them to believe the sodomy angle."

Harper exploded. "Goddam you, Nilsson, who do you think you're talking to? I told you I'm no g-d homasexshul and that's not what happened."

"Calm down, I didn't mean it. I know you're not."

"Look," Harper said. "You need to understand. We were on a hunting trip, the three of us, that's all. Gone for a week and got ourselves a little drunk. How could we know there were secret goddam telescopic lenses spying on us? Who could predict it, in our own goddam country, no less? Tell me who doesn't drink too much on a damned hunting trip. That's what they're all about! So stop accusing me of what you don't know a g-d thing about—"

Nilsson interrupted his diatribe. "If you're not careful, Harper, it'll be the end of your career. You won't be able to convince the folks back home you didn't break your marital vows, and nobody'll be able to come out in support of you. They'll vote you out of office and send you back to raising pigs and soybeans faster than you can count the toes on a sow's foot. So settle down. Let's talk about how to get that money out to where it will stop these rumors and stifle those photographs once and for all. We need that money to protect our liberties, not clean up after you."

"I already know how to take care of it. I'm flying out of here tomorrow morning to take care of the whole g-d mess."

"What about the money?"

"Talk to Zak Browning. He's in charge. I got enough stashed away to take care of things at home. When I get back to D.C., you need to see my PAC gets reimbursed."

Chapter Eighteen

Honolulu, Hawaii

Tom Kerrigan pulled up to the BeachSuites Hotel on Waikiki's Beachwalk Street, grabbed his overnight bag from the seat next to him and handed his car keys to the athletic Hawaiian valet who held open his car door.

"Take good care of my baby," he said, wrapping a twenty-dollar bill around his keys.

"Thank you, sir. Don't worry, she's in good hands." The valet grinned as he stuck the bill in his pocket.

Tom tried not to whistle with satisfaction or was it anticipation? He wound his way past the lobby's potted palms and bubbling fountains to the elevators and glanced at his watch. *Don't want to be early and seem anxious. 6:30. Punctual to a fault.* By the time he reached Alicia's twenty-second floor room he'd be a few, fashionable minutes late.

They'd spent an enjoyable day together touring Honolulu, ending up at the beach not far from her hotel. As the shadows grew long and the afternoon sun began to fade, he invited her to dinner followed by an evening of dancing. She agreed and even suggested they meet at her hotel for a swim in the spectacular outdoor pool. Afterward, they could change for dinner in her room and leave from there, she'd told him.

Tom hoped her suggestion was an invitation. After dropping her off at the hotel shortly before 5:00 and promising to be back by 6:30 with his swimsuit and a change of clothes, he'd raced home, packed a bag and returned on time. Slightly apprehensive, he stepped off the elevator onto the twenty-second floor, surprised that he'd come down with a case of nerves. Not like he hadn't done this before. He checked his hair in the foyer mirror and headed to her room with its outside view of the pool below and the ocean beyond. He took a deep breath and knocked on the door.

"Who is it?"

"Special delivery," he replied, smiling at her artifice.

Alicia hid behind the door as she swung it open. He stepped inside, and she gently pushed the door closed, stepping out to face him. He turned and stared at the white and gold bikini she wore. The translucent wrap hid nothing. The shades of aqua and seafoam green in the cover-up highlighted the hue of her blue eyes. Her short, blonde hair framed her porcelain doll face. Tom sucked in his breath, which seemed to please her.

"Like what you see?"

He nodded, feeling like an adolescent at the speed of his physical response.

"Wait 'til we get to the pool and you see my backstroke."

He knew she was teasing him. He stepped over and pulled her to him. "How about showing me your breaststroke instead," he whispered, knowing it sounded corny, but he didn't care. Here was an opportunity for the taking, and he wasn't a patient man. They could go for a swim later. He lifted her chin and kissed her lips lightly, then with more insistence as he parted her lips with his, tasting the softness inside.

§

At least he's charming, Alicia thought. *Whatever it takes to convince him to go with me tomorrow.* She might as well enjoy the evening, too. If only she could eliminate the dark thoughts of the morning from her brain. Why couldn't he be on her side? And why was the Agency forbidding her to talk to Henry about this operation? She wished she could call him right now. Nobody could dispel doubts and provide encouragement better than Henry, and Alicia was plagued with doubts. This mission was so unlike any previous operation, but times were changing, and the Agency was changing too. Still, so many things puzzled her. Like the phony resignation and the play-acting with Henry at Langley.

And Tom Kerrigan bothered her, too. No way was he the monster the dossier depicted. She had a difficult time picturing him as an international terrorist, a cold-blooded killer selling nuclear weapons to terrorists. She was good at sizing up people, and Tom was a mismatch. For a brief moment, she entertained the thought of trying to convert him, but it was a silly idea and she had an assignment. *No backing down now.* That's what Henry would tell her. *Do your job, don't think about it.* Her job was to gain Tom's complete trust by tomorrow morning when they would take his boat on a scuba diving trip. Her instructions were to deliver him to a particular place by a specific time.

Setting aside her worries, Alicia murmured her pleasure and yielded to him, surprised at her own passion. For reasons not clearly understood, the thought of leading him to his death in the morning increased the intensity of her response to him. She leaned her head back against the door and closed her eyes. When Tom picked her up and carried her to the bed, resisting never entered her mind.

§

Tom stroked Alicia's face, rolled over and gave her a light kiss. "How about that swim now?"

"That was nice," she said, sitting up and dangling her feet over the edge of the bed. "I feel energized."

"Me, too. Where are you going? Are you leaving me?"

"Just hopping in the shower. I'll be out in a few minutes, and then we can inspect this swimming pool I've heard so much about." She bent down and picked up her bikini from the floor holding it up as she walked to the bathroom. "Let's see if I can keep this on my body for more than ten minutes this time."

"Is that a challenge? Because I might not be up to the task."

She ignored him and stepped into the bathroom, closing the door behind her. Tom waited until he heard the shower running before he rolled out of bed and began his search. He rifled through her closet and her dresser drawers. Alicia's purse lay in the second drawer down in the back, covered by a shirt and a light jacket. He removed the bag, picturing its placement in his mind. A quick look and he found the gun, lifted it out and removed the cartridge before returning it to her purse. As he returned the gun, he adjusted its position to match the image in his brain and covered it with Alicia's neatly folded clothes.

If he was spending the night with her, which he planned to do, he had no interest in a middle of the night surprise. At least, not one of the killing kind.

Chapter Nineteen

Congressman Jake Harper, R-TX, Killed in Early Morning Plane Crash
By Kenneth Sayers | ASSOCIATED PRESS

LEXINGTON, KY – United States Representative Jake Harper died early this morning when his twin-engine Cessna crashed and burst into flames over a densely wooded area of the Daniel Boone National Forest near Morehead, Kentucky. The Congressman, who piloted his own plane and was alone at the time, had radioed ahead for permission to make an unscheduled landing at the Morehead-Rowan County airport.

According to airport officials, they received a distress call from Harper at 11:17 last night reporting problems with his fuel gauge. Witnesses several miles from the crash site reported seeing a small plane flying erratically. Federal Aviation Administration records indicate the Cessna 335, which was manufactured in 1980, had no prior incidents and was up to date on its maintenance schedule. The crash is under investigation by the FAA and the National Transportation Safety Board.

Congressman Harper, one of the most colorful members of the U.S. House of Representatives, was a six-term Texas Congressman noted for his unconditional support of the Iraq war and his controversial recommendations to bomb Iran's nuclear sites. Recent rumors linked him to a scandal involving gay sex at his hunting cabin, though the much heralded evidence in the form of covert photographs never materialized. Congressman Harper is survived by his wife, one daughter and two grandchildren …

Bluemont, Virginia
Mount Weather Conference Room

Zak Browning and Bjorn Nilsson waited over an hour before

entering the Mount Weather conference room for their meeting with Fred McGuire, who began with an unusual, commendatory gesture.

"Good job with Harper. Nice and clean," he told his visitors as the three men sat together in the comfortable easy chairs at the end of the plush room with the fake windows. "It's doubtful the administration will look too hard into Harper's crash. They'll be as happy as we are to see him gone. Goddam sonofabitch couldn't follow orders. Got greedy. Can't have that. Could have ruined everything," he shrugged and lit a cigar, offering the box of Cuban Montecristos to the others. "Maybe he did, we don't know yet. Can't be certain how much information has gotten into the wrong hands. Had to make an object lesson out of him," then he smiled, leaned back in his chair and puffed a series of smoke rings before continuing, "But let's forget about Jake Harper. That's not what's bothering me."

Zak looked up, confused. He thought they'd come to this morning's meeting to discuss ways to control the press coverage surrounding Jake Harper's plane crash and how to turn it to their advantage by blaming the crash on the radical left. Raise the fear factor about a left wing takeover of the country, that's what they needed to do. "What am I missing here?"

"Henry Larson," McGuire said. "He knows something."

Zak sat back in his chair annoyed to learn someone inside the Agency had delivered news to McGuire. Who had bypassed him? He was supposed to be the person notifying the Raptor about any exigencies within the organization. Unhappy about the direction of the conversation, he asked, "What does Henry know?"

"Don't have an answer to that, but he's putting together a team to work on a highly classified operation. Headed up by Dan Chavez."

"Doesn't mean it has anything to do with our plans," Nilsson said.

Zak turned to Nilsson. "Chavez was Malcolm Hall's best friend."

"I know who Dan Chavez is," Nilsson said, unable to keep the sarcasm from his voice. "He's the first person Hall's wife called when she got home from the hospital. We had her under surveillance, but Chavez interfered, and now she's disappeared. We think Larson's got her stashed somewhere."

Zak ignored Nilsson and directed another question to McGuire. "What did you hear and how did you hear it?"

"You're not my only mole inside the Agency," McGuire said, upbraiding Zak with a look of disdain.

"Are you blaming me for the Malcolm Hall incident? You know as well as I do we had to get rid of him, and the timing couldn't have been better. Misdirects the public's attention. We need that right now."

"Too many mysterious deaths can raise suspicions," McGuire snapped.

"Only if they're connected." Zak paused. "Connected politically. Besides, there's nothing mysterious about either a plane crash or a heart attack, and certainly nothing connecting Hall and Harper. That's the beauty of it."

Nilsson interrupted. "Who told you Larson knows something?"

"That's my business." McGuire said, nodding his head at Zak. "He's not my only inside source."

Zak recoiled, but replied to Nilsson with a calmness he didn't feel. "Whit, no doubt."

"Whit's a fool. You know more than he does," McGuire sneered. "But we need him."

"The more Bjorn and I know about who our friends are inside the Agency," Zak said, struggling to contain his anger, "the better we can do our jobs, unless you don't trust us." Had the source, whoever it was, been tasked by McGuire to keep tabs on him or on Nilsson or both? *The Raptor would do that. He trusted no one.* The thought gave Zak pause, but now that he knew about another mole inside the Agency, it wouldn't take long to flush out the person's identity. He could eliminate his allies and of the remainder, the number of people close enough to keep track of Henry Larson *and* who could report on Zak Browning's actions would be limited. He'd work on the problem when he returned to the office.

McGuire ignored Zak's comment. "Have you talked with Larson this morning, gotten his reaction to the Harper incident?"

"Not yet. I can call him now, see what he has to say."

"Not now. I don't want to increase his suspicions. See what you can find out when you get back to the office. I want to know if Henry has a bead on you. He knew about your lunch with Harper. Had to."

"I'll take care of it," Zak said. "Let's move on."

McGuire's eyebrow flew up, but he turned to Nilsson. "You have everything in place?"

Nilsson nodded. "Explosives are strategically located in the Metro. If Chun's assassination doesn't send the President here for safekeeping then we'll set off the bombs one by one. We can deliver the EMP generator to the Congressional Office building anytime."

McGuire looked puzzled. "EMP generator?"

"It's a device that produces pulses of electromagnetic energy that can destroy sensitive electronics in computers and microprocessors," Nilsson replied.

"How fast can they take the place down?"

"I have a work crew on standby now. We can't take down the whole building, but we can knock out enough computers to cause a panic. That's all we need. It'll take three or four months to repair that much damage. Anything else?"

"Not at the moment," McGuire replied, a thoughtful expression replacing his normally sinister demeanor.

Nilsson changed the subject. "What was the problem with Harper, anyway? I thought he was on our side."

"We weren't pleased with his little extortion ploy yesterday," McGuire said. "Can't have would-be traitors in our midst, especially not greedy ones."

"They're all greedy, aren't they?" Zak asked, a tight-lipped, half-smile turned up one corner of his mouth.

"Who? Traitors or Congressmen?" Nilsson asked.

"Congressmen," Zak said. "Traitors are idealists. Super-patriots, usually." He glanced between his two companions. "Like us, for example."

"We're not traitors," McGuire growled, "but you're right, we are patriots. Somebody has to save the damn country from going down the socialist road to oblivion. If we don't do it, who will?"

Zak barely heard McGuire, his thoughts focused elsewhere. *How much did Henry know and what was he doing about it?* Glancing between Nilsson and McGuire, Zak recalled his father's advice: *Remember son, you can't trust those who don't trust you.* Zak had his sources, too—ones the Raptor knew nothing about. And he disliked would-be traitors as much as the Raptor did.

Chapter Twenty

6th Floor Langley

"Holy shit!" Bob Randolph stared at his computer screen inside the NCS network security offices, furious at the flashing blip dancing before his eyes. "Damn North Koreans," he swore out loud again. *What did they hack now?* Randolph picked up the secure phone and punched in the five-digit number to his boss's office.

Henry's assistant, Connie Lang answered Bob's call. "The boss is tied up on the other line, Sweetie. Can it wait until he's through, or is this an emergency?"

"Both," Randolph told her. "If he gets off the phone before I get there, tell him I'm on my way up."

"Roger that, Bobby," Connie said, "I'll look forward to your visit." He could hear the smile in Connie's eyes.

"No fun in the sun this time, Baby," he said, "strictly business."

Bob was hopelessly in love with his boss's assistant, an impossible situation since she was married, though not happily, to a well-connected businessman in the D.C. area. As far as he could tell, she liked flirting with him, but that was as far as it went for her.

Complicating matters even more, Connie was almost twenty years his senior. She never told him the exact number, so he hacked her computer once, just to find out. Nineteen years, two months and five days. Bob didn't care. She was smarter than almost anyone he knew and that alone made her beautiful in his eyes. But her well-preserved looks helped, too. He jumped on any excuse to visit with her, although today he needed no excuses.

Bob stormed out of his office and bypassed the elevator bank for the stairwell, cursing to himself the whole way. Henry would be furious when he heard about the network break. He stopped at the top of the stairs, wondering if he should have contacted OS before sharing the news with Henry. *Find out what they know, if anything.* No, Henry needed to know first, he decided as he pushed open the stairwell door and stepped onto the marble tiled seventh floor hallway.

The Agency thought they hired the best and the brightest, but their network still had holes. Maybe the CIA should start hiring Chinese programmers. Either that or re-label the whole sorry security system outside of his Directorate's control. Hide Top Secret files in the unclassified section and shove the everyday stuff, which included the majority of the classified crap stored in Agency databases, into files marked Top Secret. *Then, let China and the North Koreans have at it. As ludicrous as it sounded, it might work.*

Deep in thought, Bob barely noticed his colleagues as he advanced down administrative row to Henry's office, angry that someone had beaten his security system and gotten as far as his front door, even if they didn't make it inside. It wouldn't happen again. He hated the thought of telling Henry, of letting him down. Henry Larson was a great guy and a terrific leader. Bob looked up to him more than to anyone else in the Agency. How a straight shooter like Henry ever ended up in the spy business was a mystery, but who could predict human nature? Certainly not Bob Randolph, which is why he preferred the company of computers.

§

Connie hung up the phone wondering what was upsetting Bob. A born geek, he directed the NCS Technology support division located on the sixth floor of Langley next door to the Global Response Center. Connie knew a lot about him, and she was impressed. His electrical engineer father had worked for General Electric in Schenectady, the first African American to set a record with the company in the acquisition of patents over a period of twenty years. He'd passed on his love of electronics and computing to his son, who built his own personal computer at age five—with the help of his father. From that point on, Bob and computers were inseparable, and by the time he was a teenager, he knew more about C++ than anyone other than the programming language's designer.

Connie sighed. He could have been rich by now if he were inclined to start his own company, a decision she wished he'd made. Maybe they could have afforded to be together now, but unfortunately, he preferred the fast-paced, secretive environment of the CIA where life was never dull. Or rather, not as dull as other jobs, he'd admitted to her with some chagrin.

But Connie liked her job—a lot. Between what she knew as

Henry's assistant and what she learned from Bob, she could fill a book on tech specs inside the Agency. It was all very convoluted and few people understood the workings the way Connie did. Unknown to most agency personnel, NCS was the only Directorate with a secure worldwide network separate from the Office of Security in the Mission Support Directorate. The two networks were connected, but access to the NCS system required special security codes, not all of which were available to other directorates, and that included staff in the Office of Security.

The separate but equal systems inadvertently denoted Directorate hierarchy with Clandestine Services occupying the top of the bureaucratic ladder. Henry Larson might be third in the chain of command after the DCI and the Deputy Director of Central Intelligence, but when it came to the exercise of authority, he was second only to the DCI. Connie knew Henry's elevated position made life difficult for him, given the jealousies and scapegoating among the myriad large egos occupying positions of power within the organization's intricate bureaucratic structure. Such was the price of power. And more than money, Connie pursued power.

Chapter Twenty-One

7th Floor Langley

The circumstances surrounding Malcolm Hall's death left Henry Larson thinking of little else but bringing home Evan Phillips. *If our suspicions are correct, we're facing a monumental undertaking here that Dan and I can't handle alone. Too many unanswered questions.*

What about Director Whitworth? It was the question at the top of his list. The new CIA Director had transferred over from the FBI. That fact alone provoked mistrust and led to the second question. *Could he be heading up the Code 21 operation?* If so, and if Henry took his suspicions and his meager evidence to his boss, the Director would know someone under Henry had hacked the computer system and Henry's ass would be grass. He'd be lucky to avoid jail for violating the State Secrets Act. The slightest leak would put his life, already in jeopardy, on the fast track for extinction. His only protection was secrecy until he had more than the bare outline of a possible false flag operation run by unidentified people with unknown goals.

Was the country confronting another *Operation Northwoods? Like the time the U.S. Joint Chiefs of Staff planned a pretext for invading Cuba in the early 1960's?* That plan involved the unthinkable—an armed attack on their own country, which could lead to an incalculable number of deaths of U.S. citizens. For forty years no one believed an arm of the U.S. government would attack its own citizens until the truth finally emerged. Henry shook his head in bewilderment as he recalled learning of the operation.

The intercom buzzed and Henry reached over to answer Connie.

"Bobby's here."

"To see me or you?" Henry knew she'd be irked by the question.

"You."

"Send him in."

As Bob stormed in, Henry ran his ringless left hand over his bald spot, a newly acquired habit in a man who seldom experienced nerves when he worked in the field.

"We've got a problem." Bob's angry stance conveyed more than Henry wanted to hear. "Damn North Korean hackers again." Henry appreciated his frustration. "We're the best spy agency in the world and we can't keep other countries from accessing our network."

"Offense is always ahead of defense. What happened this time?"

"Similar pattern. Intrusion came in through the Czech Republic. My guess is it's a pirate scene-operated proxy running inside a topsite in Eastern Europe or elsewhere. Who knows? Without opening the machine myself I can't say much more."

Henry listened to Bob's story with feigned interest.

"Too many breaches of the system these days," Bob complained. "Hard to keep up. And In-Q-Tel isn't helping matters bringing in too many outside partners tasked with providing solutions that ought to be handled on site. Can't keep track these days of how many people have keys to the city."

"Same service provider we tracked down earlier?" He could answer the question for himself.

"Don't know. Prague's a dead end, network-wise. The box is probably used for Czech locals, but the Eastern European pirates are deep in bed with Asia and passwords are easy enough to send around. I'd guess whoever did this picked Prague hoping to avoid watchdogs. Security through obscurity. You know. We do it ourselves."

Time to divert Bob's attention away from the Czech Republic. "What about China?"

"More likely North Korea, but could be China. It's reasonable. I'd place my money on hackers out of Jiaotong University. The pattern's common. Find a proxy nobody's monitoring and bounce through it. If I could crack open the box and look at the logs, and if I were running the thing it wouldn't have logs, it'd just bounce to another proxy, probably in Poland."

"Any evidence of damage?" Henry wanted to know exactly how much Bob knew.

"No significant hits, apparently. But they got through our first DMZ into a low-security account on the gateway machine, god knows how. I say apparently, because one never knows. According to the activity log, they touched two unclassified files and then tried the usual privilege elevation tricks to get out to the network. I don't think they got out, but I can't be sure."

Henry felt a surge of relief. "Sounds like not too much to worry about except how to keep them out in the future." He needed Bob to know he took the matter seriously, but not so much he turned him into a pit bull. Dan Chavez knew the system nearly as well as anyone, but everyone makes mistakes. Dan might have left fingerprints when he hacked into Bob's network using it to infiltrate another Directorate's files. Covering your tracks is a little like hanging wallpaper. Press a bubble down here, and one pops up there. Hide a bit over there, evidence turns up here.

If Dan did commit an error hiding his intrusion into the Information Directorate files, Henry sure as hell didn't want the finger pointing his way. Not yet, anyway. All hell would break loose once the Office of Security learned of the intrusion. Henry had little faith in his counterpart at the Support to Mission Directorate or SM as it was known in CIA lingo.

The new SM Director didn't know his ass from a telephone jack. Lacking the technical smarts for his job made him insecure and therefore dangerous. Henry had fought a formidable battle to maintain his own technical operation independent of OS, and he couldn't afford to ignite a new fight. To make matters worse, OS had been trying to get their hands on Bob Randolph for years, a point of disagreement that led to more bad blood between the two Directors. Bob was the Agency's best tech, bar none, and he belonged to Henry, who meant to keep it that way for exactly the reasons he now faced.

"Don't misdirect your time," Henry cautioned. "Though we need to button up tighter."

Bob gave him a quizzical look.

Henry recovered quickly. "No excuse for anyone finding their way into your network, even low level areas. I don't care if they're the best damn hacker in the world."

"When do you want me to report it to Security?"

"Let's wait until we learn more. I don't want either of our necks on the line over a matter that turns out to be nothing, or at least nothing we can't resolve ourselves."

"I hear you." Bob gave Henry a worried look. "I did find one more bothersome thing."

"How so?"

"Odd burp in the access logs. Over a minute where the logs indicate nothing happened. Nothing, nada, zip. No file updates, no web access, nothing. An empty minute."

"What about a restart?" Henry felt his chest constrict.

"I checked the logs, no restart."

"When was the missing minute?"

"Around midnight." Bob fidgeted displaying his agitation. "You know the odds against an empty minute?"

"It can happen."

"Shit happens, Henry. Not empty minutes."

"I'm only pointing out the possibility."

"Anything's possible. I could win the lottery. Happens all the time, but not to me. Empty minutes happen, too, but not on our system."

Henry took a breath, pushed his chair away from the desk and rested his hands on top of his head while Bob continued his rant.

"My best guess, and I know I'm obsessive, but I think somebody wiped the logs. What could they find in one minute? It doesn't make a lot of sense. I tried to ease into telling you because I'm convinced they never got past the DMZ. At least, I don't want to believe they did or we're dead. Or, I should say, I'm dead."

"Better stay with it then," Henry sighed. He'd hoped for more time before Bob discovered Dan's intrusion. "For your own protection, you need to keep this between the two of us. I want nobody, and that means *nobody*, knowing about this until we can explain the who, what, when, where and how much."

Bob nodded. "Okay. Thanks, Boss."

"Besides, I'm betting it's nothing." Henry tried to maintain an aura of calm. "Probably some smart college kids flexing their muscles, but we can't take chances. Keep me posted on what you find."

"No problem. And thanks for giving me some time to investigate, Henry, especially when I've just let you down."

"No apologies necessary." Henry felt a twinge of guilt. He'd like to tell Bob the truth, but he didn't dare. Not yet.

"I have a nagging feeling things may be worse than I think," Bob added, "but I'll let you know if anything turns up. I just hope my suspicions are wrong."

Henry closed the door behind him. *The limb I'm sitting on just got shorter.* Security would find the encroachment sooner or later. Better to have it uncovered by one of his own people so he could control the information flow. Still, it was worrisome having Bob find Dan's intrusion so soon.

Chapter Twenty-Two

Honolulu, Hawaii

Tom woke up early despite his late night and lack of sleep. The day greeted him with the news of Jake Harper's plane crash. It was everywhere—headlines in the paper, a running commentary on CNN with more information about Congressman Harper's life than anyone other than his most loyal constituents wanted to hear.

"I met the Congressman a couple of times," Alicia told him, checking the clock as she dressed. "Don't know why I'm admitting it, though."

"Did he hit on you?" Tom stopped, and let out a snort. "Based on recent rumors, I guess I'm the one he would have hit on, but I never met the guy."

"He did hit on me, as a matter of fact," Alicia said, "which I also hate to admit about a Congressman, but he wasn't the first. Please don't doubt my patriotism, but he was a first class jerk."

Tom knew the truth of her statement better than she did, and jerk was not the word he would use to describe Jake Harper. He walked over and put his arms around her, marveling at how he felt. "You don't think I'm a jerk for hitting on you, do you?" He lifted her chin so he could look into her beautiful eyes.

"Did you hit on me?" she said, smiling up at him. "I thought I was the one who hit on you."

He tried to kiss her but they were both laughing too hard. Alicia checked her watch for the third time. "If we want to do any serious diving today we'd better have some breakfast and get out of here. How far to your boat?"

"I told you last night, about thirty minutes. Won't take long. Do you want to eat at the hotel or go elsewhere?"

"No time for dawdling. Let's see what they have to offer downstairs."

Tom reached for her again wanting one last kiss, but he could tell her mind was elsewhere. He noticed her dramatic change of attitude.

As though their planned scuba trip were business instead of pleasure. He decided not to dwell on it, even though she never lightened up throughout breakfast, withdrew into herself, reading the paper for most of the meal. Tom tried to reach her, but the Alicia of yesterday and last night had disappeared, and another person inhabited her body. He'd seen something similar before and it worried him. They left for the Maunalua Bay marina straight from the hotel restaurant, Alicia checking her watch again as if she were on some sort of schedule. Tom watched her but said nothing.

§

"Nice toy," Alicia said, admiring the twin engine *Island Runner* as Tom unloaded their scuba gear and helped her on board. *Looks like a drug boat,* she thought, wondering about the purchase price.

"Used to belong to a drug runner, but I got out of the business," Tom said, laughing at her disconcerted looked. "Just kidding. It did belong to a former drug dealer, but that person wasn't me. I got a good deal because these boats aren't in demand anymore. Today, the traffickers go for specially built little numbers with hollowed out shells and six or eight outboard motors lined along the back. Name of the game is outrunning the narcs."

Alicia had no comeback. She wondered how much was true. Maybe he was a former drug runner in addition to working as a political assassin. The wealthy businessman pretense was a good cover. Besides, the two occupations went together. She wished he were an ordinary businessman, but the dossier she'd been given said otherwise, identifying Tom Kerrigan as the leader of an organization intent on using violence to overthrow the U.S. The organization led up to the highest levels of government, including a person recently elected to one of the highest offices in the land.

Tom started the motor and pulled slowly out of the East Harbor. Alicia reached for her purse and opened it, noticing Tom's apparent anxiety. She removed her typed vacation itinerary. She could tell he suspected her. She would have to be careful, keep the purse nearby since it contained her only protection. No time for a case of nerves now.

Alicia unfolded the paper. "Here's what my itinerary says about scuba diving today … "

Tom interrupted her. "I have my own secret diving places. I thought you might like to dive Baby Barge and look for shipwrecks and green sea turtles."

His unexpected suggestion increased her nervousness. She needed to talk him out of his dive site and convince him to go along with hers, cajole him into doing what she wanted. Resorting to threats wouldn't work. Once they reached the Caves, Tom would be kidnapped and kept unaware of her involvement. She couldn't risk endangering herself. Better to abort today's plan and try again tomorrow.

"I thought this was my vacation and you were my *guide*." Alicia gave Tom a pleading look. "Diving at Spitting Caves was my number one priority on this trip, and I know you don't want to disappoint me."

Tom shrugged. "No problem. We can do shipwrecks tomorrow, if you like. Makes no difference to me, and you're right. It's your vacation. Spitting Caves, here we come. It's a ways from here, you know."

Alicia did know. She checked her watch again. They were on schedule.

"How about sitting here with me," Tom said, tapping the seat beside him at the helm of the *Island Runner*, "and tell me more about yourself."

Alicia leaned close to his ear. "I think I'm getting hoarse trying to talk over these engines. Do you mind if I lie in the back and sun myself instead?" She needed to relax, practice mind control. This assignment had become more difficult than she anticipated. She'd made a mistake. Allowed herself to like Tom Kerrigan. That wouldn't do.

"Go right ahead. I'll let you know if I see anything interesting."

Alicia held onto the seatbacks for stability as she maneuvered her way to the back of the boat. When she turned around, the rushing air from the speed of the boat distorted her face, blowing out her cheeks like a funhouse fan. She stretched out on the back ledge, letting the sun drench her body. The fine spray of mist off the front of the boat cooled her skin, preventing a sunburn, or so she hoped. She tucked her purse by her side and glanced at Tom's back. So, Tom Kerrigan wanted to know more about her. What would she have told him about herself? The desire to be honest led her to wonder what it would hurt to tell him the truth. He wouldn't live long enough to blow her cover.

She also wondered how he'd react if he knew she wasn't the person she appeared to be any more than he was. Her thoughts drifted back to George Washington University and the risk her father took to provide her with advance access to the SAT exam. He was Superintendent of Schools in their county, rising through the public school ranks from a high school math teacher to principal to assistant superintendent.

Alicia knew he longed to be appointed to the President's cabinet as Secretary of Education. She hoped to help bring that about, pay him back for everything he'd done for her.

He had surprised her the day he brought home the purloined copy of the SAT questions. It was a Tuesday evening. She'd just returned home from her summer internship, which allowed her three days of practice before taking the Saturday exam.

"You've got a straight-A average," her father explained during her junior year, "and I'm not letting all that hard work go to waste. Life is not about beating the system," he reminded her, not for the first time, "it's about using the system. Remember that, and you'll succeed." She knew his philosophy by heart, having had it drummed into her head from an early age.

She turned him down. "I can't do that, Daddy," she said, struggling with the temptation. "I just can't. Please don't make me. I'll do okay, I promise."

Her father gave in to her wishes and she rewarded him by achieving a near perfect score, gaining her entrance into any elite school she chose. Not surprisingly, she'd always been a good student. The teachers at her exclusive private school, which included her mother, heaped attention and praise on her all the way through school, delighted with her high achieving, teacher-pleasing personality traits. Always a good test taker, her SAT results were not unexpected, though everyone who knew her would be surprised to know how close she had come to cheating.

Alicia twisted her head to the side watching Tom Kerrigan again, so intent on speeding to his assignment with death. There were similarities between them, but something about the man didn't add up. The real Tom Kerrigan and the dossier on him were a mismatch. In person, he was no monster. In fact, the opposite. A shiver ran through her at the thought of his death. Tomorrow morning she would wake up alone to face a world devoid of Tom Kerrigan. How soon before someone in his organization rose up and took his place, continued his nefarious activities threatening the safety and security of the America she loved? Tom's death might be only the beginning. How and where would it all end?

Tom turned around and winked at her, a half smile crossing his lips. The sadness in his eyes seemed to reflect her own feelings. At least they hadn't assigned her to kill him. She was only the messenger, not the person tasked with pulling the trigger and ending his life. Something to be thankful for, she thought, closing her eyes and enjoying the warm sun on her body. The rocking motion of the boat calmed her anxieties and without realizing it, she fell sound asleep.

Chapter Twenty-Three

Washington, D.C.

After his strategy meeting with Henry, Dan Chavez left home contemplating the two missions he had to accomplish by the end of the day. He'd dropped his wife off at Dulles Airport the night before to catch a plane to Rapid City, South Dakota for a weeklong trip to visit her parents. He missed her already. Funny, he mused, how quickly the platonic love for a sister-in-law could turn into the passionate love he felt for his new wife.

"Take care of yourself, Babe," he'd told her, separation anxiety already setting in.

He'd checked in with her again this morning, heard the grief in her voice over the news of Malcolm's death. He wished he could be there to comfort her. "How could something so awful happen after all she's been through over her son?"

"Life's not always fair," Dan replied, still in pain himself over the death of his friend.

"I want to come home, sweetheart," she said, "to be with you and to help Cheryl. She needs me."

"I want you here, too, but that's not possible right now. Cheryl's had to postpone the funeral services, anyway, and you need to stay put."

"Why?"

"Extenuating circumstances that I can't go into right now." Dan paused for a few seconds trying to frame his next words in a way that would cause his wife the least trauma.

"Listen to me carefully—"

She interrupted. "You're scaring me."

"I'm not trying to frighten you. What I'm about to tell you is precautionary, nothing more."

He gave his wife the name of an FBI agent who would be stopping by her parents' house to arrange security for her and her family.

"This means you're in danger again," she said, her voice trembling.

"Did someone kill Malcolm?"

"I have a dangerous job," he replied, ignoring her question. "You know that, but there's nothing for you to worry about at the moment. You can reduce any danger to me by promising me you and your parents will follow the FBI's instructions. Okay? This is a temporary situation and when it's over, I'll fly out there and bring you home."

He ended the conversation by telling her how much he loved her. He knew his request terrified her, but there was nothing he could do about it. More important was the necessity of ensuring her safety. The circumstances surrounding Malcolm's death might have heightened his normal paranoia, but he was taking no chances, especially not with the woman he loved.

Instead of heading north in the direction of Leesburg, he turned toward D.C., stopping first in McLean where he rented an economy car. *Easy for someone in the Agency to have attached a tracker to my car. If so, I plan to make their life difficult.* It was imperative that he not be followed for the next couple of days, and for that, he needed a clean vehicle. At the rental counter, he gave the agent an alias, one provided by Henry. Anyone calling the rental company on "official" business pertaining to a rental by Dan Chavez would learn that no one by that name rented a car from their agency.

With the right information, Dan knew anyone could track a rental vehicle. Car companies took no chances when it came to theft these days—too easy to drive a rental across the border where the vehicles disappeared into a Mexican black hole. To combat the problem, companies routinely installed GPS trackers, often in the most obscure places, making the devices difficult to find and even more difficult to remove. The tracker wouldn't be a problem. Dan removed a small jammer/blocker-anti tracking device from his jacket pocket and plugged it into the car's cigarette holder. *That should take care of the GPS issue.*

Inside the car he prepared for the worst, removing his gun from the holster on the back of his belt and placing it within easy reach. He drove slowly out of the rental lot checking all the cars in the vicinity and committing to memory as many as he could. He was known for his prodigious memory, a reputation he deserved, and a talent he credited to his Native American upbringing with its oral history traditions. Memorization came second nature to him. He knew dozens of Chiricahua myths and legends. The creation stories of *Ussen, Child of the Water, White Painted Woman, Killer of Enemies and the Mountain*

Spirits, were written on his heart. He could repeat verbatim the story of why the bat has short legs.

Taking the Leesburg Pike to Route 66 east to D.C., he watched the rearview mirror for a familiar car, eventually noticing a black SUV that kept two to three cars in back of him. His heart raced. As soon as he found an opening, he'd smash the pedal to the floor and see if the car kept up. A dangerous tactic on highways as busy as these, but the traffic also gave him an advantage. He could use the other cars to run interference. Not too different from his college days as a running back. At least this time he had no passenger to worry about.

Weaving in and out of lanes, Dan pushed the car up to seventy… then seventy-five… eighty. He ignored the honking horns and middle fingers from drivers he cut off, concentrating on his driving with an occasional glance in his rearview mirror. He could see the SUV keeping up. Adrenalin shot through his system. No way were they going to catch him. Someone in D.C. might die today in a road rage shooting, but that person would not be Dan Chavez. He reached over for the Glock he'd laid on the seat, sliding it closer.

With the Fairfax Drive exit coming up, Dan moved quickly to the right. Without signaling, he sped off onto the exit, one he knew well, its ramp long enough to slow his car to a reasonable speed before he hit the traffic ahead. In his mirror, he watched the SUV skid sideways as the driver struggled to turn onto the exit ramp, spinning out of control instead. Turning one hundred eighty degrees, the SUV's red brake lights flashed in Dan's mirror as the distance between his car and the chaser increased.

Dan wove between cars on the busy street, quickly turning onto a side street that led to the entrance of a local community college. Entering the campus, he noticed an open handicapped parking spot. He slammed his vehicle into the slot. Grabbing his gun off the seat, he jumped out and ran into the building. Once inside, he slowed to a walk and struggled to control his breathing as he strolled into the nearest office. He entered the office and casually nodded to the receptionist seated a few feet from the door.

"Good afternoon, sir, can I help you?"

Dan opened his hand and displayed his federal ID. "Daniel Chavez. Federal agent. I'd like you to contact your campus security office. Ask them to send two cars here right away. I need their help."

"Certainly. Right away, sir." The young woman reached for the phone, no questions asked and punched four numbers. "There's a federal agent standing in my office. He says he needs your help and wants you to send two cars here immediately." She looked up from the phone. "He wants to speak to you," she said, handing Dan the phone.

"This is a national emergency," Dan told the voice on the other end, volunteering his name and a number, which they could call to verify his identity, "and I need you to hurry. Two cars and as many men as you can spare." He knew he was overstating the nature of the danger, but his life was at stake. For him, that constituted a national emergency.

Dan had barely hung up the phone before two members of the campus police appeared at the door, one a large African-American woman who outweighed her partner by at least twenty pounds, in Dan's estimation.

"What's this all about?" she asked, clearly the senior partner.

Dan motioned them into the hall, closing the office door behind him.

"I wish I could explain, but the operation's classified. What I can tell you is that my car is parked in a handicapped spot in the front of this building. I'm on my way to D.C. and I need to leave campus without being followed. Think you can help?"

"No problem," the woman said. "We'll block one end of the street and guide you out through our service entrance. It's well screened. Will that do it?"

"It should."

The woman held out her hand. "Give me your car keys."

Dan held back. He was puzzled. Were they playing along only to take him into custody, thinking he was a nutcase? They could verify his credentials. He reached again for his wallet, but she waved him away.

"We checked on you on our way over here and we're with you on this, so don't worry. I'm gonna move your car to the other side of the building once we block off the street. That way, if anyone's watching they'll think we're impounding your car. We'll head for the service entrance from there."

Dan grinned at her. "We could use you over at the National Counterterrorism Center."

She smiled back. "I'll keep it in mind. Probably pays better than here."

Chapter Twenty-Four

Northern Virginia

Finally free of his pursuers, Dan drove north to the Leesburg Executive Airport to greet the plane carrying Evan Phillips. On the way, he listened to the news report of Jake Harper's death. Mindful of his suspicions when it came to politicians dying in plane crashes, Harper's incident met none of his previous criteria. No left-winger, Jake Harper was the polar opposite—a rabid neocon, who had recently threatened to leave the Republican Party and join the Tea Partiers for reasons Dan had yet to understand. It was one of those things he would have asked the Congressman next time they met, except that Dan's dislike of Harper was so intense he avoided the man whenever an event brought them within speaking distance.

Jake Harper represented everything Dan found wrong with the D.C. political establishment: the money, the lobbying, the culture of entitlement. Harper's accidental death came as no surprise, given the Congressman's high-risk personality and propensity to imbibe. He must have left D.C. before midnight, Dan thought. *Had Harper fallen asleep at the plane's controls?* It was a logical question, given Harper's notorious drinking habits. Dan guessed the alcohol from an evening of imbibing wouldn't have had time to fully metabolize before he placed his fat, autocratic ass in the pilot's seat for his final flight home.

Dan glanced at the dashboard clock. He still had time. Unsure whether he'd lost the tail, despite all the help from college security, he detoured into Dulles airport and parked the rental in the long-term lot. *Plenty of time to pick it up later*. He hauled out the roller bag containing his disguises and dragged it into the terminal. Following the signs for ground transportation, he located the Trademark Car Rental Agency.

A young woman in a dark gray suit and Kelly-green blouse waited on him. Her broad smile and perfect teeth reminded him of his ex-wife, but he blocked the memory and kept his mind on the task at hand. He spoke to the attendant in French-accented English, giving his name as Marcel Deschenaux and address Rue Victoria, Trois-Rivières, Quebec, Canada. He paid with a Visa card, flipping open his passport for identification. Neither the fake passport nor the phony credit card had been issued by the Agency. Both had come from his personal stock, the one he kept for emergencies such as this. This was the first time he'd been forced to use them.

Dan's teardrop fedora covered his head down to his eyebrows, giving him a dapper look. A pair of Ray-Bans shielded his eyes and a graying mustache and beard covered the lower half of his face. He apologized for his light cotton gloves, telling the attendant he'd picked up a fungus doing some work on his septic system, and the blisters seeped. "Nasty business," he said. "Next time, I'll hire somebody to do my dirty work."

The young woman gave him a sympathetic look. "I'm so sorry."

Dan smiled his thanks. "I'll need the car for two days. Does Trademark have a grace period?"

She nodded. "One hour."

"Good enough. Do you have a map that can get me into D.C.?"

The attendant reached under the desk and retrieved a one-page map. Using her pen, she pointed out the directions.

Dan thanked her for being so helpful, adding that he was finding Americans to be friendlier than he'd been told to expect. She grinned and said she hoped he'd enjoy his visit to D.C.

When it came to disguises, he thought, his Native American heritage was a bonus. Hard to finger his ethnicity.

The white, nondescript sedan was not one of his favorites, but he wouldn't be driving it for long. Tossing his suitcase onto the passenger seat, he reached into the bag for a manila folder labeled "Trademark Car Rental." He slid the paperwork into his folder and returned it to the suitcase. Attaching the anti-tracking jammer completed his mission. He left Dulles Airport and headed north for the remaining twelve-mile drive to Leesburg.

He turned off the Dulles Toll Road at the second exit from the end and practically coasted down Sycolin Road to the airport's small terminal. He passed up a wide-open parking spot near the entrance of the half-empty lot, settling instead for a narrow slot wedged between a van and a Toyota Prius. Dropping the rental car keys into his manila envelope, he left for the airport without locking the car. If someone stole it, all the better, though it wasn't likely to happen within the half-hour or so he'd spend waiting for Evan's arrival.

He scanned the area inside the Leesburg airport and located the camera aimed at the nearest men's room. Opening his roller bag, he activated the pinhole camera jammer. The device would block all video signals from 2400 MHz down to 900 MHz, the normal range for security cameras. He entered the men's room and walked to the last stall, wheeling his bag behind him. Seated on the toilet with the suitcase between his legs, he removed his hat and sunglasses, pulled off the fake beard and mustache and stuffed them inside the bag. He changed his shirt and ran a comb through his black hair before donning a baseball cap and a new pair of sunglasses to complete his second disguise.

Mission accomplished, he removed a soft-sided duffel bag from his suitcase and stuffed the roller bag inside, zipped it up and left the washroom as a different person. Back in the main lobby, he headed for the Trademark Rental Car desk where an obviously bored twenty-something guy greeted him.

Dan requested an SUV for the week, "preferably black, with tinted windows."

"One of our narco cars," the rental agent joked.

Dan glanced at the young man's name tag. "I assure you, I'm no drug-runner."

"Spy, then?" The young man named Eli gave him a quick grin, enjoying his game.

"Not that, either. But I might give it a try in my old age." He handed over another false ID, again from his personal stash, since Agency rules prevented the production of false driver's licenses in the U.S. This one identified him as Scott Foster, residing at Spring Valley Cove in Jacksonville, Arkansas.

Eli examined the license. "Not too many spies in Arkansas, I bet," he said, as he ran Dan's second Visa card of the day through the card reader.

Dan nodded, anxious to move away from the topic of drug dealers and spies

Eli laid the paperwork on top of the counter for Dan's signature.

Dan declined the insurance and signed his name, almost forgetting his new identity. No need for gloves this time because he had no intention of returning the car. At least, not in a condition that would allow investigators to find fingerprints or DNA evidence. Besides, by the time Trademark received notice of a fraudulent credit card, they'd realize the car had been stolen.

"So, you're dangerous then?"

"You might say so."

Eli grinned as he pulled out the carbon copy to save for his files. He seemed uncertain what to say next and resorted to, "Thank you, Mr. Foster. Nice talking to you and have a good trip."

"Thanks," Dan replied, almost adding 'you, too.' "Oh, I almost forgot." He reached down and pulled the manila envelope out of the outer pocket of his bag. "I found this on the sink in the men's room. Says 'Trademark' on the outside, so I assume it belongs to you. And from the sound of it, you'll probably find car keys inside." Dan held onto the folder as he dumped the keys and paperwork onto the Trademark counter.

Eli shook his head in disgust, "People."

Having completed his business at the Trademark counter, Dan walked back to the lobby and looked for the conference room he'd reserved. He and Evan could talk freely there, reasonably safe from prying eyes and ears. Even then, he was taking no chances. He'd brought along a jammer and a legal pad to communicate. The second page of the lined tablet contained a warning he'd scribbled: *Say nothing, we're in danger.* He counted on Evan's training. If not, their lives wouldn't be worth the price of a movie ticket.

Seated next to the window, Dan shaded his eyes from the glow of the morning sun as he watched the gleaming white executive jet glide in for a landing, bringing Evan home for the first time in nearly five years. Several minutes passed before the door of the plane opened and a curved set of steps dropped to the ground. The plane's lone passenger appeared on the top step, pausing to look around as though he were in a strange land and needed help to get his bearings. Dan wondered if that's how he felt.

Chapter Twenty-Five

Maunalua Bay, Hawaii

"Looks like shipwreck territory coming up," Tom said.

Alicia jumped up. Had she been sleeping? Her brain was foggy. He should be telling her that Spitting Caves was coming up. "What do you mean?" She reached for her purse.

"I swung by the Caves while you were napping, but spotted a couple of other boats moored there. I decided we needed a little more privacy for our dives. We can do Spitting Caves tomorrow. Actually, I'm not certain there's a shipwreck here," he admitted, "but it's a good spot for turtles and sea biscuits. One of the most beautiful dive sites in the world."

How could she have fallen asleep and trusted him to take her where she wanted to go? Something was wrong. She needed to regain control. One thing was for certain, she wasn't going on a deep-sea dive alone with him. Too dangerous. Even in the hotel they'd never been completely alone. Her backup was everywhere. She scanned the horizon. Not a boat in sight. Her protectors were back at Spitting Caves waiting for her. "I shouldn't have fallen asleep."

"I understand. We cheated Hypnos last night. I'm a little sleepy myself."

She hesitated. "Oh yes, as in hypnosis. See how tired I am? But it's not that. I'm feeling really nauseous. Should have known better than to lie down and let seasickness sneak up on me." Alicia leaned over the boat's railing. Her distress with herself made throwing up a distinct possibility. Tom cut the motor and went to her, putting his arms around her from behind. Her heart sped up, fear creeping in. She moved to pick up her purse lying on the seat, but Tom held her close.

"Just lean over the edge, honey. I'll hold you so you won't fall in."

"I need to sit down." She moved away again. "Please, Tom. My legs are weak. If I don't sit, I'll fall down." She collapsed her body, breaking his hold. He guided her to the seat, helping her down. She reached out and caught hold of the seat cushion nearest her purse, turning so her body fell on top of it. Leaning over, she put her head between her knees. "Oh, God. I'm sorry. I know I'm ruining our day, but I think we need to return to shore."

"No problem." Tom stood up and wound his way to the front of the boat.

Making a split-second decision, Alicia retrieved the gun from her purse. Before Tom could start the engine, she raised her voice and demanded, "Head back to Spitting Caves."

He turned around and stared at her, a look of surprise and hurt on his face. "Are you sure you want to do this?"

"I have no choice."

"Then you should have brought along a loaded gun."

Alicia cocked an eyebrow. "I did."

"Have you checked lately?"

"This morning. I keep an extra clip in my makeup case. Fits perfectly into my lipstick holder. I don't take chances and I'm not a novice, Tom, despite what you might have presumed."

"I didn't presume. Now what? You're going to shoot me and dump my body overboard? I also took precautions this morning," he said, lowering his voice. His stare burned into her heart. "My friends are retrieving your fingerprints and DNA from the hotel room right now. They know I'm with you. If I turn up missing, you'll be arrested for murder before you can figure out how to leave the island, and I don't care how powerful your friends are."

Alicia glared at him, unable to speak.

"That is, if you even come back alive," Tom said. "I'm betting they're perfectly willing to sacrifice you in order to get me. They're not the people you think they are. Turn me over to them, and we're both dead. You've been conned," he shrugged, as if the truth were obvious, "big time."

Alicia knew he was trying to save his life by putting doubts in her head, but they were reasonable doubts. This mission was not the way the Agency normally worked. She thought back to everything that had bothered her, beginning with the requirement to resign from the Agency, then the contract relieving them of any responsibility for her or for her actions. It meant they would hang her out to dry without a second thought. They'd done that to her once already, but would they kill her to save the Agency's reputation? New doubts ratcheted through her brain. Tom's argument made more sense than she wanted to admit.

"We're on the same side," Tom continued, "You just don't know it."

"You're CIA?" Alicia asked, remaining on alert and barely disguising her skepticism. Her index finger hovered above the trigger balancing the gun's aim against the rolling of the boat in the gentle ocean waves.

"I didn't say that. Let me show you my ID. Don't worry, I'll move slowly so you know I'm not reaching for a gun." Tom pointed to the seat cushion. "I'll slide this cushion off the seat in a way that allows you to see my hands at all times." He slowly pushed one of the seat cushions onto the floor of the boat. "Now, I'll lift this panel. You may have to move to the side in order to see the metal box inside. I won't lift the panel until you're ready."

Alicia slid along the back seat of the boat and leaned to the right. Tom lifted the panel and waited. She leaned forward, her eyes locking on the metal box.

"I'll lift the box and hand it to you."

"No. Set the box on the floor and move to the front of the boat. Face me while I retrieve the contents of the box. Is there a key?"

"Yes."

"Then use your key to unlock it before you move it to the floor."

"No problem. It's in my pocket." Tom placed his hand in his pocket.

"Withdraw your hand slowly," Alicia ordered, "or you're dead. One sudden move …" Her voice trailed off. Maybe she should remind him of her marksmanship medals.

Tom complied, holding out the key in his open palm.

Alicia barked her next order. "Unlock the box, but don't open it."

Tom followed her instructions, inserting the key and clicking open the lock. He backed slowly to the front of the boat, his eyes on Alicia as she reached for the box.

Chapter Twenty-Six

Leesburg, Virginia

Evan Phillips stood at the top of the landing trying to figure out where he was. No one on the plane would reveal their destination, and Henry had said only that Dan Chavez would meet him, but didn't say where. He spotted the small sign reading "Leesburg."

Virginia, he thought. He knew Leesburg. The town was one of his favorite places to visit when he lived in D.C. Only a forty-five minute drive from the city and you were in a different world, a different century. The houses in the historic district resembled a sleepy, southern town in the 1800's. Evan was a history buff, and he knew the city's past was anything but quiescent and tranquil, especially during the Civil War years.

He thought about the town's colorful history. Situated in Loudon County, a scant two miles from the shores of the Potomac River, Leesburg once formed the border between the United States of America and the Confederacy. A recipe for turbulence. The local population had been nearly as divided in those days as the country was today. Loudon county's representatives to the 1861 Virginia Secession Convention had voted against, supported by villagers in neighboring towns, who mustered for the Union. However, the men of the township of Leesburg offered overwhelming support for the Ordinance of Secession and raised several Confederate cavalry units.

Evan tried to orient himself to his involuntary return to the D.C. area. This flight was a first. He puzzled over the circumstances, including his landing destination. Diplomatic or military transport usually flew into Camp Peary or one of the nearby military bases. The Leesburg destination cleared up one puzzle, though. It explained the reason they landed in Boston once his transport arrived in U.S. airspace. The Notice to Airmen rules prohibited foreign diplomatic flights into or out of Leesburg due to its location within the boundaries of the Washington Metropolitan Special Flight Rules Area.

But why Leesburg? What was Henry up to now? Evan could only wonder as he reached for the railing to steady himself as he climbed down the stairs.

§

Evan looked thinner than Dan remembered as he watched his colleague traverse the plane's steps, his legs shaky from sitting too long or maybe numb from the trauma of his recent ordeal. Dan felt a twinge of guilt over Henry's methods for bringing about Evan's return, but he quickly rationalized it away, reminding himself that soldiers sometimes are caught in the middle of a skirmish and suffer wounds in defense of their country. Dan watched Evan step off the bottom stair and head straight for the terminal door without a glance at the large expanse of windows where Dan stood waiting and watching. He reached the door as Evan pushed it open and strode in. The two men shook hands and hugged.

"Glad to see you, man," Dan said.

"I sure as hell hope you aren't responsible for what happened to me over there, because if you are …" Evan let the sentence dangle and Dan took advantage of the opening.

"Shithead. Why are you accusing me of something like that? I'm your friend."

"I don't have any friends. Not any more. You know that better than anyone."

"Let's go." Dan pointed to the conference room. "We're meeting in here for a few minutes. I reserved it so we could talk." Dan held open the door.

"What's going on?"

Dan put a finger to his lips and handed Evan the yellow pad with the top page folded back so the handwritten message stood out.

"Henry knows how much you need some rest and relaxation," Dan said, switching on the portable radio and adjusting the dial to a talk station with a small amount of static crackling in the background. He took back the yellow pad and wrote *keep talking while I write*. "But first, fill me in on what happened to you over there," Dan said, as he wrote words very different from those driving his verbal conversation.

After a few minutes spent exchanging written notes, Dan and Evan left the Airport through the glass doors nearest the Trademark desk. Rental agent Eli held the door and followed them into the parking lot, pointing out Dan's newly rented SUV in the Trademark section.

"The one with the dark tinted windows, so no one will see you drive away," Eli joked.

"Maybe you'll get lucky one of these days," Dan told him, "and rent a car to a real James Bond."

"Maybe so," Eli chuckled. "Have a good trip wherever you're going. Gotta go check license plates." He held up the car key from Dan's Dulles rental. "Good thing there aren't too many white cars out here." He gave Dan a questioning shrug. "Why are some people such jerks?"

"I don't know," Dan said, bristling at being tagged a jerk even if the insult was unintentional.

"What was that all about?" Evan asked.

"Kid's got a thing about drug dealers and spies. I think he watches too much TV." Dan clicked the unlock button and Evan placed his small bag on the floor and settled into the front seat.

Dan knew by the size of the bag Evan planned to spend no more than a couple of days stateside. Maybe they'd get lucky and both could return to their normal work schedule in a few days. Right now, though, he needed Evan's help uncovering the truth about Malcolm's death. He opened the driver's side door and climbed in. Neither man said a word. They could talk later, once they agreed on how to set in motion Henry's plan.

Evan's presence had reduced Dan's anxiety levels already. Evan had some high-level contacts Dan lacked and he knew how to improvise, exactly the type you want covering your back in any operation. No one could have apprehended Evan in Prague without inside help, which Henry had provided. Dan wished they hadn't been so hard on him, but at least they'd followed Henry's orders and drugged Evan before inflicting the injuries, all of which were minor. Evan never felt the blows, only the after effects. Not much different than undergoing minor surgery.

At least, that's how Henry had rationalized it to Dan. The problem was keeping Evan from learning the truth. He might never forgive Henry, but a lot was at stake, and Henry needed to keep his case officer on his side. The information Dan had pulled out of the *Code 21* file made his skin crawl, if Malcolm's interpretation were anything close to accurate. A major assassination plot was underway, but on what timetable? They'd identified at least some of the targets, but the where and when remained a mystery.

Dan started the SUV and waved to young Eli, who went from car to car, methodically checking the license plate on each white automobile. Dan wasn't certain whether Eli could see him wave through the tinted windows because he never waved back. He watched the young rental agent close in on his target. Only two cars to go. Dan steered his SUV in front of the row of cars so Eli could back up the rental without waiting for them to drive by.

He watched Eli climb into the Dulles airport rental car and pull the door shut. In the next moment, time slowed to a standstill. Dan could imagine Eli inserting the key into the ignition and turning it to the right. What he couldn't anticipate was the ensuing explosion that rocked him and Evan from several cars away. A sick nausea coursed through Dan's body. *No time for puking now.* Thoughts of the young Eli, blown to eternity and back, sent stabs of pain into Dan's rapidly beating heart, but he stepped on the gas and drove straight for Sycolin Road as though neither he nor Evan saw or heard the devastation left in their wake.

As Dan turned out of the parking lot, he texted Henry: *We have a mole.*

Chapter Twenty-Seven

Maunalua Bay, Hawaii

Alicia felt a knot tighten in her stomach. "Okay. Tell me how we're on the same side, and this better be good." She kept the gun pointed at the middle of Tom's center of mass as she reached with her left hand to slide the metal box toward her.

"My I.D. is inside," Tom said. "Special Agent, Federal Bureau of Investigation, Washington, D.C. field office. Counter-intelligence," he added.

The I.D. Alicia lifted from the box matched Tom's words. "Phony I.D.'s are a dime a dozen these days. I'll need more than that to convince me."

"I'm working undercover."

"Trouble is, you're working undercover for the wrong side. I know all about the rogue government operation to squelch opposition. I know you're supposed to kill the Vice-President and blame it on Iran, then rig the elections and turn the current administration into a virtual dictatorship before the American people know what's happening to them," Alicia paused for breath.

"Go on," Tom said. "I'd like to hear the rest of what you know. How does this rogue government operation propose to accomplish the takeover?"

She gave him a suspicious look, trying to decide whether or not to continue. She might as well, nothing to lose. "By nationalizing everything once the country's involved in a war and distracted. They're starting already, pushing through nationalized health care. Next, they'll nationalize the whole financial system under the guise of a bailout. The oil companies and telecommunications industry come next, in the name of saving money for the consumer. Finally, they'll turn the National Guard into a Federal police force."

"Lies and half-truths. Let me give you another point of view," Tom said. "It's called the truth. But first, I think you joined the Agency intending to serve your country. Am I right?"

Alicia nodded, still wary.

"I also think someone in the Agency, your boss or maybe your boss's boss, came to you and said you'd been selected for a special mission."

She nodded again, wondering where he planned to go with this.

Tom paused and took a deep breath. "And then he told you the special mission required an extraordinary cover story. Am I right so far?"

"Yes, but—"

"Hear me out. The 'extraordinary cover' required you to hand in your resignation to the Agency, no explanations given."

Alicia's heart began to pound. So far, Tom was right on target. She thought back to how she'd agonized over the request to hand in her resignation, but in the end her worries had been unfounded. Every month since she'd left, the Agency had deposited a paycheck to her bank account, even though it came through a shell company rather than directly from the government. But the Agency handled many transactions that way—at least that's what she'd been told.

"Cooperative case officer that you are, you followed instructions. The only problem was you were duped. You are one hundred percent correct about a rogue operation, but it's being run *against* the current administration not *by* it, and you're part of that illegal operation. You know as well as anyone the laws that prevent the Agency from acting on home soil. Have you considered the fact that you can be tried for treason if you're caught? And you will be caught, and so will everyone inside and outside the government who's a part of this. I'm not the only one who's managed to get inside one of these cells."

Alicia could feel anger rising within her. Her cheeks flushed and her heart pounded. *Was he telling the truth?* She had to admit she didn't know. What he suggested was her worst fear, the nightmare that woke her week after week, ever since she'd agreed to take on this highly unusual assignment. She thought back to the offer. Tom was wrong about one point. It hadn't originated with her boss or even within Henry's Directorate, but from Intelligence—Zak Browning's Directorate. It *did* seem odd to her at the time, but the Agency had odd ways of doing business. Her colleague, the one who reported directly to Henry, sat in on the meeting as Henry's representative. *That* was the person who convinced her of the offer's veracity.

Thinking back to the offer, she reviewed in her mind her brief resignation discussion with Henry. If Tom's version were true, then her conversation with Henry made more sense. She'd assumed he was play-acting as she'd been told to expect, but Henry's behavior was out of sync with his personality. Ignoring her instincts, she'd followed orders, or what she'd thought were orders. Perhaps a huge mistake on her part. Why hadn't she trusted Henry, double-checked with him about everything? Because she was captivated by the flattery and the fat salary, that's why. How could she have been so gullible?

Her thoughts returned to Tom Kerrigan. Was he on the level, or was this a test of some sort? Either way, she couldn't risk placing all her trust in him and add a second big mistake to the first one. She needed to figure out how to keep him at bay until she could get in touch with Henry. Reaching Henry would be difficult, especially if Tom's version of events was correct and she no longer belonged to the Agency. She could try to call using her previous code, see if it still worked. Meanwhile, she still had to deal with Tom.

"You spin a good tale, but I'm not sure I can afford to believe you," she said, keeping the gun on him. "I'll believe it when I hear it from Henry."

"I'll put you in touch with him when we hit shore, but one more piece of information for you. I work at the National Counterterrorism Center where Dan Chavez is currently stationed. Maybe you don't remember the name, so I'll remind you. Evan Phillips saved his life in Iraq."

Hearing Evan's name even now caused a lump in her throat. "Why didn't you tell me that earlier?"

"Doesn't matter now, because we're out of time. We've got company coming from the direction of Spitting Caves, and they're coming up fast. We need to get out of here, darlin', right away. We both have targets on our backs." Tom turned around and with one hand grabbed the wheel, reaching for the ignition key with the other. He glanced back over his shoulder, his hand on the starter. "Time to fish or cut bait."

Alicia agonized, knowing her life was on the line either way. With thoughts of Evan on her mind, unwanted as they were, she followed her instincts and lowered the gun. "Start the boat."

Chapter Twenty-Eight

Leesburg, Virginia

Dan glanced over at Evan, seeing him recoil from the savagery of the blast, his lips locked in tight revulsion.

"Jesus," Evan said, "what bastards. This is worse than either of us anticipated. We could have a civil war on our hands here."

"Time for Plan B," Dan said, checking his rear view mirror for a tail and spotting none. "They won't follow us from here and risk being seen. Unfortunately, Sycolin Road's the only exit. They'll pick us up outside the airport."

"Depends. Maybe they'll assume you died in the blast. Obviously, they didn't realize you hired a different rental car."

"Maybe, maybe not. They tracked me this far, despite my precautions. I must be losing my touch."

"Do they know about me?"

"I'd say no way anyone could know," said Dan, glancing back again, "since neither Henry nor I have told a soul, but I had a tail coming out of the Agency. I thought I lost 'em in D.C. I don't know how they found out about you."

"Must have had somebody on you twenty-four hours. Waiting for the right opportunity. I'll wager on a watcher at the airport who knows we survived."

"Maybe. Let's see if we have company once we hit Sycolin."

"Here I thought I'd left car bombings behind in Europe."

"Whoever's running the *Code 21* op is no different than the terrorists you left behind. Dregs of humanity. Don't care who they kill as long as they achieve their goals." Dan dug in his pocket for the burn phone and handed it to Evan. "Here's the number," he said, calling out a local phone number as Evan punched in the digits.

They reached Sycolin Road and turned north. No tail yet, but Dan had to be certain. He hung a right at the next road, which took them into a residential section. A few quick turns and he'd pull into a driveway large enough to swing around and face the road. They'd sit still for a few minutes and wait to see who drove by.

Dan knew every nook and cranny of Leesburg. He'd lived there with his ex-wife. Small house on Wirt Street. Turning right onto Curtin Place he noticed a light colored sedan, a suburbanite's car creeping around the bend behind them. As he made the next turn, the sedan pulled into a driveway. Maybe the driver lived there, maybe not. An intersection loomed ahead. Santmeyer Drive. Dan turned onto it speeding up, praying for streets empty of kids. His goal was Kincaid Boulevard, but first he needed to give the slip to any possible tail.

A row of trees appeared about five hundred feet ahead. Exactly the shield he needed. He checked the rearview mirror again. Clear, so far. Immediately beyond the trees he braked and careened onto a concrete driveway, making a sharp u-turn and narrowly missing a collision with the homeowner's garage door.

He parked nose out and took his hands off the wheel. Exhaling noisily, he reached for his phone and punched in a number. "Five C, Roger, estimate three to five," he said, disconnecting the phone without waiting for a response.

"Used to think you were too paranoid for your own good," Evan told him, slipping a silencer onto the Glock 27 in his right hand. "I apologize."

"Can't be too careful in this business, as I think I've mentioned before." He glanced at Evan as his eye caught a movement from the left. A Toyota Camry with tinted windows drove past. *The suburbanite car.* Its brake lights flashed for a split second, an unconscious foot tap by the driver when he encountered their parked car. *A mistake.*

"Ex-military," Dan said. "Let's get a trace on the plate."

"Amateurs," Evan replied, typing the license number into his phone.

The Toyota turned right onto Macalister exactly as Dan hoped. Misjudge his intentions, assume he would continue straight on Santmeyer, or turn around and go back to Sycolin Road. Instead, he'd continue to wind around the residential neighborhood. He could picture the Toyota screaming along Macalister to the next intersection in time to make the turn back.

Dan pulled out of the driveway with his lights out and followed the Toyota onto Macalister. The sedan was out of sight by the time they made the turn. He crossed his fingers and made another right onto

Melody, hoping he guessed right about the Toyota's whereabouts. *No Toyota.* Dan breathed an audible sigh of relief and slammed his foot on the accelerator, careening left onto Sandy Landing. Another quick right and then a squealing left-turn got him onto Kincaid Boulevard traveling north.

"They won't find us now," Dan said.

"Nice double-back."

"Old Indian trick."

The hint of a smile broke through Evan's somber demeanor. "It still works."

"No time to get a tracking bug on this car at the airport or they wouldn't have risked following us. Good information to know."

"They can't be Agency or Bureau or we couldn't have shaken them so easily."

"No assumptions at this point. It's not *olly olly oxen free* yet," Dan said. "If the Toyota shows up again, take 'em out. Can't risk them getting us first."

Evan nodded and reached for Dan's assault rifle as they sped along Kincaid Boulevard, the beige Toyota only a bad memory. Nearing the cul-de-sac at the end of the street, Evan cracked his window. "Helicopter coming our way."

"We're almost home," Dan said, executing a sharp right turn onto a gravel driveway in front of a featureless boxy structure obscured by shrubs and trees. "Charlie's place."

"Charlie?"

"Charlie Hedgecock. We call him '*that Leesburg sonofabitch.*'"

The garage door opened and Dan pulled in. The door swung down behind them.

"Charlie's the only person in the world more war weary than I am. Ex-military, ex-Agency, ex-Bureau." Dan paused, "at least I think he's ex. One never knows, with Charlie."

"Why did you and Henry bring me back if you had this guy?"

Dan rolled his eyes. "For a lot of reasons. He's twice your age, for one thing and second, think 'Q' not Bond."

The grin on Dan's face forced a smile from Evan, only his second since Prague. "I suppose I'm Bond?"

"Close enough for me."

Chapter Twenty-Nine

FAA Investigating Congressman Harper's Plane Crash
By Jennifer Styles | CAB News Online [20 minutes ago]

LEXINGTON, KY – FAA investigators arrived within the past hour to investigate the crash site where Congressman Jake Harper died when his twin-engine Cessna crashed and burst into flames…

Evan exited the car first. Dan followed him out, extending his hand to the white-haired fellow sauntering their way. Charlie was clad in khaki shorts and a gray tee shirt that read UVA in large blue and red letters across the front. His feet sported clunky, backless Birkenstock sandals. The man's sinewy body belied his age, which Dan never really knew but guessed at mid-to-late sixties. *Must have been a runner in his younger years,* Dan thought.

Charlie ignored Dan's outstretched hand and hugged him instead.

"Hey, man. Glad you made it. Had me worried." Charlie stepped back and stroked his salt and pepper moustache as he appraised Evan. "You okay?" His olive green eyes bore in on his two visitors.

Charlie had a look in his eye that gave off the impression of a pit bull trained to kill on command, Dan thought, which sometimes unsettled him. He'd met him his first day on the job at the NCTC when Charlie offered to serve as his mentor. "You'll need somebody to show you the ropes around here," Charlie had told him, "and since I only work here on special assignment, which I don't have at the moment, I've got the time."

Charlie had kept his word and smoothed Dan's integration into the NCTC, which Dan appreciated, even if Charlie could be more than a little overbearing. Today, he appreciated the backup.

Dan turned to Evan. "Meet the best damned Special Forces officer this country's ever had. Charlie Hedgecock." As the two men shook hands, Dan turned to Charlie. "And Evan, here, is you thirty years ago. He's Henry's top man."

Dan stood back watching the two former military men look each other over. At slightly over six feet, Evan had two and half inches on the older man, but their bodies were mirror images—taut and muscular. Charlie's ruddy face contrasted sharply with Evan's dark complexion. One hinted at recklessness, the other a darker, more measured persona .

Given the urgency of their mission, Dan hoped Henry's confidence in Charlie was justified. The three would have to work fast to prevent a national calamity. Evan was here on a short-term loan. He'd be back in Prague within a week, Henry's wishes notwithstanding.

"Let's go where we can talk," Charlie said, motioning them to a basement stairway. He took a key from his pocket and slipped it into a keyhole above the combination lock. He winked at Evan. "Can't be too safe." Holding the heavy door open for his two guests, he ushered them down a concrete stairwell that resembled a bunker more than a basement. "Welcome to my lair."

They entered a well-lit office space with three workstations and a copper chain-link cage attached to the back wall. Dan could hear the ventilation system pumping fresh air into the underground confines. "A Faraday cage?" he asked, pointing to the copper contraption in the rear of the basement room.

Charlie nodded. "You got it. We can talk in there." He opened the door to the eight-foot-square low-ceilinged cubicle with its copper chain-link top, sides, and metal floor designed to keep out critical electromagnetic radiation. The cage was furnished with a card table, four chairs and a desk, all painted copper, a testament to Charlie's sense of humor. A small computer sat on the desktop along with a handset, both connected to a thick black cable that disappeared into the back wall of the room.

"We're encased in copper," Charlie said with pride. "What's said in this room stays in this room. I don't care how damned sophisticated the telecommunications systems are and I should know, since I designed most of them. You're on, Chavez. What's this all about?"

Dan's pupils dilated to cope with the low-level light conditions as he rested his elbows on the table. The lines in his face tightened and his eyes flicked back and forth between Charlie and Evan. "The last time something of this magnitude occurred was in the mid-nineteen thirties," he said.

Charlie raised an eyebrow. "You're going way back. That was a helluva time in Europe, followed by a helluva war."

"We're talking about what happened in *this* country in the thirties," Dan said. "Wall Street's plot to overthrow FDR and set up a dictatorship like the ones in Italy and Germany. Some of the plotters even traveled to those countries to study their techniques. In the name of stopping communism. And they came damn close to achieving their goal. Owned enough of the media to manipulate the thinking of the 'dumb' Americans, as they called them. Add in the American Liberty League set up by du Pont and J.P. Morgan to defend the Constitution they intended to tear down, and it looks a lot like what's going on today. The group even managed to infiltrate the churches and organize a de facto militia among disgruntled ex-military..." Dan sat back, looking directly at Charlie, "sound familiar?"

Charlie nodded and Dan continued. "Today, they're fighting socialism and taxation, or at least that's what they tell the people. Bailing out Wall Street with taxpayer money doesn't count. Socialism is when the government helps the poor instead of the rich."

"I keep up with these anti-government groups," Charlie said. "I can tick them off for you, starting with *Free-Market Americans* and ending up with the *Birthrighters* and the *American Patriots*."

"And don't forget CAB News and Sigma Services," Evan added.

"You forgot a big one," Dan said, "Are you ready for the shocker?"

"Lay it on me," Charlie said.

"The Agency."

"Director Whitworth? I don't believe it." Charlie shook his head. "I know the man. Ex-Marine, like me. Our paths crossed many times. He's a straight arrow."

"I know you know him," Dan said, "and it's one reason I'm here, along with wanting to save my hide. But for all I know, Whitworth's involved in this mess, maybe heading it up."

A startled look crossed Evan's face, but he said nothing.

"Think a conspiracy is being run out of OS?" Charlie asked.

"Security? Do you know something I don't?"

"Rumors, that's all."

Dan raised an eyebrow. "We'll need more than rumors, Charlie."

Chapter Thirty

Maunalua Bay, Hawaii

Tom gunned the supercharged 400-horsepower engines of his *Island Runner* and headed for the nearest safe haven. If only they could only make it in time. He should have been more alert, should have kept moving in the direction of his destination rather than shutting down for a cheery chat with last night's bedmate. At least she listened to reason, which was a step in the right direction. How far he could trust her was uncertain, but he hadn't much choice. And neither had she, whether she realized it yet or not.

He motioned her forward, yelling instructions when she reached him. "Lift the other seat." He took his hand off the wheel and pointed. "There's an MP5 and an assault rifle in there. Do you know how to use them?"

"Yes," she shouted back.

He hoped to God she was telling the truth. "Take the one you want and give me the other," he yelled, "then lie down on the seat and keep your head down. This baby has bulletproof shields and I'm raising them now. There's a place for your gun barrel between the panels."

Clear, acrylic-like panels rose up from within the boat's hull.

"Are these panels Plexiglas?"

"No," Tom hollered back, "aluminum oxide. Military grade. Harder than glass. They'll stop an AK-47 bullet." He glanced back over his shoulder. The chase boat was gaining, closing the distance gradually but steadily. He needed to get around Diamond Head to a spot near Kapiolani Park where they could hide the boat. An escape car waited for him inside the park, but he worried whether they'd make it in time.

Glancing at the back of the boat, he saw Alicia lying flat on her stomach propped with boat pillows so her body lay just below the rim of the boat and beneath the edge of the Alon panel, the rifle shoved through the curved arc at the joint between the sections. Tom figured she could handle a gun. Her choice of the assault rifle over the submachine gun lifted his spirits. The rifle was the smarter pick, since it required more time to aim, which he couldn't do while driving the boat. She appeared unruffled, the way he was in dangerous situations where after the first jolt of adrenalin shot through his system, calmness would sweep over him, his blood pressure would lower and his senses would grow more acute. The killer instinct, he called it. He had it, and looking at her, he decided she had it, too.

§

Tom's assurances provided Alicia little comfort. She prayed he knew where he was going and prayed the *Island Runner* was a faster boat than the one closing in on them. She adjusted the rifle in the open circle between the panels, resting it on the edge of the hull. Molded to curve with the body of the boat, these panels were clearly not standard issue, even on military vehicles. More likely installed to outwit drug runners.

Alicia watched the chase boat creeping nearer. Did her pursuers know what they were in for? She could hit a bull's eye dead center at a thousand feet. She had no idea what destination Tom had in mind, but she spotted Diamond Head coming up. *Too far away.* The pursuit boat would catch them before they reached land. Tom's life and her own were in her hands.

She looked through the semi-automatic's telescopic site. The gun was a familiar one, a military sniper rifle like the one she used in training, with a range of over half a mile. Disabling the boat would be her primary mission, unless the boat's occupants started firing on them. In that case, she would shoot to kill.

She could see Tom out of the corner of her eye. He was balancing the MP5 on top of a specialized rotating bracket attached to the prow in front of the steering wheel. The mechanized bracket lifted the gun to a level just above the bulletproof panel that protected Tom. She wondered whether he was left or right-handed, not that it really mattered. He could steer with either hand and probably shoot with either hand, as well. Not like he had to manage the M110 she held in her hands, she thought, returning her attention to her target.

"Ear plugs," she screamed at Tom in an attempt to be heard over the roar of the engines, "do you have any?" Tom shook his head. She tore off two small strips from her bathing suit wrap and stuffed them in her ears.

One advantage she had over the occupants of the chase boat was their expectation that she would support them, not fire on them.

Knowing Tom was alone with her, they might anticipate some random shots from Tom, but driving the boat made him less effective. Alicia would use that advantage to save their lives. She had to prevent the boat from closing in. She steadied her aim. Time to stay focused, permit no distractions. She took a deep breath and felt the calmness flow through her, felt her senses sharpen.

She wished she could calculate wind direction with a finger in the air, but the gusts flowing over the boat made it impossible. She studied the waves and the spray from the boat's wake and watched the birds sailing the wind currents above the water. Satisfied, she snapped the magazine in place and took aim. *Ptoo-Craack!* The sound echoed off the water. Alicia's first bullet hit the front of the chase boat at or near the location of the inboard engine. She congratulated herself on guessing right about the wind.

You people messed with the wrong girl.

§

Tom saw Alicia's bullet hit. He was impressed with the accuracy of her shot, but his frustration levels continued to rise. His boat was running at full throttle, but the pursuit boat was closing the distance between them. Diamond Head loomed straight ahead. They'd make it only if Alicia could provide enough diversion. Tom heard the retort of a second shot, but this one hadn't come from Alicia. He felt no impact on the boat and knew it had missed.

§

Alicia heard the return fire, too, which only heightened her determination. She sighted on the driver. Maybe he was somebody she knew, maybe not. It didn't matter now. She fired. The bullet missed the driver, but tore a hole in the boat's windshield. Her shot was answered by an explosion in the water less than fifty feet away and to the rear of their boat, telling her more about their pursuer's weaponry than she wanted to know.

§

"Grenade launchers," Tom shouted. "Take them out! Hurry! "

He knew everything was up to Alicia now. His MP5 was useless at the current range, which he estimated at less than a quarter mile and closing. She was a pro. Two out of three shots hit their target at that distance. Tom wished he were that good, but he didn't begrudge her talent. He was happy to have persuaded her to change sides since his life was now in her hands. He watched Alicia click in a second magazine and fire rapidly, taking less time with her aim. On her next shot, the driver fell back and the boat slowed. Tom breathed a sigh of relief, but kept the *Island Runner* throttled up. Even if another driver took the wheel of the chase boat, the delay would be enough to reach the place near the park. He hoped the right people were there waiting for him.

Chapter Thirty-One

"Keep going!" Tom shouted. "Disable the damn boat."

Alicia slipped another cartridge in the rifle and fired again, timing her shots between the splashes from the grenades landing farther and farther away from their boat.

Tom craned his neck to the left as the shots rang out, hollering back to her. "You did it." His face broke out in a large grin, "you did it, baby. They're dead in the water, literally."

She let out a long sigh as she stared at the boat over the top of the telescopic site. Yes, the boat had stopped, but where was the rest of the crew? The space between them grew wider. She turned her attention to the gun, which she withdrew from its resting place in the Alon panel's gun-hole. As she pulled the rifle away, she glanced over at Tom. He stood with his back to the steering wheel, the submachine gun pointed at her chest.

Her heart clenched. She'd made the wrong decision. A wave of nausea swept over her.

"Lay the gun across your open palms and slowly lower it onto the seat." He tipped his head to indicate he meant the seat directly in front of her. "I'm not planning to kill you, but I will shoot if you make the wrong move, and I won't stop until I run out of bullets."

Alicia said nothing. She was too busy praying he wouldn't kill her. No way, in her position, could she swing around and get off a shot before he pulled the trigger and ended her life. She held out the gun and struggled to a sitting position with the rifle horizontal in her arms. She pushed herself to her feet and took one step forward. Leaning over the back of the seat, she placed the gun on the seat cushion.

"Now," Tom ordered, his voice quieter than before, "put your hands on your head and sit down on the seat opposite while I retrieve the gun. You're smart enough to know that if I wanted to kill you I would have done it by now, so just follow my instructions, and we'll both be home safe and sound in another ten minutes."

He stepped forward, keeping the gun aimed in her direction. She watched him bend down with his knee on the seat in front of the one containing the rifle.

She wondered if she could move on him when he reached for the rifle.

"Don't try it, sweetheart," Tom said. "I want to spend more glorious nights with you and not in heaven." He retrieved the rifle and took a step backward as he spoke. "One last thing," he said, "place your head between your legs and your palms flat on the boat floor. And stay that way while I help myself to the contents of your purse." He winked at her. "In case you thought I'd forgotten about it."

Alicia's heart sped up again. Did he plan to kill her now? Shoot her in the back when she leaned over because he couldn't look her in the eyes when he pulled the trigger? She sat immobilized, staring at him, not wanting to follow his instructions.

"Trust me, please," he said, as if he were reading her mind. "I'm telling you the truth when I say I want to spend more nights with you. Just do as I ask."

Alicia complied. From the corner of her eye she could see Tom walk up and look at her, then take another step toward the back of the boat. She held her breath.

"Ah, got it," he said, stepping away. "You can lift your head now, but I don't want you to move. See where we are? Almost to the Park. Do we know who's waiting for us there?

"No one, as far as I know," Alicia said. "Since no one expected you to come back from our outing alive."

"Including you, correct?"

"Including me. May I sit up now?"

§

A wistful look crossed Tom's face. "In a minute," he said. "After I stow the artillery. Turn your head around and look out the back of the boat." He opened the door of the *Island Runner's* center console, his gaze never leaving Alicia as he gently laid the M110 and the MP5 inside. He placed Alicia's gun in his left pocket, turned the wheel to the left and slowed the boat so they wouldn't run out of fuel this close to his goal.

"You can turn around and sit up now," he said, "then answer one question for me. Since I didn't kill you when I had the chance, you know you can trust me. Tell me. How do I know I can trust you?"

"I guess you don't."

Tom returned his attention to the wheel, watching the scenery fly by. He barely heard Alicia yell to him from her seat at the back of the boat. "You've driven past Kapiolani Park."

"So this isn't your first time in Hawaii after all, is it?"

"No," Alicia admitted. "I grew up here."

"Explains a lot. I'm changing our destination, in case the wrong people are at the park waiting for us." He wished he could see inside her head, know for certain whether she was a willing participant in the plot to kidnap and kill the Vice-President or whether she'd been duped, as she claimed. He hoped the latter, but he needed to get her into FBI headquarters so they could question her. He wasn't up to the task of interrogating her himself.

"Where are we going?"

"Outrigger Hotel's marina." He took out his phone.

"Who are you calling?"

"Our rescuers," he said, thinking how relieved he'd feel when he reunited with his colleagues. Undercover work was grueling, and this job had been the worst. Maybe it was time for a desk assignment. He'd been working counterintelligence for more than ten years. Time for younger men to take over so he could concentrate on more intellectual endeavors, maybe quit and take a job with his father's foundation.

Tom's rescuer answered the phone. "Hey, it's me," Tom said. "Yeah, we're both still alive. I'm heading for the Outrigger's marina. Meet us there?" He paused to listen.

"Tom!" Alicia screamed as a flurry of bullets hit the side of the boat.

"All hell's breaking loose," Tom shouted into the phone, "get a boat out here if you can." He throttled up the *Island Runner* and reached into the console for the guns. Alicia was at his back grabbing for the rifle. He handed it to her and remounted the machine gun onto the top of the console.

The new craft, a dark blue cigarette boat, came from the direction of Kapiolani Park. I was right to worry, Tom thought. *They were at the Park waiting for us. We've got a mole.* The blue threat streaked toward them, close enough to launch a grenade into the *Island Runner,* if they had the capability. Tom held his breath. No grenades sailed their way. *One thing in our favor.* He wanted to head into shore, but the boat firing at them was running parallel to the shoreline, cutting off their access. They're trying to drive us into a trap. He swung the boat in a sharp U-turn that threw Alicia off her feet.

"Sorry," he hollered. "Can you get off a shot?"

"Not if you keep knocking me on my ass."

He could see her working frantically to load another cartridge into the M110. He knew it was the last one she had.

"Need more ammo," she screamed.

"Under the seat." Tom pointed with his foot.

The boat from the Park swung around and followed them, but its turn was not as tight and it lost its advantage. Tom steered the Runner toward the shore, closing the distance between the two boats.

"Come on, assholes," he shouted, "we're ready for you."

Another round of bullets bounced off his armored boat. Knowing they were out of range, he nevertheless pulled the trigger, sending a spray of bullets hitting the water in front of the boat, which momentarily disoriented the driver. The maneuver gave Tom the running room he needed. He heard the crack of Alicia's rifle. He saw her standing on the seat firing over the top of the Alon panel. Her first two bullets were off target, but the third hit its mark. The speedboat kept coming. Tom swung the boat around so it faced his pursuers. He raced toward them with his machine gun blasting sprays of ammunition back and forth.

In the background he could hear Alicia cursing as she hunted for reloads for her rifle. He couldn't stop to help her now. He reloaded the MP5 and pulled the trigger again. At some point, he heard the crack of Alicia's rifle echoing in the background. The chase boat, now straight ahead of them, stopped firing and bobbed in the water, its engines dead. The raw silence starkly amplified the previous cacophony and left Tom with a ringing in his ears.

"We're going in," he shouted to Alicia, nosing the boat straight for the nearest marina. He dialed a second call. "Looks like a change of venue. We'll meet you at the Diamond Head Beach hotel instead. Can you beat the cops there?"

Harbor boats with red lights flashing and sirens blazing streamed out from three different places along the shore. Two headed for the stranded boat, a third was aimed straight for them. Tom turned around to warn Alicia, but she lay unconscious, sprawled on the seat behind him. There was blood everywhere.

"Oh, God, no."

Chapter Thirty-Two

Drug-related Car Bomb at Leesburg Airport
Staff Writer | CAB News Online
Breaking News, one minute ago…

Leesburg, VA. A car bomb thought to be associated with a drug deal gone bad, exploded at the Leesburg Executive Airport this morning killing an airport employee. The victim's name is being withheld until authorities can notify next of kin. An investigation into…

Leesburg, Virginia

"Looks like everything's up to us," Dan said, wishing he trusted Whit as much as Charlie did, or trusted Charlie as much as Henry did. *What a damned mess we have on our hands.*

"You remember who broke up the FDR plot, don't you?" Charlie asked.

Dan nodded, hoping to stem a lecture by Charlie. The man grated on him. Too cocksure. *All he does is ask questions. What we need are answers.*

"Marine Major General Smedley Bradley." Charlie chuckled. "With a name like Smedley he had no choice but to become a Marine. I assume this conspiracy plot includes assassinating the President?"

This isn't a game, Dan thought. "We think that's the eventual goal, but they may want to clear the way first," he paused, "take care of a few preliminary removals. Seems Henry's on the preliminary list. Of course, it could mean he's losing his job, but after this morning's incident at the airport, I'm convinced Malcolm was right. He uncovered a hit list. It might not include my number, but I know my name's on it. Don't know what they plan to do about the President or when because we don't know who's behind it or what they have in mind."

"Might want to keep the President alive," Evan said. "Use him as a figurehead leader and let the fictive enemy kill him off later, if need be.

The South American model."

Charlie scratched his head. "Hard to believe. If it weren't for the car bombing at the airport I might not have bought your story. Evidence is pretty skimpy. Another reason you should go directly to Whit."

"Even harder for me to swallow, too," Evan acknowledged, "despite my regular dealings with military coups in the rest of the world. But think about it, Charlie. The audacity of the plan is a good reason to *suspect* Whit. He's the only one with control over both Security and Mission Support, and a coup running out of the Agency would need the help of both units."

"We need to go down our list of possible conspirators, one at a time," Dan said, "and begin ferreting out links. Something I can start working on at NCTC headquarters."

"You can trust Whit," Charlie reiterated, continuing his defense of the Director.

Dan ignored him.

"I'm inclined to agree with Charlie," Evan said. "The DCI is too new to the Agency for one thing, and look what happened the last time we had a new Director. Agency people kept the DCI in the dark for almost a year about illegal activities surrounding the torture issue."

No one spoke for several minutes. Dan turned several ideas over in his mind trying to arrive at truth through the force of logic. "Makes it hard to trust anyone at the Agency, another reason I'm glad you're here," he told Evan. "We need to find out if any of Henry's people are involved. On the way up here, I contacted my FBI friend and told him we want to talk with him over at NCTC. Not only is the Bureau clean, he said, but they've got an undercover operation underway in Hawaii. Seems they're running down an assassination plot targeting Vice-President Chun on his visit there next week. Fibbies thought the plot originated with al-Qaeda. I told them I think it's related to this g-d Code 21 operation, which the Fibs knew nothing about before my call."

"Damn," Charlie said.

"The good news is the Bureau's already on alert." Dan raised his hand to keep Charlie from interrupting. "I've enlisted a couple of operatives out of the Special Activities Division where Evan and I both have contacts. We'll see what we can learn. Whoever's behind this surely made some failed approaches to people in those agencies. Maybe we can scrape up a sleeper who had an offer they dismissed as a joke or maybe a trap. If so, they might be more likely to talk to you, Evan. How about giving one of them a call?"

"Will do, but I'm worried about the airport incident. We have to assume people know I'm home and helping you and Henry. Means I have a target on my back, too."

"Ever since the explosion I've been trying to figure out where I fouled up," Dan said. "I never told anyone you were coming back, and Henry was careful not to channel your flight through the normal routes, Camp Peary or Boiling Air Base. No way for anyone to track things out of Stuttgart either. Henry made the arrangements through his brother-in-law and the flight plan only covered the flight to Boston. Even if someone learned about your flight home they'd reach a dead end at Boston."

"They were a closed-mouthed pair, the pilot and co-pilot," Evan said. "Wouldn't even tell me where we were going."

"On orders. Just trying to protect your life. Let's assume they, whoever *they* are, knew you were flying home and knew I was picking you up," Dan thought out loud, sorting through the possibilities cluttering his mind. "They'd have been watching my house all night, but I wasn't there." He paused, "On the way here, I checked constantly for a tail. Never noticed one, so I assumed everything was okay. Somewhere, I made a mistake."

"If you made a mistake, it has to be your first," Evan said.

"Can't worry about the past, but when I find the bastard who murdered that poor kid, I'll kill him with my bare hands."

"What a pisser," Charlie said. "I see why you came to me. Need all the help you can get."

"Only took two people," Evan said, "to break up the plot against FDR. Major General Smedley Bradley and his reporter friend."

"We've got friends, too," Dan said, "so let's get busy contacting them. My blood's boiling."

"I have a question, Charlie," Evan said. "If Henry can't be sure where the DCI stands, how is it you think you can?"

"I served with Whit for years at the Bureau," Charlie shot back, "I know him like I know the back of my hand. I understand Henry's caution, but we need to think about things the other way around. If Henry goes to Whit, why should the DCI believe *him*? Whit hardly knows Henry, and his evidence is slim. The rental car incident won't prove a thing. From Whit's point of view, maybe Henry arranged to have the car blown up and polish off the two of you."

"Charlie's right," Dan said. "Henry's the best person to contact the DCI, bring him up to speed. If he's clean like Charlie believes, Whit can go to the Whitehouse directly. Neither the President, nor the Vice-President is safe until they're in the hands of the right people. Whit will know who to trust."

"Let's hope," Evan added. "They may have someone on the inside of the Secret Service, too."

"I doubt it." Dan gave a quick shake of his head. "Those guys don't turn. What's worrying me is whether the military's involved in this so-called training exercise. You two make your phone calls so we can get rolling."

Chapter Thirty-Three

Cone Memorial Hospital
Honolulu, Hawaii

Alicia lay on a bed in a private room at Cone Hospital as the nurse's aide checked the bandage encasing the middle of her body.

"Am I your first female bullet wound?" she asked.

The aide smiled. "No, but you're my first one today.

"Is there anyone here waiting to see me?"

"You mean the guard stationed out in the hall?"

"Guard?"

"Yes. Normally, we'd have to contact the police for a bullet wound, but they arrived here on their own."

"No one else?"

"Not now, but if you're asking about the FBI agent who brought you in, he said to tell you he had another emergency and he'd be in touch as soon as he could. He stayed until the guard arrived."

Alicia had a foggy recollection of Tom in the room telling her about another emergency, and then she'd drifted away. Hard to distinguish dream from reality. Her brain was a fog. She struggled to remember her conversation with Tom on the ride from the pier to the hospital. Must have been a dozen FBI agents and police waiting for them at the dock. The ambulance arrived almost immediately, which no doubt saved her life.

"How bad is my injury?"

"A superficial wound, but you lost a lot of blood, which sent you into mild shock. That's usually a bigger problem than the wound, so I'm glad to see how well you're coming out of it. Amazing how quickly an I-V can do its thing. You'll heal up just fine, but the scar will be noticeable in your bikini, unless you decide to visit doctor sellout."

"Dr. Sellout?"

The nurse's aide grinned. "Plastic surgeon."

Alicia tried to smile, but her lips weren't responding to normal brain commands. "I think I blacked out when it happened," she said, her mind reverting to the moment on the boat when she felt the bullet hit and knock her backwards. In her next waking moment, Tom was docking the boat amid screaming sirens and mobs of people yelling and cursing. She remembered him lifting her from the back seat and carrying her ashore, asking people to move out of the way, and then she lost consciousness again.

"I seem to have passed out a couple of times."

"Shock. Probably from the emotion associated with someone shooting at you. People pass out from a lot less."

"I can't remember how long I was out." Alicia hesitated again, trying to clarify what she wanted to ask the nurse.

"Affects your memory when you're in and out like that. This is the second time you've come to. I hope you're awake for good this time."

"How long do I have to stay here?"

"They're keeping you tonight. Maybe another day or two, depends. We need to watch you while the drugs wear off and we get you rehydrated. Then you can go home." The young aide hesitated, unsure of the legal status of her charge. "Or, at least, we'll turn you over to the HPD officer waiting to see you." She smiled down at Alicia. "He's almost as good looking as your FBI agent. How do you do it?"

"Blonde hair," Alicia mumbled, trying to keep her speech from slurring. She wasn't interested in the Honolulu Police Department guard waiting outside the door. She wanted to see Tom.

"Maybe I'll give it a try," the aide said, flicking her mouse brown hair with her fingers.

Alicia barely noticed. Her thoughts were on Tom. When would she see him again, she wondered? *What had he told her?* She remembered more about what she'd told him. Her mind reeled back to the ride in the ambulance and Tom's whispered questions, which she tried to answer when she was conscious, but she kept going to sleep. They whispered about the assassination plot and her assignment to kill Tom. Her whole body went weak at the thought of how close she'd come to betraying her country unknowingly.

They kept their voices low so the EMTs couldn't overhear. Tom explained how he was working undercover with the conspirators and his cover must have been compromised, which is why the plotters sent her to kill him. That much she did recall. Worst of all, she now understood how she'd been duped into resigning her post at the Agency and joining their operation.

How could I have been so trusting, so stupid?

"Easy," Tom had told her. "Following unusual orders is part of the job," not that his answer succeeded in easing her conscience. At least she hadn't killed an innocent person, but she came awfully close, something she would have had to live with for the rest of her life. And probably not a long life at that, she thought. *They planned to kill me when they killed Tom.* She wondered what happened to everyone in the two boats, the fake case officers and agents linked to…to what? *What the hell was going on?* She had to stay awake, think, protect herself, but the medicine was making her drowsy…she was back in the ambulance…

"The doctors will have you as good as new in no time," Tom said, reaching over and stroking her hair away from her forehead, "and you and I will live happily ever after."

"Really?" she said, her voice still barely above a whisper.

"I'm just kidding about the happily ever after part," he said, leaning down and kissing her parched lips. It was her favorite memory of him.

Shaking herself awake, Alicia abandoned the dream world and began to plan her escape.

Chapter Thirty-Four

Leesburg, Virginia

Dan Chavez paced the computer room while Evan phoned his SAD pals. Within a few minutes, the door of the Faraday cage clicked open and Evan walked out. "Got some interesting news."

Dan could see him struggling with his emotions. "Good news or bad?"

Evan shrugged noncommittally. "Turns out an agent by the name of Tom Carter is heading up the Hawaii operation involving some of our favorite goons. Seems it was Sigma Services that had an assassination team in the Vice-President's home state waiting to greet him on his next visit. Carter just flew into D.C. from working undercover in Honolulu under the name Tom Kerrigan. Blew the operation wide open. And here's the kicker. A former Agency officer was involved. A woman. Seems she believed she was still in the employ of the Agency, working undercover for them. Claimed she'd been told that Vice-President Chun was a traitor working as a double agent for China and had to be taken out. Assassination was to go down as a false flag operation to be laid at the feet of the Iranians."

"How was she duped into believing that?"

"Someone inside the Agency got to her. Told her she was being reassigned," Evan continued. "As part of her cover she would have to submit her resignation. Seems she bought the story hook, line and sinker. Since the monthly paychecks kept coming, she never thought to question the scheme. She's going by the cover name of Alicia Michel. Sound familiar?"

Dan nodded, sensing the turmoil Evan must feel inside as he revealed the name of the agent. "Mickie." Neither man spoke for the next few minutes as Dan contemplated this new twist, "which means the Agency person was someone high up in the hierarchy, high enough to earn the trust of one of our best former operatives."

"Explains why she seemed to drop off the planet," Evan added.

Dan noticed a trace of wistfulness in Evan's voice. He knew the pain of losing Mickie still cut Evan to the quick, even though Dan felt he was better off without her. In an unguarded moment, Evan once confided to him that he never understood Mickie's split personality—the loving lady versus the jungle creature, a wild thing, dangerous even. She might have been a gun for hire, Evan had said, she could be that cold and calculating. The trait served her well in her Agency job, Dan thought, but it wasn't much for sustaining a marriage. *Hard to maintain a marriage in our business, anyway.* Henry was a good example. Struggled for twenty years before he and his ex called it quits. Evan and Henry had a lot in common. Neither fully recovered from the death of their marriages or had gotten over their ex-wives.

"What else did you learn?" Dan asked, wanting more details on the Hawaii operation.

"Mickie's in a hospital in Honolulu being treated for a bullet wound. Lost a lot of blood, so it's touch and go. Carter ordered round-the-clock surveillance for her before he left. Thinks she's a target. Said some of the Sigma guys are dead, but nobody's certain if they managed to nail everyone. Apparently, Carter thinks not and has no idea how long it will take to find out. His boss ordered him back here to help protect the Vice-President in D.C. Carter wouldn't leave until he'd put everything in place to assure Mickie's safety."

"Jesus," Dan said, feeling sorry for both Evan and Mickie, but annoyed at the Bureau for not sharing information on the Hawaii gig. What else were they keeping to themselves? He would meet with Carter as soon as he had a free minute and give him a piece of his mind over not sharing. Once this operation ended, he'd make his wife happy and resign. He lacked the heart for this dirty business. The specter of Eli's death would haunt him forever. Maybe he'd find himself a quiet IT job in a family-friendly city out west. Start a family, live a normal life.

"We're to meet up with Carter at your place," Evan added, interrupting Dan's reverie, "and pick up Henry from the safe house and bring him along."

"When?"

"ASAP."

Charlie exited the Faraday cage, having missed the conversation about Alicia. Looking grim, he said, "Just finished talking to Whit. Secret Service received intel about an assassination attempt on the Vice-President that traced back to the Agency. Whit said he thought it might be one of Henry's ops."

That's why no one at the NCTC came clean with me, Dan thought. "They're wrong about Henry and I intend to prove it."

"Whit said rumors have been circulating inside the Agency that Henry's undergoing psychological problems. Nobody knows the source of the gossip, but Whit wants Henry back at Langley pronto, for his own safety. And he's to go straight to Whit's office—no passing Go, no collecting his two hundred dollars."

Dan was in no mood for Charlie's humor, which grated on him. Being around Charlie made him uneasy in a way he couldn't explain. "Henry can't be in two places at the same time, unless he has quantum properties I know nothing about. I'd like to keep him with us."

"Then you'll have to take it up with Whit," Charlie said.

Dan paused, the uneasy feeling returning. *Was Henry stepping into a trap?* Realizing he might be overreacting, he agreed. Henry had to return to Langley at some point, anyway. Now was as good a time as any. "Okay," he told Charlie, "we'll go get Henry and drop him off at Langley. Then you can drive us to my office to meet with Carter. But if this is a trap, Charlie, I'll be back for your scalp."

"No worries," Charlie said. "Let's roll."

Dan glanced over at Evan, wondering what he thought about Mickie popping up in his life again. *At least she was a continent away. Evan had enough to do without the complications that came with Mickie.*

"You'll like my car," Charlie said, "it's outfitted with bulletproof everything. Bought it when I was in Iraq and decided to bring it home with me. And now, thanks to you, I finally get a chance to use it."

The trio wound their way through Charlie's sprawling ranch house. "Where are you hiding it?" Evan asked.

Charlie grinned, obviously appreciating the question. "I have a second garage attached to the back of the house. Always good to have two escape routes."

"Expensive layout you have here," Dan said, wondering where Charlie came by the money for what he called his "little spread."

"Not too bad," Charlie replied, "hired my friends to help me build it. They needed jobs when they got back from Iraq and my projects seemed to fill an emotional need as well as a financial one. We had a good time. Follow me."

Charlie led them to a metal door in the laundry room off the kitchen. With the push of a button, the door slid open to a parking garage that housed two cars, one a black, bulletproof Hummer. Charlie walked over to a small computer on a workbench in one corner of the garage. After checking a series of screen images, he returned. "My surveillance equipment," he explained, climbing back into the Hummer. "Lets me check the outside surroundings every twenty-four hours. I took it back to your arrival. Nothing suspicious, except for you two." He turned and pointed to the Hummer. "That's my baby. 2006 H3. Go ahead, get in."

Dan elected to sit in the back, determined to escape Charlie's incessant chatter. Evan slid onto the orange and black leather seat next to Charlie. "Put your seat belts on," Charlie ordered, "we don't need some nosy cop stopping us for a seat belt infraction."

"How much does this thing weigh?" Evan asked.

"Before the bulletproofing, about forty-five hundred pounds. The steel plates and reinforced windows added another thousand pounds." Charlie glanced over his shoulder at Dan. "There are weapons under every seat," he said, pressing the button for the automatic door opener, "if the need arises."

Dan retrieved a semi-automatic, removed the cartridge and inspected it before re-inserting the clip. He hoped Charlie's extraordinary precautions were superfluous. He'd already used up eight of his nine lives. As Charlie backed the vehicle out of the garage, Dan's mind ran to the dark memories of the young rental agent being blown to bits only hours earlier. If only he could turn back the clock…

Not the first time he'd wished that, as images of his first wife flashed through his brain. Memories flooded back: of returning home from Iraq at the end of his deployment, sickened by the war and determined not to re-up, despite the consequences to his retirement, when he received more bad news. His wife, Janice was dying of cancer. Janice Whitelance Chavez belonged to the Oglala Lakota Sioux tribe. She'd grown up on the Pine Ridge Reservation in South Dakota, legendary for the discovery in the 1970's of water polluted with high levels of radioactive contamination from nearby uranium mining. In the years since, her family had lost several relatives to early death and disease as a consequence of mining company negligence. Anger flowed through his body each time he revisited the scene in his mind.

Whether Janice's cancer and infertility stemmed from the same cause was a question the doctors couldn't, or wouldn't answer, though Dan had insisted he knew. Nevertheless, he gambled again, marrying his wife's sister three years later. He spent the first two of those three years working with the *Defenders of the Black Hills* project until a CIA recruiter knocked on the door of his apartment in Rapid City and invited him to D.C. for a meeting with Henry Larson, the CIA's Director of National Clandestine Services. He first told the recruiter to fuck off, then relented and asked for a couple of days to think it over. After lengthy conversations with his wife's family, he agreed to a meeting with the DCS. The recruiter handed him a round-trip airline ticket. Dan later congratulated Henry on his acumen. Had the ticket been one-way, Dan remembered telling him, he'd never have accepted the invitation.

In D.C., Henry wooed Dan with the help of one of his comrades in arms—Evan Phillips, a former Navy Seal who'd saved Dan's life in Iraq and now worked for the CIA in Eastern Europe. The pair convinced him the Agency was desperate for his techno-geek skills and aptitude for languages, both of which he credited to his bi-lingual childhood growing up on the reservation. Dan remembered all of Henry's arguments persuading him that he owed the country his talents. Henry was an adroit salesman. Before leaving Washington, Dan had signed his life away.

And now here he was, putting his life and Henry's on the line again. He held on as Charlie's Hummer hit the street. He hoped Charlie was right about Whit. Henry's life depended on it. Maybe all of their lives.

Chapter Thirty-Five

Cone Memorial Hospital
Honolulu, Hawaii

A second nurse's aide entered Alicia's room shortly after the first one left.

"I need to use the bathroom," Alicia told her, "can you help me?"

"Certainly. Take hold of my arm, and I'll help you up." The aide put her hand under Alicia's arms for support. "Now, swing 'em over the edge. That's right. Now just sit here a minute." She patted Alicia's arm and asked, "Okay, now? Let me know if you feel too weak to stand."

Following the aide's instructions, Alicia was surprised at how strong she felt. She sat on the edge of the bed longer than necessary, letting the young woman think she was weaker than she actually was.

"How are you doing?"

"Not bad. Just want to let the blood circulate back to my head before I stand up. Where are my clothes, anyway?"

"Hanging on a hook in the bathroom. Your shoes are under here," the aide pointed to the nightstand, "and your purse is in the drawer. I think your friend took a couple of things with him, though."

Alicia wondered what items Tom took away. She slid off the bed to a standing position and leaned on the aide's arm. She felt a little shaky, but not too bad, considering..

"Can you manage this?" the aide asked, as Alicia eased her way to the bathroom door."

"No problem."

"I'll be right outside the door if you need any help."

"Thanks. I think I'll be fine." Alicia held her hand on the door as it closed. She found her underwear and put it on under the hospital gown, leaving her shirt and pants hanging on the hook. She washed her hands and splashed cold water on her face, then reached for a paper cup from the holder on the wall. *Need to drink water, plenty of water.* She filled the cup twice, drinking slowly so the water stayed down.

Drying her face, she stared at her image in the mirror. She looked a mess and her side hurt, but it wasn't as painful as she expected. *Only a flesh wound. I must have passed out from shock. I'm turning into a wimp.* She hoped the nurse hadn't doped her up too much because she needed to be able to think straight and stay awake.

If the nurse offered additional meds, she'd refuse to take them. She had a high pain tolerance and the ache in her side was manageable. A few exercises would help her regain strength, get her blood flowing and increase her adrenalin. She grabbed the sink with one hand and stretched her legs, holding onto her side with her free hand. After flushing the toilet twice, she left the bathroom and walked slowly to her bed for the aide's benefit.

"Are you feeling okay? Not too dizzy?"

"No, I'm doing much better, thanks to you." Alicia smiled. "Would you mind walking with me to the hallway so I can meet the palace guard?" A shadow of the officer's back darkened the frosted sidelight next to the room's door. It was enough to tell her whether or not he was seated in the chair outside her room.

The aide hesitated, but Alicia had already turned toward the door. "Sure," she finally said, "you seem to be doing pretty well. You must be a quick healer."

"I hope so." Alicia leaned on the aide's arm more than necessary. "Mostly, I feel tired, like I could sleep for a week."

"I understand. Let me get the door." The young woman swung the door back and kicked the stopper down.

The Honolulu police officer stood as Alicia stepped into the hallway. She glanced around, taking in the location of the elevators and the nursing station. Luck was with her. Her room was at the end of the hall beside the elevators and stairwell and to the left of the nurse's station in the middle of the circular ward. The room numbers began with three. She'd rather be on the first or second floor, but the beneficial hall layout was more important.

Alicia extended her free hand to the guard. "Hi, I'm your charge."

The young man shook her hand. His nametag told her his rank, which surprised Alicia. He seemed young to have made sergeant already. Meant he was good at his job. She'd keep that in mind.

"And your middle name?" she asked.

The guard grinned. "You from here?"

"Born and bred."

"*Keaka*," he added, confiding his Hawaiian name. "Means *the shadow*, and you?"

"How fitting." Alicia grinned at him. "*Puanani*."

He smiled back. "Pleased to meet you, beautiful flower."

Alicia shrugged. "My parents were hippies, what can I say?"

The nurse stepped in. "It's time to put you back to bed for a long nap." She looked over at the guard. "She's exhausted. Told me she'd like to sleep for a week, but we'll at least let her sleep until tomorrow morning."

"I am exhausted. I can hardly stand," Alicia said, hoping both people believed her. "Pleasure meeting you, Keaka. Nice to know I have a shadow."

The two women returned to the room, but not before Alicia took one last look at the hallway area. This would be easier than she expected, as long as her shadow cooperated. She took the aide's arm and shuffled back to the bed.

"We have a mild sleep inducer for you right here." The nurse's aide reached for the cup on the nightstand and handed Alicia two white pills.

"I don't think I'll need these. I can barely keep my eyes open."

"They'll keep you from waking up periodically. You need a long, deep sleep for healing. Besides, doctor's orders."

The aide poured water from the nightstand pitcher into a plastic glass. Alicia pretended to place the pills in her mouth as she accepted the glass of water. She drank it down and thanked the aide for taking such good care of her.

The young woman smiled and left the room, quietly closing the door behind her. Alicia could see her form standing in front of Sgt. Taylor, probably telling him Alicia was asleep already. At least that's what she hoped. She watched through the frosted glass until the image of the aide vanished and Sgt. Taylor's head dropped back to reading his police magazine. She waited a few more minutes, in case the aide might return to check on her, then Alicia began her escape.

Five minutes later, satisfied the aide was safely gone, Alicia retrieved her purse from the nightstand and checked to see what might be missing. Only the gun, which wasn't an immediate problem since she had two more stashed elsewhere. The cell phone languished in its proper pocket, and Alicia retrieved it, checking the charge. Next, she punched in Sgt. David "Shadow" Taylor's name, along with the hospital phone number displayed on the landline next to her bed. Thank goodness Tom had arranged for a private room.

After digging out a comb and secreting her purse under the pillow, she removed the last of her belongings from the nightstand drawer, gathered up her shoes and socks and headed for the bathroom where she finished dressing and combed her hair. She could feel her strength returning, which was good since she would need to move quickly. For another minute or two, she stood at the sink gently moving her feet up and down, heel to toe, before heading back to bed. Turning onto her side, she removed her purse from under the pillow, stuffed the comb back inside and tucked the purse under the blanket beside her. Then, she placed her phone call.

Chapter Thirty-Six

Washington, D.C.

Director of Intelligence Zak Browning was all business as he sat in the leather chair opposite the custom desk in his father's office in Arlington, Virginia. No son could be prouder of his father's success. According to the Private Equity International's PEI50 report he was reading, ZGB Capital was the world's third largest global private equity firm after The Carlyle Group and Goldman Sachs, with more than thirty billion dollars of equity capital under management. The firm employed over two thousand investment professionals, who managed thousands of portfolios concentrated in Europe, East Asia, and North America. Very impressive.

In addition to its financial investments, mostly oil-related, the company focused on leveraged buyouts, venture capital, and equity accounts outside the U.S. Zak always bristled when Agency personnel questioned him about what they considered the company's two dubious practices: employing a number of high-ranking political figures from the U.S., Canada, and Great Britain, including former U.S. Presidents and British Prime Ministers, and reaping immense profits from the U.S. invasions of Iraq and Afghanistan. Was Zak to blame for U.S. wars making his father rich? Oil and defense contracts were ZGB Capital's life-blood, but *someone* had to bankroll the nation's warmongering. From Zak's point of view, it might as well be his father's firm.

"Where do we stand?" ZB, Sr. asked, the rich timbre of his voice reminding Zak of the late, great Charleton Heston, whom he resembled both in looks and prophetic demeanor. Now in his early seventies, ZB could pass for a man ten years younger. Zak's father worked at keeping fit, a daily routine that included a swim in his private indoor pool, a half-hour workout with his personal trainer and a jog around his outdoor track, no matter the weather—a demonstration of his inner toughness. His father's reputation for ruthlessness matched that of almost any living dictator. Zak, though a little more erratic, worked hard to assure everyone he was cut from the same mold.

Chairman of the Board as well as CEO, ZB had founded the company in his late thirties when Zak Jr. was still in college. Zak recalled vividly the day the company's founding partner died of heart failure. He knew the controversy surrounding the partner's death. The widow's accusations eventually proved unfounded. She'd backed away after learning of the death benefits provided by the company, attributing her earlier allegations to stress over her husband's death. At the time, the financial sector assumed Zak would join the firm as a senior partner, but he chose the military instead, a decision suited to his long-term interests as envisioned by his father.

"We're not there yet," ZB said, bringing Zak back to the matter at hand, "but we're getting close. The country is split down the middle. Neither side trusts the other, and as long as we can focus that mistrust, we have control."

"CAB media has done their job well," Zak said, always ready to compliment his father. "Your decision to buy out their franchise was pure genius."

The two men smiled, mirror images of each other.

"CAB lets us swing public opinion in our favor," ZB said. "What's important is to maintain the illusion of a democracy. As long as the people believe they live in a democratic society they can be manipulated."

Zak nodded, awed as always by his father's genius.

"By the way," ZB said, "I listened to McGuire on CAB News yesterday, spouting off on the merits of torture. The man's delusional. I wish he knew how to maintain a lower profile."

"I've talked to him about his public appearances, but since he thinks he's running the show, he's not inclined to listen to my advice."

"The puppet who believes himself the puppeteer." ZB grinned. "He should have been born in a banana republic where he could have risen to dictator and ruled with an iron hand. The position suits him. If he thinks he can pull off that kind of rule in the U. S., he needs a few more appointments with his shrink."

"He's dangerous," Zak told his father, not for the first time.

"Once we leak the news about the sabotage of Harper's plane, McGuire's days will be numbered. He's the left wing's number one target these days. What's the story on Chun, anyway?"

Zak shrugged. "As soon as I know something, you'll know something."

Chapter Thirty-Seven

Northern Virginia

Dan studied the surrounding area as Henry emerged from inside the safe house, glancing around as if he expected trouble. Charlie pushed a button that opened the back door of the Hummer and motioned Henry inside. Once Henry settled onto the back seat, Dan lowered his voice. "Any idea why Whit didn't call your secure phone about returning to the office?"

"Not a clue," Henry whispered, "and I don't like it. It's not like Whit to send orders through an intermediary, especially someone outside the Agency."

"Have you tried to call him?"

"Yes. His assistant said he was out of the office, but she confirmed the meeting. Said a car would be waiting at the gate for me. I told her not to bother, I'd call my office for a car once I got there."

Dan stared out the window at the dismal Washington streets, wet with rain. The weather matched his mood. "I don't like the sound of this, either. Guess we're stuck with playing it by ear." He reached for the phone in his pocket. "Need to call my office. Tom Carter's back in town with some news, and I need to talk to him."

"Good news or bad?"

"A bit of both," Dan said, briefing Henry about Mickie. The news appeared to shock Henry, not a reaction Dan ever witnessed prior to today.

Charlie drove past CIA headquarters and made a U-turn at Merchant Lane heading north on Dolley Madison. At the entrance to Langley, he pulled in and swung around so the Hummer's back end stopped at an angle about ten feet from the front of the bright yellow main gate. Henry opened the back door and stepped out.

Dan watched Henry take a deep breath before he climbed out of the car. *He's steeling himself against the unknown.* Dan rolled down the window. "Hang on," he said, calling Henry back to the Hummer. "Give me a call right now on your cell and keep the line open so we can hear what's going on when you get to the gate. We'll park around the corner."

Shielded from the gate by the Hummer, Henry took his m-trix3 out of its case and speed dialed Dan, adding, "I'm really not expecting a problem. I go through this gate every day."

Dan leaned his arm on the window ledge, hesitant to acknowledge the sense of irony he felt at having qualms about the place that for the last few years had served as his sanctuary. Based on Charlie's assurances, he shouldn't be expecting trouble, but he couldn't rid himself of a nagging sense of unease about Whit. "You're okay, then?" he asked Henry.

"I'm fine. Let's hope there's not a car waiting for me because that might mean trouble. When I get to the guardhouse, I'll call my office for transport," he said. "Calling ahead might have alerted the wrong people."

"Good luck," Dan told him, hesitant to let him enter alone. He wondered if he should walk Henry to the gate, but decided against it. "I'll be in touch."

"And watch your back," Charlie added.

Just what Henry needed to hear, Dan thought, as if we aren't worried enough.

"We've never had an assassination inside Langley," Henry replied with a cynical grin, "and I've no intention of becoming the first." He tucked the m-trix3 back in its hip case, leaving the connection to Dan open. "Once I reach the gate, no talking," he told the group. "I don't want tiny voices emanating from my belt buckle." With that, he grinned and walked away, lifting his hand behind him in a half wave.

"Pull out," Dan barked.

Charlie stepped on the gas, making a right turn north onto Dolley Madison. Less than fifty yards along the highway he pulled the Hummer to the side of the road, parked and cut the engine. The heavily treed area shielded them from sight of the guardhouse. Dan turned his speaker to the "on" position so everyone could hear Henry's conversation with the gatehouse guards. Then, he took a deep breath and waited.

§

Henry pushed open the yellow barrier and approached the guardhouse. He was in no hurry, wanting to give Charlie time to leave the area before he faced the gatekeepers. He stooped to tie his shoe, hoping Charlie would remember to cut the motor on the Hummer. He could feel the pounding of his heart as he bent down. *Was Whit really on the level, as Charlie believed? And not involved with the plot to overthrow the U.S. government?* Henry wished he were as certain as Charlie, but he couldn't seem to dispel his normal skepticism and embrace an untested trust in the new DCI.

Henry's mind raced, thinking about all the deaths. Malcolm, the poor kid in Leesburg, and Jake Harper. He was having second thoughts about accepting Harper's death as an accident. Had the plane been sabotaged? Hard to know when it came to plane crashes. Maybe the Congressman had been involved in this conspiracy and had a change of heart. It wouldn't surprise him. Henry wracked his brain, reviewing recent news headlines in his mind, trying to recall if anyone else with political or governmental ties had died recently. He'd check on it when he reached his office.

The only bright spot in his day was having Evan home, which gave him a renewed sense of security. He wished they hadn't been so rough on him in Prague. He'd take care of that matter later, after this was over. His thoughts turned to the future, wishing not for the first time in his life that he could read minds. *Was Whit on the level? What the hell.* He'd know soon enough.

"Afternoon, sir." The military guard saluted Henry, aware he was former military. The Agency's gatekeepers were the best of the best and their memories often astounded Henry. Most knew hundreds of Agency employees by name and rank.

"Afternoon," Henry replied, removing his wallet and displaying his Agency ID. From the corner of his eye, he noticed the guard from the next booth moving toward him. A knot formed in his stomach. *Charlie guessed wrong about Whit.*

"I'll call my office for a car," Henry said.

"Not necessary, sir." The second guard took Henry by the elbow. "We have one over here."

"Please take your hand off my arm," Henry said, warning Dan and Evan about the guard's demeanor. "I prefer to call one of my own staff to pick me up."

"We have orders, sir. We apologize. Please follow me."

Henry stood his ground. "What's going on here? You have orders? What kind of orders?"

"Orders from the Director, Sir. You're to come along quietly, or we will resort to force."

Henry knew Dan and Evan would hear enough to know he was being taken prisoner. He followed the guard, wondering where they were taking him, who was behind it, and how long he had to live.

Chapter Thirty-Eight

Washington, D.C.

The Secret Service agent sitting to the right of the Vice-President glanced around nervously, in sharp contrast to the calm demeanor of the man he'd been sworn to protect. Knowing there was trouble ahead made the job harder, not easier. In addition to carrying out his sworn duty, Agent Myers admired the new Veep. Easier to put your life on the line for someone you admired.

What had surprised him the first time he met Allen Chun was his height. At six-one, he was tall for an ethnic Chinese, and his slim build made him seem even taller. Dr. Chun was a handsome man whose expansive smile enhanced his considerable charisma. He had no trouble winning friends and influencing important people, including his bodyguards. Meyers knew the Veep's supporters felt *he* should be the new President and believed he would have won the Presidency had his name appeared first on the ticket. They were probably right.

Agent Meyers had been in charge of the Veep's security since the day after Election Day. He'd made a point of knowing everything there was to know about the man who placed his life in his capable hands. The Hawaiian born Dr. Chun, an economist and Nobel laureate, continued to write his weekly column for one of the country's leading newspapers, in spite of his extra duties as Vice-President. His foreign-born wife, an attorney in the Justice Department, had held onto her job for more than twenty years despite swings in the Washington power structure. Agent Meyers felt his job would be easier if she'd just quit, but that wasn't her style. The couple had one daughter, a graduate student at Harvard majoring in international business. They were a family not lacking in self-esteem, he mused, which made them a target among those who mistrusted the highly educated, preferring instead to idolize movie stars, televangelists, and country singers, or political candidates "just like themselves."

Meyers had been around the Veep long enough to know that with

Allen Chun there was no middle ground. He was a crusader whom most of the public loved to love and some of the public loved to hate. Today would find them among friends, or so it might seem, but Agent Meyers knew differently. When the Vice-President had stepped into the limousine parked under the portico outside the White House, four Secret Service agents in addition to Meyers joined him, one seated on either side in the rear seat, two facing across from him and a fifth occupying the front passenger seat.

"Isn't this overkill?" the Vice-President had asked, seemingly annoyed at the extra security measures that might restrain his contact with the people he served.

"Can't take chances," Meyers replied. "We've had a tip. Might be something, might not."

The limousine eased out of the gate and headed for the dedication ceremony for the New Life Senior Residences at Marlow Heights, a 36-unit affordable housing development for low-income senior citizens in Washington, D.C. The Vice-President's schedule, posted daily on the whitehouse.gov website, indicated he would tour the project before dedicating the buildings.

"Big crowd," Chun said, leaning across Agent Meyers to look out the window.

"I'm not a fan of crowds."

Chun brushed aside his remark. "These people are my supporters. I'm not worried."

Meyers exchanged glances with the agent sitting across from him as the limousine pulled up to the curb and they were besieged by a swarm of cameras, microphones, and a crowd chanting the Vice-President's name.

Meyers and the Secret Service agents, with the exception of the driver, exited the limousine and waited for the security crew in the car behind to spread through the crowd before opening the door for the Vice-President. Meyers waited by the limousine's back door, scanning the crowd of multi-ethnic faces, looking for anyone suspicious. He never worried about accusations of profiling. Of course, he profiled. One nearby face worried him, and he flipped on his mic. "Move closer to the Middle Eastern guy in the red shirt." He waited. "Yeah, you got him. Keep an eye on him."

Satisfied everyone was in place, he bent down and opened the door. "Mr. Vice-President."

Chun stepped out of the limousine and waved to the crowd, smiling broadly. Reporters shouted questions as the crowd chanted: "Chun…Chun…Chun.'" He pointed to the woman with the NBC News microphone who was calling his name, "Allen, Allen."

As the Vice-President turned toward her, Meyers felt him crumple over. His heart pounded. He grabbed Chun before he could hit the ground and pushed him back into the limousine, shielding him with his body as he turned on his mic again and shouted, "We're headed to the hospital. Keep us posted."

§

The Secret Service agent nearest the man in the red shirt felt himself being hemmed in by the tight knot of people straining to see the Vice-President. He'd moved to within three feet of his target when he saw the man raise his arm as if to fire a gun, but the would-be assassin had no weapon. He was pointing his finger. *What was happening?* The agent heard a loud pop, looked over his shoulder at the limousine and saw the Vice-President disappear at the same time he smelled the odor of gunpowder. He turned around and saw the man in the red shirt. He'd pushed and shoved his way to the rear of the crowd and was running away, fast.

The agent, a former running back for the University of Pittsburgh, sprinted after him. Catching up, he dove and tackled his quarry, taking down innocent bystanders in the process. *Collateral damage. Couldn't be helped.* Within seconds, two additional Secret Service men appeared out of nowhere and helped subdue the assassin. Bending the man's arms behind his back, the agent snapped cuffs on his wrists, stood him up and pushed him forward. The agents held each arm, steered the prisoner to a black SUV and shoved him none-too-gently into the back seat.

The SUV driver reached for his radio and clicked on the mic. "We got the bastard."

Chapter Thirty-Nine

Breaking News: Assassination Attempt on U.S. Vice-President
Staff Writer | CNN Online [10 minutes ago]

WASHINGTON, D.C. – Confusion reigns in city as officials try to calm the nation's capital after a blatant attempt to assassinate Vice-President Allen Chun. CNN reporters have been unable to learn the condition of the Vice-President...

NORTHERN VIRGINIA

"Dammit all," Charlie said. "Not Whit. What do we do now?"

"We continue to NCTC. Evan and I are meeting with Carter. He's waiting in my office," Dan said. "You might have bet wrong on Whit, but I'm not wrong about Tom Carter. His blood runs red, white, and blue. I'd trust him with my life. No way in hell would he be involved in a plot to take down the government."

Charlie gunned the Hummer back onto Dolley Madison heading west toward Lewisville Road and the Counterterrorism Center. As he made the turn, Dan's thoughts strayed to his sister who used to teach English at a nearby private school. He tried to remember the name of the Department Chair, a nice guy. She'd been at the school on 9/11. Dan remembered her story about Saudi commandos entering the school and scooping up the Saudi Prince's children.

"Let's not dawdle," Dan told Charlie, trying to speed up their trip. "I'll watch for cops, you keep your foot on the gas." The words barely left his lips before sirens screamed in the other lane and a row of police cars streaked past, heading for D.C.

"What the hell... " Charlie slowed the Hummer as the line of cars raced by.

Dan reached for the car radio. "Let's see if we can find out what's going on."

"Hang on," Charlie pointed to the dash. "I've got a police scanner in here." He pressed a button on the dash. The radio crackled for the first few seconds before they heard the word "…assassination," followed by an address and the code 10-12, which meant "be discrete, visitors are listening."

"I'm calling back to the office," Dan said, "find out what the hell's happening."

Charlie ignored him and tuned the radio dial to a local FM station. "Should have listened to you in the first place. We'll probably learn more from NPR than from the scanner."

No sooner had Dan hung up than his phone rang. He picked it up. "Carter here, Dan. Where are you, partner?"

"Heading your way on Dolley Madison. What's going on?"

"Assassination attempt on Vice-President Chun. You might run into problems getting here. Glad you called. Just got in myself, but I'll phone down to the gate and tell 'em to speed you through. D.C. is a mess."

"What happened?"

"I'll fill you in when you get here. Phone's not secure."

Dan hung up and tuned his ear to the report on the radio as the announcer came on with the news of the hour:

> *"NPR News update at 5:00 p.m. At 4:49 this afternoon, a gunman attempted to assassinate Vice-President Allen Chun as the Vice-President prepared to dedicate a new senior citizen center. We're waiting for a report from the hospital spokesperson about the condition of the Vice-President…"*

Dan listened carefully to the NPR report. "Chun survived the assassination attempt or the news would be reporting his death."

"I'm not as optimistic as you are," Charlie said. "Comes from old age, maybe."

"I'm not an optimist either, Charlie. Just trying to assess the situation. We need to get to my office, fast."

"We'll be there in fifteen."

Evan glanced back at Dan. "I'm still hoping Charlie's right about Whit."

"Me, too," Dan replied, looking as grim as he felt. *What next?*

Emergency traffic and blocked roads added twenty minutes to the normally twelve-minute trip to the other side of McLean and the new National Counterterrorism Center headquarters, known locally as Liberty Crossing.

Charlie stopped at the main gate. "Let me know if you need me for anything," he said, as his two passengers got out slamming the doors behind them.

"I'll call you," Dan replied, tapping the window, a signal for Charlie to take off.

Inside the NCTC building, Dan led the way to his office. He glanced over at Evan as they entered the large, well-lit corner office, the stamp of high status in any organization, but even more so in D.C. Dan noticed the young woman standing in the corner as he and Evan greeted the movie star handsome man sitting in the chair behind Dan's desk. Tom Carter came around to the front of the desk to shake hands with Evan.

"How was your trip in from Honolulu?" Evan asked.

"Fast. Caught a military flight and slept the whole way. Don't even know what day it is."

Dan turned to Evan. "I want you to meet someone."

The dark-haired young woman stepped forward. Dan made the introduction, "This is my colleague, Elena Petrova." A startled look crossed Evan's face as Dan added, "but then, I believe you two know each other from an earlier encounter?"

"We've met," Elena said, her dark eyes shielding any emotion she might have felt, "although Mr. Phillips may not recall the circumstances. And whether he does or doesn't, I want to apologize." She glanced down at Evan's bandaged left hand. "They weren't supposed to be so rough on you."

"Sonofabitch. So it *was* my own people." Evan gave Dan an accusing look. "Did you order this?"

Chapter Forty

Liberty Crossing
McLean, Virginia

Images of the dinner meeting in Prague flooded Evan's brain. The beautiful woman who sat at his table and dropped her handbag. His memories stopped there. He should have known. He did know, but refused to accept it because of his friendship with Henry and Dan. No one could have reached him that easily except his own people. There would be hell to pay the next time he saw Henry, provided he was still alive. An involuntary shiver ran up his spine. A string of profanity left Evan's lips, despite his efforts to contain himself.

"Calm down, Evan, please," Dan said. "Henry needed you back here fast, and he wanted to prevent tipping anyone off. We decided the best route was to make it seem like someone blew your cover and you were returning home for a little R&R rather than coming back on assignment to help us fight these goddam terrorists inside our own country."

"What drugs did you use?" Evan demanded, unwilling to be pacified so easily. He wanted to slap Elena Petrova across her pretty Czech face, if indeed she was Czech. He didn't know. He wouldn't forgive Henry or Dan for this, at least not any time soon. *When I said I had no friends I was more correct than I realized.*

"Nothing dangerous," Elena told him, her voice calm and reassuring. "An anesthetic, that's all, so you wouldn't remember what happened and wouldn't feel anything. Same sedative doctors give for a colonoscopy," she said in a matter-of-fact tone.

"Right," Dan said. "Think of it as minor surgery."

Evan wanted to say "*fuck you*," but held his tongue. "You have people here who can handle this problem. Why drag *me* into it?"

"Sigma is the first reason," Dan said. "We're still trying to piece everything together, but you worked alongside those guys in Iraq. No one knows the leadership better than you, or has more of their respect."

Evan shrugged. "Which means I can't exactly go undercover for you in order to investigate them."

"Not our plan. We can't wait that long. Things are out of hand already with the attempt today on the Vice-President's life. We didn't know it would start this soon. The assassination attempt on Chun was scheduled to occur in Honolulu when he made his trip next weekend, but once we shut down that operation they must have panicked and tried to take him down in D.C., moved up their time table."

"Is he still alive?" Evan asked.

Carter nodded. "He's fine. Secret Service had him tightly surrounded and outfitted with a flak jacket. It was a desperation attempt. One of the bullets nicked his arm, which is why they raced him to the hospital. We aren't releasing any details, other than he survived the attempt. We want them off-balance as much as possible."

Dan turned to Evan. "All the evidence we've assembled so far points to a wide-ranging plot designed to take over the Presidency of the United States. Am I right?" He glanced at Carter, who nodded. "We know Sigma's involved, but at what level is still an unknown. Is it a rogue outfit, or is it being run from the top? We need somebody who can reach Sigma's leadership, talk them down, convince them they're on the wrong side in this fight and they'll lose if they continue down this path."

Evan's expression remained impassive, listening as Dan continued.

"Rumors are that Sigma forces now outnumber our armed forces, so they may think they're a match for us. But they're not. We're counting on you to convince Sigma to switch sides, because if we have to sic the U.S. military on those sonsabitches, we'll kill every last one and make sure they die a slow and painful death." He paused, and Evan broke in.

"You said Sigma was the first reason I'm back here. Is there another reason?"

"There's always another reason." Dan smiled and continued, "Our puzzle's not complete. What we've learned from Tom's operation in Honolulu added more pieces for us, but I'm worried we're still in the dark."

Evan took a deep breath. "I have a feeling Henry knew more than he was saying."

Dan shrugged. "You know Henry. He doesn't like to share, but to his credit he didn't know the full scope of the operation, and neither did I. You know how everyone plays the game around here. The less information released, the less that can fall into enemy hands. Henry can't override his training. No offense to you, me or Tom. Someone at the Agency appears to be involved, which is why Henry felt he had no choice but to bring you home. Not an easy decision for him."

"Henry covers all his bases, doesn't he?" Evan turned around, glancing between Dan and Tom. "Does this mean we can assume Henry's safely stashed somewhere?"

Dan shrugged. "I'm not certain. Charlie's the only person one hundred percent convinced of Whit's innocence. If Charlie's wrong, Henry's in deep doo-doo right now, and I hope we can extract him in time."

"Better lay the rest on me," Evan said, feeling a little mollified, given the severity of the situation. "What's the second reason I'm back in D.C.?"

"We think there's a link between our home-grown troubles and at least one of the terror cells you've been investigating in Prague. Don't know how long it will take to track things down on that end, but when you go back, that's your long-term goal. While you're here, we need you to concentrate first and foremost on talking down Sigma. So, what do you say, Evan old pal? Think you can make them an offer they can't refuse?"

"I guess we'll see," Evan replied.

Chapter Forty-One

6th Floor, Langley
NCS Network Security Office

Bob Randolph scrolled down the long list of statements on the log displayed on his computer screen before reaching for the phone and dialing Connie. He gave a sardonic sniff as he glanced over the rest of the information in the file. *Problem was the lack of details.* Continuing to stare at the file, he was stunned by Henry's revelation the previous night in which he'd explained that the illegal hack had originated within his own Directorate and on his orders. He was even more shocked when Henry cautioned him to watch his back now that he knew.

Why couldn't he wring more accurate information out of these damned files beyond an indication of who was being targeted? No how, what, or when, and no mention of who might be carrying out the operation, although Bob and Henry both suspected Zak Browning. The folder resided within the DI's files, but there were other reasons to suspect Zak. Everyone knew he'd doctored intelligence information in the past. Just couldn't get the goods on him. Bob would obey Henry's wishes about keeping the files a secret, but he would continue investigating on his own. He needed to be careful, and he wanted to talk with Henry again, somewhere safe and as soon as possible. He pressed the phone to his ear, listening to it ring. He was about to hang up when Connie answered.

"NCS Directorate, Connie Lang speaking."

"Is the boss back, yet?"

"No." Connie hesitated for a few seconds. Long enough to cause Bob to wonder about the pause. *Was there something she wanted to say, but felt she couldn't?* Whatever it was, he'd find out sooner or later. He was crazy about Connie, but he also knew she had a devious streak. She cheated on her husband with impunity and bragged to Bob about her convincing lies. He often wondered if she were playing the same game with him, having grown more suspicious lately when he noticed inconsistencies in some of her stories.

"I have bad news," she finally said.

Bob held his breath. "What's that?" He thought he knew what might be coming, but her announcement was worse than expected and the element of drama in her voice surprised him.

"Henry's been arrested."

He tried to absorb the shock. Bad news of the worst sort. Her reaction bothered him and he tried to put his finger on it. He said nothing for almost a minute.

"Are you there?"

"I'm here. When did this happen?"

"About an hour ago."

"Where?"

"He was walking in the front gate. Tried to call up here for a car to pick him up, but Whit had a military unit waiting to meet him. Can you believe it?"

"No," Bob answered, already monitoring his words. "Keep me posted, okay?" He wanted to hang up, search the database again and figure out what he could do to help Henry.

"Can I give him a message?"

"Just wanted to check in with him about the assassination attempt on the Vice. See if there was anything I should be doing."

"I can transfer you to the DI's office, if you want."

"That's okay. I can contact Zak on my own. Should I be talking to him?"

"I would if I were you, unless you want him to think you're in on whatever Henry's done."

"What has he done?" Bob listened carefully as she hesitated again.

"I don't really know, sweetie, but you know Henry. It could be anything. He isn't much for playing by the rules. Pushed his luck a little too far this time, I imagine."

"Thanks for letting me know. I need a few minutes to collect my thoughts, then I'll catch up with the DI." He had no intention of contacting Zak.

I need to keep a low profile, he thought. I may be in as much danger as Henry. *Time to leave for home and hope there's no military vehicle at the gate waiting for me.*

Chapter Forty-Two

Bob left the Agency without incident and turned north for home, checking his rear view mirror constantly. A few miles later, he turned south and headed for the city. Once inside D.C., he meandered through the maze of city streets until he was reasonably certain no one could have followed him. In the event he was mistaken, he'd take his pursuers to a popular tourist destination where they could spin their wheels trying to locate the elusive Bob Randolph.

Pulling into the Smithsonian parking lot off Independence Avenue, he sat in his car surveiling the vicinity before getting out and locking up. The walk from his parking spot to the Smithsonian Metro station was a short one, but he jogged to the entrance, taking the stairs down two steps at a time. After purchasing the necessary tickets, he took the first train that entered the station. He'd ride the cars, exiting and re-entering at the least populated stations and checking for a tail each time.

After an hour or more of hopping trains and armed with the knowledge no mere mortal could have followed him unseen over that time period, he emerged back onto the D.C. streets heading for his intended destination—a Georgetown brownstone on N Street NW belonging to his friend, Mark Harju.

Bob and Mark belonged to a hacker group that went by the name Phrack-U, a faux epithet playing on the popular symbol shared by the hacking community. He'd joined the group initially with the goal of sniffing out illegal activity. Over the years, his role changed as he became friends with the members. They were an elite cadre known as *gray hatters*, hackers with good intentions like their *white hat* counterparts, but who in emergency situations might commit an illegal act more characteristic of the *black hatters*, the criminals who gave hacking its bad name. Until today, the group's activities had never crossed the line into prosecutable activities. That was about to change.

The small band had been together for the past three years. All worked for one or another government agency and all were employed in network security jobs. They were a tight-knit band of brothers and sisters—two members were women, who helped each other out of tight fixes in their work lives, as well as their private lives.

Bob knocked on the front door, checking the area constantly for signs of danger. He hadn't dared to phone first, nor had he found time to buy a disposable phone. Sweat poured down his face while he waited for his friend to answer. The muggy air made it hard to breathe, but his wait was short. The door swung open almost immediately.

Blonde-haired Mark Harju stood in the entrance, the picture of a Greek god, or maybe the Finnish god Ukko, the thunder deity responsible for drizzling honey from heaven to earth. Bob looked him over, wishing not for the first time that Hollywood's central casting would sign Mark to play himself and thus rid the populace of their stereotypical geek imagery. However, knowing Hollywood, the only roles open to Mark would be surfer boys in beach movies.

"Hey homeboy, you look awful," Mark said, standing aside and waving Bob inside.

"I feel as awful as I look," Bob answered. "Do you have some time for me? It's urgent."

"No problem, dude."

Mark motioned his friend through the brownstone's dining room and kitchen to the room that served as a veritable communications outpost furnished with the latest technology, including jury-rigged laptops, tracking devices, iPhones, and PDA's with built-in exploit platforms engineered to automatically launch code-execution manipulations.

Mark was single and gay, having vowed never to marry, even though D.C. had finally legalized gay marriage. "I'm tied to the high tech life," he gave as his excuse, which may have been true, but Bob knew how much Mark hated commitments. He seemed to switch jobs every three to five years. Sometimes for better advancement, but more often because he needed a change of scenery. Fortunately, his monumental talents kept him financially solvent.

Mark's eyes focused on Bob's worried look. "What's the problem?"

"I'm struggling with how much I can share without committing a crime. But the country needs your help and if I don't tell you what I know I'll be committing an even worse crime." Bob paused, waiting for Mark's response.

"I'm in. Nothing leaves this room."

Bob took a deep breath and began. "Our system's been compromised, which pisses me off royally. Target was a set of files stored in a database outside my division. Files are disguised to look like a training exercise, but it may be a planned operation, a coup."

"Government overthrow kind of coup?"

Bob nodded. "Possibly involving the assassination of high-level government officials. Files have a code name, which should make our work easier."

"Which is?"

"*Code 21*."

"Sweet," Mark said, running a hand through his blonde hair and wrinkling his nose in distaste. "Code for *Windows is removing this device*. I wanna kill these people just for coming up with that name."

Bob allowed a grim smile to cross his lips. "From what I've been able to track so far, there's more than one outside organization involved as well as someone inside the Agency. We need to start at the top—figure out the key players."

The keys on Harju's computer clacked before Bob could finish his sentence.

"Any initial suspects?" Mark asked, his characteristic impatience on display.

"The usual, beginning with Sigma Services."

"Good guys turned bad? We can start by tracking the communication networks. Find out who's tapping into the files. See where that leads."

The two worked through the evening. The breakthrough came just before midnight.

"Good work," Bob said. "I owe you."

"Okay, then," Mark replied. "Let's hit the sack."

Bob gave him a startled look and Mark laughed. "I'm not hitting on you. I know better. I have a guest room with a comfortable bed. You can sleep there tonight and spring for breakfast in the morning."

§

Early the next day, the pair walked to Mark's favorite café two streets away where Bob bought breakfast, paying in cash rather than a credit card that could be tracked. The pair ate in silence, neither discussing the previous night's foray into the CIA's communications network and beyond.

On the way out of the restaurant, Bob picked up a newspaper and paused at the headline. He skim-read the article. It's started, he thought.

Chapter Forty-Three

Honolulu, Hawaii

"Cone Clinic and Hospital, how can I help you?"

"May I have the nurse's station, third floor surgical ward, please?"

"Just a moment, please, I'll connect you."

"Thank you." Alicia kept her voice low.

"Third floor nurse's station."

"Good afternoon. This is the FBI calling, Tom Carter's office," Alicia said. "We've placed a Honolulu police officer guarding the room of one of your patients. His name is Sergeant David Taylor. Would you tell him that Mr. Carter needs to speak with him immediately?"

"Certainly. And who is calling again?"

"Agent Tom Carter's office, Federal Bureau of Investigation."

"Just a minute, please."

Alicia turned toward the door and pulled the sheet up around her shoulders, keeping the phone hidden under her hair. Through the frosted glass panel she saw a form appear in front of Sgt. Taylor, who stood up immediately. Alicia kept her eye on the door handle and when it started to turn, she quickly closed her eyes, pretending to be asleep.

She heard the door open and assumed the nurse was looking in on her. As soon as the door closed, she checked the glass panel. The shadowy forms had disappeared. Alicia slid out of bed, grabbed her purse and hurried to the door. She needed to reach the stairwell while Sgt. Taylor's back was to her room. Opening the door a crack, she saw him walking toward the nurse's station, giving her just enough time to slip out and around the corner. She glanced back once to see Sgt. Taylor reach for the phone before she ducked into the stairwell. Grabbing the handrail for an extra second to stabilize herself, she held the stairwell door with her foot, ensuring that it shut quietly.

"Dave Taylor here," the sergeant's voice said in her ear.

Alicia adopted a high-pitched southern accent. "Sgt. Taylor? This is Tom Carter's assistant." She tried not to sound breathless as she eased her way down the stairs. "Would you please hold? Agent Carter will be with you in one minute." She turned the corner on the second floor and rotated the phone upward so she could still hear the sergeant on the other end, but he couldn't hear her heavy breathing.

As she reached the bottom floor, Dave Taylor asked, "Tom, Tom, are you there?"

"He's coming," Alicia assured, unwilling to risk saying more and raise the Sergeant's suspicions. She turned the handle on the first floor door, relieved to see that it opened onto the hospital's main entrance. Today was her lucky day.

With exaggerated calm, she strolled over to the front doors, which slid apart as she approached, allowing her to walk out of the hospital and into the sunshine and freedom. She stepped onto the sidewalk and dumped the phone in the trashcan beside the doorway. Still out of breath, she walked as fast as she could manage, holding her side the whole way as she flagged down a taxi. She gave the driver an address one block from her parents' house.

She hated dumping her phone, but the police might use it to triangulate her location. She couldn't risk phoning her mother either, in case her parents' landline was bugged. Better if no one knew her whereabouts. Her saner side told her a tap on her parents' line was unlikely. And since the Agency no longer had an interest in her, at least not until yesterday, they had no reason to track her. Nevertheless, she was taking no chances.

As for Tom, the FBI hadn't had time to install a listening device on her parents' line. Besides, she'd never told Tom where her parents lived, and he was on a plane flying back to D.C. By the time he learned her parents' address, she'd be long gone.

"Here we are, miss," the cab driver said, stopping at the intersection she'd provided.

Fumbling in her purse for the fare, Alicia checked the streets for watchers. Homes in the upscale neighborhood came with large driveways. Residents, as well as visitors, rarely parked on the street. A traditional stakeout would be easy to spot. Satisfied the coast was clear, she paid the cabby and eased herself out of the vehicle, walking casually down the block holding her wounded side. At the next corner, she turned up the driveway of the house next door to her parents' and walked around to the back, where she checked again for surveillance. Everything appeared normal and she cut across the yard and onto the terrace outside her mother's kitchen.

The back door was unlocked, and she went inside, forgetting about her altered appearance. Her mother came around the corner at the sound of the door and jumped back in fright.

"Mom, it's me." Alicia said.

"Mickie, you scared the daylights out of me. I didn't recognize you." Her mother reached over to embrace her before Alicia warned her about the bullet wound.

"You can hug this side of me," Alicia said. "Is Dad home?"

"Yes, he's downstairs on his computer."

"Great, let's go downstairs. We need to talk."

Chapter Forty-Four

Breaking News: Iranian Assassin Captured
Staff Writer | CAB News Online [12 minutes ago]

WASHINGTON, D.C. – The Federal Bureau of Investigation announced the capture of Haffez Shirazi, an Iranian terrorist accused of attempting to assassinate Vice-President Allen Chun. The White House still refuses to release to the public the condition of the Vice-President.

Liberty Crossing
NCTC Headquarters

Evan sat in Dan's office listening to his phone conversation. When Dan finally hung up, he turned to Evan with a surprise announcement. "Looks like we got lucky. Just got an assassin dumped on our doorstep. I'm guessing he's somebody you know."

Evan was on the verge of exhaustion coming off the long flight from Stuttgart and the stress following his arrival in the States, but he knew the sooner he helped wrap up the mess in D.C., the sooner he'd be able to go home. *Funny to think of Prague as home.* "What's his name?"

"Haffez Shirazi. He's been charged with the attempted assassination of Vice-President Chun. Before they haul him off to a military holding cell, they dropped him off here for preliminary questioning."

Dan motioned Evan to follow him. They left Dan's office together and caught the elevator down to the interrogation room. Evan stood in front of the one-way glass watching Shirazi, who was seated at the table in the interrogation room checking his watch every few minutes.

"I know him," Evan said. "Shirazi's not his name. First name's correct. He's Haffez Shahrzad."

"Thought you might have run across him," Dan said. "Claims he's a member of the Iranian Revolutionary Guard. More likely he's one of the terrorists Iran's exporting these days."

"He's Iranian and a terrorist, but he's *anti*-Iranian," Evan said. "Runs with the political opposition in Iran. MEK trained. Fanatical about getting rid of their President. Hates the Supreme Council of Cultural Revolution with a passion that borders on insanity."

"They're all insane," Dan said.

"He used to be Mujahideen, but he left the MEK. In his last job in Iran, he worked for the election of the opposition leader. When they lost the election, he had to get out of the country. Last I knew he was working with one of the pro-western anti-Iranian groups in Eastern Europe. We crossed paths in Prague."

Dan smiled. "See why you're here? The bastard's been passing himself off as the opposite. A pro-Iranian anti-American loony-tune."

"Not surprising. Probably intends to sacrifice himself in hopes of luring the U. S. into a war with Iran, or at the very least drawing us into providing support for the Iranian resistance movement. I'll have a chat with him." Evan grinned. "He owes me."

Dan reached over and turned the key, unlocking the door to the stark twelve-by-fifteen foot room. Evan entered the cell and extended a hand to Haffez who jumped up and threw his arms around him.

"My friend, how did you get here? Who told you about me? Are you here to get me out of this place?"

"That depends," Evan said, gently pushing Haffez away, motioning him to sit back down.

Instead, Haffez bowed politely. "After you, my friend."

Evan crossed to the other side of the table, pulled out a chair and sat. "I'll answer your questions after you answer mine," he said in a business-like tone. "First, what are you doing in this country, though I have a good guess, and second, what was your role in the attempted assassination of the Vice-President of the United States?"

Evan watched Haffez bow his head and shuffle his feet under his chair as he ran his hands over the metal chair's padded arms, pretending to be lost in thought. Finally, he glanced up with a puzzled look on his face. "It's a long story."

"I'm not going anywhere, and it looks like you aren't either, so let's get started. Give me your version of events, and I hope you're not in as much trouble as I think you are."

"Now that you're here, I'm not so worried." The hangdog expression on Haffez's face almost brought a smile to Evan's lips.

"You should be worried. I don't know how much I can help you, but I know I can't do anything until I know what you've done. And no holding back on me." Evan paused. "If, even once I think you're lying to me, I'll get up and walk out of here and you won't see me again. Ever. And then you'll be damn lucky if you aren't exported to Romania for some local work on your teeth and nails."

Haffez winced. "You're my friend. You wouldn't let that happen to me."

"I *am* your friend and I want to save you, but only as long as you tell me the truth. So, let's stop stalling and get to it." Evan waved his hand for Haffez to begin. "And don't drag it out. I'll ask for details if I need them. Get started with the basics."

Haffez took a deep breath and sat straighter in his chair with a look of resolve. "I came to the States about a week ago on assignment. My organization is very angry at the new American administration because they're trying to negotiate with my country. What we want is for them to overthrow the government and stop trying to befriend them, which is a stupid idea. Why are the Americans so stupid they want to be friends with the devil?"

Haffez reached his hands across the table in a gesture of supplication familiar to Evan, who nodded, letting Haffez know he understood. "How did you get into the States?"

"By car."

"From Prague?" Evan's words dripped with sarcasm.

Haffez smiled. "I flew into Canada, and a friend drove me down here."

"You crossed the border where?"

"A little town in Maine, where my friend lives. Half of the town is in Canada and the other half in the U. S. It's a handy place to live."

"Name of the town?"

"I can't remember."

Evan raised an eyebrow.

"Honest, I'm not lying to you. I can't remember, but if you show me a map I could probably find it."

"The place is not important. At some point, I may want your friend's name. What have you been doing here and with whom?"

"My friend took me to meet with Sgt. Ben Strickland, former U. S. Army—"

Evan interrupted. "Who does Sgt. Strickland work for now?"

Haffez smiled again. "You're kidding me, right? Old friends of yours. You don't know him?"

Evan shook his head.

"When you came in I thought Sgt. Strickland called you to come and help me."

"Why would he do that?"

"He put me up in a hotel, and I've been working with him on a strategy to convince the United States government that it is in their best interests to overthrow the Iranian infidels, even if it means bombing strategic sites in my country."

"You want the U.S. to bomb your own country?" Evan glanced over at the one-way glass window and shrugged. "Nobody seems worried about collateral damage these days."

"It has to be done."

"And you expected to accomplish this task by assassinating the Vice-President of the United States and blaming the assassination on Iran?"

"First, I wasn't the assassin. I only pretended to be the assassin so we could blame the Iranian government. It was Sgt. Strickland's idea. He was supposed to fire the shot standing beside me, but another soldier came in his place. That made me nervous. The soldier fired the shot and when he did, I ran."

"And you were dumb enough to go along with this charade? Or was this the only option, other than suicide bombing?"

"I wasn't supposed to run. I was supposed to pick up the gun and let the authorities capture me, but I was afraid the soldier might shoot me after he shot the Vice-President, so I ran."

"Without doubt, shooting you was the plan. Then he could take credit for killing the assassin. At least you had sense enough to get out of there. What was supposed to happen after your capture?"

"Sgt. Strickland told me the authorities would be required to let me go because I was an agent of a foreign country. That's why I thought you were here. To facilitate my transfer out of the country."

Evan sighed and reached for the yellow tablet and pen lying on the far side of the table. He slid it over to Haffez. "Write down everything. Details of this and any other plots you know about, including timetables: what, where, how and when. After you finish I want a list of everyone involved. Names, lots of names. Everyone you worked with or met in the States and those outside the States, including your Canadian friend.

When you're done, I'll come back and look over the information. After I check your facts and see if you've told the truth, I'll do what I can to get you out of here and send you home."

"I don't want to go home. I want to go back to Europe. Please." Desperation colored Haffez's voice at the mention of being deported to his home country where Evan knew he would face a quick trial and certain death.

"I'll see what I can do after I read your report. Remember, the words you write down on this piece of paper may be the most important bit of writing you've ever done. Important to you and important to me." Evan stood up and walked around to Haffez's side of the table. "Let me see your hands."

Haffez held out his hands, palms up. "Why?"

Evan took both hands and turned them over. "I want you to take a long, hard look at those well-kept fingernails and imagine how painful it would be to lose them." He glanced from Haffez's hands to his face. "One by excruciating one."

"You make bad jokes, my friend."

"I'm not joking," Evan said, turning to leave the room.

Haffez Shahrzad a.k.a. Haffez Shirazi picked up the pen and began to write.

§

Back in Dan's office Evan reported on Haffez's story.

"He's writing his memoirs," Evan said. "Maybe when he's done we'll be able to figure out who this Sgt. Strickland is."

Dan grinned. "Good going. I knew you'd get him to see the light. Now, on to task number two. Sigma."

"I can't wait."

"I'll be running the operation, providing backup, etc. Nothing for you to do but convince Sigma's leadership to make the right decision. Turn on the charm, like you did with Haffez. I have confidence in you."

"Might not be that easy, especially if he's surrounded by his goon squad."

"They'll stand down or else."

"It's the *or else* that worries me."

"Not a problem," Dan said. "Now get on the horn and call your old pal Nilsson. Make a date for breakfast. Then, I'll let you get a good night's sleep. NCTC's providing your room and board and I'll meet you back here tomorrow morning, bright-eyed and bushy-tailed."

Evan raised an eyebrow.

Dan grinned. “Old Indian saying.”

Chapter Forty-Five

Mount Weather Conference Room

On the stroke of eight, Shadow President Fred McGuire distributed copies of his distillation of the President's Daily Intelligence Brief to the four members of the Executive Cabinet. He never provided the Shadow Cabinet members with access to the original document due its highly classified status, or so he told them.

"As you can see from the summary before you," he stated in his usual clipped tones, "our country is in grave danger. The CIA has uncovered a network of Iranian terror cells operating out of Eastern Europe, headquartered around Prague. They're planning an assault on the United States that will make al-Qaeda's 9/11 attack look like child's play."

McGuire's noisy intake of breath let his message sink in as he paused long enough to allow those around the table a quick read of the report summary. He waited until all eyes focused on him before letting the next shoe fall, anticipating the stunned distress that would paint the faces of those assembled when his next announcement reached their pre-programmed ears.

"The CIA believes these terrorist groups may have access to Iran's nuclear weapons and in fact, may be an arm of the Iranian government." The Executive Cabinet members stared at him in silence as he continued. "The CIA and Homeland Security have requested the President and the National Security Council to issue a Code Red Alert for the country. However, the Executive branch is pushing back." McGuire stopped talking and surveyed his audience. "Does anyone have a question or comment before I continue?"

"I do, Mr. President." The Shadow Secretary of Defense spoke up. He was usually the first to do so and always the first to agree. "What can be done if the President sticks his head in the sand and refuses to take these threats seriously?"

"That's precisely the reason I'm bringing the matter to your attention today."

"Do we have the authority to do anything about it?" This question came from the Secretary of the Interior, who, like his counterpart in Washington, knew virtually nothing about foreign policy. McGuire couldn't have cared less. More important was the man's unflinching support. The Interior Secretary knew how to say yes with a smile.

McGuire hesitated, and Shadow Attorney General Jack Vanderstory, a former lawyer with the Justice Department, broke into the conversation with a loud objection. "The answer is '*No.*' We have *no* authority to interfere with the actual governing of the country unless there is a catastrophic event that precludes the elected administration from carrying out its functions."

McGuire did nothing to hide his displeasure. "Let me point out," he shot back, his voice dripping with sarcasm, "the term *catastrophic event* has never been clearly and legally defined."

"True, up to a point," Vanderstory countered. "However, the accepted definition implies the death of the executive branch's elected officials."

McGuire stood his ground. "I differ with that interpretation." *Not the first time I've had to make this argument.* "If an elected administration fails to uphold its sworn oath to protect the country's population from destruction, especially under threat of nuclear attack, I would define that condition as constituting a catastrophic event."

"The problem with your interpretation," Vanderstory persisted, "is how to go about demonstrating the proposition that an administration is *failing* to do something, such as failing to protect the country to the point of inviting or provoking an attack. Even *you* can't prove a negative."

"I acknowledge the sarcasm," McGuire said, "employed by those who can't back up their position with reasoned argument."

Vanderstory refused to be intimidated. "By your reasoning, we should have prosecuted the Bush administration for ignoring the warnings about al-Qaeda and failing to prevent the 9/11 attack."

The Attorney General's reply stung the Raptor to the quick. He'd been worried for a long time about Vanderstory, who was not a patriot, in McGuire's view of the term. *That's the trouble with attorneys like Vanderstory. They were too conservative, locked into the past with no vision. The country was under siege from the left and he wasn't about to let people like Vanderstory turn the country into a goddam communist state.*

Somebody had to do something about it, and screw the consequences. The nation needed strong leadership, not a bunch of niggling pansies afraid of their own shadows.

In McGuire's mind, he was the man to provide that leadership. He surveyed the faces at the conference table. As far as he could determine, Jack Vanderstory was the only holdout, the only member who hadn't warmed to the idea of quietly replacing the country's governing structure, if you could call the current administration's race to socialism "governing." *Taking the country down the European road to destruction, willing to subvert our whole free market system, in the name of caring for the lazy masses.*

Raging with anger, McGuire struggled to maintain his imperturbable demeanor. Never allowing his voice to rise, he replied with calculated disdain. "You're proving my point," he argued. "We can't let something like 9/11 happen again, and we may be the only people with the knowledge and the power to prevent the next attack. We're patriots. We have a responsibility to the country. I won't stand by and allow this great nation to be defeated by a third-rate, out-of-control, godless nation like Iran. Now is the time to act. Before it's too late."

"Act legally," Vanderstory insisted, "or we become part of the problem."

McGuire's complexion reddened. If he could eliminate Vanderstory right now, he'd do it. What a shithead. When this meeting ended, he would contact his people about the problem. Vanderstory loved fast cars. It's a wonder he hadn't wrecked that fancy Porsche before now, the way he raced over the back roads of northern Virginia.

McGuire watched for reaction at the table, pleased to see no change in the others' demeanor. They were an arrogant bunch, each person at the table convinced he could perform better than his appointed or elected counterpart and dreaming of the opportunity to prove it. As far as McGuire was concerned, they were right. They *could* do a better job. All they had to do was listen to him and not some pissant, pusillanimous lawyer like the pretender Attorney General, James Cornelius "Jack" Vanderstory.

"Acting legally is a subjective judgment when it comes to saving the nation," McGuire replied, maintaining his matter-of-fact tone. "Was dropping the A-bomb on Japan a legally justifiable act? No, but it was a necessary one. There are times, in the protection of the nation, where legality is not an issue."

"I say we go directly to the military." The Secretary of Defense pounded his fist on the table in a gesture of defiance, letting everyone know he was on the Raptor's side and had run out of patience with the Shadow Attorney General. "Show our military leaders the evidence, give them a good reason to go over and bomb the goddam towel heads to kingdom come and back again."

"Iranians are Persians, not Arabs," Vanderstory said, offended by the towel head slur.

"It's too early to release our information to the military, Sam," McGuire told the Secretary of Defense, "Not a risk we can take at this point. Keep in mind, we're the country's only protection." He adopted his most somber tone. "It's imperative for us to devise a solution to the country's security problem first, then implement that solution with impunity."

The Shadow Secretary of Defense is a loyal soldier, McGuire thought, but impatient and impulsive. *Not traits I need right now. Besides, I can't afford to contact the military at this point in the operation. If word leaked out to the military about these plans, given their recent leadership changes, they'd kick my ass from here to the moon.* An image of the current Secretary of Defense popped into McGuire's mind. He was an old adversary, but not for long. McGuire had placed his name high up on the removal list. Bile rose in McGuire's throat at the thought of him. He wouldn't know a patriot if he fell over one. Good thing he hadn't been in charge of World War II or we'd all be speaking German today.

The Raptor knew of a few genuine patriots in the Armed Services. They would stand with him today if he told them his plans, but they were no longer in power, and he couldn't risk a leak. Not yet. He'd recruit their support when they understood it was safe to do so. *Once I have full legal control of the government, I'll order the military to bomb the shit out of Iran and save the United States of America, whether or not the country has sense enough to save itself, but that option comes later. First job is regaining control of the country, then I can put my own people in charge of the military.*

McGuire took a long breath before addressing Vanderstory's objections, expressing agitation for the first time. "Legalities be damned. The Constitution is a peacetime instrument, a guide to governance when the country is not under mortal threat. War has no rules. Rules of war ended when Truman dropped the bomb on Japan, and it was the right thing to do. We're at war again, and it's our turn to do the right thing. We're the only ones who can turn this country around, bring it back from the edge of the abyss."

"As for the specifics of our endeavor, what do you have in mind?" the Shadow Secretary of State asked.

"I'll let everyone know at the appropriate time," McGuire said. "Now, one final matter." He'd worked himself into a frenzy on purpose. It helped convey the urgency of his message. "I'm sure I don't have to remind all of you of the restrictions regarding the conversations that occur during our meetings inside this room. You understand that, don't you? Our discussions are classified. Nothing leaves this room." McGuire made visual contact with the four people at the table, his eagle eyes watching as each person, with the single exception of Jack Vanderstory, signaled his agreement.

Chapter Forty-Six

Liberty Crossing
NCTC Headquarters

The iPhone alarm rang at 8:00. *Feels like the middle of the night,* Evan grumbled to himself, reaching over to silence the annoying ring tone. He'd had a fitful night, unable to shut down his brain, which insisted on reviewing Shahrzad's testimony from the previous night. Today promised more of the same. Evan's phone call to Sigma Services' Bjorn Nilsson had been pleasant enough on the surface, but the call ended with Nilsson expressing his reluctance to meet for breakfast due to a busy schedule. He'd finally agreed only after Evan indicated he might be flying back to Prague soon and would have no other opportunities.

Nilsson's worried, and he should worry, Evan thought, getting an early start on being pissed at his former friend. The last two days had the quality of a nightmare. Almost as bad as the night terrors he'd experienced after leaving Iraq. *The country's going to the dogs.* He wondered, not for the first time, whether the country was headed for another civil war. *How can we expect the Middle East to overcome thousands of years of hostilities when we can't overcome our own disagreements from the last hundred and fifty years?*

Thinking about the condition of the country made him glad to be living overseas. A flash of guilt accompanied him to the small bathroom in the NCTC on-site living quarters. The comfort of the accommodations had surprised him. His quarters were the size of a standard motel room, but with a more comfortable bed and a better smell. Elena was bunked in the room next door. Evan wondered if she'd slept any better. Probably.

As he crawled in the shower and adjusted the water temperature, he reviewed his approach with Nilsson, deciding to take his chances on the direct approach. Dan wanted to wire him and provide a bulletproof vest. Evan had agreed to the wire, but not the vest. No way to make it inconspicuous on a body as lean as Evan's if Nilsson insisted on a pat down.

Evan had scheduled the breakfast meeting for 9:00 at a small café in nearby McLean. Even Nilsson wouldn't attempt a hit in a restaurant. At least, Evan thought with gratitude, they weren't meeting in Nilsson's offices where all bets would be off. He stepped out of the shower, dried off and wrapped a towel around his waist while he shaved. He was surprised to see how much weight he'd lost over the last few weeks. He'd bulk up now that he was back in the States eating oversized, fat-infused American meals.

His thoughts returned to his dinner in Prague with Elena Petrova. She was an attractive woman and on the right side, a thought that comforted him. Maybe he'd see her again in Prague under better circumstances. He remembered being struck by her presence when she'd walked into the restaurant that night, poised and stunningly beautiful. It was the reason he'd dropped his guard. Lesson learned. It wouldn't happen again.

His cell phone rang, and he left the bathroom to answer it.

"Evan, Bjorn. Say, I'm running late this morning. Lots of appointments. Can we make it lunch instead of breakfast, and can you come to my office? I've already called down to the caterer and they're preparing a spectacular meal for us to celebrate your homecoming. What do you say?"

"Sounds pretty good to me," Evan said, without breaking stride. Nilsson would read the least bit of hesitation as a warning sign. "What time, and where do I find your office?"

"Let's say 1:00 o'clock. Can you wait that long to see me?"

"Sure. Just rolled out of the sack. It'll give me time to catch up on my email and have a light breakfast. Where do I find you?"

"I'll send a car to pick you up."

"No need. I've got wheels, and I have some errands to run, so I'll be out and about." Both men understood the game, which so far they'd played to a draw. Evan wondered if Sigma was triangulating the phone call, trying to pinpoint his location. He expected so. He needed to hang up. "I've got a GPS, just give me … Evan hung up the phone, cutting himself off in mid-sentence. He'd call back after a minute and complain about his cell phone provider always dropping his calls. Sigma would have to re-start the triangulation.

Meeting Nilsson at his office meant a major shift in strategy. He'd prefer having Dan along for company, but that would put Nilsson on notice. Nilsson needed to believe this was a social call and not about business.

His phone rang before he finished re-dialing.

"Hey Buddy, what happened?"

Evan grinned to himself. "Damn provider drops my calls every time I turn around. Just give me the address and office number. I've got a lot to do today, and I hadn't planned to waste the whole day on a bastard like you, even if I am looking forward to seeing you."

"Here you go, Buddy." Nilsson rattled off an Arlington address. Evan used his shoulder to hold the phone against his ear as he wrote the address on the note pad lying on the bedside table.

"Got it. See you at 1:00," Evan said, hanging up without waiting for a response from Nilsson. He quickly slipped into his clothes before dialing Dan.

"Dan, we've got a problem."

"Morning, Evan. How did you sleep?"

"Not great. Did you hear me?"

"I heard you."

"Nilsson changed the meeting time and place on us. Wants me to meet him for lunch at 1:00 o'clock in his office. Kept me on the line trying to pinpoint my location, which he may have accomplished. I don't know for certain, even though I cut off the conversation twice."

Dan paused a long time before responding. "Well, you're right about a problem. They'll pat you down so you won't be able to take a weapon in with you. And they'll check you for wires, but we've got a little number they won't find unless they check where the sun don't shine."

"Oh, shit."

"Yeah, that can be a problem. Better watch what you eat." Dan snorted. "I've got some clothes for you, too, compliments of the Agency. Ultra lightweight ballistic underwear that'll withstand anything other than heavy artillery."

"I'm not planning on taking a hit, but I'll wear it, just in case."

"Don't worry. I'll have you covered and I was kidding about the location of the bug. I've got a wristwatch for you, outdated as that is, and a pair of eyeglasses. Even if they examine both, they'll have no way of detecting the listening devices. Belt buckle, too. We'll load you down so we can keep track of everything. And we're well acquainted with Nilsson's office digs. We'll be there backing you up if they try anything, but I'm not worried. I have confidence in your persuasive abilities."

"We'll see. If he's traced my location, matters will be a lot more difficult."

"You've been in tighter places overseas."

"No kidding. I'll be down to pick up my new clothes in half an hour or so. Have a couple of calls to make first."

"When you get here I want to talk to you about Shahrzad's epistle. We found a few inconsistencies."

Evan groaned. "I was certain he'd take my advice and deliver accurate information."

"He's Iranian. Lying is second nature. What made you think anything else?"

"His manicured nails."

Chapter Forty-Seven

Mount Weather

Jack Vanderstory stared directly into McGuire's eyes, refusing to acquiesce. He had no intention of keeping this meeting and its subject matter to himself. Not only was he not sold on McGuire's position, but he was worried the man had gone off the deep end. Worse than illegal, what the Raptor proposed was treason. Apparently, Vanderstory was the only person at the table who recognized McGuire's plan for what it was and the only person who hadn't agreed to spend the next couple of days at Mt. Weather on the Raptor's orders. Quite the opposite. He was returning to D.C. No way could they hold him prisoner here. Not yet, anyway. Not without giving themselves away.

On the trip back to D.C., he'd place a few phone calls hoping to convince someone to listen, willing them to believe the story he had to tell. It might be a hard sell. No one bought into conspiracies these days, even though they were woven throughout the fabric of politics. The higher the level, the more egregious the treachery and the more unbelievable the acts. He knew he had to find the right people. *Where better than the agency that dealt with conspiracies on a daily basis*? He'd head over there and talk his way inside.

No stranger to dangerous situations, Vanderstory recognized the pangs of fear rising within him, but he'd experienced true terror in his life and emerged victorious. Adrenalin was his friend. Compared to Vietnam, breaking out of Mt. Weather would be a cakewalk. First item on his agenda was to be clever about his escape. He remained in his seat, taking notes and listening patiently to one rant after another, some by the Raptor, others by his sycophants. When the coffee and pastries cart arrived, Vanderstory excused himself for a trip to the men's room, leaving behind his favorite briefcase and the papers he'd strewn about his place at the table. No one would be fooled for long about his return, but the ploy would buy him some time. All he needed for his getaway were a few minutes head start. His Porsche would handle the rest.

He left the Raptor's conference room and raced outside to the parking lot, careful about being watched or followed. So far, he'd spotted no one, or at least no one who seemed to care about his exit. But he knew the Raptor cared and underestimating the man was not in Vanderstory's nature. Reaching his car, he opened the door to the driver's side and leaned in for his raincoat before walking to the back of the vehicle and lifting the trunk lid. He tossed the raincoat over the gun resting on the trunk floor and transferred the coat-covered rifle to the front passenger seat, using his body and the open car door to shield his actions from security cameras. Returning to the back of the car, he slammed down the trunk and glanced around again before settling himself into the sports car's bucket seat, pressing the lock button and starting up the motor.

Paranoia was a trait left over from Vanderstory's days in Vietnam. He'd never bothered to cure himself because he felt it kept him safe. The war had taught him many things, among them, the depths of human depravity. Made it difficult to trust. Vanderstory understood the capacity of the human heart in a way known only to those with firsthand experience of pure evil. Inside the car, he removed the canvas cover and loaded the gun, placing it across the seat with the handle toward him. He checked the rearview mirror before starting up his black Porsche 911 and maneuvering it along the Mount Weather macadam roads, trying to calm his nerves and concentrate on his driving. The main gate came into view, the first test. He pulled up to the gate, one hand on his gun butt. The last time he remembered this level of fear he was a Second Lieutenant fighting in the jungles of 'Nam, where the enemy was equally elusive.

The guard opened Mount Weather's main gate, and he breathed a sigh of relief, but he wasn't home free yet. Pulling onto the country road, his mind reviewed portions of the conversation from the meeting he'd just left. He thought about the people he should contact, who he could trust. Couldn't go to the D.C. police. They'd dismiss his accusations as the same crazy stuff they heard on a daily basis. CIA was out, too, given McGuire's ties to Zak Browning, another wingnut. Vanderstory had no contacts at the FBI and besides, he thought FBI agents were a sketchy group. Images of J. Edgar Hoover popped into his head. A genuine Fascist, in Vanderstory's view. He settled on the NCTC, but finding a route to someone he could trust would take time. Could he manage to get his message across, he wondered, before McGuire called out the dogs, arranged a drive-by shooting or a convenient auto accident—a favorite for ridding the world of political enemies, no questions asked?

Nearly out of view of the main gate, Vanderstory checked his rearview mirror, and his heart rate doubled. A black SUV exited Mount Weather and turned in his direction. Good thing he'd driven the Porsche today. The car was made for Grand Prix driving, a race he knew how to run. Double-checking the SUV's intent, he slammed the accelerator to the floor. No time for taking chances. He watched the SUV speed up and felt his heart rate begin to slow, the way it did in battle when his nerves turned to steel.

He kept the pedal to the floor, appreciating the car's engineering as it rounded the curves with ease. Were they planning to run him off the road, he wondered? If so, he had a few surprises of his own for the driver whose vehicle was no match for his on the snaking back roads of Virginia. Someone might land in the ditch, but given the centers of gravity of the two vehicles, Vanderstory knew he wouldn't be the one digging himself out. He'd survived the Viet Cong. What did Sigma, or whoever his pursuers were, know about survival compared to that?

The Porsche spun around curve after curve as it pulled away from the SUV. The problem, he realized, would be the traffic lights he faced once he made it to the main road. He couldn't count on outrunning the SUV there. Had to take the bastards out before he reached the highway. Keeping the pedal to the floor, he gradually increased the distance between his Porsche and the chase vehicle. He needed time, and he needed the right place. He checked the rearview mirror again. The SUV was out of sight most of the time now, but they knew his destination, knew they would catch him once he left the two-lane country road and turned onto Route 7.

The location he'd been anticipating appeared ahead, the site his Vietnam angel had prepared for him. He slammed on the brakes, nearly flipping the Porsche as he swung into a break in the tree cover that lined the side of the road. No time to hide the car. Only time to grab the gun. He reached over for the XM8 assault rifle. Outside the car, he crouched down using the open car door for cover, resting the gun on the window ledge. He could hear the SUV approaching at full speed. He'd just made it. He crossed his fingers, hoping they wouldn't see him until it was too late. They would be looking for him straight ahead, his biggest advantage.

In the flash of an eye, his moment of truth arrived. He had the

SUV in his gunsite. Vanderstory pressed the trigger of the automatic rifle, aiming first for the tires, then the windshield on the driver's side. As the SUV spun out of control in front of him, he aimed again and hit the second front tire. The careening black mass flipped end-over-end down the road, finally veering off to the side and landing in a clump of trees. He wasted no time assessing the damage. Jumping back in the Porsche, he swung it around in the opposite direction and took off. He thought he heard a gunshot, but by then he was out of range and on his way back to D.C. over a route few non-locals knew.

In an effort to restore normalcy to his day, Vanderstory reached up and fingered the metal figure dangling from his rearview mirror, any lingering doubts about the SUV's purpose in pursuing him erased. "Thank you, my angel," he whispered, bringing the talisman to his lips and kissing it.

Chapter Forty-Eight

Loudon County News-Herald.net
Drug Shootout Near Round Hill
Author: Mary Gauthier
Last updated: 2 minutes ago

Sounds of gunfire on a rural road near Round Hill startled local resident, Henrietta Baker, who called police to report the incident. "It sounded like a war, Mrs. Baker said, and . . ."

NCTC Headquarters
Liberty Crossing

Evan left his room and called Charlie for the second time that morning, but got no answer. He wondered where Charlie had gone and why he hadn't communicated before leaving. His questions were answered when he entered Dan's office to find Charlie and Elena sitting opposite Dan's desk. Elena looked even more gorgeous than Evan remembered, discomfiting him momentarily.

Charlie sang out the first greeting. "You finally dragged yourself out of the sack. We've been waiting down here for hours."

"More like ten minutes," Elena said, smiling as if they were the only two in the room.

Was she trying to disconcert him? "What's going on here that I don't know about?"

Dan stood behind his desk studying the mass of papers splayed across the top. He glanced up as Evan entered the room. "Elena, your fiancée will be joining you for lunch."

Evan objected. "Nilsson won't like it. He's already changed the time and place on us. Can't trust what he's got in mind."

"I think she'll serve as a distraction," Dan replied, "keep Nilsson off-balance."

"Also, I'm a judo expert." Elena grinned at Evan again. "I can provide protection."

Charlie hooted. "I love this woman." He turned to her and asked, "Will you marry me?"

"She's engaged to me," Evan said, the words leaving his lips before the monitor in his brain had time to activate. Not since Mickie had a woman had this effect on him. *What's the story with me and dangerous women? Mickie should have been a lesson.* I'm a slow learner, he thought, surveying Elena's outfit and trying not to imagine the figure beneath.

Evan caught the look on Dan's face. "I'm glad you approve," Dan said, his tone surprising Evan, "but it's only temporary."

Evan wondered if Elena and Dan might be an item. If so, the affair was being conducted under the nose of Dan's new wife. Evan thought about Mickie. She never cared whether her conquests were married, either. "How do you want this to go down?" Evan asked, returning his thoughts to business.

"No difference, except you show up with Elena, introduce her as your fiancée Darlene Peters, and say you wanted to surprise Nilsson if he asks why you didn't tell him you were arriving with company."

"Maybe he'll buy it, maybe he won't," Evan said.

"Elena's charms will disconcert him. He'll be more careful what he says around her and how he says it. At least, at first."

"Maybe. I'm still not comfortable putting her in that situation."

"Not to worry. I have a tactical team already in place. I commandeered a Dominion Power truck and a few uniforms. They've been *working* in the area for the past hour going from building to building. They'll enter Nilsson's place a minute or so ahead of you. The least sign of trouble, and they have orders to storm Nilsson's office. Let's hope you can keep that from happening."

Evan nodded. "Makes me feel better about having company, but Nilsson's as unpredictable as he is paranoid. The power company ploy may spook him."

"We won't give him time to be spooked."

Evan reviewed Dan's plan, searching for weaknesses. "Once we arrive, I assume you want me to string him along for a while before I drop the bomb about his involvement with the *Code 21* operation?"

"Yes. I want his defenses down. With Elena along, he may be more likely to dismiss his version of the Praetorian Guard, and we can avoid trouble."

"He won't do that voluntarily," Evan said, playing out the scene in his mind. "At some point, I'll request a confidential conversation with him."

"And if he wants to dismiss Elena along with his goons?"

"If he does, I'll object. Tell him that what I have to say requires a witness, so she stays, the goons go."

"He may not buy that, either," Charlie ventured.

"We'll see."

"In any case, we'll have you covered," Dan said, glancing at Charlie, "and we'll even let the Leesburg sonofabitch tag along so we have an extra pair of ears covering our listening devices."

"I can provide more than a listening ear," Charlie said. "I'm not ready for the retirement home yet, you know."

"Pity the home when you are," Dan replied.

Evan noticed a hard edge to Dan's bantering with Charlie and wondered how long the two had known each other. He also wondered if Charlie had intimate knowledge of Dan and Elena's relationship. He'd figure out a way to ask when this mess was over. Meanwhile, he wanted the group to engage in some play-acting exercises. Test out a variety of scenarios he and Elena might face when they confront the head of Sigma Services with the news that the NCTC had Nilsson and his organization in their sites. *Never hurts to prepare for the worst.*

§

A few minutes before 11:30, Evan embarked on the Sigma mission with his new fiancée. Elena had changed her clothes and looked more seductive than ever, and he tried not to think about it. Dan walked the pair out to the parking lot. *Protecting his property*, Evan thought, with some degree of irritation.

"We can't arm you," Dan told Evan," but I have armed her, something only the three of us know."

"Are you telling me we have a leak?" Evan asked.

"Not sure. I'm looking into it. I'd like to know why Nilsson changed the time and place of your meeting."

"It's not out of character. Nilsson's paranoid. Maybe I should handle this alone."

"My cosmetic bag comes battle ready," Elena said, "you'll need me if there's trouble."

Dan handed the car keys to Elena. "Take your time getting there," he told her, "and watch your rear view mirror. My men and I need as much time as you can give them."

Evan knew his way around Washington and normally preferred to drive, but the landscape had changed in the four years since he'd lived in D.C., and as Dan pointed out, they needed to reach Nilsson's office on time, but not before reinforcements were in place.

"If they know you're leaving from here," Dan continued, "they may be watching to see if anyone follows you. Disabuse them of the idea, even if it means stopping along the way for takeout coffee. We'll be equally careful. If we're about to have a showdown with Sigma, I want it to be on our terms."

"Don't worry," Elena told him, clicking the unlock button of the silver Honda Pilot SUV with black tinted windows.

"Car's a little conspicuous," Evan said.

"I know," Dan replied. "Just trying to keep them in doubt." He opened the driver's side for Elena, and she slid in. Evan walked around to the passenger side. He heard Dan tap twice on the window of Elena's door after he shut her inside. "Good luck, you two," he said, and walked away without turning to watch them leave.

"Nervous?" Evan asked as Elena started the car, checking on all sides before backing out of the parking place.

"I'm not the nervous type. Besides, I know your reputation."

"I'll take that as a compliment."

"It's meant to be, and again, I apologize for what happened in Prague."

"All part of the game."

She stopped at the NCTC main gate and surveyed the area. Before pulling out, she reached over and placed her hand on his. "I hope we can be friends."

"I hope so, too," Evan said, adding, "if Dan doesn't object." He could have killed himself for letting that slip out. He was losing his cool, out of practice with women for way too long.

A look of surprise crossed Elena's face, and he felt a hot flash of embarrassment. "I'm not involved with Dan, if that's what you're asking," she replied coolly. "He's not my type and besides, he's married. Happily, I understand."

Evan decided on an honest reply. "I'm afraid that's what I was asking and not too subtly, either. My turn to apologize."

"No apology necessary." A half-smile played on her lips. "We're colleagues, and I'm looking forward to getting to know you."

Lewinsville Road loomed ahead, a high traffic area. Evan watched the mirrors. So far, nothing indicated a tail. "Me, too," he said, feeling as tongue-tied as a schoolboy, "getting to know you, I mean."

He knew he was tumbling off a dangerous precipice, but he couldn't stop himself. Just like when he'd fallen for Mickie. He glanced again at the side-view mirror. Still no one following them. Maybe Nilsson hadn't pinpointed his location, after all. Today might be his lucky day.

Chapter Forty-Nine

Georgetown, Virginia

Zak Browning entered the restaurant at noon and greeted the maître d' with a handshake and an affectionate hug. The two men had been friends for years. Thanks to Zak, the man earned a fat, part-time salary working with the Agency whenever and wherever Zak needed him. The Georgetown restaurant on Wisconsin Avenue was a popular one with Washington's in-crowd, which gave the maître d' access to a wealth of inside information useful to Zak.

The DI followed his friend past the elegant mahogany bar to a small table in the least crowded section of the dining room. "I have a corner table for you." The maître d' lowered his voice to a whisper. "He hasn't arrived yet."

The two Secret Service men accompanying Zak made their way to the section of the bar nearest Zak's table. They removed the "reserved" sign from each seat and placed each sign face down on top of the bar. The bartender slid them off the bar and out of sight.

Zak felt elated. The world was his oyster! He could hardly contain his excitement over the new world order he and his father were in the process of instituting. He could imagine the look on Henry Larson's face when he confronted him, realizing that his days of lording it over him had come to an end. *Same for today's lunch companion.* He might harbor visions of himself as President of the United States, but that prize would not be his to claim. Zak liked the way his father phrased it, "the puppet who imagines himself the puppeteer."

Within minutes, Fred McGuire arrived, accompanied by his personal security team. The maître d' apologized for the crowded conditions and showed McGuire's two Secret Service agents to an empty table near the front of the restaurant, out of sight of Zak. The security men surveyed the restaurant.

"Where's the Raptor's table?" one of the agents asked.

"The one in the corner. Mr. Browning's there now." The maître d' turned around just as Zak stood and waved.

"Security in the last two seats at the bar," the second of McGuire's agents added, "Correct?"

The maître d' nodded and apologized. "Sorry we're so busy. Will this table do?"

The two agents ignored him and remained standing as McGuire impatiently made his way to Zak's table. They waited until he sat down, ensuring he remained in their line of sight before agreeing to the table the maître d' provided. Nodding a subtle greeting to their counterparts at the bar, they finally took their seats, rearranging their chairs for the most comprehensive view of their surroundings.

"Why this place?" McGuire asked as soon as he sat across from Zak, neglecting to shake hands or otherwise engage in a polite exchange. His tone registered annoyance at the lunch location, which made Zak even happier about his choice. He realized, not for the first time, that he truly hated the pompous ass seated across from him. No way was he allowing McGuire to gain the precious seat Zak and his father had so long coveted. President of these United States.

"For starters, the food's great. And I thought it would do us good to get out of the rut."

"I like ruts," McGuire replied, obviously peeved, "ruts are familiar and comfortable, that's why they're called ruts."

"There's an alternative view."

McGuire looked up from the menu. "I suppose you intend to tell me."

Zak grinned. "A rut's a grave with the ends kicked out."

McGuire's dour expression remained. "We need to get on with business. Too many things going wrong."

"Nothing's gone wrong that we can't fix."

The waiter approached. "Are you ready to order?"

McGuire complained the menu choices were heavier than his usual lunch fare. Later, Zak would be unable to remember what either man ordered.

"I know you like your shot before lunch," Zak said, removing two mini bottles of Macallan's and two shot glasses from his coat pocket. He set both bottles in the middle of the table, the half-full bottle near him and the full one facing McGuire. "So I brought you something to whet your whistle." Zak leaned over and opened McGuire's bottle, pouring the whisky into the shot glass and glancing up in time to see the Raptor's eyes light up.

Before handing the full glass to McGuire he lifted his empty glass and handed it across the table. "See my latest shot glass from the Agency gift shop? Can't let the rest of the world make money off our reputation without taking a cut of the tourist trade ourselves." Zak grinned as McGuire took the glass with the CIA logo, rolled it around in his fingers and shook his head in mock disgust before handing it back to Zak.

"Cheapens the Agency, in my mind. Not like you need the money, with your unlimited budget."

Zak grinned. "Can't have too much money. Drink up."

"You must want something," McGuire said, reaching for his shot glass.

"Only to keep you happy." Zak's heart raced as he returned the Veep's bottle to his pocket. He unscrewed the lid on the bottle in front of him and poured a small amount for himself, which he rolled around in the glass before downing the contents. He watched the Veep raise the glass to his lips and languidly tip his head back, emptying the contents down his throat. He chased his drawn-out swallow with a long, open-mouthed sigh that seemed to last for the eternity McGuire now faced.

"Ahh, that one stung all the way down," McGuire said. In the next instant, his eyes widened. Zak reached for McGuire's shot glass and palmed it in his left hand, tucking it in his pocket with the speed of a prestidigitator.

"Are you okay?" Zak asked, sliding the remaining bottle and shot glass over to McGuire's side of the table.

McGuire grasped his chest. "I ah, I ... " The words froze on his lips. His gaze grew panicky.

Zak jumped up. "Call 9-1-1," he shouted to his two aides. "Get an ambulance here right away. I think it's his heart." He looked back over his shoulder and saw McGuire hunched over the table face down. Zak issued another order, this time to the Raptor's Secret Service aides who were rushing over to assist. "Get him on his back. He needs CPR. Hurry."

The two men lifted their charge off the chair and laid him on his back on the hard, marble floor. The older of the two men began pressing McGuire's chest with both hands. The other agent bent his ear to his face, listening for the sound of a breath that never came.

As the EMTs loaded the ex-Vice-President on his last stretcher ride and wheeled him out the door, the older agent turned to Zak. "I'm sorry, sir, but I'll need to collect the table's contents. Do you mind?"

Zak nodded. "Go right ahead."

"Thank you, sir. Let me know if there's ever anything I can do for you."

"I will," Zak said, watching as the agent gathered up the half-full whiskey bottle and the empty shot glass, conveniently bearing only whiskey residue along with his and McGuire's fingerprints. "Let's go," Zak told his security men, following McGuire's agents out of the restaurant.

As he passed the maître d', who stood in front of a gold tasseled rope holding back the crowd of restaurant onlookers, Zak shook his head, working to produce a sad expression. "He was a great man," he said. "We'll all miss him."

Chapter Fifty

Arlington, Virginia

CEO Zak Browning, Sr., welcomed his guests into his private dining room in the ZGB Capital building in downtown Arlington, Virginia, informing them in a veiled manner of how privileged they were to be invited. The room, which had been decorated by his wife's firm, exuded luxury and power.

The design mimicked the State Dining Room in a castle he and his wife once visited on a tour of the British Isles. Antique crimson velvet covered the seats and backs of the faux-eighteenth century chairs, highlighting the rich color of the mahogany arms and legs. A red and blue nineteenth century Persian carpet covered the center of the dark-stained hardwood floor under an elegant oval table that could seat as few as eight or as many as twenty. ZB Sr. appreciated the effect of the decor on his visitors.

The four men seated in the palatial room had barely begun to enjoy the extravagant lunch, catered by one of D.C.'s four-star restaurants, when Zak Browning, Jr. strode into the room. He pulled out an empty chair and collapsed into it, breathing heavily. A worried look crossed his father's face.

"Things are going from bad to worse," Zak told the men staring at him. "I just came from a lunch meeting with Fred McGuire. He's had a heart attack. Keeled over onto the table right in front of me right after we placed our orders."

"Will he be okay?" The COG Shadow Secretary of Defense nervously fingered the handle of the steak knife at his place setting.

"He's dead," Zak replied, averting his eyes from his father's gaze before letting out another long, exhausted breath and stretching out his legs.

Defense looked puzzled. "Why were you having lunch with McGuire today? We were expecting you here."

ZB Sr. glanced at the man, wondering if the question was a veiled accusation, but Zak appeared unflustered. He bent down and opened his briefcase, retrieving a manila folder. "McGuire gave me this. It's a rundown on the status of the setup at Bluemont." Zak read down the sheet of paper, ignoring the outstretched hands begging for a copy. Glancing up, he said, "top secret classification. Can't share, but I can summarize."

"If McGuire's out of the picture, does that mean you're running the show?"

Zak glared at Defense. "You have a problem with that?"

"I'm not sure."

ZB Sr. broke in, not wanting a confrontation at this point. The Shadow Secretary of Defense needed to be handled, not alienated. ZB reached over and placed his hand on the man's arm. "Let's see what Zak has to say." He could feel Defense relax. The man wasn't stupid. He knew where his future lay. ZB Sr. shot his son a warning look.

"I'm sorry," Zak said, apologizing. "I'm a little on edge. McGuire's death shouldn't change a thing. Everything he knew, I know. I'll need you to stay in close contact with me at Bluemont so you can help coordinate Sigma and the military. I'm relying on you to keep them in line. When they hear about McGuire, try to reassure them."

"They'll want to know who they're putting in office, if not McGuire."

"Tell them we'll decide once we get the President to Mount Weather and under our control."

"Who *are* we putting in office?" Defense asked, a slight edge to his voice.

"Me." Zak said. His response was followed by a long silence.

"So, from your point of view," Defense snapped, "things aren't going from bad to worse, but bad to better. Will there be an autopsy on the body, or are you in charge of that, as well?"

ZB stepped in again, hoping to ease the Shadow Secretary's anxieties. "Let's not go there. Zak had nothing to do with McGuire's heart attack, for God's sake. They were out in a public restaurant, surrounded by enough Secret Service to protect the Queen of England. We're here to make important decisions about running the goddam government of the United States of America, not politicking with deacons in the church down the block. Either you're on board or not."

Looking shocked at the dressing down, the Shadow Secretary of Defense straightened in his chair. ZB knew when to play tough and when to be consoling, one of many talents that helped him keep ZGB Capital at the top of the world financial heap. Before Defense could respond to the rebuke, Zak reached across the table and mimicked his father's behavior, placing his hand on the Secretary's arm. "We need your support. This is no time for doubts. Are you with us or not?"

"Do I have a choice?"

"Of course," ZB said, interrupting his son. "But I thought we'd made our choices after the last election. You can always change your mind. However, I fail to see why you wouldn't appreciate having my son occupy the highest office in the land. That can only mean good things for you. Direct access to power, for starters. Isn't that what you've been working for all these years?"

The Shadow Secretary of Defense took an angry breath and turned his gaze on Zak. "Tell me what you want me to do," he said.

"I need to be assured Sigma is one hundred percent on board," Zak replied.

"I'll do what I can with Bjorn Nilsson, but they're an independent bunch. My influence is limited."

"If we believed that, you wouldn't be here," ZB said, reminding the Secretary he would hold him accountable. He knew the man would take advantage of any weakness in the current structure, no doubt coveting the high office for himself, but that wouldn't happen anytime soon.

"Nilsson will be on the phone as soon as he hears the news of McGuire's demise," Zak added. "When he calls you, tell him we want a meeting with him here, in this room, before the day is out."

"I'll do what I can."

ZB shot the Shadow Secretary of Defense a dark look, his voice quietly urgent. "Today. Here. In person."

Chapter Fifty-One

Arriving in downtown Arlington, Elena and Evan's SUV crept past the five-story steel-and-glass structure housing the administrative offices of Sigma Services.

"Let's not park in their garage," Evan said, "don't want to get caught like rats in a trap."

"It may take us a while to find a parking spot around here. I'll head over to the courthouse, there's usually something there." She glanced over at him. "It means we'll have to walk a few blocks, but I could use the exercise, get the adrenalin flowing."

"Good idea to get the kinks out, anyway. We may have to move fast in there." Evan was well acquainted with Nilsson's *take no prisoners* tactics. He wished he were meeting with him alone. Despite Dan's assurances, he hated the responsibility of another person, especially one he'd never worked with before. "I hope Dan's team is as good as he says they are. What are you packing, anyway?"

"Two of the lipsticks in my purse are miniaturized derringers, but I'm counting on you to pull this off strategically so weapons won't be necessary," she said, as a smile crossed her lips. "My lipsticks aren't very powerful, despite the Agency's claims."

"We'll have to play it by ear. But this will be a new experience for Nilsson, too. "Confronting him on his own territory may make him cocky and even more unpredictable."

"You really think he'd try to take us out in his office in the middle of Arlington? Might be a little hard to explain."

"Not for the head of Sigma. He and his goons can testify that we never arrived and they're as perplexed as anyone else about our disappearance. They'll doctor their surveillance cameras and scream frame-up. Meanwhile, we'll be sleeping with the fishes in Chesapeake Bay."

"If you're trying to scare me, you're not succeeding."

"Just making sure you realize what we're up against."

Elena swung the Honda into a large parking lot opposite North

Uhle. "This looks promising. Lots of people coming and going from the courthouse." Halfway down the left row a set of taillights flashed. "Somebody's leaving, just for us." Elena stopped, waiting for a red Civic to pull out so she could swing into the vacant space. "Ready?" she asked, switching off the car and gathering her purse.

"They'll want to look through that."

"Not going to happen." She swung the small bag defiantly over her shoulder as she got out of the car and pressed the lock button. "Even if they end up examining it, what are they going to find? A couple of lipsticks. If they ask to open them, I know a few embarrassing lines that might make them back off."

"These guys don't embarrass."

"Then I'll take out a tube, open it and run it over my lips. The Agency's good. There's real lipstick inside these babies." She shot Evan a knowing look as she strode beside him.

Memories of Mickie popped into Evan's head. Mickie would be excited in this situation, not deliberate and thoughtful. Same job, same training, two very different women. Somehow, he couldn't picture Elena wearing Mickie's favorite t-shirt with "born to kill" stenciled across the front. He hated that shirt. Mickie loved it.

Three blocks away they entered Sigma's building. An enormous round desk occupied the center of the marble-tiled entrance foyer. Two men in Dominion Power uniforms stood at the desk talking with the guard who pointed off to his right. The workers lifted their bags of gear and headed in the direction the guard indicated as he turned his attention to Elena and Evan. His hard stare monitored their every movement as they approached his domain. Evan estimated the guard's age at sixtyish, with the workout routine of a twenty-year-old. The military haircut and bearing told Evan all he needed to know about the man's employment history. All business, the guard ignored their greetings and asked for identification as he slid the blue notebook toward them, his index finger marking the spot for their signatures.

"We have a 1:00 o'clock appointment with Bjorn Nilsson," Evan explained.

"Doesn't mean you don't have to sign in."

Easy to tell we're in Sigmaland, with that attitude. Evan returned his ID to his wallet and signed the guest book below Elena's neatly printed "Darlene Peters" name. The rest of the page was blank. Not a good sign. Evan wondered about all the appointments that prevented

Nilsson from meeting him for breakfast.

"Fifth floor," the guard said, motioning to the elevator bank. "Elevator's that way."

Evan was surprised at being able to reach Nilsson's floor without the aid of a key in the waiting elevator until they stepped inside and noticed all the floor indicators blanked out, except for floor number five. He pushed the only button. Within seconds the doors slid open directly into an office reception area.

A uniformed guard stood near the elevator. Evan and Elena nodded to him as they walked past, approaching the reception desk manned by an ex-Marine, Evan guessed.

"Mr. Phillips?" the Marine receptionist said, omitting any greeting.

Evan nodded.

"Mr. Nilsson thought you were coming alone." *An accusation more than a statement of fact.*

"I know. I wanted to surprise him. This is my fiancée, Darlene Peters."

"Miss Peters." The jarhead nodded slightly in Elena's direction. "I'll let Mr. Nilsson know you're here. Have a seat over there, if you'd like."

Elena sat in the designated chair a few feet to the right of the Marine's desk. Evan remained standing, letting everyone know he wasn't anticipating a long wait. Almost immediately, the door to Nilsson's office opened and he strode out, hand extended. Shorter than most people expected and not as blonde, his coloring still suggested he might have been a towheaded child. His most striking features were the icy blue eyes, which cut straight to a person's soul or cut them in half, depending on the situation.

"Hey, pal," Nilsson said, smiling and grasping Evan's hand.

Evan returned the firm handshake, wondering how long before Nilsson patted him down in a weapons search.

"Good to see you," Nilsson said, giving Elena an appreciative glance as she stood modestly behind Evan. "And who is this? I didn't know you were bringing company."

Evan's face lit up in a broad grin. "I wanted to surprise you. This is my fiancée, Darlene Peters."

"Really? When's the big day?"

"Christmas," Elena said, taking the hand he held out to her.

"You know how to pick the pretty girls."

Elena's game smile provided Evan a brief moment of amusement.

"Come on into the office," Nilsson said, nodding at the elevator guard who followed them inside. Nilsson stood aside, allowing the trio to enter the office ahead of him. He closed the door with deliberation and pointed to a dining table by the window. The table was set for two. "I'll add another place," he told Elena before turning to Evan. "Say, pal. Do you mind if Curt, here, pats you down for weapons?"

Evan scowled. "Yes, I mind. This is nonsense." He took Elena by the arm. "We're out of here, sorry. Maybe we can have a social lunch after your next visit with your shrink. I think you need to renew the scrip for your paranoid pills."

Nilsson grabbed Evan's arm. "Just humor me, will you? You know how I am."

Evan glared at Curt. "Go ahead, you sonofabitch. But watch where you put your hands. Touch the wrong body part, and I'll break your wrist." Evan dropped Elena's arm and stood with his legs apart while Nilsson's bodyguard patted him down.

"He's clean. What about the girl?"

Evan bristled and reached for Elena, moving her behind him. "No, you don't." His face contorted with anger as he confronted Nilsson. "Do you want to visit with me or not? Because I'm already at the end of my rope with you."

Nilsson looked chagrined and waved his hands at the bodyguard, dismissing him. "They're friends, don't worry." He shut the door behind Curt and apologized to Elena, who told him not to worry about it. "Guess that means your boyfriend's told you about me."

"He's my fiancé."

Good response, Evan thought.

"So," Nilsson said. "Where'd you two meet, anyway?"

"In Prague," they replied in unison.

"Prague. One of my favorite European cities." He turned to Elena. "Where'd you live there?"

"On the hill, near the castle."

Evan interrupted Nilsson's cross-examination. "I came to see you for three reasons."

Nilsson took his eyes off Elena and turned a tight-lipped glance on Evan. "Go ahead."

Evan knew Nilsson hated relinquishing the upper hand. In a social situation, he would have softened his approach, but they were running out of time, and this visit wasn't social. "First, I wanted you to meet

Darlene, let you know I'm planning to go the marrying route again. Second, I wanted to see for myself that my old friend is the same person I knew in Iraq."

"I am. Why would you think otherwise?"

"Because I don't like what I'm reading about you in the news lately or what I'm hearing behind the scenes."

"Ignore it. You can't believe everything you read. Damn press can't get anything straight." Nilsson sucked in his breath. "And your third reason? The one I suspect I won't like?"

"*Code 21.*"

Chapter Fifty-Two

Sigma Services Headquarters

Elena watched Bjorn Nilsson's face freeze at the mention of *Code 21*. Her heart raced as he leaned forward and reached under his desk for the call button. Without changing expression, she slid her hand into her purse and wrapped her fingers around the armed lipstick.

"Don't do it," Evan told Nilsson, stopping his motion before Nilsson's hand located the button. "We need to talk to you without your goons present. They may not like what I have to say."

"I can deal you in, no problem," Nilsson said, resting both hands on top of his desk in a gesture of accommodation.

Elena shifted position in her chair, withdrawing the lipstick hidden in her hand. Evan leaned forward, suggesting the offer might interest him.

This isn't going well. Elena sensed Nilsson wasn't buying her fake identity now that he knew why they'd come. She wondered if Dan's worry about a leak might be correct. Something in Nilsson's behavior suggested to her that he might have been tipped off.

"What role would I play?" Evan asked.

"Whatever you want." Nilsson shrugged, reminding Elena of the don in a *Godfather* movie. "There's plenty to do, and I can set you up after the job's finished so you never have to work another day in your life."

Evan's look suggested he might be considering Nilsson's offer.

Nilsson leaned back in his chair. "Tell me what you want."

Elena sat perfectly still, keeping a close eye on Nilsson's hands, which were moving ever so slightly across the desk. She readied herself to move.

"I want you to help us," Evan said, "break up this *Code 21* plot so we can keep our democracy intact. Save your revolution for another country. One that needs it."

"And if I don't agree?"

"If we can't talk you into joining us voluntarily, we'll have to take you with us when we leave."

"You and what army?"

"The United States Army."

Nilsson looked around in mock fear. "Funny, I don't see any soldiers. All I see are you and one well-stacked broad, who's supposed to be your fiancée, but is probably a CIA whore. I don't think that's gonna do it." Nilsson reached under his desk again.

Evan jumped to his feet, and Elena moved behind Nilsson as two Sigma soldiers in the outer office burst into the room, Glocks pointed at Evan.

"Tell them to drop their weapons or I'll blow a hole clean through your head," Elena instructed Nilsson in a calm, firm voice. He started to turn around. "Don't move," she said, sending a swift kick to the back of one knee that caused him to grab his desk in order to regain his balance. At the same moment, she ducked behind him, using his body as a shield. "Tell your goons to lay their guns on the floor and back out the same door they came in."

Nilsson stood frozen in place.

"Do as she asks," Evan said. "She's a lot like Mickie. She'd sooner kill you than look at you."

The lines around Nilsson's mouth hardened as he directed his bodyguards to follow Evan's orders. "Lay your weapons on the floor by the door and wait for me outside. I'll handle things in here."

The two men squatted down and placed their Glocks on the floor in front of the door. They backed out slowly, one of the guards reaching up for the doorknob and slamming the door shut behind them. Elena kept the derringer on Nilsson, who backed away from the desk.

"Watch out!" Elena screamed to Evan, as she aimed her lipstick at Nilsson's left foot, firing off one shot to stop his movement. Evan dove for the Glocks, grabbing one and rolling away from the door. Nilsson shrieked in pain and collapsed onto his desk chair, cradling his wounded foot in both hands as he struggled to remove his boot.

Evan almost reached the opposite wall before a hailstorm of bullets burst through the bottom half of the office door. The barrage sent shards of wood and metal into the room like shrapnel from an exploding frag grenade. Evan's body contorted in pain, but he managed to keep the Glock aimed at Nilsson. A volley of gunshots, screams, and shouts erupted from the outer office. Elena hoped the pandemonium signaled the arrival of Dan's men. She forced herself to ignore the racket and focus on her immediate surroundings.

"Are you okay?" Elena asked, wanting to go to Evan, but fearing if she moved away from Nilsson he would go for the weapon in his desk.

"Not sure," Evan gasped.

Elena could see blood oozing from beneath his body. She knew he'd been hit, but where and how badly she couldn't tell.

"You sonofabitch," Evan muttered before his eyes rolled back in his head.

Elena took a step in his direction as the office door flew open and Dan exploded into the room, his weapon aimed at Nilsson. "Lean over the desk! Spread 'em," Dan bellowed.

A wave of relief swept through Elena. She pocketed the lipstick pistol and ran to Evan as Nilsson sprawled his upper body across the desk, arms outstretched. "She shot me," Nilsson whined.

Elena glanced back at Dan, "It's a flesh wound. In his foot," she said, rolling her eyes and waving her hand as if it were nothing. "Evan's been shot."

"She should have killed you," Dan told Nilsson. He kept his gun trained on Nilsson as he edged toward the spot where Evan lay.

"Evan, can you hear me?" Elena asked, getting no response. She felt Evan's neck and found a pulse. Her fingers shook as she undid the buttons on his jacket and his shirt. *Where the hell is he wounded?* She ran her hands over his upper body, encountering a wet, sticky area on his left side, just below the Kevlar undershirt. "He's been shot in the side. He needs an ambulance."

"It's downstairs," Dan said. "EMTs are on their way up now. Are you okay?"

Elena barely heard the question. "Help me turn him. We have to stop the bleeding." She struggled to rotate Evan and reach his wound as the medical technicians arrived.

"Step aside, ma'am," one of them said, but Elena barely heard the order.

"Help him," she said, "he's been shot. He's dying."

"We know. We're trying to help him now."

Dan reached for Elena's arm and helped her up. She gave him a stricken look. "He can't die," she said, covering her mouth with her hand.

"They'll take good care of him," Dan said. "Are you okay?"

"I'm fine. It's Evan. He needs help."

Dan held onto her arm as they followed the stretcher into the elevator. Elena barely noticed the officer handcuffing Nilsson and lowering him onto a second stretcher. Nor did she notice the other EMTs working in vain on the two jarheads lying on the reception room floor. The only person in her field of vision was the unconscious man on the stretcher in front of her, his mop of dark hair the only visible part of his body. She reached over and ran her fingers through it, brushing stray hairs from his face, which was now covered with an oxygen mask.

Dan pointed at Nilsson. "Bring him to NCTC," he ordered from the elevator. "We can bandage him up there." He turned to Elena, still staring at the stretcher. "Evan will be fine, don't worry. He'll have the best care available and he's a tough sonofabitch. Not the first time he's been shot. Made it through the last time and managed to save my life in the process."

Chapter Fifty-Three

Honolulu, Hawaii

A knock on her bedroom door woke Mickie with a start minutes before her phone alarm was set to ring.

"Honey, I hate waking you this early, but I promised," her mother said, as an old Beatle's tune sounded on the iPhone next to Mickie's bed. She reached over and shut off the alarm.

"I'm awake, Mom, thanks for the backup." She wished she could roll over and sleep the day away, but the luxury of sleep wasn't hers to enjoy. Not yet, anyway.

After sharing parts of her story in the early hours of the previous evening, she'd finally put an end to her parents' endless questions and convinced them to stop worrying about her. So much she couldn't tell them—*had a shootout with some bad guys in a boat, Dad. Traitors to their country. Had to take them out.* Her mother would have a heart attack knowing what her precious daughter had done in the name of her country. *Water over the dam now.* Sometime around midnight, she'd reversed roles and sent her parents to bed, kissing them goodnight in the way she had done since childhood.

The bedroom door opened slightly and her mother's voice drifted across the room. "Can I fix you some breakfast, dear?"

"Sure. Give me a few minutes. I'll be down after a nice, long shower."

"What would you like to eat?"

"Whatever you want to fix." Mickie smiled to herself. Her mom was a great cook and she loved to surprise people at breakfast. *No wonder I never learned to cook.* Who could compete with her mother when it came to spectacular food? She lay still listening to her mother retreat down the stairs, enjoying the sound, which brought back so many comforting morning memories.

Time to face the day. She threw back the light blanket and turned over, the ache in her side excruciating, but she dared not take any pain meds that might make her drowsy. She needed to stay alert, not give in to feelings of exhaustion. She wondered if Tom Carter was catching up on his sleep in a Washington, D.C. hotel or struggling to stay awake in some godforsaken FBI office in the bowels of the J. Edgar Hoover Building. With thoughts of Tom on her mind, she dragged herself out of bed, crossed the room into her private bathroom, turned on the shower and reached for her phone, punching in a number from memory.

"Mickie." The voice on the other end of the call registered no surprise. "Are you okay?"

"I'm fine," she lied.

Several minutes later she hung up, having extracted a promise: "I'll take care of it."

Satisfied, she stepped into the shower, leisurely washing her hair and gently scrubbing her aching body before rinsing and toweling dry. Changing the dressing on her bullet wound took a few minutes, but a cursory examination showed the injury to be healing nicely. The doctor's neat, even stitches would leave a small scar, but nothing that would interfere with wearing a bikini, despite the nurse's warning. Before going down to breakfast, she retrieved a backpack from her closet and laid it on the bed. She had a lot to do today, most of which hadn't been part of her plans, at least not as of last night. *Story of my life.*

After stuffing the necessary items into the pack, she dressed, swallowed three Advil with a glass of warm water, inhaled a deep breath to calm herself and headed downstairs to the kitchen to face her parents.

"Good morning, sweetheart." Both parents greeted her with the same smiling words along with a hug and kiss.

"Did you sleep well, dear?" her mother asked.

"Slept great. How'd you guys sleep?"

"Not very well," her mother said, but her father insisted her mother had snored the night away.

Mickie surveyed the platters of food laid out on the table. "You've outdone yourself again, Mom. It may take me all day to eat this."

"That's the idea," her mother said. "I hope you won't be leaving us again right away."

"I am, Mom, I'm sorry. And there's one other matter I need to discuss with you."

"Is it bad news?" her father wanted to know.

An ironic smile played across Mickie's lips. "It is and it isn't."

"Lay it on us."

"Thanks for understanding, Dad." Mickie's voice dropped. She wondered if the house had been bugged, but decided it probably hadn't. "You may get a phone call that something's happened to me. Don't believe it. Just go along. And don't worry. I'll get in touch with you and here's how."

Mickie explained her plan, which included one of her favorite drop boxes on the island, one her parents knew nothing about, until now. The only people familiar with the drop site were dead. "Just to ease your minds, I'll leave you a message that I'm alive and well. I may leave more than one message. You can check the site every other day, but try to be surreptitious. Change the time of day, change the direction of your approach. Resort to disguises, arrive on public transportation one time, your car another, a taxi another. Remember the procedures I taught you a long time ago."

Tears rolled down her mother's face. "You're in danger again, aren't you?"

"Mom, you know the story. I'm not in any more danger now than I've ever been. Please hang in there for me, and I promise you better days ahead."

After breakfast, Mickie's parents drove her to the airport where she kissed them good-bye and told them not to wait with her. Inside the terminal she took the escalator down to the rent-a-car counter and rented a red Corvette convertible.

"Would you like a map, Mrs. Philips?" the attendant asked.

"No thanks, I know where I'm going."

Leaving the airport, Mickie turned the sports car toward the Kamehameha Highway. *Ah, this will be fun. Haven't driven a 'vette in years.* She loved speed, and the car invited fast driving. She should have slowed down when the passing driver honked at her, but she was having too much fun. *Just have to handle that next bend.*

Shortly before the bend, a large SUV emerged from an overlook and pulled in front of her. The driver tapped his brakes, continuously slowing her down. *What's he doing? Signaling me?* She pulled out to go around him, but a car coming in the opposite direction forced her back into her lane. She glanced in her rearview mirror and saw a second SUV racing toward her. *What the hell?* As she reached the bend in the road the rear car rammed her from behind. She grasped the steering wheel, turning the wheels to her left, but the SUV overpowered her.

Her last view was of blue sky and green trees as her car plunged down the mountainside.

§

Three police cars blocked traffic on both sides of the Kam highway, their red and blue lights flashing in the bright afternoon sun. One officer emerged from the side of the cliff and climbed back onto the road.

"Looks like a red convertible. Hard to tell the make. It's a long way down. Nobody could have survived."

Chapter Fifty-Four

Arlington, Virginia

After the Shadow Secretary of Defense left the ZGB building, Zak followed his father into his office and plopped on the couch in his usual place, adopting his usual posture.

"Our meeting was successful," ZB said, "wouldn't you agree? I think we can depend on Defense to carry out his assigned tasks."

"To the best of his ability," Zak snorted, lighting up a cigar and reaching across to light a second *Bolivar Inmensas* for his father.

"Don't worry about him," his father replied, drawing on his cigar. "We need the COG's support and they need us. Symbiosis. Like bacteria in a cow's stomach."

Zak's cell phone sounded. He checked the caller ID listing the name of the Deputy Director of the CIA, not one of Zak's favorite people. "It's the DD. Probably calling to tell me about McGuire."

His father nodded. "Better answer it."

"Browning."

"Zak. We need you back at Langley ASAP."

"What's the problem?"

"Whit's called an emergency meeting of all the Directors. Big trouble brewing, possible assassination attempt on the President. We may be accompanying him to Mount Weather when his train comes through. If so, Whit wants all of us on it. Where are you, anyway? We've been trying to reach you."

"My father's office. I can be there in half an hour, depending on traffic. What else have you heard?"

"Told you everything I know at this point. Whit says it's top secret. Can't tell anyone, and that means no one, not even your father and not anyone in your Directorate. Nobody. Agreed?"

"Sure. I'll stop by my office and then head down to Whit's."

"No stops when you get there, the boss said. Not even the head."

"Okay, I'll see you shortly."

The line went dead before Zak could ask another question.

"What's the matter?"

"Whit's called me back to Langley about a threat to the President who, it seems, is packing up for a trip to Mount Weather. We're supposed to join him."

Zak's father grinned. "You see? Everything's proceeding according to plan. I told you Whit would come through. I had guarantees from a source that's solid. Who's the *we*, by the way?"

"Agency Directors. It's top secret. Can't mention it to anyone." Zak emulated his father's grin. "I'm not even allowed to talk to my people about it. I'm wondering why Whit's called us in now. Way ahead of schedule."

"Maybe it's time to give Bjorn Nilsson a ring? He's supposed to meet with us later today."

Zak paced his father's office, worrying. *I don't like being kept in the dark. Information is power.* He flicked cigar ashes into the crystal ashtray and turned to his father. "I've spent my entire career manipulating intelligence information to my own ends and now intel turns up that didn't come from my people. I don't like it."

"It came from Whit. Don't stress over the small things. Everything's on target. The President's headed to Mount Weather a little ahead of schedule. That's a good thing. Besides, it's a reasonable response to the assassination attempt on Chun and the information Haffez is feeding them. Getting the President to Bluemont is a major coup. So, it's happening a little early. You can deal with that."

"You're right." Zak collected himself. "I'll call, see what's going on with Sigma and Bjorn Nilsson."

"Too bad McGuire kicked off so soon," his father said, "or we could find out if everything's ready at Bluemont."

"I've got it covered," Zak said, trying to rein in his annoyance as he phoned Nilsson.

"Bjorn," Zak shook his head, mouthing the words "no answer" to his father before leaving a message with Nilsson's answering service. "Something's come up and I need to arrange a different meeting time and place today. Give me a call ASAP. If you can't reach me, call my father."

Zak paced the office as his father swiveled his chair around to his desk.

"I don't like this. Something's not right," Zak said, thinking aloud, not persuaded by his father's reasoning.

"You worry too much."

"You're probably right," Zak said, removing his vibrating cell phone from his pocket. He made a face at the identity of the caller. "What now?" Rolling his eyes at his father, he took a deep breath and answered the call. "Yeah, what's up? Uh-huh, Uh-huh. Which girl? Uh-huh. Okay. Just sit tight for now, I'll get back to you."

"Honolulu," he told his father. "I've taken over McGuire's operations. Seems everything he touched out there has gone bad on us. I'm trying to verify a death, but my lines of communication have been compromised by the infiltrator."

"The girl?"

"Yeah. Died in a car accident, but she's not the problem. FBI agent by the name of Tom Carter apparently blew things open. Bureau's shipped him back to D.C., but they can't keep him under wraps forever. He did a lot of damage and he knows too much."

"He doesn't know about you, though, right?"

"Everything traces back to McGuire."

"What about Sigma? Can they handle the schedule change?"

"No problem. They're pros. When the President arrives at Mt. Weather everyone will know what to do."

"You're sure?"

"I'm sure." Zak sat back in his chair looking thoughtful. *Nothing to worry about, really.* His father was right. Things were coming together despite the *glitches*, as his father called them. Complicated plans always come with complicated problems. The secret is to push forward, overcome the obstacles. "By next Monday," Zak assured his father, "the United States of America will have a new government, and the people will be grateful. Sit back and enjoy the ride. I'm about to make you richer than Croesus, or if you prefer, richer than Warren Buffet."

Chapter Fifty-Five

Disgruntled employee attacks Sigma CEO
Staff Writer | CAB News Online [2 minutes ago]

WASHINGTON, D.C. – A former army ranger employed by Sigma Services attempted to kill the company's CEO today and died in the attempt. A second employee also died trying to save Sigma CEO Bjorn Nilsson, who was slightly injured in the melee. The employees' names have not been released due to . . .

Dan helped Elena into the back of the ambulance carrying Evan to the Virginia Hospital Center in Arlington after assigning one of his agents to ride up front on the short journey. "I'll check in with you later," he told Elena, stepping aside while the ambulance driver closed the back doors.

As the emergency vehicle sped off, Dan hummed a Native American prayer he'd learned as a child when his parents took him to visit the White Mountain Apache Reservation to hear the prayers, absorb the rituals, and learn about the medicinal plants of his people. When he returned to his office, he would perform a smudging ceremony, burning sage and sweet grass he kept on hand for such occasions, and pray for the purification and healing of his good friend—the man to whom he owed his life.

Afterward, he would pocket a smudge stick and take it to the hospital, hoping to avoid the nurses long enough to light the stick and pass the smoke over the injured body of his friend. By the time the nurses noticed the unusual odor, he'd have accomplished his mission. He'd think of an explanation later. Right now though, his main goal was to pry information out of Nilsson. Time was running short. Buses carrying the *Birthrighters* and the *American Patriots* protestors would leave for D.C. in the morning. He had a lot to do and the biggest problem was learning every detail of the planned coup in order to stop it piece-by-piece and in a way that prevented public panic. Too much disturbing news flying over the airways these days. It was keeping the country in a state of perpetual fear, never good for a democracy.

He walked over to the ambulance bearing Bjorn Nilsson. The attendant was about to close the rear doors when Dan stopped him. Addressing the EMT inside busily bandaging Nilsson's foot, he asked, "How bad is the wound?"

"His boots saved him. Small caliber bullet barely got through the hard leather. Looks to me like he's got some nasty bruising, but that's about all. He may have a fracture, but we won't know until we X-ray."

"And if it's fractured? What's the treatment?"

"Wrap it up. Give him a medical boot to wear until it heals, that's about it."

"Good. Then, fix him up with what you have here and take him back to Liberty Crossing. I'll be there shortly. Park in the underground garage and wait for me."

"Sure thing."

Dan turned to the National Guard officer waiting to speak with him.

"We have the building secured, sir. As instructed, we've given out the story that a disgruntled Sigma employee tried to kill his boss."

"That's a good approximation of what happened," Dan said. "Don't let anyone leave the building until we've finished interrogating Nilsson. I'll get back to you. Nice work, officer. You guys may have saved a bloodbath here."

"Thank you, sir."

Dan returned the guardsman's salute and headed for his car, motioning three of his agents to follow him. "The rest of you stay here and work with the Guard. See if you can learn anything new from the employees. With the excitement over, they'll want to talk to somebody new, feel they're a part of it all. That's how people are. Take advantage of it."

Arriving at NCTC headquarters, Dan pulled into the limited access underground parking garage. He and the agents accompanying him strode over to the waiting ambulance, its red and blue lights producing an eerie strobe effect in the semi-darkness of the cavernous enclosure. As Dan approached, the ambulance driver shut off the flashing lights and walked around to the rear of the vehicle, pulling open the back doors. Dan looked inside and addressed the EMT sitting next to Nilsson.

"Can he walk?"

"Sure, with a little help," the EMT replied.

"Okay, pull over next to the elevator. We'll meet you there."

The driver shut the doors and climbed back into his vehicle, flipping on the strobe lights again as he followed Dan and his men to the steel reinforced elevator module in the center of the garage. The structure always reminded him of a spacecraft portal and the flashing red and blue lights only accentuated the illusion. The EMTs lifted Nilsson's stretcher to the ground and helped him off. *What a wimp*, Dan thought, watching Nilsson gingerly trying to put weight on his bandaged foot. *Why is it the most hawkish warmongers seem to be the biggest sissies?* Reminded him of a bellicose ex-Vice-President who wangled half a dozen deferments during the Vietnam War, but had no compunctions about sending the country's young men out to die for causes that had little to do with protecting the nation's security.

The country would be a better place, Dan thought, if only his ancestors had won the battle to keep their land. *Cochise might have made a good President. And peyote would be legal.*

Chapter Fifty-Six

**VIRGINIA MEDICAL CENTER
ARLINGTON, VIRGINIA**

At the Virginia Medical Center Evan received VIP treatment, having been rushed into emergency surgery immediately on arrival. Elena and Tom Carter sat together in the surgical waiting room hoping to talk to a doctor or hear a report soon.

"How about I go find us some food and a cup of coffee?"

"I don't know if I can eat, but coffee sounds good," Elena said, as her companion left her sitting alone, waiting anxiously for news about Evan. She surveyed the waiting room and counted the number of people in an effort to calculate the number of surgeries underway. At least ten. Busy place.

Hospital waiting rooms were all the same and she'd spent plenty of time in them, one in particular—Albany Med in upstate New York where both her parents had died. She became a familiar face in the wards and after graduating from Duke, had even considered applying to medical school, but life got in the way.

Tom's voice cut into her reveries, and Elena glanced up from the magazine in her lap, the one she wasn't really reading.

"Bad luck," he told her on his return, "cafeteria closes at 2:00 and doesn't re-open until 4:30, so we're stuck with vending machine fare. I hope you like who-knows-how-fresh turkey and provolone on whole wheat."

"It's my favorite." She smiled at him as he handed her the sandwich and coffee.

"Coffee's hot, careful. And the sandwich comes with a pickle, so it can't be all bad. Plus, I sprang for chips." He reached into his jacket pocket and brought out a bag of spicy tortilla chips. "I tried not to crush them too badly, but it was a lot to juggle." He gave her an apologetic grin, the smile lighting up his face and causing her to notice his good looks. FBI recruiters seemed to have an eye for Hollywood types, she thought.

"No news on the surgery?" he asked, washing down a large bite of turkey sandwich with a swallow of coffee.

"Nothing yet, but it's still early."

"So," he glanced over at her, "tell me about yourself, Elena Petrova. That's a pretty name."

"Thanks, it's my grandmother's name. I never knew her. She died young, something that seems to run in my family." She slipped a chip in her mouth, hoping it would appease the hunger pangs that cropped up as soon as she saw food. Tom appeared ravenous, finishing half a sandwich before she'd managed to down her first bite. Her reply seemed to surprise him, probably the matter-of-fact way in which she stated the peculiar truth about her family heritage.

He paused from wolfing down his sandwich to look at her. "Early death runs in your family?"

"Unfortunately, yes. My grandparents and both my parents died in their fifties. My dad from a heart attack and my mother from cancer. I wasn't blessed with the world's best genes."

"Not something I would have guessed," he replied. His smile held a hint of sympathy. "How did the Agency snag you, anyway?"

Elena noticed how he kept the subject away from himself and wondered if sharing personal details made him uncomfortable. The FBI types she knew could be pretty dispassionate; another character trait she suspected recruiters favored. She wondered what it said about her? Except for Evan, who seemed not to fit the stereotype. She'd found him warm and comfortable in their ride together from the NCTC to Nilsson's office. They'd clicked, and she'd felt an instant connection she'd never experienced before with any man. He just *had* to make it through this operation.

"The Agency," Tom repeated, "how did they get their claws into you?"

"I'm not exactly sure. A recruiter contacted me in my senior year at Duke, asked if I'd ever thought about CIA work. Of course, I hadn't. They brought me to Langley, wowed me with promises of exotic travel and adventure and promised to pay my way through law school if I signed on with them. It was an offer I couldn't refuse."

"Would you do it again?"

"Actually, I would," she said, adding, "despite days like today," she hesitated, "or maybe because of these days. I like fighting for what's right."

Beethoven's *Emperor Concerto* interrupted their conversation and Tom reached for the cell phone in his pocket. "Carter here." He listened, cocking his head as if to be sure he heard the caller correctly. "Say again?" Another pause. "Mickie? Are you sure?" Pause. "Can you put a hold on things until I get back?" He slouched forward, took a deep breath and returned to the conversation.

Elena wondered if the Mickie in the conversation was Evan's former wife. Probably not. There were many Mickies in the world. What was the likelihood?

"Okay, thanks for letting me know." Carter stuck the phone in his pocket and stood up. He seemed to move in slow motion. Turning to Elena, who could see he was upset, he said, "Excuse me for a minute. I need to splash some cold water on my face. I'll be right back."

What if the Mickie he mentioned *was* Evan's ex-wife? Had something happened to her? Carter never mentioned gender. She couldn't tell if he was talking about a man or a woman. Whatever, or whomever the call was about, he seemed devastated. *Was Carter involved with Evan's ex?* The more she thought about it the more likely it seemed. Tom Carter had been working undercover in Honolulu, Mickie's hometown.

The mention of Mickie set off a movie reel in Elena's head bringing back memories of her first encounter with Evan at the counter-terrorism workshop. Like Carter, Evan was handsome as a movie star and seemed to enjoy star status at the Agency. The crowded workshop was full of eager new recruits hanging onto every newly-coined term Evan delivered in his lectures and demonstrations. No chance he'd ever have noticed her. Besides, he was engaged to the pretty brunette in the front row. The one with the know-it-all, abrasive attitude.

At the time, Elena wondered what Evan saw in her beyond her attractive figure. Later, when news spread around the Agency about Evan's divorce, Elena wasn't surprised. He was an intelligent man who needed more than a great body to satisfy him, an opinion borne out of jealousy more than any certain knowledge about the couple's relationship. Elena had considered whether she might stand a chance with him. All she needed was the right opportunity.

Whatever drew her during those workshop sessions hadn't faded over the years. The account of his newly single status had prompted her request to transfer to Prague, hoping to work with him, hoping he hadn't found a new love in his life. And then the Agency wrecked her plans with that nasty first assignment before she even had an opportunity to meet him. She nearly bagged the job and resigned when she learned what might happen to him, but she'd hung in there and now she'd been given a second chance. She had no intention of blowing it.

Tom Carter returned and picked up his coffee as he sat back down. "I'm sorry," he said, as if a show of emotion required an apology.

"I can tell you received some awful news. I wish I could help. If you want to talk about it, please do."

"A colleague of mine in Honolulu. She died this morning." Tom leaned his elbows on his knees, his head in his hands. He sat that way for a few minutes.

"I'm so sorry for your loss."

"You might know her," he said, "she used to be with the Agency. Allison Michel, or rather, Allison Parker. She goes by Mickie."

"Evan's ex-wife?"

"You know her, then?"

"Only by reputation. We were in a workshop together once, but I never met her, not officially. Sounds like you were fond of her."

"More than strictly business, I guess."

She gave him a sympathetic look. "It happens."

He shook himself as if to brush off the bad news.

Elena wished she could summon the appropriate words of comfort, but the awkward moment passed thanks to the young Pakistani in surgical scrubs who approached and introduced himself. Tom and Elena stood up, and the three shook hands. "I've completed the surgery on your colleague," he told them, "and he's in recovery doing well. I have complete confidence that you can stop worrying about him. He's lost a lot of blood, which was our main problem, but the bullet missed any major organs. Chipped some bone from his hip, but that's the most serious damage. He's a lucky guy."

Odd to describe a shooting victim as lucky, Elena thought, but the doctor delivered the news she wanted to hear. "When can we see him?"

"He'll be in recovery for another hour, maybe two, then they'll take him directly to his room. You can see him there. We're keeping him overnight, maybe two nights. We'll see how he progresses. Need to keep an eye on his fluid levels, make sure no infection sets in. An orderly will come for you when they wheel him to his room."

Elena stretched out her hand. "Thank you so much, doctor."

They stood together watching the doctor leave the waiting room before Elena collapsed into a chair. Her emotions were getting the better of her.

Tom Carter sat next to her and put his arm around her shoulder. "Guess Evan's more than strictly business for you, eh?" She nodded and leaned against him for emotional support, relieved this hospital was more forgiving than Albany Med when it came to claiming the people she cared about.

Chapter Fifty-Seven

NCTC Headquarters
Liberty Crossing, Virginia

The ragged crew led by Dan Chavez straggled out of the elevator, a limping Bjorn Nilsson slowing their progress as they made their way to the end of the long hallway and Dan's prized corner office. "We'll be in the conference room," he told his surprised assistant when the group entered.

"Do you need anything?" the young man asked, watching with a wary eye as the procession entered the room behind his desk.

"Coffee, for now."

"Right away, sir."

Dan's assistant picked up the phone and ordered down to the cafeteria, asking them to send up coffee, tea, and sandwiches.

"Have a seat," Dan told Nilsson, waving a hand toward a chair near the middle of the table. The EMTs stood by awaiting instructions. He excused them, suggesting they return to their center, the medical emergency offices located in another wing of the NCTC. "I'll call you if I need you."

Dan closed the door and motioned the agents to chairs around the rectangular table. He moved to the seat across from Nilsson who sat rigidly upright, signaling his defiance.

"We can do this one of two ways," Dan said. "The easy way or the hard way. I suggest you opt for the former because your foolishly contrived plan to overthrow the government of the most powerful country on earth is being ripped to shreds as we speak."

A contemptuous grin spread across Nilsson's ruddy, Scandinavian face. "If that were true, you wouldn't have me here trying to pump me for information."

"Information. That's the operative word," Dan replied, "and if you don't wipe the sarcasm off your ugly face, one of us will have the pleasure of doing it for you."

Nilsson's expression changed to obstinacy, but Dan ignored it and continued, his voice chillingly low and soft.

"Let's return to what I told you earlier, since you seem to have some difficulty believing the truth when you hear it."

Nilsson shifted in his seat as Dan spoke.

"I'm familiar with Sigma's political stance on enhanced interrogation techniques when the country is in danger of a terrorist attack, and you might be surprised to learn that I agree with you on the issue." Dan paused to let his words sink in. "It's one of the positions we share." He smiled at Nilsson who stared back, as though daring him to follow through on the implied threat. "So, what I'm getting at is this. You should have no problem if we employ those techniques on you, should you refuse to cooperate with us."

"You wouldn't risk it," Nilsson sneered.

Dan nodded to the agent sitting next to Nilsson who lifted his revolver and pistol-whipped Nilsson hard across the side of the head before Nilsson had time to raise his arms in defense.

Nilsson shrieked and screamed for help. "They're trying to kill me," he shouted, moisture forming in the corners of his eyes, one drop leaking out and running down the side of his nose.

"This is a soundproof room," Dan said, "no one can hear you but us, and we're not your friends, so we're not inclined to help you. Scream all you want."

Dan leaned back in his chair waiting for Nilsson to regain his composure and then laid his Glock on the table for Nilsson to see. He enjoyed the look of uncertainty on Nilsson's face. Dan resumed speaking in reasonable tones. "Now, I don't believe in water-boarding and even if I did, we don't have the facilities here, but we do have the means for inserting painful pieces of molten steel into various parts of your anatomy, beginning with your knee caps." Dan turned to look at his agents in mock horror.

As the three agents nodded their heads, Dan added, "Wouldn't it be a shame to learn this asshole's bodyguard shot him in both knees before we burst in to save his ass? If that happened, he'd probably never walk again."

"Nice play-acting," Nilsson blurted with a bravado Dan suspected he didn't feel. "But I know the rules. I know what you can get away with and what you can't. You think you can scare me, but two days from now I will bury all of you, and—"

Before Nilsson could finish his sentence, Dan jumped up and screamed, "Take him down. I'll shatter his kneecaps myself."

The agents on either side of Nilsson grabbed him and threw him to the floor, the first one pistol-whipping him on the opposite side of his head, which caused another shriek of pain. The third agent knelt on Nilsson's feet, pinning his legs to the hard floor while the first agent reached down to pin Nilsson's arms.

Dan bolted around the table and stood looking down at Nilsson. "Last chance, scumbag," he said, sucking in his breath and spitting out the word, "Geronimo."

He waited for a reaction, but Nilsson maintained his silence. Dan spit out, "You know that name? Crazy Injun. He was my great grandfather and I inherited his crazy Apache genes. Now, tell me. How many kneecaps do you want to lose? One? Two?" He paused, glaring down at Nilsson, "Or none?" When Nilsson failed to reply, Dan lowered his voice to a whisper. "Listen closely. I'm gonna count to three and if you don't say *uncle* before I reach three, I will put a bullet through your left kneecap."

He leaned over and placed his gun a foot above Nilsson's left knee. "I'll give you a few seconds to think about it, but whatever you do, don't doubt me, because I will do what I say." He paused, grinning down at the defiant Nilsson, "Honest Injun."

Still no response.

Dan counted. "One," he said, waving the gun in small circles over Nilsson's kneecap, "two … "

"Okay!" the terrified Nilsson screamed, "Okay!"

"I knew you'd see it my way," Dan said, walking around to his side of the table. "Put him back in his chair so he can be comfortable while he answers my questions." Dan watched the agents lift a limp Nilsson by the armpits and slap him down in the chair. Dan could see two lumps forming on the sides of Nilsson's head. Both had turned an angry red. *He'll have a nasty headache tomorrow*, Dan thought, with some satisfaction.

Two of Dan's agents stood alongside Nilsson's chair waiting for their boss's next directive. "Please stay," he told them with exaggerated courtesy, "in case our friend has a change of heart, which I sincerely hope he doesn't, because next time, I may forget that I know how to count." He looked over at Nilsson and raised an eyebrow. "Honest Injun."

Chapter Fifty-Eight

Virginia Medical Center
Arlington, Virginia

"He's still in recovery, Charlie," Elena said into the phone. "I haven't left the waiting room yet. They should be moving him to a private room shortly. He's been here nearly two hours." She ended the conversation by giving Charlie directions to the second floor waiting room.

Several minutes later, Charlie charged out of the elevator accompanied by one of Dan's men. Elena couldn't miss his entrance. Bigger than life, voice a little too loud.

"I expect you all know each other?" Charlie asked, waving his arms at everyone.

Elena remained seated while Tom stood and shook hands with both men. "I hear I'm being relieved," he said.

"You heard right," Charlie told him. "The boss needs you back at work. We're here to take your place."

Tom turned to Elena with a rakish grin. "Did you hear that? It takes two men to replace me." His humor cut the tension in the air, which Elena expected was his intention. Tom directed his next comment to Dan's man, a CIA agent and longtime friend of Evan's. "He's on the mend."

"He's a tough ole' cat," the agent replied, "but I'm afraid he's used up more than half of his allotted nine lives. Time to consider an office job, I'd say."

"Good luck with that suggestion," Charlie chortled.

"Keep an eye on him," Tom said.

"Don't worry, we're not taking any chances," the agent said. "NCTC is sending over a private nurse to supervise his care, and any food delivered to his room will come in from our sources. We're keeping a tight watch."

"You think someone might try to kill him in here?" Elena hadn't considered the possibility, despite her nagging fears.

"As I said, we're not taking chances."

"Time for me to split," Tom said, turning to Elena. "Bureau's calling."

Elena watched him go, wondering if Evan knew about Tom's involvement with Mickie. She guessed not and hoped no one planned to tell him about Mickie's death any time soon, or at least not until he was healed. Emotional stress could set him back, and she wasn't about to let that happen.

Curious to know if Mickie's death was general knowledge, she decided to ask. "Have either of you heard about Evan's ex-wife?" Both men shook their heads. "She died early this morning, but I don't want anyone telling Evan."

"How'd you learn about it?" the agent asked.

"Tom received a call here a short time ago. He was pretty upset."

"Hadn't heard about it," Charlie said, looking surprised.

Elena wasn't surprised about Charlie, but she doubted the truth of his companions' response. The agent clearly had no interest in discussing the matter and she dropped the subject.

Charlie continued with a few more questions, but stopped asking when no one answered. The three spent the next few minutes reading magazines and discussing the weather and other trivial topics before the desk receptionist approached and spoke to Elena. "Your patient is being transferred to room 421 in the surgical wing. You can meet him there."

Before Elena could thank the woman, the CIA agent took off for the stairs. "They were supposed to contact me," he called back, "when he left recovery."

The receptionist gave Elena a look of dismay.

"Our patient is supposed to be under guard," Elena explained, her heart pounding. "Can you call up to recovery?"

"It's not a worry," Charlie said, pointing to his companion disappearing into the stairwell, "he's on his way to the room now. If Evan's not there yet he'll head down to recovery and be there before Evan arrives."

"I'll call and see if the patient has left recovery yet," the receptionist offered. "There's an inside phone at my desk."

"Let's do that," Elena replied, still anxious about Evan's safety. "Charlie, you stay with me. If Evan is still in recovery, they can hold him there until one of us arrives to escort him to his room."

The receptionist placed the call and explained the situation. "I see," she said. "No, that's okay, there's a guard on the way to his room now." She hung up and added. "He's probably in his room by now, I apologize for the mix-up."

"Not your fault," Elena called back as she ran for the elevator. *If there was another guard, why hadn't he arrived with Charlie? Or, why hadn't he checked in with Tom and me?* She was growing more nervous by the minute, pressing the elevator button continuously until the doors finally shut.

"Stop worrying," Charlie said. "He'll be okay."

"Aren't you concerned?" she asked, as the elevator made its way far too slowly to the fourth floor.

"Not really. This place is pretty secure. Besides, no way would anybody know more about Evan's whereabouts than we do. We'll probably arrive in Evan's room and find him awake and asking for his clothes so he can get up and leave."

Elena smiled, but she wasn't feeling reassured. Once they left the elevator on the fourth floor, she broke out in a run following the sign that read, *Rooms 420 - 430*. Evan's room was the first on the left past the nurse's station. She crossed her fingers and prayed as she hurried past the desk and opened the door to Evan's room, wishing Charlie weren't lagging behind.

"He's here, he's fine," the young CIA agent said, carrying a chair toward the door where he could sit and monitor traffic coming and going from Evan's room. "The NCTC nurse is tending to him now. He arrived a few minutes ago and provided the escort from recovery to the room. Guess no one told him we were downstairs waiting for word."

"Not surprising," Charlie said, "there's a lot going on. We should wait out here until he's finished," he told Elena. "Give him some privacy."

Elena could hear the male nurse speaking to Evan in a low voice, but she couldn't make out the words, other than recognizing Evan's voice muttering "unh-unh." The nurse's feet shuffling around under the blue curtain surrounding Evan's bed caught her eye. Something was wrong. She bolted toward the bed and pulled back the curtain. "Who are you?" she screamed, grabbing hold of the nurse's arm as he prepared to insert a needle into Evan's IV.

Startled, the male nurse glared at Elena, yanking back his arm and swinging the hypodermic needle past Evan's body. Elena hung on, but the man recovered quickly, turning back to finish his task just as the young agent burst back into the room. Taking advantage of the distraction, Elena landed a hard kick to the back of the imposter's knees, sending him sprawling across the floor. The agent ran over, locked onto the man's right arm and wrenched it behind his back, nearly breaking the man's wrist. Elena dropped to her knees on the back of the struggling man's legs as the agent grabbed his left arm and jerked it back.

"What the hell?" Charlie said, entering the fray.

A pair of handcuffs dangled from the agent's right hand. He bent down and snapped the cuffs around the man's wrists while Charlie moved over to help Elena hold down the man's legs. "What happened here?"

Elena stood up. "He tried to kill Evan."

"How do you know?" Charlie asked.

"What the hell?" Evan half-sat half-leaned sideways in the bed, looking down at them.

"She just saved your life," the agent said, "from this bastard."

"If I had any money," Elena added, "I'd bet this piece of shit was at the Leesburg Airport when you landed, intending to blow you to kingdom come and back." She nodded to Charlie who turned to help the agent struggling to subdue his prisoner and make a phone call at the same time.

"Want me to inflict more pain?" Charlie asked.

"No dude, we're good." The agent glanced over at Elena. "What tipped you off?"

"The shoes. They're the same shoes Bjorn Nilsson and his thugs wore today." Elena walked over to the bed and reached out for Evan's free hand. "Doctor says you're going to be fine."

Evan nodded, still in a drugged state from the operation. "Thanks," he managed to say before dropping back to sleep.

Chapter Fifty-Nine

Breaking News: Former Vice-President McGuire dead at age 66.
Staff Writer | CNN Online [2 minutes ago]

WASHINGTON, D.C. – Former Vice-President Frederick McGuire suffered a heart attack while lunching in one of Georgetown's elite eateries. For the past ten years, heart trouble has plagued "the Raptor," as he was known to friends and associates. After a quadruple by-pass last year, his doctors . . .

NCTC Headquarters
Liberty Crossing, Virginia

Dan paced the conference room like a caged tiger, glaring at his captive. He was glad Bjorn Nilsson had decided to take the easy route. He'd have hated wrecking the man's kneecaps. He hadn't planned to shoot him and mess up the office, but he would have smashed his kneecaps with the butt of his gun. Broken them one at a time if the SOB hadn't come to his senses. Dan needed to know the location of the blast sites before word got out about Nilsson's capture and some gung-ho Sigma rednecks took matters into their own hands.

"The bomb sites," he said, "where are they and when are they set to go off?"

Nilsson hesitated long enough for Dan's agent to raise his gun, threatening another blow to the head. "Hang on, hang on, I'm thinking."

"Think faster. How many, where, and when? Stop stalling, or so help me . . ."

"First one's in the Metro, McPherson Square, Fourteenth Street. Midnight tonight."

Dan went ballistic. "Goddam it, are you fucking out of your head? Attacking your own fucking country? I should put a goddam bullet through both of your fucking knees right now."

The agent next to him reached up and touched Dan's arm. "Calm down, boss. We're getting people on that one now, let's get the rest of the information."

"I want some guarantees," Nilsson said.

"I'll give you a goddam guarantee," Dan said. "If one of those bombs goes off, I'll kill you myself and I'll take my goddam time doing it. How many more are out there and where are they?"

Nilsson named the remaining three bombsites, providing precise locations and detonation schedules, all set to go off at different times: two in the middle of the night, one on the following night. Nilsson had had the audacity to point to the nighttime scheduling as proof of his concern about collateral damage, only contributing to Dan's rage. As details about each site emerged, the agents sent the information to the bomb squads, the first detachment already on its way to McPherson station, currently being evacuated by the Metro authority.

When Nilsson finished, Dan asked, "You're sure that's all of them?"

"If there are any more," Nilsson replied, "I don't know about them."

"Who would know if there are others?"

"My head of military operations."

Dan handed Nilsson's phone back to him. "Put it on speaker and get him on the line. Give him my story about events in your office today."

Nilsson tapped the screen on his phone. His underling answered on the first ring with a question. "Where the fuck are you?"

"We had a situation at my office. One of my guys went berserk. Who knows why? It was pretty nasty. I'm calling to check on things. We have four events scheduled, right? Is that it?"

"Jesus, isn't that enough? How many innocent people do you want to take out?"

Nilsson gave Dan what amounted to a sheepish look. "I don't want to kill any innocent people, but shit happens. We're in a war here."

"It's not a war, it's a damned coup. I'm starting to have second thoughts, frankly."

Dan motioned Nilsson to wrap up the call.

"Look, I've got to go. Talk to you later." He hung up before hearing a reply.

Turning to the agent on his left, Dan instructed, "Send somebody over there to pick him up." The agent hurried out of the room as Dan reluctantly praised his captive. "Good job," he said, wanting to encourage Nilsson in his current cooperative attitude. "Now, let's turn to this American Patriots demonstration. Tell me all about Sigma's plans."

"First, I want to know what I'm getting out of cooperating with you."

"Beyond your life?"

"You know what I'm asking. I can provide information to you, or I can turn Sigma around to help. I think you should encourage me to do the latter. I run a powerful organization, and making a martyr out of me will only make your job harder. I know that for a fact, and so do you."

Dan turned thoughtful. "I won't acknowledge your point, but I do want Sigma back on board supporting the United States government independent of whether or not you're fond of the administration in power. Remember, I can arrange to void all your contracts tomorrow, which will shut down your operation in a fuckin' heartbeat. Without U. S. government funding, you guys are nothing."

"We have other sources of income," Nilsson ventured.

"I know all about your other sources of income. You know what will happen if we arrest you and your goons and word gets out that Sigma Services was involved in an attempted coup to overthrow the U. S. government? You'd be back here begging me for protection, pleading to save your skin. The Defense Department would sever all contracts with Sigma. There goes your company's big bucks. The Justice Department would try you for treason, a mandatory death penalty. Congress would re-institute the draft and pull your independent contractors back into the U. S. Army to work twice as hard for one tenth of their current pay. If the government doesn't get you, your own men would string you up. So, don't try to intimidate me into making deals with you."

Dan stopped pacing the room and turned to face Nilsson, hands on hips. "Now, start spilling your guts, and maybe I'll come up with a way to save your miserable, fucking hide." He yanked out a chair across the table from Nilsson and sat down hard. "Go ahead, get started," he said, flicking his fingers at the sides of his head. "I'm all ears."

§

Half an hour later, an exhausted Dan Chavez left the conference room and headed straight for the men's room down the hall, leaving Nilsson in the hands of his agents. He splashed cold water on his face in an effort to reinvigorate himself. He wanted to leave and drive to the

Virginia Hospital Center to see Evan, but he had to finish questioning Nilsson first.

After Elena called to report on the results of the surgery, he'd sent Charlie and one of his men over to the hospital to keep her company. He needed Tom back here to help coordinate operations while he dealt with Nilsson. The man was psychotic, and trying to be civil drained Dan's emotional energies.

Dan reviewed Nilsson's testimony about the bombs. So far, Nilsson had responded truthfully. They'd found two of the bombs and defused them. They'd located a third, which was in the process of being disarmed. A search remained underway for the fourth and final explosive device planted by Sigma operatives. However, Dan needed to extract more information from Nilsson about the extent of what appeared to be a wide-ranging conspiracy. He intended to learn the identity of all the conspirators, and he steeled himself for the ordeal ahead, alternating strategies of coercion, cajoling and even flattery if it produced the desired results.

When Dan stopped by his office to check for messages, his assistant delivered the news about Fred McGuire's death from a heart attack. Ironic that he was lunching at one of his favorite Georgetown eateries. *Another damned heart attack.*

Before he could wrap his mind around this latest contingency, Tom Carter walked into his office with more news. "We just caught ourselves a lucky break."

Dan nodded. "You mean about McGuire assuming room temperature? I'd say the whole damn country caught a break with that one."

"Heard it on the radio on my way back here."

"What's your best guess about this heart attack? Another Malcolm Hall fuck-over or the real thing?"

"Brought you a guest who might be able to answer that question."

"Who's that?"

"A walk-in. Big-time Washington lawyer by the name of Jack Vanderstory. Didn't know if you'd remember his name, since the appointment was done on the QT. But when the ex-Pres named the members of the COG, Vanderstory landed the slot of Shadow Attorney General."

Dan shook his head. "Vaguely remember him. What's his role in all of this?"

"Bureau's had him on ice until you or I had time to debrief him. I quizzed him on the way over. He's got a tale to tell, including an attempt on his life along the back roads near Mt. Weather. Old Vietnam vet. Said he neutralized the assassins and hightailed it to the Bureau with a story he thought no one would believe."

"Does he know who tried to take him out?"

"Sigma. Says he has proof. He's confirmed our theory about a wide-ranging plot to take over the government. Goal is to spread enough fear to send the President to Mt. Weather, then place the country under martial law. The assassination attempt on Chun today was the start."

"Christ, what's next?"

"I was hoping you could tell me."

"If I can't, maybe Nilsson can."

"Nilsson's cooperating?"

"You might call it that."

§

Dan returned to stage two of his interrogation, pumping Nilsson for details about Sigma's role in Saturday's Patriots' demonstration on the Washington Mall. The NCTC, FBI and CIA worried about the outcome of the event, knowing they couldn't call it off and had to rely on crowd control. Extra troops from the National Guard had been called to the city, most of whom would arrive on Friday.

Dan believed they were ahead of the game with regard to the weekend. He'd finally convinced Nilsson to call off the dogs and rein in the Sigma unit scheduled to infiltrate the Patriots' protests and turn a peaceful demonstration into a full-fledged riot. He'd applauded inwardly as Nilsson chose to use his suggested excuse for canceling the weekend's operation—a change in political strategy.

"Listen to me," Nilsson told his underling on the phone, anger rising at the objections coming from his subordinate. "I've come up with a different approach that will yield better results. Think about what I have to say, and you'll see the logic of it. And even if you don't, I expect you to do it my way." Nilsson paused to listen to the voice on the other end of the phone and gave a short laugh. "That's right, my way or the highway. That's never gonna change, you know that. Here's the thing. We need a peaceful demonstration this weekend to provide us with cover for the upheaval that's about to come. We have to be seen as blameless, and the way to do that is to become the peace-keepers." After a few minutes, Nilsson appeared satisfied he'd accomplished his mission and hung up. "We're good."

Dan nodded his approval at Nilsson's performance, pleased to have convinced the Sigma CEO to buy his argument about a nonviolent Sigma Services. "You could be portrayed in a new light, peacefully demonstrating for democratic change. Turn public opinion in your favor, because right now they hate you."

Now for stage three, Dan thought. "Your intel, so far, appears to be on target. Let's keep it that way, and maybe you and I can become friends."

"I need some pain pills."

Dan handed him two Advil.

"I need something stronger."

"Need to keep your mind clear," Dan said, pressing the buzzer on his intercom. "Now that we've taken care of damage control, there's another matter we need to clear up." He spoke into the receiver, "Send in Jack Vanderstory." Dan noticed the change of expression on Nilsson's face at the mention of the Shadow Attorney General. *Good. He knows what's coming next. Let's see him squirm his way out of this one.*

"Vanderstory told me he can't wait to testify against you in a court of law."

Chapter Sixty

Virginia Medical Center
Arlington, Virginia

Charlie and Elena sat together in the hospital room watching over Evan, comforting him the few times he woke up. A new guard had been posted outside the door, this one military police.

"Scary looking," Elena remarked to Charlie about the young man.

"That's the idea," Charlie said. "Nothing to worry about with him out there."

Elena almost said "that's what you said earlier," but she bit back the comment, not wishing to hurt Charlie's feelings.

Sometime before 5:00, Dan walked in looking exhausted. "How's he doing?"

Elena responded first. "Nurses and everyone say he's doing fine. Doctor came in once to check on him and said the same thing."

"Do you mind giving me a few minutes alone with him?"

"Sure, no problem, but he's sleeping," Elena said, as she and Charlie got up to leave.

"Give me a heads up if you see a nurse about to come in the room, okay?"

Puzzled, Elena rolled her eyes at Charlie as they left, neither daring to ask for an explanation. I'm getting too accustomed to following orders, Elena thought to herself as she pulled the door closed, giving Dan his requested privacy.

Out in the hallway, Charlie headed for the men's room while Elena stayed back to intercept any nurse about to enter Evan's room. The MP who sat stiffly in a gray metal chair guarding the door stood up when Elena and Charlie emerged from the room.

"Everything okay?" he asked.

"Just taking a break," Elena told him.

She paced the hall, tempted to peek through the small window in the door to see what Dan was doing, but she resisted, at least for the first minute. Overcome with curiosity, she finally turned and looked in. What she saw fascinated her. Dan was holding what looked like a smoking cigar, which he passed back and forth about a foot above Evan's sleeping form. She could see Dan's lips moving, but she was unable to make out the words, even though she'd always been good at lip reading. Must be some sort of New Age rite, she thought, until she remembered Dan's Native American heritage. Realizing he might be engaged in a religious ritual and she was invading his privacy, she moved away from the window and returned to pacing the hallway in front of the room, maintaining her watch for approaching nurses.

A few minutes later Dan opened the door. "You can come in now," he said, motioning her inside. "Thanks for waiting. Where's Charlie?"

"Men's room," she said, walking over to the chair next to Evan's bed. "What's that smell?" The smoke odor was so obvious she had to ask.

"A smudging stick. The smudging ceremony is used by my people for spiritual and physical cleansing and in healing rituals."

"Smells like herbs of some sort. I like it. Very calming."

"Yes. Sage and sweet grass. Sage drives out bad spirits and sweet grass brings in the good. The smoke from sweet grass carries our prayers to God."

"I hope it works," Elena said, turning to look at Evan. "He looks so peaceful."

"He won't be so peaceful once the sedative wears off," Dan said. "He'll be chomping at the bit to get out of here."

"What's that smell?" Charlie asked, entering the room and parroting Elena.

Before Dan could answer, Elena responded. "Dan performed a curing ceremony for Evan. Sweet grass and Sage. The smoke from the herbs is carrying our prayers up to heaven."

"Whose prayers?" Evan asked, opening his eyes and glancing from one visitor to another. "What's going on?" he mumbled. "You having a party?" He tried to shift himself up on one elbow. "Ow, can't do that," he complained, emitting a few choice epithets as he lay back down.

"Medicine must be wearing off," Charlie said.

Elena took Evan's hands in both of hers and lowered her voice. "It's a prayer meeting," she whispered. "We're praying for you to get better so you can get the hell out of here."

Evan turned to look at her. "My prayer, too."

Charlie muttered, "Nope, I was wrong. He's still drugged up. Not the praying type."

"I'm glad to see you're back with us." Dan smiled at his patient. "We've been worried about you."

"Sorry," Evan said.

"No apologies necessary," Elena told him, knowing his apologies were for the benefit of Dan and not her.

"Where do things stand?" Evan asked. "Did you get the SOBs?"

Dan pulled up a chair alongside Elena. He kept his voice low. "If you're up to hearing about it, I'll fill you in on what we know so far."

"Shoot," Evan said, his voice gaining strength.

"It's complicated. A lot of people with big egos and big plans to take over the White House," he said. "Gotta be a first. We don't have everything nailed down yet, but for starters, the asshole who tried to kill you today …"

Evan interrupted. "Kill me?"

Charlie explained. "Pain meds are messing with your memory. Sigma goon came in posing as a nurse, tried to slip a Mickey into your IV." Elena winced at Charlie's choice of slang. "But Elena caught him and saved your life."

"We convinced him to roll on his bosses," Dan said, "figured the orders must have come from Nilsson, but not so. Seems Fred McGuire, who kicked the bucket yesterday thanks to a heart attack over lunch, was commanding what he called a 'removal operation' using Sigma contractors. To cover his ass and convince the contractors their actions were legal, orders went out from inside the CIA. The goons thought they were working for the Agency to combat a government conspiracy instead of running one.

"What about the Hawaii operation?" Charlie asked, unaware of Elena's desire to avoid any conversation about Honolulu and Mickie.

"Seems McGuire put together the Honolulu team that Tom Carter infiltrated."

"Where's Tom? I have some questions for him."

Dan leaned closer to Evan. "Bureau sent him back to Hawaii to clean up the mess out there, but if you get a good night's sleep tonight I'll come back in the morning and tell you the rest of the story."

"Can she stay?" Evan asked.

"I can stay," Elena said, taking no chances Dan would send her on another mission.

Chapter Sixty-One

Local Woman Dies in Auto Accident
By Associated Press and Honolulu Star-Bulletin staff

Honolulu: Alicia Michelle Parker, daughter of Mr. and Mrs. Anderson Parker died early this afternoon when her rental car plunged off a cliff on the Kam Highway near…

Dan left the hospital room wishing he could go home and crash, but the day wasn't over and he still had too much to do. His head was swimming from the nasty events of the last few days, but at least Evan was on the mend. Probably only needed another day in the hospital. Funny how he and Elena seemed stuck on each other already. He wouldn't have predicted it, not after the way she sold him down the river in Prague. Had to have hurt his pride, but he seemed almost blasé about her involvement. *More angry with Henry and me.*

Elena was a lot like Mickie, but without the hard edges, Dan thought. Mickie was made of steel. During her time at the Agency, her colleagues referred to her as Wonder Woman, whom she somewhat resembled, but the appellation referred less to her looks than her abilities. She was good at everything and during her short time in the Agency she had made a name for herself. *Smarter than most of her colleagues and twice as tough.*

Elena was a different type entirely, adventurous but not reckless. And she had a soft side to her personality, unlike Mickie, though he'd only met Mickie a couple of times. What he knew of her, he knew by reputation. She and Evan were once considered the Agency's glamour couple. Dan remembered how proud Evan had been to introduce his wife, bringing her around to his office on one of their furloughs home from Europe. Mickie's demeanor had surprised him in that first visit. She seemed almost shy as the three of them sat around the office talking and sharing stories. Later, he learned Mickie's reserve concealed a tigress underneath. He often wondered which persona first attracted Evan.

Her animal aura, no doubt. Evan liked to court danger.

Following the couple's divorce, the rumor mill ramped up. More stories filtered in about Mickie than anyone could handle. Gossip claimed the divorce crushed Evan, and he considered leaving the service. But Henry convinced him to stay, and Mickie made the decision even easier by resigning. Surprising the conditions under which she turned up again, he thought. He wished someone else had been given the job of phoning her parents about the car crash, but he'd had to bite the bullet and make the call.

Mickie's parents reacted as any parent might. "When will her body come home to us?"

"More bad news," Dan said, explaining that Mickie's body was government property, temporarily. "She'll be treated with respect," he'd explained, "and at some point she'll be buried in the plot of your choosing. The government may let you know when that happens. They may not. I'll do what I can."

"We appreciate your help," her parents said, their sadness resounding across the continent.

He wanted to say more, but the words escaped him. He'd been responsible for the story of her accident in the Honolulu paper. The Agency had called and asked him to contact the Honolulu police department, who contacted the local papers. On Agency orders, the police refused to provide details until crash investigators finished their work. By the time that happened, Dan hoped the newspaper people would have forgotten all about the story.

The papers listed her occupation as a sales representative for a major pharmaceutical firm, one of the CIA's favorite cover occupations. Dan would have refused to do the Agency's dirty work if Mickie had remained their employee. As it was, he had to handle it. Dan wondered how Evan would deal with the news.

He'd felt sorry for Mickie's parents, knowing she was an only child, a fireball descending to earth for a short, brilliant time. He wondered if she'd return as some exotic bird flying over the harbors and volcanoes of her native Hawaii, occasionally visiting her parents' back yard bird feeder. Whatever her new form, he believed her spirit hadn't gone away but remained on earth. He didn't know how he knew other than he could feel it in his bones.

Dismissing thoughts of Mickie, Dan climbed into his SUV and drove out of the hospital garage, his mind on the many tasks left to wrap up before he could head home for a good night's sleep. He wished his wife would be there to greet him, but at least she was in a safe place away from the turmoil in D.C. *What a beautiful woman she was.* He felt inordinately lucky.

A ringing phone jarred him back to the present.

"Chavez."

The voice of his assistant responded. "You're needed at Langley ASAP, sir."

Chapter Sixty-Two

Langley, Virginia

Zak Browning pulled up to the gate at Langley and flashed his ID, even though he'd known the tall, gaunt guard with the military haircut for years.

"Afternoon, Mr. Browning," the guard said, bending down to look in the window before waving Zak through. A good sign, Zak thought to himself, knowing Henry Larson hadn't been so lucky.

He wished Whit would tell him what was going on with Henry, but everyone was buttoned up tight. Maybe his father was right about over-reacting, but the number of things going wrong worried him. *Too many leaks. Hard to keep secrets in an operation this big.* Nevertheless, he realized the scope of the operation was its strength. Even the most cynical investigators within the Agency or the Bureau would have a tough time wrapping their heads around a plot involving so many people. If one dropped by the wayside, like the death of the Raptor, another would take his place. It was a strategy Zak had counted on from the beginning, and he was counting on it now.

Reaching into his inside jacket pocket, he dug out his m-trix3, steered with his left hand and dialed Bjorn Nilsson again, sliding the thumb of his right hand across the screen to Nilsson's number. *Still no answer, dammit. Probably at his girlfriend's again. Spends too much time with her. Need to do something about her when this is over. The woman's a slut, not worthy of Nilsson.* Zak thought about a solution as he pulled his car into the slot next to Henry Larson's empty parking space.

Where was Whit holding Henry? Bile rose in Zak's throat at the thought of him. Henry was the reason he'd requested a transfer into Intelligence where Zak found information easier to handle than people. Most of all, he enjoyed the power that came with controlling information, sifting and spinning what the politically powerful knew and didn't know, a trick he learned from his father. The financial world was no different. Money begat power, and information begat money, epitomized by the insider trading laws habitually ignored by those at the top of the investment community to the detriment of low-level investors and the country at large. What mattered was management's bottom line and the freedom to gerrymander the proxy system to control stockholder-voting power, a game at which his father excelled.

Why should loyalty to country be expected of multinational corporations? Zak wondered. They had no allegiances, apart from the bottom line. *The stockholders expected it.* Besides, patriotism was an archaic value, over-rated and useful mainly for manipulating the masses and seeding the military—a military tasked with protecting corporate interests at home and abroad. Zak knew all this and had no problem with it. He and his father saw the world the same way.

Zak flicked the car key button twice and listened to the beep telling him his BMW had locked itself. He wondered how long before cars held conversations with their owners. *Your car is now locked, Mr. Browning, what would you like me to do next?* We're about to that point, he thought, reflecting on the female voice from his GPS. The normalcy of the surroundings renewed his confidence and Zak strode into the new headquarters building with a lighter step, making his way to the bank of elevators as he nodded and returned greetings to Agency personnel he passed along the way.

Reaching the elevators, he punched the *UP* button and waited in front of the polished steel panels. Glancing down he studied his feet, admiring his $1,500 Italian shoes. It was one of his few accommodations to vanity, only because the shoes were comfortable and he did a lot of walking on Langley's hard, marble floors. The elevator arrived and Zak stepped in, pressing the indicator for the seventh floor. Spotting the young woman running toward him, he quickly pushed the button to close the door before she reached the elevator. He preferred to be alone in elevators due to a slight case of claustrophobia. The doors closed and the confining space sped its closeted inhabitant to his seventh floor destination.

Zak emerged from the elevator and strode down the empty, marble-tiled hallway to Whit's office two doors away from his own. He wanted to bypass the Director's office and proceed to his own suite, but Whit's orders prohibited any stops. Not wanting to anger his friend, he decided to follow orders. He opened the clear glass, bulletproof door to Whit's reception area, stepping into the space dubbed *The Evil Office* by Agency personnel. Whoever coined the phrase possessed an intuitive sense of humor, and the epithet had stuck. Zak used the term so often he'd nearly forgotten its connotation.

Whit's assistant greeted him as he entered. "Afternoon, Mr. Browning."

"Afternoon, Marie."

"The Director is expecting you. Go right in." Marie motioned to the set of double doors leading to Whit's inner chamber.

Zak took a deep breath and pushed open the doors to *The Evil Office*.

Chapter Sixty-Three

7th Floor, Langley
Office of the Director

Zak nodded a greeting to Henry as he passed by his chair on his way to shake hands with the Director. *So this is where he's been keeping Henry. Looks like Henry's yet to realize he's under arrest. Whit should have let me know how he was handling this.* "Afternoon," he said. "What's going on?"

"Have a seat, have a seat," Whit said in his repetitious style, a continual source of amusement among his colleagues. Missing was his usual broad grin, Zak noticed, replaced with a mask of serious concern. "We're in the midst of a crisis here. A crisis. We all have targets on our backs, targets on our backs."

Zak monitored the responses of his nemesis as Whit spoke. Zak read confusion and wariness on Henry's face. Clearly, he doesn't realize he's a rat in a trap, but something's starting to sink in. The only question remaining is when does Whit plan to snap the trap? Zak began to relax and asked in his best, naïve fashion, "What do you mean targets on our backs? Are we in immediate danger here? And if so, from whom? Al-Qaeda?"

"We're not certain," Whit replied. "Not certain. I can't believe your people haven't kept you up on the latest intel. Where have you been? I've been trying to reach you."

"It's been a rough time," Zak said. "Had to deal with McGuire's death. Massive heart attack. Nothing unexpected, given his condition, but it was upsetting. Spent some time with my father. What intel came in that I've missed? And from where?"

"From the Bureau via NCTC. Seems the assassination attempt on Chun is part of a larger plan aimed at taking over the Presidency. We've notified the White House to send the President immediately to Mount Weather for his own safety. And he needs to remain there until we've sorted things out."

The look on Henry's face lit a candle in Zak's heart. Larson seemed to be swallowing Whit's story hook, line and sinker.

"The train should arrive within the hour. We all need to be on it."

The office door opened, and Whit's assistant ushered in Dan Chavez.

Zak was the first to speak, looking up at Dan. "Why Chavez?" he asked, adding, "No offense, man."

"Need someone who can monitor the security networks once we reach Bluemont," Whit replied.

"Sounds reasonable," Zak said. "I'd like to go back to my office and work on a few things until we're ready to leave. Check if any new intel has crossed my desk."

"Can't do that," Whit replied. "For your own protection, everyone's protection."

"You mean we're not safe inside our offices inside this building?" Zak knew he had to play along. *Can't have Henry asking to go to his office and provoke a standoff here instead of at Bluemont where we have military backup. Whit's doing a good job of playacting. Worthy of an Oscar.*

"That's right," Whit said, "that's how bad the situation is."

Zak stood up, pretending to be angry. "I can't believe that, Whit. If *you* don't trust my people, *I do.* I'll take my chances in my office."

"Can't let you do that, Zak. National security's at stake here. I'm afraid we're prisoners in this office until the train arrives from D.C. to ferry us to Bluemont. How about we have some tea and sandwiches while we wait."

"Then shouldn't we be in the bunker?"

"We're good here." The DCI reached for his phone and pressed the intercom button. "Marie, can we get some tea," he paused and looked around the table. "Is tea okay, or would anyone prefer coffee?"

"Coffee for me," Dan replied.

"And for me," Henry said.

"Tea," Zak said.

"Two coffees, two teas, and some sandwiches. Whatever's in the fridge. Yes, ham and cheese on rye is fine. And pickles, add some pickles. Thanks, Marie."

Zak sprawled in his side chair staring out the window at the uncharacteristically empty courtyard below, legs stretched out in the manner of his father, his mind on the future. With McGuire out of the way, there was no one to stop him. He and his father would be in charge of the most powerful country in the world. The thought made him giddy, but he needed to maintain a calm exterior.

"When is the subway train scheduled to arrive?" he asked, maintaining the illusion he was in the dark about everything instead of sitting in the engineer's seat driving the train, "and who'll be on it?"

Whit checked his watch. "No schedule, really. As soon as the White House loads up, they'll contact us and we'll head downstairs. We'll have less than five minutes to board. No dawdling once we get the word. No dawdling."

"I'm surprised they're stopping here if Langley is as insecure as you're claiming," Zak said, just to keep Whit on his toes. *Can't let him get off track or he might say something he'll regret.*

"I get your point, Zak, but the train will be heavily armed, as will our underground area, which is being secured right now. I don't like being holed up here anymore than you do, but I have my orders."

"Who's coming in on the train?" Zak asked, as if he didn't know.

"The President, Vice-President, and Secretary of State. That's it, as far as I've been told."

"Chun? He's out of the hospital?" *This was news someone forgot to tell me. Heads will roll when I get back to Langley.*

"Oh yes, he's fine. Wore bulletproof clothing under his suit the day of the assassination attempt. Ended up with a few bruises, but that's it. The assassination was supposed to occur in Honolulu on his next visit home, but the bureau foiled that attempt. Forced them to go after him in D.C. where we had tighter control over Chun's movements."

Zak sat a little straighter, drawing his feet under his chair. "The Bureau. So that's the reason information's bypassed my office."

"One of the reasons," Whit replied.

"And the other reasons?"

"Apparently, there's a leak coming from within the Agency."

"Highly unlikely and even if there is a leak, it's not coming from my side of the fence." Zak turned to the window again, a study in indifference. *Why is Whit discussing leaks inside the Agency? He runs at the mouth too much. I may need to replace him sooner rather than later.*

"It's happened before." Whit walked over to the window and stared down at the object of Zak's fascination. "Whoever it is, we'll catch them eventually."

"In that case, shouldn't we be staying here working on it instead of riding out to Bluemont?" Henry asked, speaking up for the first time since Zak entered the room.

Zak never turned to look at him.

"They're not letting us investigate ourselves," Whit said. "Conflict of interest and all that."

"In case the leak came from one of us?" Henry asked, glancing over at Zak.

"It wasn't an Agency operative who tried to kill Chun," Zak said, unable to contain himself at Henry's loosely veiled accusation. "The shooter was an Iranian terrorist. If anyone's involved in a conspiracy to overthrow the U. S. government, it's Iran in cahoots with al-Qaeda, or maybe you haven't kept up with the President's daily briefs, Henry." Zak sent a look of disdain Henry's way.

"As a matter of fact, I've read them all," Henry replied.

Chapter Sixty-Four

"Like the trumped up connections between Al-Qaeda and Iraq, the links between al-Qaeda and Iran aren't any more substantive," Henry said, continuing the discussion of the President's Daily Brief.

Zak shot Whit a startled look. The plan was to confront Henry at the Mount Weather facility, not here. Or was Whit leading Larson to the edge, then pulling back for the pleasure of watching him squirm? If so, he had succeeded. This was the first visible sign of discomfort on display. Zak's posture resumed its previous, disinterested stance. "Doesn't matter whether al-Qaeda and Iran are working together or separately. Their goals are the same. Destruction of the U. S., then overthrow of the rest of western civilization in order to institute a world-wide Islamic republic."

"You might be right about their goals," Whit said, "but Iran and al-Qaeda aren't why we're locked up in this room today." The trenchant tone of Whit's words suggested he might not be sharing everything he knew.

"I don't know how NCTC, the Bureau, or anyone else made the jump from an Iranian terrorist's assassination attempt on the Vice-President to a homegrown conspiracy with links to the Agency," Zak said. "Somebody's been reading too many Baldacci novels." Zak stood up and glanced toward the door in the back corner of the room. "I need to use the can."

"Sure, go ahead," Whit said.

Marie arrived with the coffee, tea, and snacks as Zak disappeared into the DCI's private bathroom. "Mr. Browning still here, or did he leave?"

"He's here." Whit tipped his head toward the corner of the room. "Just set them down, Marie, we can serve ourselves."

"As you wish, sir. Is there anything else?"

"Not now, thanks."

"I'll be right outside if you need something more." She pointed to the square Styrofoam box as she left. "Pickles are in there."

Zak left the bathroom and joined the quiet group nibbling on sandwiches and pickles. Finishing only half his sandwich, he looked around Whit's office, wondering what goofy stunt Whit would pull next. But before he could ask, the call came in announcing the approach of the subway train. A minute later, Marie opened the office door and informed everyone of the arrival of the Marine guards who would escort them to the basement.

A jarhead escort to the DCI's private elevator, Zak thought. *Whit's not taking any chances.*

"The whole country's on a red terror alert," Whit explained, "and that includes us. We can't be too careful."

The subway cars pulled in as the DCI's contingent stepped out of the elevator mere feet from the edge of the tracks.

"We're in the last car," one of the Marines said, pointing at Zak and Dan and motioning them to the back of the train as the first subway cars passed by. The darkened one-way windows prevented anyone on the outside from seeing into the brightly lit cars. Zak wondered which car held the President and Vice-President.

"We're in the next car up," the other Marine told Whit and Henry.

"You're splitting us up?" Zak asked, registering his protest.

Whit looked over and shrugged. "Not my show." He motioned Henry to precede him into the next-to-last car. Dan followed Zak to the caboose, or the place where a caboose would be if this were a normal train.

Zak turned to the Marine. "Why back here?"

"Not enough seats up front, apparently," the young man replied.

Must be the arrangements McGuire made, Zak thought, stepping into the car filled with Marines. He hated being denied the pleasure of watching Henry squirm in the other railroad car, knowing he couldn't worm his way out of this situation. *The final solution.* Visions of World War II German prisoners on their way to concentration camps flashed through Zak's head and for a few brief seconds he felt trapped, his mind playing tricks again.

Zak glanced around the railroad car. Not much choice about where to sit. Three seats remained, none by a window. *That was a good sign. Better protection away from the windows.* Zak claimed the seat closest to the door. *If the Marines could save three seats together in one car, why not save six?* Military decisions, Zak thought, no rhyme or reason to half of them. That would change when he was in charge of the country. As for getting to that point, the plans were in place. When the train arrived at Mount Weather, everyone knew what to do. Moving up the schedule was actually an emotional relief. The goal was to get the President to Mount Weather, and now the President was on the train headed to Bluemont. It almost felt surreal.

Having Henry Larson along was an unexpected bonus. No need to take care of him later, Zak thought. He would give Larson a choice: play ball or be arrested and charged with espionage; a no-brainer. Zak had confidence in the march of events once they reached Bluemont. He'd double-checked everything with his father by phone from Whit's bathroom. Even if someone inside the Agency were monitoring his phone, the call to his father would sound innocent. Everything was in place despite the schedule change, his father had assured him.

Zak felt confident about the military higher-ups waiting at Bluemont. They would take over once the train arrived. The contingent of Marines sitting across from him had no idea they would soon receive new directives from their superiors the minute they stepped off the train. That wasn't a worry. Marines were trained to act, not think. They would respond based on their most recent orders. Zak breathed a sigh of satisfaction at the thought of the coming scenario. Larson's overbearing days were coming to an end. Zak took comfort in knowing that soon he, Zak Browning, would be the person holding all the cards. He leaned his head against the back of the seat and closed his eyes, imagining the scene taking shape at Mt. Weather in preparation for the President's arrival.

Chapter Sixty-Five

Bluemont, Virginia

The subway train pulled into the Mt. Weather station, the end of the line. One of the Marines in the last subway car got up and walked to the back of the car, stopping in front of Dan Chavez.

"Please wait here, sir, while we de-board Mr. Browning."

Dan nodded and leaned back in his seat, casting a disparaging glance at the snoozing DI.

The Marine Sergeant Major gave Zak's shoulder a light shake. "We've arrived, sir."

"Oh, sorry. I must have fallen asleep. Too many late nights, I guess," Zak said, rubbing his eyes. *Once we get through this weekend, maybe I can get to bed at a decent hour, catch up on my sleep.*

"We're disembarking from back to front, sir. Our car is the first to unload." He waved his arm in the direction of the open door. "After you, sir."

Zak stood up and moved toward the door. As planned, he thought with relief. *I exit first and take control.* "Thank you, Major. Please stand by. There'll be further orders for you shortly."

"Yessir." The Marine saluted sharply as Zak stepped out of the subway car onto the platform at Mount Weather. He noted the three star insignia on the uniform of the Marine officer waiting to greet him, a Lieutenant General, not someone he knew, which might have raised an alarm had not the Sergeant Major just saluted him and followed instructions about de-boarding. The Lieutenant General walked over and saluted. Zak relaxed.

"Lieutenant General Warren Todd at your service, sir."

"Thank you, General. Everything in order here?"

"Yes sir. I'll escort you to your quarters and place a guard at the door for your security. Once we have the President and Vice-President quartered, I'll return for you." The Lieutenant General saluted again.

"Thank you, General," Zak said. Following the General through the underground corridor, Zak could feel his chest swell with the pride of accomplishment. To taste absolute power, he mused, is an incomparable experience. His thoughts turned to the future. Airports and public buildings would one day bear his name. Annals of today's event would validate his brilliance as well as his patriotism. Where in recorded history had anyone pulled off so extensive and peaceful an overthrow of so powerful a government? Not Napoleon, not William the Conqueror, not even the twentieth century robber barons. Wealthy as they were, they lacked the military contractors, media control and grass roots organizational structure that Zak commanded.

His mind drifted to his plans for the country. He would turn the United States of America into a haven for the competent, the best and the brightest, those able to restore America's greatness. They would be rewarded, put into positions of power. He planned to eradicate the do-gooder non-militant left and mold America into a mirror of its former self, the most powerful and fearsome country in the world. Time was of the essence. China's power had to be checked. Iran had to be subdued and brought into the new century, their nuclear ambitions destroyed, even if it meant bombing every possible nuclear production plant in the country. After that, Africa. Another check on China, which was gaining a stronghold on the Dark Continent.

"Watch your step, sir."

"Thank you, General," Zak replied, stepping into the elevator as the Marine Lt. General held the door for him. Two young Marine Privates followed the pair into the elevator and introduced themselves to Zak, as requested by General Todd.

"They'll be right outside your door," General Todd explained, "if you need anything."

"I'll be fine," Zak said. "Have a few calls to make while I'm waiting to hear back from you."

"Sorry, sir. We have all communications in and out of Mt. Weather shut down temporarily. In fact, we're collecting cell phones from everyone. Don't want calls leaking through the system and causing problems." The General held out his hand for Zak's phone.

Zak hesitated. "I'm in charge here, General, so there's no need to confiscate my phone."

"Yes sir, I understand. But I'm in charge of the military operations. Securing the communications system is a military responsibility. The President of the United States is required by law to acquiesce to Secret

Service and Military when he is in danger."

"You believe I'm in danger here?"

"Yes sir. If the President realizes what's happening before we can lock him down, he will issue orders that countermand yours. I'm trying to see that doesn't happen, which is why all wireless underground communications channels have been shut down, with the exception of one emergency channel."

The elevator doors slid open and the General preceded Zak into the hallway, his hand extended, waiting for the requested instrument. Zak hesitated briefly, then dug in his pocket for his phone. He disliked handing it over. Without it, he felt naked, vulnerable. He understood how the President felt when the Secret Service said he had to give up his Blackberry after his inauguration. Like the President, I should have refused, Zak thought, but it was too late now.

"We don't have time to make the special arrangements necessary to permit you to hang onto your phone," Lt. General Todd explained, in what Zak perceived as an effort to calm his fears. "Remember what happened when the President took office and wanted to keep his Blackberry? Took some time to retrofit his instrument."

Zak shook his head. "I do understand, General, no problem." *I should have thought ahead and made those arrangements, but McGuire never kept me informed.*

Zak and Lt. General Todd continued down the hall to Zak's living quarters. *Who knows how long I'll be here, a week, maybe longer.* Zak congratulated himself on having stocked the refrigerator with his favorite foods once he realized a few days earlier how dependent he would be on the contents of the food and drink stores at the facility. He'd also thought to load the room's bar with essential beverages. In fact, he could use a drink right now. He needed to have a clear mind and calm demeanor when he met with the President.

"Here you are, sir," General Todd said, as one of the Marine Privates unlocked the door to Zak's quarters and held it open.

Zak nodded his thanks and strolled into the room, the General following behind. "You know your orders, correct, General?"

"Yes sir. I'll keep you posted." General Todd saluted again and walked out. Before closing the door, the two Marines moved to either side of Zak's apartment door and saluted as the General walked away without saying a word.

Inside the room, Zak walked over and flipped on the television, surprised to see a picture light up the screen. Obviously, the communications' lockdown didn't include television, which was coming in on cable. Zak wondered why the military hadn't shut the cable down, too, but decided they must have only sealed the outgoing network. *Understandable. There might be a fly in the ointment, some agitator at Mt. Weather not one hundred percent on board with the new regime. The military wouldn't want such a person broadcasting their thoughts to the outside world. Good thinking on the part of General Todd.* Another circumstance Zak should have anticipated, but hadn't. *Well, that's why we have a military, to deal with security issues.*

Zak liked General Todd, thought maybe he would promote him to Chairman of the Joint Chiefs of Staff once he took over the Presidency. Of course, that would require promoting him to Four-star General status first. Not a problem, and it would make the Marines happy. They'd been shafted for years on the Chair appointment, having only one Marine named in the fifty-year history of the position. Good to keep the Marines on your side, Zak thought, particularly when the politics of the new administration promised to be hairy. Sigma Services and the U. S. Marines. Who, besides illiterates in Africa and the Middle East, would dare take on that combination?

Satisfied at how well the program at Mt. Weather was proceeding, Zak sat down to watch CAB News, but the news of the day held little interest for him. More monumental proceedings were occurring right outside his door. Zak was anxious to join the fray, settle scores once and for all. Revenge was a collateral benefit of the day's takeover, and it would be sweet when it arrived, particularly when it came to Henry Larson. I'll nominate him asshole-in-chief, Zak thought, smiling to himself. He shut off the television and stretched out on the bed. General Todd should be coming back with news shortly. Until then, Zak decided to take advantage of the peace and quiet and grab a short nap.

Chapter Sixty-Six

A gentle knock on the door woke Zak from a fitful sleep. He checked his watch. Nearly 6:00 o'clock. He'd only slept for half an hour.

"Hang on. I'm coming." On the way to the door, Zak stopped in the bathroom and splashed cold water on his face.

"We're ready, sir." General Todd called out from the hallway as he waited for Zak to join him. "I've assembled everyone in the conference room," he said, as Zak left his room. "They're waiting for you."

"The conference room? I thought I was supposed to meet with the President."

"We're following Shadow President Fred McGuire's schedule, sir. Isn't that what you expected?"

Zak fumed. He'd emailed a revised schedule after McGuire's death. *Why hadn't they received it?*

"No. I'd sent a replacement schedule, but apparently something's happened to it. It's not important. We can meet now. Maybe that's better, anyway." Zak followed General Todd to Fred McGuire's favorite conference room, the one with the webcam window overlooking the streets of D.C. "Join us, if you'd like."

"Thank you, sir, I will."

Zak and the General entered the room and took their seats, nodding to the members of the COG Executive Committee seated around the table, all but Vanderstory. Zak wondered what Sigma had done with him, but it didn't matter now, anyway.

"You know why we're here and you know what's about to happen," Zak said, nodding a greeting to each person at the table. "I hope you feel prepared for the jobs ahead of you. We've a lot of work to do to restore America to its former standing in the world. We, you and I, are the chosen ones to make it happen."

"Has the President been informed?" someone asked.

"Not yet," Zak said, "but I will meet with him soon. His first task will be to effect the resignation of Vice-President Chun and name me as his replacement."

"What if he refuses?" the Shadow Secretary of Defense asked, looking skeptical.

"I plan to make him an offer he can't refuse," Zak said. "Either Chun resigns, or we see that he commits suicide. Those are the alternatives the President faces. I have confidence he will ask for Chun's resignation."

"What reason will he give the public?" asked Defense.

"An explanation they're already inclined to believe." Zak was losing patience. "The President will display a birth certificate for the Vice-President showing his birthplace to be Taipei, the capital of Taiwan. We have a copy of the new certificate and a document that explains its origin and the manner in which it has been kept secret from the public."

"So, the Birthrighters were correct all along," the Shadow Secretary of Interior commented, to Zak's amusement.

Zak shot the man a disdainful look. "If that's what you choose to believe, fine. The important thing is for the American public to believe."

"And if the President doesn't capitulate?" This question was from the Shadow Secretary of State.

"He'll be assassinated." The room fell silent. "Collateral damage," Zak explained with a shrug of the shoulders, "and a very low toll, considering the nature of this operation." He glanced around the room, locking eyes with each person at the table, silently mobilizing their acquiescence.

"How long before we take our rightful positions?" the Secretary of State asked.

"That depends," Zak said. "I'm expecting the current cabinet members to resign immediately. As they do, you'll be moved into their positions. The obstinate will be encouraged to leave, which may take more time. I'm anticipating having everyone in place within a month's time. A military attack on Iran should move things along dramatically." Zak looked over at Lt. General Todd, who nodded. Zak continued. "The first bomb run is scheduled to deploy sometime within the next two to three weeks."

The Shadow Defense Attorney spoke up again. "What if the President refuses to go along with our plans even after Chun is out of the picture? And why do we need him, anyway?"

"He'll go along in order to save the lives of his children. We need him with us—to give inspirational speeches, keep the public informed, play his role."

A knock on the door interrupted Zak, and he motioned General Todd to answer it.

The young Marine aide from the hall stood at attention. "Time for Mr. Browning to meet with the President, sir," he told the General.

Zak stood up and faced his audience, telling them with great pomp, "As that courageous military hero of World War II and the Korean War, General Douglas MacArthur once promised to the nation of the Philippines, '*I shall return.*'"

With that, Zak turned and followed the military aide out of the conference room and down the hall to the President's Mt. Weather quarters. Lt. General Todd followed behind. Reaching the door at the end of the hallway, the Marine aide knocked and stood at attention again as he waited for his counterpart to answer. A second Marine aide opened the door, the two men saluting each other. "Come in," he said, pointing the way for Zak.

The empty reception area resembled the waiting room outside the White House Oval Office. Zak followed the young Marine to the back door of the room. Rather than knocking, the Marine held open the door and motioned Zak inside. The President and Vice-President's chairs held two men, who were sitting with their backs to the door. Zak stepped inside. A confused look crossed his face as the men spun around. Henry Larson and DCI Whitworth glared at him.

"I'm not interested in dealing with these two right now," Zak said, his arrogance spilling over as he regained his confidence. "I need to meet with the President first." He directed his words to the Marine aide. "Take them away until I'm ready for them."

The Marine aide remained in place.

"Did you hear me?" Zak demanded, his voice rising. "Get rid of them. Now!" His face turned red as the Marine made no move toward Henry and Whit.

Zak turned to leave and encountered Dan Chavez, who stood in front of the door. "Get out of my way," Zak barked, reaching for the door handle. Dan's swift hands had Zak against the wall with his hands behind his back before the Marine aide had time to reach him. The Marine slapped a pair of handcuffs on Zak and walked him to the center of the room.

"What's going on here?" Zak sputtered. "I'm in charge. I'm ordering you. Call General Todd."

"Lt. General Todd is with us, Zak," Whit said in a matter-of-fact tone, "Now, have a seat, have a seat." He pointed to an empty chair next to Henry.

"What do you mean with *us*? You're with me, and you're not in charge. *I* am."

"I have something to show you," Whit said.

Zak spit obscenities at Dan and the Marine aide as they took him by the arm and dragged him to the designated seat.

Henry held a remote control in his right hand. He lifted the clicker and pointed it at the oversized flat-panel TV mounted on the opposite wall. Zak watched with revulsion as an image appeared on the screen of the conference room he'd just left, showing him entering the room. He heard himself greet those gathered around the table with the words, "You know why we're here and you know what's about to happen. I hope you feel prepared for the jobs ahead of you ... "

"Shall we continue," Whit asked, "or have you seen enough?"

Zak slumped in his chair, unable to speak.

Henry took over. "You know what this means. You will be tried for treason and sentenced to death. Your father's fortune will be useless when it comes to saving your reputation or saving your life. Is that clear?"

Almost in a stupor, Zak nodded. For several minutes, Henry and Director Whitworth waited, neither saying a word, allowing the gravity of the situation to sink into Zak's deranged brain. Finally, he looked up directing his words to Whit. "Give me a way out. I know you're prepared to do that. Am I correct?"

"Yes," Whit said, "you're correct, but it's conditioned on your responses to our questions."

Zak nodded again.

Henry began the questioning. "Did Malcolm Hall die of natural causes?"

"No," Zak said, his voice a hoarse whisper, "aconite poisoning."

"And Jake Harper?" Whit asked.

"Dirt in the plane's fuel tank."

"Who doctored the fuel tank?"

Zak hesitated. "Sigma Special Forces."

"The Hawaii operation to assassinate Chun?"

"Sigma Special Forces unit under the direction of Fred McGuire. Nilsson knows who runs it. I was only peripherally involved."

Whit drew a long breath. "We'll give you a few more hours to provide us with a complete account of each person and Agency involved in this cabal, their roles and any plans yet to be enacted. I expect you to include every aspect, in exquisite detail. Keep in mind, we know most of it already, so we can check your accuracy. There's a laptop in your room. A Marine guard will keep you company. Cooperate, and we'll give you your out. Try to screw us, and you'll be on trial for treason faster than you can say Benedict Arnold. Do you understand?"

Zak's look of desperation said everything.

"And don't forget to include your father's role in this," Whit added.

"My father's not involved. Never has been. He knows nothing."

"As you wish," Whit said, motioning the Marine guard to escort Zak to his room. "Time to write your memoirs."

Chapter Sixty-Seven

Top CIA Official Dies in Auto Accident
Staff Writer | Washington Post

Arlington, Virginia. Zachary Browning II, son of the CEO of ZGB Capital and Deputy Director of Information at the Central Intelligence Agency, died in an automobile accident in the early hours of the morning. According to witnesses, his car went out of control and plunged into the Potomac. Divers are searching for his body. CIA Director Edward Whitworth expressed his sadness and promised to release more details once . . .

Virginia Medical Center
Arlington, Virginia

Shortly after 8:00 in the morning, Dan entered Evan's hospital room, nearly knocking over a nurse carrying a tray of empty dishes. He found Elena perched at the bottom of the bed, her hands on Evan's feet. Evan was propped up in bed flanked by Charlie, who sat in a straight-backed chair looking concerned.

The nurse turned and glanced over her shoulder at Evan. "You won't get better if you can't get some rest. Why don't you tell these people they have five minutes before you kick them out and go back to sleep?"

"Thanks, I'll do that," Evan said, as the nurse left the room. He winked at Elena, "except for you."

Dan strolled over to the bed and stuck out his hand. "You're a fast healer, my man. You look great."

"Must have been the sweet grass," Evan grinned. "I feel pretty good. Doc said I could go home today as long as I have someone to take care of me. Trouble is, home's across the water and I can't afford a private nurse on the lousy salary the Agency pays me."

"He's coming home with me," Elena said. "I can take care of him as long as you talk Henry into giving me some time off."

"I expect I can arrange that," Dan said. "I plan to take a few days off myself."

"Sure, leave me with the cleanup work," Charlie added.

"Not all of it," Dan said. "By the way, Henry's on his way over."

"Don't tell me he plans on holding a meeting here," Elena said.

"He's bringing Haffez Shiraz by for another chat with Evan. Trying to patch the holes in his story."

"What time's he coming?" Charlie asked.

"Said he'd be here," Dan checked his watch, "around 8:30, so we have a few minutes yet."

Charlie stood up. "Good. Means I have time to grab some grub, since I haven't had breakfast yet. How's the food here, anyway?"

Evan rolled his eyes. "If you're hungry, it's great."

"Wait up, I'll come with you," Dan said. "I could use another jolt of caffeine. Can't seem to wake up this morning."

"Too much partying," Evan called out as Charlie and Dan left the room together.

In the hall outside, Charlie motioned to the men's room door. "I'll catch up with you downstairs," he said, "I need to hit the head."

§

In the parking garage underneath the hospital, Henry's SUV pulled into a handicapped spot next to the elevator, with Bob Randolph at the wheel. An MP in the back opened the door and motioned his seatmate out of the vehicle.

"Take him up to Room 419. It's empty," Henry said. "Hold him there 'til I call for him."

The MP and his shackled prisoner walked over to the elevator as Bob and Henry drove away to hunt a parking space.

Two floors up, Henry spotted a vacant parking spot. "There's an empty place," Henry said. "Your lucky day."

"Let's hope it's *our* lucky day," Bob replied, swinging into the vacant slot and cutting the motor.

On the long walk across the garage to the bank of elevators, Bob asked, "Who is this Haffez guy, anyway?"

"Our star witness. He's got an interesting story to tell, but it's full of holes. We're still trying to fill in the missing pieces. Evan knows Haffez from his European operations, so I thought I'd bring him over here. Give Evan another shot at questioning him, see if we can learn something more than we know now."

Stepping out of the elevator on the fourth floor, Henry led the way to Evan's room. The young officer guarding the door to the adjoining rooms looked up as they approached.

"You look tired, Sergeant," Henry said to the young man. "Need to get to bed earlier, cut down on the partying." Henry smiled as he flashed his credentials and pushed open the door of the room next to Evan.

"Yessir," the officer replied, standing up to salute.

When Henry entered the room, Haffez Shiraz jumped up. "I saw him. I saw Sergeant Strickland," he said excitedly.

The MP sighed. "Yeah, I can't shut him up. We passed this old geezer in the hall and Haffez here kept yelling for me to stop the guy, put him under arrest. I figured he was trying to create a diversion so he could get away."

"No, no!" Haffez gave a violent shake of his head as he addressed Henry. "He's here. I saw him. Sergeant Strickland. I told you he was a friend of yours."

"Calm down, Haffez," Henry said, then turned to the MP. "Describe the guy for me."

The MP shrugged. "Old hippie. Jeans, sandals, t-shirt. Harmless."

"Not so harmless, I think," Henry said. "Stay here. I'll be back."

Henry left the room as he dialed a number on his phone and motioned Bob to follow him. "No answer," he said, pushing open Evan's door and breezing into the room with Bob Randolph in tow. "Where's Charlie?"

"Thought you might have passed him," Evan said. "He left a few minutes ago. On his way downstairs for coffee."

"Shit. Just what I thought." Henry picked up his phone. "Is Charlie with you?"

Dan answered. "He was. Went to the can."

"Stay with him. Make sure he comes back here. If he doesn't come back voluntarily, hog-tie him."

"Something wrong?"

"Damn right there is. He's our Sergeant Strickland."

"Shit. Hang on, I'll see if I can find him."

Henry signaled his impatience to the group as he waited to hear back from Dan.

"He's running, Henry. I'm going after him."

§

Dan raced across the hospital lobby's marble floors yelling orders into his cell phone. "Contact hospital security," he said. "Tell them to block all the parking exits. Don't let anyone in or out." Through the large glass doors he could see Charlie sprinting across the back lawn toward the parking garage. *Why, Charlie? Why would you do this?* Dan struggled with the news of Charlie's treachery.

Bursting through the door to the outside, the glare of the morning sun nearly blinded him. He flipped down his dark glasses and drew his gun, calling out "federal agent" to the puzzled people he ran past. Nearing the garage, he saw Charlie disappear into the lower level. Less than fifty feet away by Dan's estimate, enough distance to give Charlie an advantage. Dan had to take the risk. He dashed across the street, using a passing car for cover, and slid behind one of the concrete posts guarding the entrance.

Charlie could be anywhere. Dan moved forward cautiously, his arms straight in front of him, both hands gripping his Glock. A frightened woman manned the glass-enclosed parking booth. Dan reached down with one hand and grabbed his credentials, holding them out for a brief second or two. She pointed to her left, and Dan motioned her down.

How fast was Charlie moving? Had he parked his armored Hummer in here? Was he heading to his vehicle, or was he setting up an ambush? A thousand questions ran through Dan's mind as he crept to his right and crouched behind a large SUV, using it for a shield. *Not as good as Charlie's Hummer, but it would do.* He removed his phone from the clip on his belt and dialed a number.

"Where are you?"

Dan lowered his voice to a whisper. "He's in the parking garage, first floor, heading left."

"He's a rat in a trap. Don't take unnecessary risks. We're on our way."

Before Dan could respond, a shot rang out. He heard the loud ping of the bullet hitting the side of his cover vehicle. He moved slightly to his left to ensure his legs were completely behind the rear wheel. Knowing Charlie, he was spread-eagled not far away hoping to catch a glimpse of Dan's feet. The bullet had missed its mark to the right. Not enough information about Charlie's location, but some.

Dan remained motionless listening for Charlie's next move. Time seemed to stand still, but only for a few moments. A second shot rang out, the bullet hitting a foot closer. *He thinks he knows where I am, but he can't be sure. I need to outwait him. Charlie's not a patient man. The longer I do nothing, the more nervous he'll be. He'll get anxious, try to smoke me out. His mistake.*

A third bullet missed by a wider mark, and Dan smiled to himself. The shot told him Charlie was guessing. *Doesn't know where I am. The advantage belongs to me now.* Dan remained on high alert, his eyes and ears monitoring the least change in his surroundings. The wait was short. A stealthy sound caught Dan's attention. He hesitated, listened, then rose up and fired a round in the direction of the noise. Charlie hit the concrete with a thud, an otherworldly scream issuing from deep in his throat. Dan ran around the car, aiming his Glock at the writhing form of the man he once called a friend. Despite his wounds, Charlie raised his gun arm.

"Don't do it, Charlie," Dan yelled. He was so close he could see Charlie's finger on the trigger as he turned his weapon in Dan's direction. Dan fired. His shot blew Charlie's face apart as the bullet from Charlie's gun sailed off in the distance. Dan turned away holding his stomach and trying to catch his breath as he heard his reinforcements arrive. He couldn't look at Charlie. He felt sick.

Chapter Sixty-Eight

Justice Department Launches Wide-Scale Investigation
Staff Writer | Washington Post

Washington, D.C. The United States Department of Justice announced a wide-scale investigation into the activities of Sigma Services. Early indicators suggest the military contracting firm may have participated in a conspiracy targeting the U.S. President. The lid of secrecy surrounding the DOJ's investigation suggests the involvement of other agencies, including but not limited to. . .

7TH FLOOR, LANGLEY
OFFICE OF THE DIRECTOR OF NATIONAL CLANDESTINE SERVICES

Three days after the revelation that had resulted in Charlie's death, Dan arrived at Henry's office and greeted Connie Lang's replacement. Henry's long-time administrative assistant had moved upstairs to the Director's office. Henry told Dan he'd balked at the transfer initially, but Whit played on his sympathies.

"I need her more than you do," Whit told Henry. "When you're the new guy on the block, it helps to have experienced people watching your back."

In the end, Henry had capitulated, but Dan suspected he'd exacted a price. What price was the big question on everyone's lips. Dan didn't know, but he did know the woman now occupying Connie's desk. She'd helped him in the past with a couple of his special assignments. According to the grapevine, she was thirty-three years old and a single mother with a ten-year-old son. Her husband was the victim of a roadside bomb in Iraq three years earlier.

Before Dan could ask how she liked her new job, Henry walked in.

"Good morning everyone," Henry said, motioning Dan into his office and nodding a greeting to his new assistant.

"Good morning, sir. Shall I make you some coffee?"

"Not your job, thank you. I like to brew my own. I even know how to wash the pot and clean up after myself. What do you think about that?" A Cheshire cat grin lit up Henry's face.

"I think I'm working in the right office," she said, flashing him a quick smile in return.

"What you *can* do is call down to Bob Randolph and tell him we're ready to start our meeting.

"Right away. Anything else, sir?"

"That's it for now. Are Evan and Elena here?"

"Not yet, sir."

Henry followed Dan into the office announcing, "Coffee time."

Dan watched with amusement as Henry fumbled around at the sink in his private bathroom cleaning the crud from the bottom of his coffee carafe. After drying the outside with a paper towel, Henry filled the pot with water and meticulously measured out three scoops of freshly ground coffee. *Tres Rios*, Dan knew, since Henry never failed to mention it.

"Nothing like the aroma of freshly brewed coffee, especially if it's *Tres Rios*," Henry said, eliciting a semblance of a smile from a morose Dan. "You know," he added, "I feel good today. First day I've felt good in a couple of weeks."

"I'm starting to feel better … " Dan said, about to say more, but Bob Randolph entered the room and Dan settled for, "especially now that my wife's coming back home."

"What's this about your wife?" Bob asked, grabbing a chair and dragging it closer to Henry's desk.

"My wife agreed to leave Rapid City and return to D.C.," Dan replied, "'in spite of the Agency, she said.'"

"You must be doing something right, dude. Maybe I'll find me a good woman one of these days, too."

"I hope so," Henry said, "then you'll have a good reason to go home at night."

Dan noticed Bob's grin fade as he posed a question Dan never would have anticipated. "By the way, Henry, am I the reason you lost Connie?"

"Nope, and I'm sure you can visit her in Whit's office now and then."

"I'm trying to move on to single ladies," Bob said, as the buzzer sounded on Henry's desk.

Bob's interest in Connie was news to Dan, but it didn't surprise him. She was the female version of a ladies' man, though Dan failed to understand what other men saw in her. Something about her rubbed Dan the wrong way. He was glad to see her gone, though he'd never share those feelings with Henry. Connie had Henry wrapped around her little finger.

"Good idea," Henry told Bob before answering the intercom. "Yes?"

A disembodied voice filled the room. "Ms. Petrova and Mr. Phillips are here."

Henry nodded at the instrument. "Yes, yes, send them in."

Bob glanced over at Dan. "He's starting to sound like Whit."

"I heard that." Henry said, as he stood up and shook hands with Elena and Evan. "You're looking a lot better," he told Evan.

"I've got a good nurse." Evan replied, winking at Elena.

Dan knew Evan had spent the last two nights at Elena's house, which explained his good spirits. As for Elena, she seemed to relish her new caretaker role, which Dan found amusing. She hadn't seemed the type to him, but what he knew about women could barely fill one of his mother's sewing thimbles.

Henry shoved aside the papers in front of him and looked around the room. "I've called this meeting because we still have work to do and I want to be sure we're all on the same page. I'll start by reviewing what we know so far. Some of you," he nodded at Dan, "know this already. As it turns out, Mickie's decision to quit the Agency was orchestrated by Zak Browning. He told her she was going undercover and the Agency had to make it look good, which is why the orders came from him and not me. She fell for it hook, line, and sinker. Let that be a lesson to everyone. I don't give secondhand orders. If you haven't heard it from the horse's mouth, then you haven't heard it. Got that?"

Everyone nodded.

Henry turned to Bob. "Why don't you tell us what you found in the *Code 21* files."

"For starters," Bob said, "the folder contained a number of files in addition to the assassination list that Malcolm uncovered. Most were receipts that made little sense until we ran down the links. ZGB Capital has offices in Berlin and Singapore among other places. Our tracers showed ZGB offices in both of those cities regularly accessing the *Code 21* files. The company's sys admins were logging into the account and leaving coded messages. Decoding revealed bank names, amounts, and account numbers for the payoffs used to finance McGuire's and Browning's operations. We've put a hold on the accounts and provided Henry with a list of available funds for the government to confiscate."

"I'm hoping some of it shows up in my budget," Henry said. "But at least we have tangible evidence of Browning Senior's involvement, and it gives us a start in terms of nailing him. Whit's already acted on some of the info, but there's a lot to do when you return to Prague."

"I'm looking forward to it," Evan said. "Anything to get out of D.C."

Henry nodded and continued.

All business, Dan noted.

"Now, the last piece of the puzzle. Dan, you want to tell everyone about Charlie?"

Dan took a deep breath, trying to erase his last memory of Charlie. "We knew we had a mole in our operation even before the disaster at Nilsson's office. Charlie was brought to my attention as a suspect because we'd kept a pretty tight lid on our operations, and some of my people felt he was the only loose cannon. I had trouble believing it, which was a mistake on my part."

Henry broke in. "Not your fault. You got him in the end."

Dan nodded, "I—"

Henry interrupted again. "Turns out Charlie had been practicing his skills as a double agent, working for us on the side while holding down a full-time job with Sigma, a small matter he forgot to tell us. Go ahead, Dan. Sorry to butt in."

"After the Charlie incident, I had another chat with Nilsson. We have him on a tight leash. Don't want to arrest him just yet, because he's more use to us informing on his former colleagues. Nilsson claimed Charlie's job was the obvious—keeping Sigma informed of our operations. According to Nilsson, Charlie came to him and offered his services, saying he objected to the socialist direction the country was taking. However, Nilsson insists Charlie was in it for the money."

Henry glanced at Dan and shrugged. "You know I can't match Sigma's pay with the budget they give me."

Evan leaned forward in his chair. "We've heard this budget story before, Henry, and we're still not buying it."

"Which brings me to you and Elena," Henry said. "You'll have a lot on your plate when you get back to Prague. But if anyone can uncover the money laundering ties between ZGB Capital and the Iranians, Saudis, Israelis or whatever other bastards are over there unduly influencing the policies of the U. S. government, you two can do it."

"I appreciate the vote of confidence," Elena said.

"And I have one request," Evan said. "Next time you want me back in the country, Henry, just call and ask, okay?"

Dan joined the laughter, the first time he'd laughed since Charlie died. After the trauma of killing Charlie, Henry insisted he schedule time with an Agency shrink. Dan had resisted until his wife changed his mind. She said she wanted to come home to a healthy husband, so he'd agreed. The laughter felt good. He needed to do more of it, he thought, as he re-focused on the meeting.

Henry continued his discussion with Evan and Elena. "I'm convinced we'll turn up more dirt once you two dig deeper overseas, and Tom ties up loose ends in Hawaii. Follow the money," he added, mimicking Whit, "follow the money."

"The Supreme Court's made that job a lot tougher," Evan replied. "Their Citizen's United decision makes my stomach churn. It's opened a can of worms. Taken the worry out of hiding dirty money. Allows anybody—China, even—to come in and buy our government lock, stock and barrel and all we can do is sit on the sidelines and watch. We might be witnessing the end of our country's great experiment with democracy, Henry. "

"I've still got hope," Henry said, adding, "One last thing. I want to congratulate every one of you for the part you played in bringing down this conspiracy, but as we've discussed, we haven't dealt this plot a deathblow, only a wound. We can't even be certain we've cut off its head. Severed an arm, maybe. Now," he waved his arms dismissively, "I've got work to do and so do you."

Everyone stood up to leave, but Henry held Dan back. Closing the door behind the others, he returned to his desk and slid his memo pad over for Dan to read. Sprawled across the top in Henry's illegible handwriting was the reminder: *call Cheryl Hall about dinner.*

"What do you think?"

The note surprised Dan, but he winked his approval. "Good idea, Henry. She's a nice lady."

Henry nodded. "My last dinner date with a pretty woman happened way too many years ago. I think I might give her a call today."

"Go for it." Dan said, adding, "that's an old Indian saying."

Henry raised an eyebrow.

Dan laughed. "From my old Indian mother."

Chapter Sixty-Nine

`Ewa Beach, Hawaii

Shortly after sunrise, Tom Carter climbed over the volcanic rock wall and lowered himself to the sandy beach on the Mamala Bay side of the house on Pupu Street. Fitting that the location of his house was next to the Naval Air Station at Barber's Point, he thought. *Not that the U.S. Navy offered any protection worth crowing about.*

*`Ewa Beach.* He reflected on the name. Like the Hawaiian dish poke, it was another of those words that separated the tourists from the natives. Sounding like *Ava*, it had two meanings: "in the direction of `Ewa Beach west of Honolulu" and "stray." The latter came from native mythology referring to the game *`ulu maika,* played with lava rocks. According to legend, a stray stone landed on the beach during a game among the gods and the place became known as `Ewa Beach. Also fitting, he mused, that a stray like me should have landed in `Ewa Beach.

Gentle waves lapped the shore as a cooling breeze drifted in from the ocean. He walked barefoot, letting the soft white sand ooze between his toes. His mind raced. Memories of the past weeks were like an eddy swirling in his brain, a turbulent vortex of grief and remorse. For several minutes, he considered dashing into the water and swimming out to sea, swimming until he could swim no more, letting the water take him to a place of no responsibilities, no regrets. Instead, he turned, and ran the length of the beach until his calves ached and his lungs burned from lack of oxygen. Nearly exhausted, he fell to his knees on the sand, gasping for breath.

At some point, he struggled to his feet, massaged his aching legs and stretched his body toward the rising sun. Making his way to the water's edge where the sand felt hard beneath his feet, he plodded back along the shore, trying to free his mind from the past and focus on the future. Nearing his beach house, he stopped and examined its beauty, its promise. Inevitable decisions lay ahead. Was he prepared for them?

He perched for a time on the prickly, volcanic wall and watched the waves roll in. The mesmerizing motion cleared his mind.

Ready to face the day, he swung his legs back over the wall and stepped onto the soft grass. Crossing the lush lawn to the outdoor stairwell, he climbed the steps to the second floor. Warm air drifted across the upper deck as he slid open the patio doors and headed for the bathroom and his morning shower. The water rained down on him, soothing his skin as he gradually changed the temperature from cool to warm and back again. He drizzled shampoo on his head and scrubbed his hair, as if to wash away memories.

After rinsing off, he stepped onto the terrycloth bath mat and rubbed himself dry. The luxurious bathroom felt like a spa, and he realized how quickly he'd acclimated to luxury after inheriting the beach house from his maternal uncle. He took his time dressing and padded out to the kitchen to prepare his yogurt, fresh fruit, and coffee. *A slice of mango bread would be perfect right now*, he thought, carrying his breakfast out to the deck.

As he sat at the round café table sipping the morning's first cup of Kona, a flutter of wings caught his attention. A snowy Fairy Tern landed on his feeder for the first time. Spellbound, Tom leaned closer to watch the small white creature pick among the seeds. It looked up, noticing him. He crushed a piece of his mango bread and held the crumbs out to the bird. It stretched its neck and ate the pieces from his fingertips, watching him with a wary eye.

Ring tones coming from his cell startled the bird and it spread its wings to the heavens. As Tom reached for his phone, he followed the tiny bird's flight until it disappeared into the blue, cloudless sky.

"Carter here."

A familiar voice at the other end of the line said, "Pack your bags. You're flying out at midnight."

Epilogue

Connie Lang reached across her desk and shook hands with Vice-President Chun. "Welcome to the *Evil Office*," she joked. "The Director's been waiting for you."

"How are you, Connie?"

"Feisty as ever. How are you, is the question?"

"I'm fine. Thank God the bastard's aim was off."

The door to Whit's office opened and he strode out to greet his guest. "Who are you calling a bastard?"

"You," the Vice-President answered, winking at Connie.

"Come on in," Whit said, waving Chun into his office. "Come on in."

The two men shook hands as Whit closed the door behind them.

"I'm sorry you were hit," Whit said, motioning Chun to one of the upholstered chairs by the window. Whit sat down in the other. "Wasn't supposed to happen."

"Are you sure about that?"

"As sure as I can be, as I can be. We ran into a few problems. Seems McGuire had plans of his own. Didn't want to play ball our way. Nothing I could do. Had to go along with shutting down the whole operation. Won't happen again."

"What about Browning?"

"I cut a deal with his father. Had to put him and his family into witness protection for a year or two. But ZB has houses all over the world. They'll live in style until we can afford to resurrect him."

"China's not happy."

"Hell, I'm not happy, but you'll be President before they know it. That'll make us all happy."

"I see you snagged Connie."

Whit laughed. "Snagged. Snagged is the right word. About describes it all right, all right. She's my mole and she's good at it. Had to reward her."

"Not all she's good at, from what I hear," the Vice-President said.

Whit raised an eyebrow. "I wouldn't know, I wouldn't know about that."

Chun nodded as if he didn't believe him.

"You didn't come here to talk about Connie, did you? Because I can hook you up, if that's what you want."

Chun guffawed. "Pimping out Connie, are you? I'm afraid I like 'em a little younger than Mrs. Lang."

"Can't beat experience, though," Whit replied. "Can't beat experience. Now, what can I do for you?"

"You can give me something to take to the Chinese," Chun said, then flashed a grin, "other than Connie."

Whit turned serious. "Tell them a better plan is in the works. And this one won't fail."

"That's good to hear."

"And tell them you'll be President before the summer's out. So they can relax and you can enjoy yourself for a couple more months. Travel. Take a trip to South America or some place while I work out the details."

"How much do I want to know?"

"The less you know, the better."

Chun stood up to leave. "Okay. I'll take your word for it and pass the message along."

###

ABOUT THE AUTHOR

Harol Marshall (named for her father's brother) grew up in upstate New York in the town of Rotterdam, a suburb of Schenectady. Her love of mysteries began when her British mother introduced her to English cozies. Credit for her interest in detective stories and political thrillers goes to her police officer father, a political junkie who entertained his family with daily stories of life on the force.

In college, Harol's short stories entertained her English professor who encouraged her to switch her major from mathematics to English. However, the prospect of finding a job after college led to a short-lived major in the literary field. After marriage and graduation in that order, she taught biology for two years before staying home until her two children started school, then returning to school herself for graduate studies.

While working on her PhD at the University of Pittsburgh, Harol conducted field research in central Mexico, the setting for the first two novels in her Anna Merino mystery series.

Harol began her career as a fulltime novelist after retiring from twenty years in academia. In addition to her mystery series, she's published several short stories, including a short story anthology, Growing Up With Pigs, about life in the 1950's. She recently completed her first full-length play titled, Our New Thing, a political satire about retired crime bosses who decide to go into investment banking.

When not writing, Harol enjoys reading, cooking, and dancing (swing and ballroom) in Greensboro, North Carolina, where she lives with her physicist husband and four cats.

For more about Harol, visit her website at: www.harolmarshall.com, or on facebook.com/harol.marshall

CPSIA information can be obtained at www.ICGtesting.com
Printed in the USA
LVOW121504200513

334653LV00013B/597/P